88

ROANOKE COUNTY PUBLIC LIBRARY
HOLLINS BRANCH
6624 PETERS CRI
ROANOKE, VA 24019 W9-ATO-964

NO LONGER
PROPERTY OF
ROANOKE COUNTY LIBRARY

LADY OF
HORSES

HISTORICAL NOVELS BY JUDITH TARR

Lord of the Two Lands

Throne of Isis

The Eagle's Daughter

Pillar of Fire

King and Goddess

Queen of Swords

White Mare's Daughter

The Shepherd Kings

Lady of Horses

0 1197 0305351 0

LADY
OF
HORSES

JUDITH TARR

A TOM DOHERTY ASSOCIATES BOOK
NEW YORK

This is a work of fiction. All the characters and events portrayed in this novel are either fictitious or are used fictitiously.

LADY OF HORSES

Copyright © 2000 by Judith Tarr

All rights reserved, including the right to reproduce this book, or portions thereof, in any form.

This book is printed on acid-free paper.

A Forge Hardcover
Published by Tom Doherty Associates, LLC
175 Fifth Avenue
New York, NY 10010

www.tor.com

Forge® is a registered trademark of Tom Doherty Associates, LLC.

Library of Congress Cataloging-in-Publication Data

Tarr, Judith.
    Lady of horses / Judith Tarr.—1st ed.
        p. cm.
    "A Tom Doherty Associates book."
    ISBN 0-312-86114-1 (alk. paper)
    1. Horsemen and horsewomen—Fiction.   2. Human-animal relationships—
Fiction.   3. Prehistoric peoples—Fiction.   4. Horses—Fiction.   I. Title.
PS3570.A655 L34 2000
813'.54—dc21   00-027653

First Edition: June 2000

Printed in the United States of America

0 9 8 7 6 5 4 3 2 1

"[The first ride on the back of a horse] probably occurred very shortly after the horse was domesticated, around 4000 B.C. . . . I think some kid—some brave, thrill-seeking adolescent—climbed aboard a docile mare who was accustomed to humans. All it took was one successful ride, and everyone wanted to do it."

—*Prof. David W. Anthony*
of the Institute for Ancient Equestrian Studies
in EQUUS 248 (June, 1998), p. 110

LADY OF
HORSES

PRELUDE

IN THE GRANDFATHERS' *time, when few yet living had been born, the People worshipped the horse, and served him, and took the gifts that he gave them: his meat, his hide, the milk of his mares. But he had not yet granted to men the greatest gift of all: the gift of riding on his back, and racing the wind.*

There was in that time among the People a prince of great beauty and strength, a child of kings, a god among men. He was the greatest of the hunters, the best of the dancers. No one was swifter of foot than he, or mightier in battle. Even before the beard had sprouted on his cheeks, he had led the young men of the People in war against their enemies, and taken skulls beyond count, so that every one of his women had a cup from which to drink, and all of his father's women, and even a handful of his younger brothers. When the People gathered to dance their deeds and to sing their prowess, he danced foremost, and his voice rose above them all, chanting his glory.

One day in the morning of the world, this prince walked out among the herds of horses. Such a thing, only a man grown and proven could do, for horses were sacred, beloved of the gods. They were tended by priests and acolytes, warded with great magics. The prince was a priest of the horse god, but of the second order, as a prince must be—for he cannot both serve the horse god in all things, and rule the People.

He was thinking on this as he walked, while the mares grazed and the foals played in the fields of grass. The Stallion who ruled them, the great king of horses, stood on his hill as he liked to do, with the wind streaming in his mane, and watched over them all.

Men, even priests, even princes, did not trouble the Stallion in his eminence. The Stallion in his turn took little notice of men, as was fitting; for he was greater than them all.

But on this day in the dawn time, in this bright morning of spring, the Stallion came down from his hill. He walked among his mares and his children, who gave way before his presence. He approached the prince.

The prince had paused at the Stallion's coming. No fear troubled him; he was a great warrior, a lord of the People. And yet he knew the welling of awe.

The Stallion stood before him. And he spoke as gods speak, in a voice like wind in the grass, like thunder on the steppe—the thunder of the herds over which he was king. "A gift I give," he said, "by the gods whose kin I am. Rise up, O man. Mount on my back."

The prince was a great man and proud, but even he was not so proud as to dare what the Stallion commanded. He spoke as humbly as a prince may, as a man before a god: "O lord of horses, how can I do that? I am but a man, and mortal. How can I mount on your back?"

"Mount on my back," said the Stallion. "Taste the wind. Take my gift and be glad."

Then the prince knew that the gift was freely given, of the Stallion's own will. And he did as he was bidden. He mounted on the Stallion's back. He tasted the wind. He became, for that while, like a god—and that was the Stallion's will, and his gift, and his great good pleasure.

Then the Stallion bade him choose companions, the greatest warriors and hunters of the People, its lords and princes, and offer them the gift in turn. "But have a care," said the Stallion, "that you choose only the best to be men, and never demean yourselves with lesser creatures; and let every man sit astride a stallion, but for boys keep the geldings. And let no woman at all, whatever her rank, trespass here where only men may go. This command I lay on you, and this gift I give: to be lords of the wind, and rulers of the world."

And so it was. The prince, who had been a lord of men, was now also a lord of horses, swift as wind in the grass, and more terrible than ever in battle. And his people prospered and grew, and spread far across the steppe. Every tribe that they met, they conquered, for they were swifter far than any man afoot, and could travel farther, and fight harder, and never succumb to weariness.

And the world changed; and men changed with it, borne on the backs of horses.

✦ ✦

The Grandmother told the tale as she was dying, told it as it had been told in the gatherings of the tribe since time out of mind— since, in fact, she was a girl.

"For I remember," she said. "I remember that prince. He was my brother."

Sparrow knew that. Everyone knew it, though most chose to forget. The Grandmother was only the Grandmother, ancient and shrunken, and, most thought, either mute or close to it. She never spoke where people could hear. Except to Sparrow. To her, who was her daughter's daughter's son's daughter, she had long told stories, wonderful stories, stories of the morning of the world.

Now that she was dying, she seemed little more than a voice and a spate of stories. Sparrow could not make her stop. She would barely sip water or the mare's milk that was the best sustenance of the People. She would not eat at all. She lived on the words she spoke.

"That story," she said as the sun sank low into evening, when the winter had closed in and the cold come down, and the earth lay deep in snow, "you know better than any. All you children do. It's the one story you live by—how the prince rode the Stallion, and made his men lords of horses.

"And that story is a lie."

Sparrow had been warming a cup of mare's milk over the fire in the Grandmother's tent, cherishing that warmth, for the cold was bitter. At first the words meant little. But as they sank in, she started, and nearly spilled the milk.

She mastered herself, careful of the cup, turning, holding herself steady. The Grandmother lay swaddled in furs, a tiny, shriveled creature—not even as large as Sparrow, who had nine summers. The life burned low in her. All that there was, was gathered in her eyes. Those were large still in their web of wrinkles, clear grey like rain, bearing in them all the memory of what she had been: great lady and great beauty, prince's sister, wife and mother of shamans.

"That story is a lie," she said in her whisper of a voice. "Oh, not that he was a great warrior and all the rest of it—that is true enough. But the Stallion never came to him and offered the great gift, the gift of the wind. That gift he took. He stole it, if you would know the truth. He seized it from the one to whom it was truly given."

Sparrow was not exactly horrified. The Grandmother had told her such truths before—hard truths, truths that laid bare the myths and deceits that men laid like veils over the world. But this one—this was the greatest of the myths, the one that surely must be true.

"There was a gift," the Grandmother said, "and it was freely given. But not to any man. It was given to a woman. And it was never a stallion who gave it. The men dream that stallions rule the herds; but anyone with eyes can see that stallions give way before the mares."

Sparrow knelt in front of the Grandmother, cradling the warm cup. The Grandmother let herself be fed a sip, then two; but no more. She was too full of words, and her life was too short. She could not waste it in drinking mare's milk.

"It was a mare who gave the gift," the Grandmother said. "A queen of mares, ruler of the herds, to be sure; and when she gave it, she was great with foal. One morning when the priests were far away, not long before she foaled, she offered the gift to a small and head-strong girlchild. She let the child clamber onto her broad warm back, and carried her about as she grazed. It was a quiet giving, with no words in it; but what need have horses ever had of words? Horses speak with their bodies. And she said, as clear as a voice in the air, 'Come, child. Mount on my back. Sit at the summit of the world.' "

Sparrow, in the furs beside the Grandmother, understood what she had been meant to understand. "You. The child was you."

The Grandmother nodded just visibly, a bare inclination of the head. "Yes. It was I. I rode the mare before my brother ever rode the Stallion. I rode her till she foaled, and after. And when she was strong again, she carried me far and fast, as a horse can—she gave me truly the gift of the wind.

"Then one day as I rode the mare, when I had grown arrogant with safety and forgotten to be cautious, one of the priests caught me. That priest, of course, was my brother: the prince who would be a legend. He was gentler to me than one of the others would have been—for what I had done was a terrible thing, a great sacrilege. I, a female, had sat on the back of a horse. To be sure, it was only a mare, but I had done it. And worse: I had done it over and over, for the whole of that long bright summer. I had not only been given the gift, I had taken it with both hands.

"There was nothing for it, my brother thought, but to take that gift from me. To claim it as his own. To become a legend, and to cause my part in it to be forgotten—for if the rest of the priests had known what I had done, they would have buried me under the earth. Nor would they have troubled to take my life first."

Sparrow shuddered. Priests still did that to people who had done terrible things, things too appalling for any lesser punishment.

"So you see," the Grandmother said a little wryly and not too bitterly, "how my brother took a truth that was less than endurable, and made it into a legend."

"It's still a lie," Sparrow said.

The Grandmother sighed, a bare whisper of breath. "Sometimes lies have to be. Men especially—they need them. Just as they need to believe that the stallion is the lord of the herd. Their spirits have little strength to bear the truth."

"That's not fair," Sparrow said.

"You are young," the Grandmother said. "Now go. Let me rest."

Sparrow intended to obey, but not before she had seen the Grandmother wrapped as warmly as possible, and fed a trickle of milk. The Grandmother was failing: she did not try to fend Sparrow off. Already her body was growing cold, though her spirit lived in it still, like an ember in a heap of ash.

She wanted to die in peace. Sparrow meant to let her; but it was hard to leave, harder than she had thought it would be. The Grandmother had been mother to her when her own mother died, had raised her when no one else would, and taught her most of what she knew. Sparrow had learned things from her that women were never supposed to know: arts and magics, prayers, powers over the world and its creatures.

A woman could not be a shaman. It was forbidden. And yet the Grandmother was a shaman, and perhaps more. To most of the People she was only the Grandmother, the eldest of the tribe, granted no such power or presence as the elders of the men were given, and accorded respect only insofar as she was let live when she could have been left on the steppe to die. And she had permitted it, because, she said, it was better to be ignored than to let the men know how much more power she had than any of them.

"You, too," she said now, as Sparrow steeled herself to go. "You have power. You are like me. The gods speak to you."

"No," Sparrow said. "No. They never do that."

"Don't lie to me," said the Grandmother. Her voice was remote, as if she spoke already from the far side of the sky. "I knew when you were born, what you would grow to be. You are of my blood, child. You are the gods' own."

"The gods don't speak to women," Sparrow said.

"The gods speak to whomever they choose." The Grandmother sighed, almost too faint to be heard. "Ah, child. They will test you— torment you. Have a care to be strong. And remember. Men cannot bear the weight of the truth. If you must lay it on them, do it gently; or veil it in a lie."

"And if I won't do that?"

"Then the gods defend you," the Grandmother said.

Sparrow left her then, for she could see that there was little life left, and no strength to bear anyone's presence but her own. When she came back, the Grandmother would be dead.

She grieved, walking out into the bitter cold and the advancing dark. And yet she was glad.

The Grandmother would wake on the other side of the sky. There she would be young again and beautiful, and strong as she had been when she was a girl. And if the gods were kind, and certainly if they were just, she would stand born anew, and a shape of light and swiftness would come upon her: a shape that was the mare whose gift she had received, but had been forced to give up. It would all be given back to her, all that the prince had taken. Then she would mount, singing for the joy that was in her. And the mare would turn, wheeling as the stars wheel, and bear her away, riding swifter than wind over the undying grass.

PART ONE

WALKER BETWEEN
THE WORLDS

WALKER WAS MAKING magic. It was only a small magic, a matter of fire and breath and a green plover's feather, and yet he set his soul in it, as if it had been a great working before all the tribe.

Keen lay in the tumbled sleeping-furs and watched. He had forgotten her, as he had forgotten everything else but the magic he was making. She did not mind. She had given him the strength to do this thing, whatever it was—she seldom asked. Her body in its deep places, the fire in her spirit, had fed his, till he rose and left her, and went to rouse the fire and work his spell.

Whatever he did, she loved to watch him. Walker was a young man, far too young, some said, for a shaman; and yet he was the prophet of the tribe, the speaker to the gods who rode on the wind, the Walker Between the Worlds. He was beautiful, too, in the way of the People: slender and tall, fair-haired and grey-eyed, his face carved as clean as the edge of a fine flint blade. When the young men danced, he danced in front of them all, and all the women envied Keen, because her husband was both graceful and strong.

Keen hugged herself amid the furs, clasping her arms tight about her breasts and running her hands down her belly. One came to rest there; the other slipped between her legs where she still throbbed gently from their loving. Maybe this time, if the gods were kind— maybe this time they had made a child.

She smiled, thinking of it; letting herself slip into a dream of a bright-haired infant, a son for his father, with Walker's beauty and his grace, and his gift of magic. From the middle of the dream, she almost convinced herself that he would be born; that he would exist. That she could reach in the furs beside her and touch him, and show him what his father did, finishing his spell, letting the feather fall spiraling into the fire, and so vanish in a flare and a brief, pungent stench.

Walker lingered for a while after his spell was done, crouching in the fading firelight. The shadows stroked the long lines of his back; they clasped his lean hard buttocks as, only a little while before, Keen's own hands had done.

When he rose, he took her somewhat by surprise. She lay still. He took no notice of her. He was smiling, a faint, edged smile. Whatever the working had been intended for, it seemed he was satisfied.

She was ready to take him back to bed again, and to do the other thing, too, that he loved to do after his workings as before; but he ignored her. He pulled on the long tunic of pale doeskin that was his right as shaman, and plaited his thick pale-yellow hair, weaving into it another feather of the plover; and then he went out, leaving her all alone in the dimness of the tent, with nothing to keep her company but the dying fire and the lingering stink of burnt feather.

+ +

Sparrow did not see Walker come out of the tent he shared with Keen, but she knew that he was out and about, just as a sparrow knows when the hawk has left his nest. The camp was different when Walker was abroad in it. People walked softer where he was, and watched their tongues. Everyone was afraid of the Walker Between the Worlds.

Sparrow was not afraid of him. But neither did she exert herself to attract his notice. She was on her way to fetch water from the river, a task not particularly urgent but demonstrably useful—not least for that it freed her from her father's tent. The wives were at their feuds again, White Bird taunting the others with her beauty and her wealth and the son who, she was certain, was swelling her belly. The rest, who had given the old man mostly daughters, were inclined to be bitter about it. And when the wives were bitter, the daughters were most likely to suffer.

Sparrow, eldest and least regarded of those daughters, kept her head down and her shoulders bent as she trudged through the camp. Her back was still sore from the blow she had caught before she left the tent, when she strayed unwisely in reach of an angry wife. She would straighten it when she came to the river, down among the reeds where no one could see, or care that he saw. Maybe she would bathe, too. Maybe she would swim. Maybe even she would visit the horses—though that would require great caution and no little store of luck.

She had to be careful while she was still in the camp, not to walk too swift or too light, or look too glad of her errand. People must see nothing but the brown shadow, the shaman's ill-regarded daughter, the little dark changeling among the tall fair tribesmen.

She had almost escaped—was almost free of the camp, and ready to slip away through the reeds and sedges of the river—but she had outwitted herself. She had strayed too close to the camp's edge where Walker's tent was.

Walker did not always see her. Only when he chose to. Only when he had a use for her.

"Sparrow," he said. His voice was as beautiful as his face, deep and sweet. "Sister. Have you come to visit us, then?"

Sparrow could hardly pretend not to have heard: not with him standing full in front of her, blocking her advance. He was a great deal taller than she, and rather broader. He was, she saw in a glance under her brows, smiling that thin smile of his. People found it terrifying. Sparrow merely glowered at it.

"What, little sister," Walker said, "no welcome for your brother? Not even a smile?"

"What do you need now?" she asked him—rudely, she knew, but she did not care.

"I could say I only needed your company," Walker said.

She snorted. "And I need your absence. White Bird thinks she's near her time. I'm to fetch water for the birthing. Or shall I tell her why I've been delayed?"

"White Bird, is it?" Walker said. "Well then, you mustn't keep her waiting. Here, I'll take one of the waterskins. The task will go the quicker if two of us do it."

Walker had never in his life offered to do anything out of the generosity of his heart—and certainly not the drawing of water, which was the most menial of labors. He needed her, then, and desperately, if he would stoop so far.

People saw him. They could hardly avoid it. They had seen him before, keeping company with his ill-favored sister; it was a kindness, they thought, and a mark of his strong spirit, that he had no shame of her company. They admired him the more and her the less, the more often he did it.

Sparrow had never cared overmuch for what people thought.

Since the Grandmother died, nine winters past, she had cared even less. She performed her duties quietly and well, because that was the least troublesome way to do it; then she had the world to herself.

Except, of course, when her brother the shaman vexed her peace. He did not do it often, which was a mercy. Mostly he went his own way, strutting among the men or making a great show of seeking solitude to perform his magics. When he came to her, it was because he needed something. A gift. A thing that he had little or nothing of, and she had altogether too much.

He walked with her down to the river, the image of noble solicitude. But as soon as the reeds had risen to hide them, he turned on the narrow path and stopped her.

She had been expecting that. She stopped somewhat out of his reach, even if he stretched his arms long, and eyed him warily. She was not going to give him anything. Not unless he asked.

Of course he knew that. He hated her for it: she saw how his eyes went narrow and cold. There was no warmth in his voice, either. "You've been dreaming again. I can tell. What is it now?"

Sparrow considered the lie that veils the truth—the lie the Grandmother had lived by. She was living one, too. She had been living it since the third spring after the Grandmother died, when her women's courses had come, and with them the dreams. And other things, things that brought her no pleasure and certainly no peace; but the dreams most of all. Her brother had not been Walker then. He had been Minnow, for the little fish that darts in an eddy of the river. But she had always been Sparrow, and no doubt always would be.

She knew better even then than to trust him. He was a slippery creature, like the little fish of his name. And yet when she woke from the first dream, the dream she knew was truth, he had been there; and in her befuddlement she had seen only the beauty of his face and the clear grey of his eyes, and she had told him what she dreamed. And he had listened to every word of it, intently, for he was their father's pupil, and was to be a shaman when his beard had grown. He had said words that she forgot almost as soon as they were spoken, words that soothed, that bade her rest, be at peace, forget the fear that had flung her into the light of morning.

Then he went away, and when next she heard of him, it was as a wonder and a rarity, a true dreamer, a shaman of power such as the People had seldom seen. But the dream he related to the tribe, the prophecy he spoke in a voice thrumming with power, was her dream. Hers, and never his.

She was still dreaming dreams. And he was still taking them and claiming them as his own. It was just as it had been with the Grandmother and the prince. No one would ever believe that a woman could do what she had done. If she tried to proclaim the truth, people would call it a lie. Then where would she go? What would she do? A woman could not be a shaman. That was the way of the world. That the gods had chosen to give her such gifts and to withhold them from her brother—that was their jest. Of course, her brother declared, she was to give those gifts to him, one by one, as each was given. He was the one who had been meant to receive them. She was but the vessel through which the gods passed them to their rightful master.

Now he demanded yet another vision. If he had a gift, it was to know when she dreamed; but this dream she had no desire to share. It was the dream she had most often. It had been the first, though she had not known it then for what it was, nor had she ever betrayed it to him. It came to her the night the Grandmother died, as a sort of death-vision—and that was what she had thought it was, until the spring, when other dreams began to come.

This dream had no fear in it, and no horror. It was a dream of pure splendor. In it, she stood on the steppe under the moon. And out of the moon came a Mare. It was Mare as the men's stallion was Stallion—greatest of all her kind, glory and goddess. She was as white as the moon, and she shone, leaping down out of the sky. The earth sighed as she touched it. The stars shone brighter in the light of her. She was splendid; she was beautiful beyond words. She was too holy, ever, to give to this man, this liar, her brother.

Therefore she gave him the other dream, the first that she had betrayed to him. "I saw it again," she said, flat and hard. "The black claw of winter, and the bitter spring. Then the summer of plenty. The bone-thin horses in the blowing snow, and the bleak plain and the dying herds of cattle and goats; and then, as always, the fat herds grazing in a field of flowers."

Walker hissed between his teeth. She thought for a moment that he would strike her. Sometimes he did, if she did not give him as much as he wanted. But this time he held back the blow. "Is that all? It's useless—worse than useless. I need something better!"

"Then let the gods give it to you," she said. "I have only this. I never ask for it. It simply comes."

His hand rose then. She braced against it. But again he did not strike. He turned instead, stiff with disgust, and stalked away.

He was still carrying the second, larger waterskin. She shrugged. It was not water she had come for, not really. She was free of him now, and would be, she could hope, for days yet. Everyone else was safe in the camp, or out hunting, or riding with the herds of horses. She had the river to herself.

+ +

She shook off the oppression of her brother's presence, the shadow that darkened her spirit when he had been at her again, stealing her visions. She was not giving him as many as she had before. If she could help it, she would give him none at all; but he was too determined for that. He needed the visions. He could not be a shaman without them.

And she could not be a shaman with them. She was a woman. She could not be anything, she sometimes thought; but that was foolishness.

For now she was free. She hid the waterskin in the reeds, in a place she had used before, and wandered down the riverbank toward a broad eddy. There, where the bank curved round an islet, was a quiet place, a pool where one could swim, or paddle in the water. The horses came there sometimes to drink, and deer, and once she had seen a bear fishing.

The People knew about the eddy, but mostly they kept away from it. A strong spirit lived there, they said. It was sacred, and therefore frightening. The only spirit Sparrow had ever sensed in that place was a spirit of peace: the lapping of water, the darting of dragonflies among the reeds.

Today she came there as unwarily as she could come anywhere—and found others there before her. She dropped down in the thicket, swallowing a gasp that was more than half rage. That so took her by surprise that she could not move, could only lie and stare.

It must have been a dare. The young men were much given to such. They were there, a whole pack of them, naked and whooping. It was a grand thing, they were telling one another, to face down the spirit that haunted this place, and swim in its pool. And frighten away the fish, Sparrow thought nastily, and drive the deer far away.

The ringleader, as always, was the king's son. He was not the tallest, but he was far from the smallest, and at an age when the rest were as awkward as yearling colts, he carried himself with lightness and grace. Even in a raw fury, Sparrow could not help but sigh as she watched him. He was beautiful. His hair was like winter sunlight, pale gleaming gold. His eyes were the clear blue of the sky in summer. His face . . .

She bit her tongue. That small pain helped her focus; kept her anger alive. Linden the prince barely knew she existed, nor ever would. She knew that, and yet she yearned after him. He was more beautiful than her brother Walker, as beautiful for a man as Keen was for a woman. When they were younger, Sparrow had believed devoutly that Keen should belong to Linden—perfect beauty mated to perfect beauty. But when Walker laid the courting-gifts in front of Keen's father's tent, Keen had let herself be given to Sparrow's brother.

"They're both beautiful," Keen had said when Sparrow taxed her with the choice. "But I prefer a man with wit as well as beauty. Your brother's mind is as marvelous as his face. Whereas Linden . . ."

"But Linden has a heart," Sparrow said.

Keen shook her head. She would never believe that Walker was as Sparrow knew him to be: beautiful to look at, ugly beneath. No one believed it. "Walker has a great heart," Keen said: "maybe not as warm as some, but he can be wonderfully gentle, and very kind. He sees beyond his own face. Linden has no such gift."

"Walker has a pretty way with words," Sparrow said; but she did not say the rest. Keen was not listening. She had wanted Walker since she was a child, as Sparrow wanted Linden. But Keen was beautiful, and her father was one of the great warriors of the People. He accepted a lofty price for his daughter, and returned it thrice over—as Walker had fully expected. Walker, who had had little of his own before he took Keen to wife, was now a wealthy man. And, to be fair, he was still kind to his wife.

Linden would never come asking for Sparrow as Walker had asked for Keen. Sparrow was both daughter and sister to shamans, but the old man's daughters were legion, and he reckoned this one of little account. She was a captive's daughter, a little dark bird among the tall fair People. She had no beauty and little grace. Her father's wives used her like a servant. There was nothing about her to draw the eye of a prince as lovely, and as empty-headed, as Linden.

She knew all that, had always known it, but she could still dream of lying in those long strong arms, and running her fingers through that pale-gold hair, and waking after a night's loving to that fair-skinned, clean-carved face. She sighed now as she watched him at play with the rest of the new-made men. They were wrestling in the shallows. Linden heaved up the Bullcalf—all the great roaring mass of him—and flung him into the water. The Bullcalf bellowed. Linden laughed. He was not particularly broad, but oh, he was strong, and lovely in his strength.

She almost forgot to be angry that they were profaning her secret place. Then she saw a figure that had been hovering about the edges, gathering courage, she supposed, to join the others. As if he had made up his mind at last, he stripped and plunged into the water, swimming as an otter swims, sleek and swift.

The others paddled gracelessly like dogs—even Linden, though his awkwardness had a certain beauty. Wolfcub, who on land was a tangle of knees and elbows, in the water was pure grace. He cut through the yelling crowd of young men, straight for Linden; tweaked his dangling rod, which Sparrow reckoned as lovely as the rest of him; and escaped just ahead of the whole pack of them.

At first Sparrow was too startled to realize what had happened. One moment the eddy was full of boisterous idiots. The next, they were all gone, baying after Wolfcub.

She let her breath out slowly. The quiet was deep. Not even a bird sang. Then, not too far away, one essayed a chirp. Then another. A fish splashed tentatively. A dragonfly ventured out above the newly stilled water. The eddy returned, little by little, to itself.

2

YOU WERE MAD to do that."

Wolfcub grinned at Sparrow. She did not need to know how painful that grin was. One or two of the young men had come close to catching him, and one had flung a stone that smote his shoulder a shrewd blow. He would be nursing the bruise for days.

"Of all the ways you could have freed this place of its invaders, tweaking the prince's rod was surely—surely—"

Wolfcub enjoyed the spectacle of Sparrow at a loss for words. "It worked," he pointed out. "I'll even live. Linden's been coveting my third-best hunting bow for time out of mind. He was happy to take it."

"Your third . . ." Sparrow glowered at him. "You didn't give him *that* one."

"It's pretty," he said. "It's carved with a frieze of leaping deer. It draws easy, too, though it doesn't shoot particularly far. Linden is so happy he's almost forgotten how he won the bow."

"And he thought it was your best." Sparrow sighed gustily. "Someday, wolfling, you're going to outsmart yourself."

"You thought I had today." Wolfcub had been lying on his stomach in the sand beside the river-eddy, to which the spirit of quiet had come back. He rolled carefully onto his back, lacing fingers behind his head, studying the play of clouds about the sun. If he glanced quickly, he could see Sparrow without her knowing it.

She was watching the river as he watched the sky. Water was her element, as the air was his. Her soul ran as deep and quiet as the river. How deep, no one knew—maybe not even she.

She thought she was ugly. She did not look like the other women: small, round, dark. Her mother had been a captive of the old people, the earth-spirits, whom the People had conquered in battle. She had been a witch, people said. If she had been a man, she would have been a shaman. The chief of the shamans of the People had taken her as was only fitting, subdued her and bedded her and got this one odd child on her. Then she lay down, it was said, and simply died—walked out of the world, Wolfcub thought, shed her skin like a snake and vanished away among the spirits.

This daughter whom she had left behind, child of a witch and a shaman, could have been all that her brother claimed to be. But she chose to slip like a shadow through the tribe, to be ignored, disregarded, forgotten. It was her protection, he supposed. It kept people from vexing her—or from discovering what she was.

She was not beautiful, no. She was a small brown bird of a woman. Her eyes were as dark as a doe's, and difficult to meet: she veiled them with her long black lashes under straight black brows. But when she lifted them to his, they came near to stopping his heart.

That was not all of her that he saw, either. Her rounded cheeks. Her firm chin. Her small strong hands. Her breasts, round and sweet, and her broad hips. Even the turn of her ankle, which for some reason he loved to see. Maybe only because it was hers.

Sometimes he dreamed of creeping out in the night and laying the bride-gifts before her father's door. And when in the morning they all came out to stare and wonder which of the shaman's many daughters he had chosen, he would turn and stretch out his hand and say, "That one." And everyone would marvel, and no one would dare to laugh, though he had chosen the least and the smallest. They would all learn then to see what she was.

But he never did it. He was too young yet. His name was not made in the world. He needed to be more, to be worthy of her.

He sighed and filled his eyes with sky.

✢ ✢

Sparrow left him drowsing by the eddy, found the waterskin and filled it, and went back to her father's tent. Her duties there, the squabbling wives, slipped over her like water over a stone.

When the sun had set and the men been fed, then the wives, then the children, Sparrow was free at last to eat her portion. She would have settled in a corner to do that, except that a flurry of whispers brought her alert. The young shaman was coming. People thought he came to see his father, but that could not be so: his father was gone, being a shaman. But Sparrow could feel his presence like fire on the skin. Walker would pause, yes, to pay his respects to his father's wives, and maybe to speak of visions. But he had no vision but what Sparrow gave him. He needed one—needed it desperately.

He was up to something. Sparrow did not want to know what it was. She slipped away under cover of the women's uproar—White Bird had decided that it was time to build the birthing-lodge, and was making a great deal of noise about it.

Even as Sparrow escaped beneath the back of the tent, she heard a woman's voice raised in welcome. Walker had come—and she had eluded him none too soon. Gods be thanked, the younger women and old Mallard who was a midwife were departing in a flock, bearing White Bird with them, for she was at her time. The men knew better than to slow or stop them.

Sparrow made herself a shadow. The camp was still very much awake, with the sun just set and the stars coming out. Some of the young men had gathered round the king's fire, singing vaunts and dancing their prowess. Linden strutted in the light, brandishing the bow that he had won from Wolfcub. Wolfcub himself she did not see. He would be wise to lie low, she thought, after what he had done to the prince.

She slipped from darkness to darkness, skirting circles of firelight. The camp dogs might have liked to follow her—she could be relied on for a kind word and sometimes a bit of meat—but she sent them back to their places. She had little enough to eat tonight, and nothing to share.

She went back to the river, meaning to hide in the reeds, eat her meager supper, and sleep as she could. But when she had made herself a lair in the rustling thicket, and eaten the seedcake and the bit of meat that had been her portion, she found herself wide awake.

She crept out onto the riverbank. The stars were bright overhead. The moon was rising, huge white full moon.

Sparrow's breath caught. This—this was—

Moonrise. It led her along the river past the eddy, then inland to the fields of grass.

She was awake, she was not dreaming. And yet this was like a dream: vividly, almost painfully clear, and yet oddly remote.

She knew where she was going. To the grass. To the steppe, and the herds of horses.

✢ ✢

The horses went where they would. The People followed. That was the way of the world, as it had been since the dawn time.

The herd that she knew best was the smallest. It had come in a few seasons before, as strays: mares without a stallion, searching for a new protector. The king of stallions had taken them in, mated with them and made them his own.

He thought he ruled them. But since they came, they and not the king led the herds in the great round of the year. They chose the pastures in each season. They drove off other mares and kept the king for themselves.

The men seemed not to know what the mares had done. That these strays were different, even the greatest fool could see. They were white or grey or dappled like the moon. Their foals all seemed ordinary at birth: black or bay, dun or brown. But as they grew, they paled, dappled, whitened.

Some of the shamans wondered if they might not be the gods' own. But Sparrow's father, the great shaman, Drinks-the-Wind, scoffed at such a thought. "All horses are sacred," he said. "These are strays, wanderers off the steppe—odd as to color, but ordinary enough else."

Drinks-the-Wind was truly a shaman as his son was not, but in this, Sparrow thought, he had no vision. Maybe because they were mares, he could not see what they were. The moon shone through them. The night wind sang in their manes.

There was one in particular. She was young; she had been born after the herd came to the People—born, in fact, at Sparrow's feet, on a night of the full moon, when the feet of gods trod the earth, and their voices whispered in the heavens. When she was a foal she was black dun—rare enough among horses, but not unheard of. But as she grew, as with the others, her color had faded, paling and dappling to silver.

Now, in her fourth summer, she was like the moon at the full. Other foals of her year had bred and borne foals of their own this spring, but she had cast off the young stallions who importuned her. Her sire, who might have driven her off as he had the rest of his daughters, had made no move against her. She grazed with her mother and her aunts and her sisters who had come to the herd from elsewhere, ran and played with the foals and the yearlings, squealed and tormented the lesser stallions.

It was she who always greeted Sparrow's arrival, lifting her head and calling as a mare calls to her foal: soft but peremptory. From the moment of her birth, she had looked to Sparrow, trailed after her when she walked through the herd, learned from her how frail and yet how strong a human creature could be.

She had grown up strong, and she had grown up beautiful. On this night she came to Sparrow under the rising moon, a white shining creature like the dream of a god. And yet she was a living creature. She was warm; she breathed. She smelled of sweet grass and sun-warmed earth and a pungency that was horse.

She came and laid her head in Sparrow's arms, and coaxed her to rub the spots that itched: along the cheeks, under the jaw, down the neck to the big square shoulders. She sighed. Sparrow sighed. They rested against one another.

The moon crept up the sky. The horses grazed or drowsed or
stood guard against the raiders of the steppe. After a while Sparrow
curled in a nest of grass at the white mare's feet. She slept there,
more deeply than she ever did in her father's tent. And in her sleep
she dreamed, but it was only the dream of the white mare. She had
lived it that night. What it meant beyond itself, she did not know,
nor did she care.

She woke in the dawn, shivering, damp with dew. The moon had
set. The mare stood above her like a white hill, head low, hipshot,
asleep. Her mane was knotted and her tail tangled with burrs. She
had never looked more mortal.

Sparrow knew then what the dream meant. Here in living flesh,
breathing the air that mortals breathed, was one of the gods. A goddess. Horse Goddess. She had taken the form and semblance of one
of her children.

There was great power in the knowing, but no fear. Not here in
the grey light of morning. Sparrow was safe, warded and protected.
No ill thing could come upon her here, and nothing touch her, unless
the mare willed it.

Sparrow sat up. The mare snorted gently, but otherwise did not
interrupt her sleep. Sparrow reached to touch the sturdy leg that
stood closest. It was dark still to the knee, though dappled with silver.
And it was quite solid.

Gods, the priests said, were things of air and naked power. They
lived in the wind and the storm, and rode the sun. Sometimes they
spoke through chosen vessels. Often they took on the fur and flesh
of an animal, or flew as a bird, bearing messages from Skyfather to
his lesser creation.

But to be born in flesh, to live in it, to be both mortal and god—
that, Sparrow had never heard of. It was a new thing, a great thing.
It was a mystery.

Was this the vision that Walker hungered for?

Her lips stretched in a mirthless smile. No; this was nothing that
Walker would think to ask for. When Walker demanded visions, he
had in mind those that furthered his cause and fed his power. She
had no doubt at all that he could use this as he used everything.

She was not going to give it to him. This was hers. The mare had
been born at her feet, had grown in her presence. The truth had
come to her, not to the Walker Between the Worlds. Let him find
his own vision. This one she kept for herself.

She rose stiffly. The mare woke with a small start, shook herself, rubbed her face on her knee. Then she turned her head and looked at Sparrow.

It was a command, as clear as if she had spoken it in words. *Get on my back. Mount and ride.*

Sparrow almost laughed. It was just as the Grandmother had said of that long-ago and older mare. Just such a command, just such an irresistible compulsion to obey. There was the mare, there was her broad pale back; and she was standing conveniently close to a low jut of stone.

Sparrow hesitated. When the Grandmother had done it, it was nothing that anyone had ever done before. Now it was a thing that only men did. That had been so since the prince took both vision and power away from his sister and made it his own. Boys learned to ride on gentle and much-scorned geldings. Men earned the right to master stallions. Women did not ride. They were forbidden the herds; forbidden to defile them with female impurity.

Indeed; and Sparrow had defied that prohibition since she was a child just barely big enough to slip away from her nurses and hide among the horses. Mares had raised her rather more attentively than her father's women had.

But she had never tried to ride. She had never been asked.

Sparrow gathered her courage in both hands. She clambered up on the rock. The mare stood still beside it. Gingerly, trying not to breathe too hard, she laid a leg across the mare's back. The mare flicked an ear at it, but did not buck or bolt as Sparrow had seen the colts do. With a sudden, almost fierce movement, Sparrow pulled herself astride.

The mare staggered a little, finding her balance. Sparrow clutched mane. The mare steadied. Sparrow clung to her, unable to move and barely able to think.

What had Linden said once in her hearing? "The world is a different place from the back of a horse."

Yes. It was. She had sat higher above the world, on the summit of a hill, in the branch of a tree that grew near one of their winter camps. And yet, to sit on the back of a living creature, to feel its warmth, how it breathed, the way it shifted to carry her weight: she had never known a thing like it.

She leaned forward a little, meaning to stroke the mare's neck. The mare advanced a step, as if surprised; then found herself walking.

Sparrow had to remind herself to breathe. That was what the men said when they taught the boys to ride. "Breathe. Don't clench. Let the horse carry you."

She tried to do that. It was harder than it had looked from a hiding place in the grass. A horse's back was round, and it rolled. At the same time it surged forward, then back. It was too much to do all at once.

It's worse if you think about it. Wolfcub's voice, clear as if he stood beside her. *You have to just do it.*

And that was the hardest thing. Not to think. Simply to do.

The mare circled the herd, walking more steadily as she grew accustomed to carrying Sparrow—and no credit to Sparrow, either; for all that she could do, she still clutched and clung. And yet she clutched less, the longer the mare walked.

The sun came up as Sparrow sat on the back of the mare. She was facing east, as it happened. The clear light fell full on her face, bathed her and the horse she rode. It blessed her. She was sure of that, as sure as she had been of anything, even to the mare's divinity. The sun smiled on her, and on what she did. She had pleased the gods.

· · · · · · · · · · 3 · · · · · · · · · ·

WHITE BIRD LABORED long and hard to deliver the child that was, she insisted, another son for her husband. It was a long enough labor that most of the women in the tribe had out of courtesy to find occasion to visit the birthing-lodge.

Keen would have avoided it if she could. White Bird was as arrogant as she was beautiful, and she had been insufferable since she began to bear children to Drinks-the-Wind. She always seemed to take particular care to remark on Keen—how they were of the same age, and Keen had yet to bear a child at all, whereas White Bird was bearing her third; the others having been daughters, and never counted except when White Bird wanted to vaunt herself over Keen.

That White Bird had caught Drinks-the-Wind's fancy when her breasts were barely budded, and Keen's father had waited till her courses came before he found her a husband, mattered little to White Bird. She only cared that she be better than anyone else, and especially Keen.

"It's because you're more beautiful than she is," Sparrow liked to observe. "She's jealous."

Keen did not think she was more beautiful than White Bird, but that White Bird was jealous, she could well believe. White Bird was jealous of anyone who had anything that she wanted, or might expect to want. And Keen had seen how she looked at Walker. Walker was young, strong, beautiful. Drinks-the-Wind was strong but he was old, and his teeth were bad. He smelled like an old man. Not like Walker, who was fastidious, and even bathed in winter.

Keen took her time in paying her respects to White Bird in the birthing-lodge, though it might cost her in courtesy: if she waited too long, White Bird would bear the child, and Keen would be known to have stayed away. That was not a wise thing for the wife of a shaman to do to the wife of a greater shaman.

On the second day therefore, which was as late as she dared, Keen gathered her courage and her store of calm, and went to the birthing-lodge.

Drinks-the-Wind's women had built it by the river in a place sacred to the women's gods, shaping it of woven reeds and making it soft inside with heaped grasses. Herbs were strewn among the grasses and hung at the entrance to the lodge. The fire that burned in front of it was pungent. Its smoke curled toward the blue vault of heaven. The gods would find it sweet, and the earth would cherish it; and ill spirits would fly far away.

Some of the women sat outside the lodge. They had been telling tales of horror, birthings that went on for days, women rent asunder, children stillborn or ill-born or cursed by the spirits. These were the tales they always told; and they were always driven out of the lodge, sometimes sooner, sometimes later.

Those who stayed within were wiser, maybe, and better able to hold their tongues. White Bird sat on the birthing-stool, swollen, sweat-streaming, exhausted. Her hair was lank about her face. Her body was gone all shapeless, great mass of belly, milk-heavy breasts, thighs parted as she strained to bear this child.

Warriors came back from battle less worn than this woman was, and her battle was not yet over. Keen almost admired her. When the pains struck, she did not scream. She grunted, that was all, and set herself to endure.

They were coming close together. It would not be long now. Old Mallard squatted down in the midwife's place and thrust a hand between White Bird's legs. The other elders leaned close. Mallard nodded. "It's coming."

Keen, spared the necessity of speaking polite words to White Bird, found herself catching the infant as it came. She was close, she was quick, and it came so fast that it caught even wise old Mallard by surprise.

They all stared at the wet and wriggling thing in Keen's hands. It gasped and choked and let out a thin wail.

"Yes," White Bird said faintly. Then more strongly: "Yes. Let me see him!"

The women glanced at one another. Keen, still holding the child, knew a moment's satisfaction as she laid the child in its mother's arms.

White Bird was so sure it was a son, that for a long moment she did not see what all the rest of them had seen. When she did, she stared. Her face went slack. So too her arms.

Once more Keen caught the child—the daughter whom White Bird had not allowed herself to foresee. It was a strong child, well formed, and large for one so young: small wonder then that it had taken so long in coming.

Keen tried to give the child back to its mother. But White Bird turned away. "That's not my baby," she said. "I have a son. Where is my son?"

Keen stood holding the child. No words came to her.

It was Mallard who said, "There, young one. There. Lie down now, and rest."

"Give me my son," White Bird said. "Where is my son?"

"Rest," Mallard said. "Rest."

Keen carried this youngest of the shaman's daughters into the light. Female that she was, she had no name, no existence till her father granted her both; and if he did not, then she belonged to the wolves and the birds of the air. What her mother wanted did not matter.

The women by the fire, seeing the girlchild in Keen's arms, sighed and rolled their eyes. White Bird was not greatly beloved. "Pity," one said for them all.

It was only a girl, but there was still somewhat they could do for her: wash her and lay her in the swaddling that had been waiting. It was a fine swaddling, of the best doeskin, ornamented with quills and beads, a swaddling for a prince. They left it open for the father to see, and because, if he chose not to grant her life, she must be laid naked on the plain for the wolves to take.

Keen had caught this child as she fell into the world. It was her place, by the gods' will if not her own, to serve as messenger to the shaman. The next time, she thought, she would be the first to visit White Bird in the birthing-lodge, and the first to leave, even before the fire was lit and the herbs scattered on it to drive the demons away.

But on this day she carried her small squalling burden from the sacred place into the camp. None of the men would be caught staring at a baby. The children, who had no need to be so proud, ran after her for a while, but babies were dull. And Keen was taking this one to the old men's circle, dullest of all the circles, and least inclined to welcome a pack of children.

Drinks-the-Wind was not like a young father awaiting a first son, so eager or so desperate that he either paced the camp till the people in it were ready to cast him out, or else snatched weapons and horse and fled till he could bear to come back again. Drinks-the-Wind was an elder, a shaman, father of many children. He might not even be aware that one of his wives had gone to the birthing-lodge—men of such stature as his could take little notice of such things.

Somehow Keen did not think White Bird would have allowed her husband to forget what she was doing. She would have made sure that he knew, and that he waited for the son she meant, herself, to place in his arms—for she had declared in everyone's hearing that she would do just that.

Keen's coming therefore would tell him all that he needed to know. That made her even less willing than she might have been, to do what had been laid on her. But she was a proper daughter of the People. She did not walk away from duty.

The elders sat in the circle as they did every morning and every noon, and every evening, too, as often as not. It was always the best place in the camp, wherever that camp might be. Here, it was a low hill that looked out toward the river. The king's tent was pitched there, beside a gnarled and ancient tree that was sacred to the spirits of earth and air. The white horsetail of the People hung from it, swaying gently in a bit of breeze.

The old men sat in the tree's shade, heads for the most part as white as the horsetail, backs more often bent than straight, and faces seamed with the passing of years. The king was one of the youngest: he still sat erect, and his shoulders were broad, his yellow hair not yet gone all grey. He still rode, still hunted, still led the People in battle as a king must do. When he could no longer do any of that, he would no longer be king.

Drinks-the-Wind was older—how much older, Keen could not be certain. Not as old as the Grandmother had been, who had died before she married Walker, but old. Old enough to be ancient. Yet he sat straight and bore his strong old bones lightly. The plaits of hair that lay on his shoulders and flowed down to his waist were white, but thick and beautiful as a woman's. He had been as handsome as his son when he was younger, it was said. He still had great beauty, the beauty of a tree in winter, stark and strong under the weight of snow.

His magic was strong, the power of his name terrible. Tribes far away from the People knew and feared him. Sometimes they sent their own shamans to seek his wisdom, as, Keen saw, some tribe she did not know had done just now: there were strangers in the circle, men smaller and darker and thicker-set than the People, bearing the spirit-bags and bone rattles of their calling. They did not speak the language of the People, but communed in signs that traders and travelers passed from tribe to tribe across the steppe.

The child in Keen's arms had hushed her crying and lay quiet, paddling aimlessly as babies do. She was much too young, and yet she seemed to be watching the stranger shamans present what must be a petition to the great shaman of the People. No one acknowledged Keen's presence. She was only a woman, standing with her eyes downcast as was proper, holding a newborn baby—a mere and unwelcome girlchild, everyone could see.

She knew some of the signs; it helped in speaking with women of distant tribes in the summer gathering, and in trading for this or that when the traders came through on their wanderings. There was trouble far to the east: a sickness in the herds, a weakness among the young men, and the hunting was poor. It was a curse, they thought, or the ill-will of a god, but none of them had power to alter it.

Drinks-the-Wind heard them out. When they were finished, he signed to them, briefly but courteously: "I will consider this. Go, rest, be at ease. My wives will see that you have whatever you desire."

The strangers left with good enough will, and perhaps some hope that the shaman's wives would be both beautiful and accommodating. Keen, who knew Drinks-the-Wind's chief wife all too well, expected that they would be disappointed. Mallard guarded her husband's honor zealously, and with it the honor—and the obedience—of his other wives. Older wives, gracious of manners but plain of face, would attend the strangers, and the younger and fairer women would be kept discreetly apart.

Then at last Keen was suffered to be noticed. Drinks-the-Wind looked on her as kindly as he ever could with his fierce pale eyes like a falcon's. She bent her head and let him see what she carried. "Here is the daughter White Bird bore you," she said. "She asks that you give her life, and make her your own." Which was not the truth, but this was ritual.

Drinks-the-Wind looked at his daughter. Keen thought she heard him sigh faintly. Then, somewhat to her surprise, he took the small drowsy body from her arms and lifted it up to the eye of the sun. "A strong child," he said, "and good to look on. Let her be Whitethorn, of the White Stone People."

So did he give his daughter life and make her a child of the People. Keen left gratefully, carrying the child, who was now named Whitethorn, back to her less than grateful mother.

✦ ✦

"I don't want it," White Bird said over and over. "Don't make me take it. Let me be!"

It was as if she had gone mad. The older wives sighed and muttered among themselves, remembering other new mothers who had been strange; but none quite as strange as this. Old Mallard sent Keen away, to Keen's relief.

Keen walked slowly from the birthing-lodge, back to her own tent on the camp's edge. Her heart was troubled. To bear a child and not want it, even if it was a girl—how could any woman, even White Bird, do such a thing?

There were tasks to be done: hides to scrape and cure for clothing, for shoes, for mending the tent; seeds of the wild grasses to grind
into flour for bread; herbs to gather and dry, some for eating and
healing, and some for Walker's magics. The boys who hunted for the
youngest shaman had brought a brace of fat ducks to pluck and clean
and roast on a spit, and one, shyly, brought a grass basket full of
berries, first of the summer, which he had gathered, he said, just for
her.

All that she had to do, because Walker had as yet no other wives,
and had taken no captive to share his wife's labors. Keen had never
minded. It was a haven of sorts, an escape from the memory of White
Bird's strangeness.

Sometimes Walker did not come back to his tent till very late, or
if he was working magic or courting a vision, he might not come
back at all. Still Keen prepared dinner for him, roasted the ducks with
some of the herbs that she had gathered, and filled them with the
berries.

Maybe the scent brought him back, the rich fragrance of roasting
duck, the pungency of herbs, the delectable sweetness of the ripe red
berries. He came walking off the steppe in the evening, with the last
light of the sun turning his hair to ruddy gold. Keen, crouched by
the fire, caught her breath at the beauty of him. He walked as light
as a red deer, as proud as a stallion.

And he was hers. He smiled as he saw her.

They were modest, he and she. She lowered her eyes as a good
wife should, and offered him the dinner that she had made for him.
He sat politely and ate it, every bite, savoring the rich fat and the
sweet marrow of the bones. Then he urged her to take a portion,
and pressed till she gave in.

She was hungry, but not for that. She ate it because it was proper,
and because it filled her stomach. It was good, she supposed. She
barely noticed. Her eyes were full of his face in the firelight, the long
clean planes of it, the beard so fair it hid little, even if he had not cut
it short. It was all she could do not to lean forward and kiss him, out
in the open where anyone could see.

Waiting made it sweeter. She had learned that since she married
him. He had taught her. It was a shaman's gift, maybe. Certainly it
was not common to young men—and young, unquestionably, he still
was.

She went first into the tent. With beating heart and breath coming quick, she prepared their bed, sweetening it with herbs and the petals of flowers. He might not come. Sometimes he did not. He might go back among the men, or return to the steppe in search of dreams.

But tonight he came almost too soon after her to be proper. She had just taken off her long tunic and slipped her hair from its braid. As she drew it over her shoulder and began to comb it out, he lifted the tentflap and stooped beneath it.

He paused just within the flap, straightening slowly. The flame flickering in its bowl of fat, the lamp that she had lit to see by, flared and brightened at his coming, just as her spirit did.

He dropped his tunic without ceremony. His body was lean, no softness in it. He was not scarred as so many men were, from war, from the hunt, from quarrels when there were no wars to fight or beasts to kill. He was all smooth but for the marks that proclaimed him a shaman: over the heart, on his belly, above his manly parts. Later maybe she would trace the curves and swirls of them, to feed his power and give him strong dreams.

He swept her up, comb and half-unplaited hair and all, and kissed her till her eyes went dark. She wrapped arms and legs about him and took him into herself, even as he stood there. He buried his face in the hollow of her shoulder, laughing softly. "O beautiful," he said. "O marvelous."

He lowered her into the heaped furs and the sweetness of herbs. She held him within her, drawing him deep, rocking gently, then with greater urgency. His body was hot against hers. His scent was musk and smoke and wild grass. He was strong in her, and hard, filling her almost to pain.

She gasped at the gush of his seed like fire in her. *Gods,* she prayed. *Gods, spirits, Mother Earth, let this be a child. Give me a child!*

His weight sank onto her, crushing her breasts. She could not breathe. And yet she clung to him, holding him inside, until he slackened and shrank and slipped out for all she could do.

He was asleep suddenly, as men could do after they had taken a woman. Keen slipped from beneath him, struggling a little, gulping air. Her breasts ached. She stroked the ache out of them, and that other ache out of her lower parts, finishing what he had begun; putting the seal on the gate, as the old women would say.

He slept. She finished plaiting her hair, languidly, watching his face in the lamplight. It was much younger in sleep, all the arrogance smoothed away, the face of a boy, a child. But the body was a man's, and the long limp thing that lay in its nest of hair, below the blue swirls and interlacings that sealed his power as a shaman.

Keen smiled to herself. Some of the women whispered that Drinks-the-Wind had patterns of power limned on his rod itself; but none of his wives would confirm it. Some things, she supposed, were a mystery, and should remain so.

4

WALKER NEEDED A vision.

He was a shaman. Someday, and soon, he would be the shaman, the chief prophet and true ruler of the People. But first he had to have visions, proof that his power was greater than his father's had ever been.

It was his curse and the gods' jest that instead of a spirit-guide, some beast or bird, stone or tree or eddy of the river, he was given his visions through the least regarded of his sisters. And she was not a willing guide. Sometimes he had to threaten her before she would speak.

In the winter just gone by, he had made a long fast. He had emptied himself till his spirit was as pure as light through clear water, and begged the gods for a new guide. They had answered him nothing at all, until he went back to the camp, drifting light as a feather, and come face to face with her. And there was the gods' answer. This was his guide. He would have no other.

Now he needed a vision. His father had not had a great seeing in more summers than most could remember; but Walker had been counting. Nine. Nine summers. Little visions, small foretellings, Drinks-the-Wind had had; and he was famously wise. No one seemed to notice that the great prophecies had gone away from him.

They had gone away. And in the way of the gods, they would come back—must come back to the one who by blood and breeding was the old shaman's heir.

The gods had made that clear, just as they had made it clear that any vision Walker had must come through his sister. He could feel the time running out. This summer was the ninth-year feast, the great gathering of tribes, when kings were made and shamans chosen, and the great sacrifices were offered up to the gods of earth and sky. To that feast, Walker must bring more than his simple self. He must have a prophecy.

He tracked his sister to one of her lairs, an eddy of the river where sometimes the young men came to swim and play. There was no one there on this day of bright and singing spring, except the one he had come hunting for. She sat on a stone, seeming no more than a stone herself, in her worn rag of a tunic, with her feet bare and her hair escaping its plait. She was no guide for a shaman to boast of, but she was all he had. He had to make the best of it.

He could tell that she was aware of him: her shoulders stiffened just perceptibly. But she did not acknowledge him. She was an odd, wild, ill-mannered creature, and no one seemed inclined to teach her proper womanly decorum.

Someday Walker meant to, but not now. Not this moment. He needed a vision.

"No," she said.

He must have spoken the words aloud, for she was answering him, still with her face turned away from him, staring out over the sunlit water.

"I will not give you a vision," she said.

"Of course you will," said Walker, softening his voice as much as he could, though he would dearly have loved to slap her. "You have visions. I feel them in you. Give them to me."

"No."

He seized her arm and pulled her about. She came without resistance. There was no fear in her face. "You must," he said through gritted teeth, "give me what is mine."

"I have nothing to give you."

"You must!" he cried. "I must have a vision. I—need—" He stopped before he betrayed himself. "I must have a vision," he repeated.

"Invent one," Sparrow said, so insolently that he struck her. She cowered under the blow, but her eyes had no submission in them.

He stood breathing hard, glaring down at her. She had grown more defiant rather than less, the older she grew. Now even force could not shift her. That much, her eyes told him. She was wise to his threats, and aware of his fear: that if he harmed her, the visions would go away.

It was time he found a husband for her. Someone strong, and not to be swayed by a woman's wiles. A man who would curb her tongue and teach her proper obedience.

As for inventing a prophecy . . . he shuddered to think of it. That was blasphemy. A shaman's power was in the truth, though he might veil it in mystery for the people's sake.

She crouched at his feet, small huddled body, wide defiant eyes. He could sense no yielding in her.

In a passion of rage and frustration, he flung up his hand. He would beat her till she bled; till she cried for mercy. She gave him no choice. He must have his vision.

A shriek rent the air, a scream of pure rage. Walker whipped about with hammering heart.

There was nothing there. The eddy was quiet, the sun unsullied. A horse, he thought, now that he could think again. A mare, driving off an importunate stallion. One of the herds must have come down to the river, out of sight round the bend of the eddy.

His heart slowed. His mind cleared. He turned back to his sister.

She was gone. The eddy was empty of her. Nor was she to be found anywhere among the People, though he looked hard and long. She had vanished from the camp, or hidden so deep in it that she escaped him utterly.

+ +

On the morning when the shamans from the east consented at last to leave the warmth and the good hunting of the People's camp and return to their cold and distant country, Walker pondered his need and his sister's intransigence. Drinks-the-Wind had given the easterners what they seemed to reckon wisdom, but Walker barely saw even sense in it. The elder shaman bade them fast and pray, and perform a ritual of cleansing over the herds, and make certain that all the hunters performed the proper rites both before and after a hunt. That would appease the gods, the old man said, and bring back the game. Then they would be strong again.

Which might be true, but any man of sense could have advised such a thing. They had not needed a full moon's journey to be told of it.

Drinks-the-Wind had grown old. And the king himself was no

longer young. Walker saw him as he set the strangers on their way. His stallion had grown thin in the winter, and the back that had been so strong was beginning to sway. The man on that back had the same look to him of age beginning to conquer his strength.

And this was a ninth year.

Walker left the camp without speaking to anyone. He needed solitude to hear the gods' voices most clearly. But as he climbed the long hill above the river, a whooping crowd of young fools thundered past on half-wild horses, with a pack of hunting-dogs baying before them. Linden the prince rode hunting with his friends and followers. Some had great hopes: they carried boar-spears.

Most of them veered wide round Walker. They were afraid of him, though they might have chosen to call it hearty respect for the shaman's power. But Linden paused. His stallion was very beautiful, deep red, but its mane and tail were the same winter gold as Linden's own long plaits; and it made a great show of fire and fierceness, though Walker, who had seen it in the herds, knew that it was not the best regarded of the stallions. It was too inclined to defer to the mares.

Deference need not be an ill thing, if it was properly judged. Walker reflected on that as he smiled up at the man on the horse's back. Linden smiled down a little uncertainly, but with a lift of the chin that spoke of proper princely pride.

"Good morning, prince of the White Stone People," Walker said civilly.

"Good morning," Linden said, without granting Walker a title. "We're going hunting. Shall we bring you back a fat deer?"

"Bring me back a tender piglet," Walker said, "fresh from its mother's teat."

Linden looked as if he did not quite dare to laugh. "That's tender meat indeed," he said, "and not easy to get hold of."

"Yes," Walker said.

"Would you like the sow's milk to cook it in?"

"That would be a dangerous thing," Walker said, "to milk a wild sow."

"So it would," said Linden. He laughed then, light and a little wild. "You'll dine on piglet tonight, seer. My word on it."

Walker inclined his head. Linden wheeled his showy beast about, laughed again and sent him thundering after the others.

Walker stood on the hilltop. His eyes followed the young men as they galloped off northward, but his mind flew far above them, looking down on them with cold falcon-eyes. They were little men, every one, and their prince was hardly greater than they.

And yet that was a very pretty creature, sitting on the back of his pretty stallion. He moved well, spoke well. He was hunter enough for the purpose. He was much too thick of wit to know fear in battle, though he had little judgment, either.

It was a ninth year, and the king was old. His son was young, very young, and not the most clever of men.

It came to Walker out of the sun, in the whisper of the wind. Shamans had always ruled the kingmaking—that was so from the dawn time. And yet, in the long ago, the king had been king for but a year, served his purpose, led the young men in battle and in the hunt, mated with the royal women. Then when his year ended, so too did he. There had been the great sacrifice then, the Stallion offered up to the gods—but he had had a rider, always. The king of stallions and the king of men had gone together before the gods, taking with them the People's prayers and their petitions, and all their tribute.

Then there had come a year of war that stretched into two, then three; and the king in that time was a great leader of men. The shamans had suffered him to live until the war was over. By then the People were accustomed to him, and he was strong among them. The shamans bowed to his power, even till the ninth year, when at last they mustered the strength of will to offer him in sacrifice.

That had begun the decline. Now a king ruled as long as he pleased, or as long as he kept his strength. He chose the time when he would die, and the shamans submitted to his will.

It was time, Walker thought, to return to the old ways. The king was growing old. His son was strong in body but weak in will. Any man of wit could play him like a flute.

Walker turned his face to the blue heaven. The sun stroked his cheeks with warm fingers. He spread his arms and wheeled slowly, as the stars wheeled at night and the sun by day. The wind caressed him, sweeter than any woman's touch.

After all, he had had his vision. It had not come in dream through his sister, nor in trance, nor after a great working. And yet it was real.

It was strong. It filled him with certainty. He was the Walker Between the Worlds. He would be a maker of kings and a ruler of the People. He would be as shamans had been in the old time, great in power and terrible in his strength.

5

WOLFCUB HEARD WHAT the shaman said to Linden, and how Linden played into his hands with almost distressing ease. Wolfcub had been going hunting himself, but alone, as he preferred to do. It was easier to track the deer without a pack of idiots baying at his back.

But once he had seen that Linden meant to bring the shaman a delicacy for his dinner, Wolfcub attached himself to the end of the riding. No one minded at all. Wolfcub was the odd one, the one who liked to hunt alone, but he was also the son of the great hunter of the People, and a hunter of prowess himself. He was always welcome on hunts, no matter what impudence he might have offered the prince.

Linden, at least, had a short memory for slights. He was an easy man, which might be a virtue, or might not. Wolfcub could never quite decide. He was carrying the pretty bow that Wolfcub had given him, for he cherished it: it was, like his horse, like himself, lovely to look at if not particularly practical.

Wolfcub, whose horse was no beauty, but hardy and sensible, shrugged to himself and made his way to a place not far behind Linden. If Linden was going to risk his neck going after a sow and her piglets, Wolfcub would do what he could to keep the fool alive. The fool was, after all, the king's son.

A pack of wild pigs had made itself a tribe some distance down the river, where an outcropping of rock gave shelter, and a little thicket of wind-torn trees offered roots to graze among. The boar had claimed the upper reaches of the hill, the sows and piglets the rest.

If Wolfcub had been consulted, which clearly he had not, he

would have preferred that they hunt deer, whose meat was sweeter and who did not turn a hunt into a battle. But there was no glory in hunting deer when there was a boar to hunt.

This one had been lord of his tribe for a hand of seasons now. This was not the first hunt he had seen. Nor might it be the last. He had killed men who came against him, taken wounds that would have slain a lesser beast, but escaped to his lair and mended, and come back in time to challenge a new hunt.

They left the horses to graze just out of sight of the boar's rock, with a handful of sullen boys to look after them. On foot then, and as softly as they knew how, they made their way toward the rock. Brighteyes, who was best with the dogs, had whipped in the leaders and bound them, so that the others followed with heads and tails low. They would have their part to play in the hunt, but not yet— not too soon.

Wolfcub hung back somewhat, still within spearcast of Linden, but out of the crush of young men. He was wary, half of the sows and their great boar, half of the shaman who had dared the prince to come here. Wolfcub did not trust the Walker Between the Worlds. That one had ambitions, he thought, beyond the simple reading of prophecies for the People to marvel at.

And maybe he wanted Linden dead. Or maybe he did not. Wolfcub was not sure, yet.

But of this he could be sure: he would do what he could to keep his king's son safe. Not for any love of the pretty idiot, but because he was the king's son. And, certainly, because Wolfcub loved Walker not at all.

At this hour of the day, their quarry rooted and idled about the base of the rock. The great sow, the mother of the tribe, cast her bulk in the shade of the trees, while her piglets played at battle or at feeding in the leafmold nearby. Other, lesser sows fed beyond them, or lay as she lay and nursed their own litters. Of the boar there was no sign.

That meant little, Wolfcub knew. The old warrior would have heard them coming from far away, and would know what they intended. He would wait and watch, and when they were off guard, he would attack.

They had to hope that they took their prey and escaped before the boar came. Though Linden might hope for something else— for the boar himself, his hot heart's blood springing over Linden's hands. The shaman had asked a thing that was mad, perhaps knowing Linden would want something madder still.

There was nothing Wolfcub could do for that, except watch and wait. Linden went in among the trees, the more fool he, rather than let Brighteyes loose the dogs to bring the sow and her litter to him. He went in and the rest followed, Brighteyes, too, and the dogs, the whole lot of them, trampling into the shade of branches, tangling themselves in underbrush.

They were men of the steppe, high-grass people. Trees were alien. Sky shielded by branches, feet tangled by undergrowth—they knew nothing of such things. Wolfcub, hunter and son of a hunter, had made himself familiar with them, the better to excel at his craft.

The lesser pigs squealed and scattered, but the great sow knew no such cowardice. Her grunt brought her piglets flocking. Most fell greedily to nursing at her udders, but one or two, bolder than the rest, watched the hunters come.

She surged up, shedding piglets. Linden laughed and taunted her, dancing his mockery. She charged.

He was not there. But his noose was—the same rope of braided leather that he used to catch his horse, and strong enough to hold an enraged stallion. A charging sow strained it, but not to breaking. He leaped to lash it round the trunk of a tree. The tree groaned as the rope snapped taut, but held. The sow dropped like a stone.

Linden sprang in to bind her fore and aft. Then, still laughing, he milked a skinful out of her, while his following pursued her piglets. They caught three; the rest were too quick or too slippery to hold.

Still Wolfcub hung back. Linden rose triumphant, brandishing his skin of sow's milk—and, with a slash so swift the sow must scarce have felt it, took the udder he had drained it from.

He should have left the sow bound; but that was a good rope. He freed her. She lunged, screaming in rage. He danced away, mocking her, but not altogether in folly: he had his boar-spear. So too a handful of others. They circled her, whooping above her squeals, laughing and singing battle-songs.

The boar came without a sound. He was huge, and yet he passed like a shadow through the thickets. His eyes were tiny and blood-red. His tusks curved thrice, piercing his lip with each curve, till they arched, spear-sharp and gleaming, on either side of his eyes.

Wolfcub saw him clearly, far more clearly than he ever wanted to see such a beast. The boar plunged straight for the one who had violated his consort. Men and dogs fell before him.

Wolfcub was ready—as ready as any man could be for such an assault. He had braced himself, and secured his spearbutt in a knot of roots. As the boar came on, he called out, a deep grunting cry like the challenge of boar to boar.

The boar heard. He veered—only slightly, but it was enough. He launched himself at Wolfcub.

The spear would not hold. No spear could. Nothing of fire-hardened wood or tempered bone was strong enough. But it slowed him. It freed the others to escape bearing their prizes, the piglet and the skin of milk, though they had perforce to leave the sow behind.

Wolfcub crouched eye to eye with the great boar. The boar was pure living rage. Wolfcub was pure blind fear. Almost he lost the power to move. The boar's breath was hot in his face, so fetid that he gagged.

That freed him. He flung himself backward, rolled, came up running, bolting toward the light.

The boar sprang after him. But the spear was lodged in its breast, amid more scars than Wolfcub dared to count. It slowed him; staggered him. He fell to his knees. His great body, so heavy in the head and shoulders, so light behind, tumbled end over end. Wolfcub darted out of its path. Even in midair the boar slashed with hooves and tusks.

When it fell, the earth shook. Wolfcub stumbled and went down. Fire burned his leg. He scrambled away.

The boar did not come after him. It did not rise. It lay, massive and still. The spear lodged deep in its breast.

Wolfcub should not stop. Should not even pause. It was feigning death, surely it was. It was the great boar, the king of boars, the mocker of all who hunted it, slayer of men and hounds and horses. It could not be dead.

And yet no breath stirred that massive body. Blood and foam stained the tusks. The stink of death overlay the stink of boar.

Like a fool or a madman—like Linden, if Linden had lingered—Wolfcub approached the carcass. No life trembled in it. What no man had been able to do, the boar's own weight and speed, and a spear lodged just so, had done and more than done. The great boar was dead.

L INDEN WAS TO come back triumphant—or dead, but Walker had no real expectation of that. A great deed, a feat of prowess, would serve Walker's purpose well.

Linden came back with the piglet and the udder and the milk, but that paled beside the greater feat: the great boar, the king boar, was dead. But Linden had not killed him, or presumed to claim the honor. The one they all celebrated, the lord of the hunt, master of warriors and slayer of the great boar, was that odd lone creature whom everyone called the Wolfcub. To be sure, he was a son of Aurochs the hunter, but he appeared to have no ambition but to hunt alone.

Then why, Walker demanded of the gods, had he decided to hunt with the pack at this of all times? It was more than inconvenient. It was maddening.

The gods were not answering. Linden, curse him, would not give way to jealousy or claim the kill for himself. He seemed delighted to honor the boy as they all did, bringing him home in procession, and gaining his father's leave to call for a feast.

Well; and that might serve Walker, in its way. People noticed a generous man. A man who claimed only what was due him, who gave honor to those who had earned it . . . yes, that was kingly, too. Walker could make use of it.

But he would not forget this one who had spoiled his plan for the prince. A boar was a great kill, one of the greatest. A man who killed a boar was a lord of the tribe. Even such a man as this Wolfcub, who heretofore had claimed little and seemed to aspire to less.

✦ ✦

Sparrow saw how Walker looked at Wolfcub after he came back from the hunt with the boar's tusks on his arms and the boar's hide for a saddlecloth.

It was not easy to get at Wolfcub. Everyone wanted to sit with him, eat and drink with him, touch him to gain a bit of his luck. Wolfcub did not look as if he minded.

That woke her temper. It was foolish, she knew perfectly well—did not every young man yearn to be honored so?—but she could not help it. She was used to seeking him out whenever she had a mind, or being sought out as often as not, by someone who walked alone as she did, and cared no more to be noticed.

Now he was the People's darling. The king had set him in the place of honor, seen to it that he was fed the best of the feast and the strongest of the *kumiss,* and offered him a very great honor: his choice of captive women. Linden the prince undertook to advise him in that. In too little a while, the two of them had vanished into the king's tent, to the grand glee of the men at the feast. The king's laughter followed them, and a blessing with it.

Sparrow sat in the shadows and simmered. Something was odd in all of this, and she suspected that Wolfcub knew what it was. And he was in the king's tent, tumbling the king's women.

How like a man, after all. How utterly like a man.

✦ ✦

Wolfcub had never meant it to go on like this. At first, he tried to tell people that he had not killed the boar, the boar had killed itself. But they would not listen. "That's your spear in his heart," Linden said. "Of course you killed him."

And that, for the rest of them, was that. None of them seemed the least displeased to give Wolfcub the honor of the hunt. Certainly not Linden, who showed every evidence of delight. He offered his knife for the flaying, and lent a hand with it, too; and he helped Wolfcub free the tusks from the great jaws and slip them onto his arms. They fit almost disturbingly well, holding him in a warm strong clasp, as if they had been a god's hands.

He did not feel any stronger or any wiser for having taken that of all lives. The boar's strength had not entered into him. And yet its power, the potency of its name, had become his. He was the boarslayer. He was a lord of hunters.

He could let himself be glad of that, since no one minded; no one stooped to envy. The wolf who walked alone was one of the pack after all. That was not so ill a thing, now it had happened. Linden was alive and whole, whatever the shaman might think of that.

The feast he had expected. To sit by the king—yes, that was the place of honor. But when the king, warm with *kumiss* and expansive with the rich fat of the boar, gave him the night's freedom of his own tent, Wolfcub's first and indeed only impulse was to bolt for the shadows.

He might well have done it, if Linden had not laughed and said, "Here, brother! I'll help you. If my father wills?"

The king smiled indulgently and waved them both away. "Go! Go. Both of you. Don't let me see your faces till morning."

Linden had Wolfcub's hand before he could prevent it, pulled him up—staggering as the *kumiss* rushed to his head, but steadier on his feet than he strictly wanted to be—and carried him off to the king's tent.

Wolfcub had never passed that flap before. When he came with his father to visit the king, the king was always seated outside by the council-fire or taking his ease in the elders' circle. The tent was his private place, a kingdom of women, and of children too young to be sent to the boys' tent.

It was the largest tent in the camp, of course, as was fitting. The floor was covered with the finest tanned leather, and with mats of woven grasses, sweet-scented and pleasant underfoot. The sleeping-furs were of the best, and there were great treasures scattered among them: weapons of rare quality, coats and cloaks beaded and embroidered in patterns as magical as they were beautiful, necklaces of bone and stone and precious shell spread atop baskets of close and intricate weaving, skull-cups inlaid with bright stones and bits of shell, drinking-gourds painted with care and complexity, and, great treasures those, clay pots, some ornamented, some plain, that had come in trade from countries far away.

There was too much to take in all at once. Wolfcub let it enter his eyes as if he had been on a hunt, to remember later piece by piece, as he chose and as it amused him.

Now what he chiefly saw were the women who waited by the king's sleeping-furs. The rest would be hidden away behind a curtain, or perhaps had gone elsewhere for the night. He never had known what women did when men were not thinking of them, nor had he known to care.

These were the captives, the prizes of battle or raids, whom the king had chosen or who had been allotted him as the best of the booty. They were not all the most beautiful, though none was ill to look on. Some, he knew from rumor, had gifts that served the king:

weaving baskets, tanning hides, cooking or singing or, as people whispered, pleasing a man in the sleeping-furs. Wolfcub did not know which of them was which. They all stood as women were supposed to stand, eyes lowered, hands folded, submissive. Most were fair or redheaded like women of the People. Two were darker. These came from the south and west, Wolfcub knew, where the little dark people lived; where Sparrow's mother had come from, taken in war long ago.

Neither of them had quite her cast of feature. Both were lovely, doe-eyed and soft-cheeked, with full breasts and deep round bellies.

Wolfcub turned resolutely away from them, and chose almost without a glance, stretching out his hand to a blur of white face and fair hair. "Well chosen!" cried Linden, whose presence Wolfcub had all but forgotten. "Beauty and skill both, and a voice like water running. You've a fine eye for a woman, brother."

Wolfcub, who had brothers enough, but none of them was this one, held his tongue and made himself look at this paragon of women whose hand had happened to be closest. She was beautiful indeed. She seemed compliant, which the dark women had not. If it troubled her to be given to a callow boy, she did not show it. Maybe he would be a relief from the old man who was her husband, and the elders to whom she must be given most often as a gift.

His body had no difficulty in wanting her, whatever his mind did and wherever it wandered. He looked about. The women whom he had not chosen had withdrawn, but Linden was there still, and one of the women, a plump freckled creature with hair as red as fire. She had a bold look, now she was almost alone, and a wicked eye, which she cast on the thing thrusting beneath Wolfcub's leggings.

"There now," said Linden, "be patient. I'll let you have him— but you have to take me first."

The woman laughed. "You're pretty," she said in a barbarous accent. "He's not pretty. But when he grows up—aaahhhh." She let the sigh go on and on.

"But I," said Linden, "am pretty now." He swept her up in his arms and, to Wolfcub's considerable relief, carried her off behind one of the curtains that divided the tent. Wolfcub had feared that he would be forced to couple in front of the king's son—and, perhaps worse, in front of the plump and lecherous woman Linden had chosen.

But Wolfcub was alone with his own choice, who was not plump and who did not appear to be lecherous, either. Indeed she seemed a cold creature, such a one as suffered a man's presence but took no pleasure in it.

Maybe, after all, he should have taken one of the dark women, or the red one. A curtain was little enough barrier, and his ears were keen. Linden was more than pleased with his choice. And his choice was loudly and emphatically pleased with him.

Wolfcub sighed. If he walked away now, he dishonored the king and insulted the gift. He faced the fair woman. She had not moved since he singled her out: hands folded, eyes downcast. The tunic that she wore was finer than some men's wives could claim, well-tanned pale leather that caught the pale gold of her hair and made her skin seem even whiter than it was. She wore a necklace of bones and stones and beads, such as a man would trade fine furs for at the gathering of tribes.

This was a favorite, then. But surely not only for her beauty, though that was considerable: skin like milk, face carved as if from ivory, and eyes set wide in it under a swoop of fair brows. Wolfcub slipped the tunic from her shoulders. It hesitated over the rise of her breasts, then slid to her waist. She made no move to stop it.

His manly parts had ascended from ache to pain. But he did not indulge them. He touched her round high breasts. The nipples hardened under his hand. He stroked them slowly. Her breath caught.

So: she was not as cold as she seemed. "Do you resent me?" he asked her.

She raised her eyes. They were clear blue, pale as a winter morning, and hardly warmer. "I am my lord's to keep or to give as a gift," she said—and yes, her voice was like water falling, low and sweet.

"I am asking you," he said, "do you resent me?"

"I have learned," she answered, "to resent nothing."

"Would you rather I went away and left you alone?"

"Then my lord would beat me," she said, "because I had failed to please you."

Wolfcub bit his lip. There was no escape, then. Nor should he have wanted one, or been as eager to find it, and yet it was so.

He sighed before he knew what he did, and shed his leggings and his good tunic that he had put on for the feast. He was nothing to enchant a woman's eyes, he did not suppose, except that he was young and lithe and honed with all his riding and hunting. She was exquisite as she rose to face him, with her tunic pooling about her feet.

She too seemed to have resigned herself to this. She did not put on a smile, but he hardly minded; he wanted nothing so false. Her eyes warmed, perhaps, as she took him in. She took his hot and aching rod in her cool hand.

It burst at the touch, in spasms so fierce he tumbled to his knees. She followed him down, still calm, not laughing at him, nor mocking him for a fool of a boy. But then she had no need. He did it for her, bitterly.

She laid a hand over his mouth before he had well begun. "No," she said. "It's no shame. Here, lie by me for a while. Tell me of your hunt."

He stiffened against her when she would have drawn him down. "You don't want to hear me boast."

Her pale brows rose. "No? And why should I not? Men are charming when they vaunt themselves. They say you are more charming than most, and can tell a fine tale when you have a mind."

"Who says that?" he demanded. It was rude, but he could not help it.

She tugged at him. This time he gave way, till he was lying beside her but at a little distance. "Women talk to one another," she said. "They say you are very pleasant to listen to, and almost as pleasant to lie with."

"You see how true that is," he said.

She shrugged. "It's been a long while since the winter fires. You're young; your blood is hot. You killed a great boar today. Tell me how you did it. Tell me everything."

Very well, he thought. Since she insisted, he told her the truth. He even told her of the shaman's challenge to Linden, which might not have been wise at all, but he did not care. "It was an accident," he said, "that the boar died. He fell; the spear pierced him. I did nothing."

"You stood fast while he came, and you set the spear where it would be most deadly," she said—very like Linden, indeed. "That was a brave thing you did. And braver yet, what you did to the shaman."

Wolfcub flushed. "I'll pay a price for that. He won't forget."

"Mostly likely not," she said calmly. "Still, it was well done. Even a shaman can get above himself, and that one . . ." She trailed off; then shook her head. "Well. That's as may be. Come now, kiss me."

She said it so suddenly and so imperiously that he obeyed her before he thought. It was a long kiss, sweet as if with honey. Her hands did wonderful things in the midst of it, stroking his back and sides, and—greatest wonder of all—rousing his rod anew, far sooner than he would have thought possible.

She drew back from the kiss, but her hand stroked his rod still. She was smiling. "Youth," she said, "is a marvelous thing."

He could hardly disagree. She opened to him, taking him inside herself, but holding him—reining him in, drawing it out, as long and fully as sweet as her kiss. When he could not bear it for one more instant, when he was ready to scream for release, then at last, and only then, she let him go.

A cry escaped him, a shout of surprise. She smiled and brought him to the end of it, till he lay gasping, spent, with all his body thrumming like the bowstring after the arrow has flown.

Gods, he thought. *Dear gods.* But not for the height of her skill or the strength of the release. No; those were to be expected. The greatest wonder, the one that would remain with him long after his body's trembling had quieted, was the warmth of her smile. There was something a little sad in it, and something a little wry. It was a wonder, a marvel of a smile.

And that, he knew, was why she was the king's favorite. For that smile.

················ 7 ················

WHEN WOLFCUB CAME out of the king's tent in the morning, he had a sheen on him that no one could mistake. Certainly the men could not, either the young ones or the old: they mocked him for it, but lightly, as men will for one of their own. The whole camp knew by then that he had chosen the woman called Fawn, who was the king's favorite.

The king himself applauded the choice and bade him share the royal breakfast, seated at the king's right hand, with Linden the prince on Wolfcub's other side.

Already people were circling, watching, weighing this new favorite. Some of his more callow brothers were strutting about in the glory of their kinship, and letting fools even more callow appoint them messengers for this favor or that. His father might have had something to say of such foolishness, but Aurochs was away on a hunt.

Sparrow hoped that he would come back soon. Aurochs was a level-headed man, as she had thought his son was inclined to be—but Wolfcub was young, and Fawn had a great name among the women for her skill in bending men to her will. She could snatch a man's wits and turn him into a blind and seeking thing, a rod with eyes, as old Mallard had been heard to mutter. Mallard had no use for Fawn. "She's not a witch," the old woman said; "she's not got the wits for that. But she has the gods' own gift for bewitching a man."

Sparrow thought that perhaps Mallard was jealous. Mallard had been beautiful when she was young, but age had not been kind to her. Fawn had a beauty that would grow old slowly and only become finer, till it was stripped to the fine white bone. She knew it, as she could hardly fail to do, but she was not arrogant about it, nor did she sneer at Sparrow as some of the captives did. She had a calm way about her, a cool acceptance of her place in the world, that Sparrow found rather more pleasing than not.

But Sparrow was not at all pleased that she had worked her wiles on the Wolfcub. Sparrow had thought better of them both.

It was not as long as she had feared, before she could get at Wolfcub. After he broke his fast with the king, he managed to slip away—but not before Sparrow saw where he went. It was a hunter's trick, but she had learned it, and from Wolfcub, no less. One moment he was there, with all eyes on him. The next, he was gone, and people had a vague memory of his murmuring about changing out of his good tunic and then maybe going to swim in the river.

The tunic was an excuse, but a true one. Sparrow caught him coming out of the young men's tent, dressed in leggings but no tunic, with a hunting bow in his hand and a quiver on his back, and a bag that held perhaps a tunic and a bit to eat and provisions for a journey,

whether long or short. He looked like himself again, awkward gangling Wolfcub with his hair in untidy plaits; the princely creature of
the night before was gone, folded away with his best tunic.

That slowed her enough that he almost eluded her. He was not
going to the river; that had been a ruse. He was going to find the
horses, and then, she supposed, to hunt as he often did.

She let him think he had lost her, turning hunter herself, taking
another and quicker way to the place where Wolfcub's ugly little
stallion liked to graze. As she had expected, the stallion was there,
but Wolfcub was somewhat behind her. She filled the time by
brushing out the beast's dirt-colored coat with a twist of grass, and
picking burrs out of its rusty black mane. It had acknowledged her
when she came, but gone back to grazing, like the sensible creature
it was.

She was ready when Wolfcub came, well and carefully apart from
the horses, favoring him with a wide and sunny smile. "Good morning, O lord of hunters," she said. "Are you well pleased with yourself
and your world?"

He blanched, as well he might, but he was never one to turn and
bolt, even from Sparrow in a temper. He stood his ground, and regarded her with exasperating calm. "Is there any reason why I should
not be pleased?"

"None at all," she said brightly. "Fawn is a marvel, isn't she?"

His eyes widened. "You know—"

"Everybody knows Fawn," Sparrow said. "Or at least, all the
women do. Men only notice women when the women are being of
some use to them."

He flushed. "Men can lose their jewels for looking at women who
don't belong to them."

"Exactly," Sparrow said.

He opened his mouth, but shut it again. His eyes narrowed.
"You're jealous."

"Oh, you want me to be?"

"You're angry," he said slowly, as if that were a revelation. "You
really are jealous. You wish I hadn't gone into the king's tent. Don't
you?"

"If you hadn't gone in, you would have insulted the king." Sparrow did not like to say it, but it was true. "Of course you had to go.
And of course you chose Fawn. Only an idiot would pass up that
chance."

"She was the closest," he said with some heat. "I barely even saw her."

"I'm sure," said Sparrow.

"It's true!" And she believed that: Wolfcub did not lie. "I suppose," he said, "she meant it to happen that way. That's part of her art, isn't it? To know such things. To make them happen."

"She doesn't often have to," Sparrow said.

"Well," said Wolfcub. "I'm a fool, if not exactly an idiot. And you're jealous."

"What have I to be jealous of? I don't incline toward women."

That made him blush scarlet, to her considerable satisfaction. He might have bolted then, if she had not been standing between him and his horse. "You don't want me," he said. "But you don't want anyone else to want me, either."

"That's ridiculous."

"Isn't it?" He stepped round her. He paused for an instant, seeing how clean the stallion was, burrs picked out of his tail, and tangles out of his mane. But he seemed not to realize how that had come about. He shrugged and slipped the bridle over his stallion's ears.

She thought he would mount and ride away, but he paused. In that pause she said, "I'm not jealous. I'm annoyed. I haven't been able to get near you since you went on that madness of a hunt. My brother put Linden up to it, didn't he? That's why you went."

Wolfcub had quicker wits than most men: he could shift the path of his thought without excessive floundering about. "Yes, that's why I went. If you knew that, why are you asking me?"

"Because I wanted to be sure. Does Walker want Linden dead?"

"I . . ." Wolfcub paused, frowning, pondering what she had said. "I don't think so. I thought he might, but . . . no. He wanted Linden in danger, but he doesn't want Linden's life. He's up to something else."

"What else?"

"I don't know," Wolfcub said.

"He's pressing me for visions," said Sparrow. "He's plotting something, you can be sure of it."

Wolfcub did not ask what she meant about the visions. He knew. He was the only one who did, or who would believe her. "He wants visions?" Wolfcub's grey eyes darkened. "And he sent the king's son on an errand that, if it didn't kill him, would gain him a fine share of honor among the men."

"Except that you overshadowed him."

"Yes," Wolfcub said. "I didn't intend to. All I wanted was to make sure Linden was safe. I never meant to kill the boar."

"The gods saw to that," Sparrow said. And when he stared at her: "What, that's a great revelation? Of course they did! My brother has to know that—and I doubt very much that he's happy."

"I know he's not," Wolfcub said, not as if it frightened him, but he did not make light of it, either. "Whatever he's doing, I'll wager it has something to do with the king. Everyone knows Linden's his favorite son."

"And," said Sparrow, "it's a ninth year."

"Yes," Wolfcub said. "You don't think—"

"I think the king is older than he was, and Linden is young and beautiful and none too quick of wit. And," said Sparrow, "I think my brother knows this all too well."

"That is not a comfortable thought," said Wolfcub.

Sparrow set her lips together. No, it was not comfortable. She had not meant it to be. "Go on your hunt," she said. "Think on this. And if you happen to come across your father . . ."

"I'll tell him," Wolfcub said.

"Do that," said Sparrow. "Now go."

But he hovered still. "Maybe I should stay. Maybe—"

"No," she said. "I'll keep watch here. Come back as soon as you can. If you bring your father with you—so much the better."

He understood. She had known he would. He might have dallied, but she fixed a glare on him, fierce enough that he had caught the reins and sprung onto his horse's back, perhaps, before he stopped to think.

"Go," she said to the stallion. The stallion, like a sensible beast, obeyed.

✦ ✦

Wolfcub looked back once as he rode away. Sparrow stood watching him, as he had expected. There was something standing behind her. At first he thought it was a cloud, or a trick of the light; then it moved. It was a horse, grey as a cloud, lowering an elegant head to nuzzle Sparrow's neck. She did not turn, did not start, but reached up with all the calm in the world, and stroked the pale cheek and the dark muzzle.

Almost Wolfcub wheeled his stallion about and went charging back, but the horse was not in the mood to listen. Wolfcub gave in, for once. He had enough to think of as it was. Sparrow with a white horse—mare, he would have wagered, and he would have laid his best spear on the herd it came from—seemed, somehow, all of a piece with the rest of it.

He went on his hunt therefore, hunting not the red deer but a man, his father who could be anywhere in this part of the world. Aurochs was wise, wiser in Wolfcub's estimation than any shaman. He would know what to make of this. He might even know what to do about it.

·········· 8 ··········

S PARROW HAD BEEN away from her father's tent too much since she reckoned it wise to stay out of Walker's sight. When she came back from seeing Wolfcub off, and then from riding the white mare wherever the mare chose, which had been farther from the herd than Sparrow might have expected a horse to go, every one of her father's wives seemed to have decided at once that they needed something from her. It was well after sunset before she was done, and they were at her again in the dawn.

"Do my hair, Sparrow! Nobody else does it as well as you do." "My best tunic—see, the beading's all torn out along the hem. Mend it, Sparrow. Mend it quickly. Our lord has asked for me tonight." "Come here, Sparrow, grind this meal, and be quick! The men will be up before the bread is made."

And on and on, through a day that stretched endless, till she ran headlong into an obstacle that grunted but did not give way.

She blinked stupidly at Keen. Keen smiled at her, a smile that knew no trouble, even in the face of Sparrow's abstraction.

Sparrow was running to fetch a basketful of dung for the cookfire. Teal had taken it into her head to prepare a delicacy for Drinks-the-Wind, the stomach of a newborn calf stuffed with grain and berries and herbs, and roasted in heaped coals. Of course she must do it this very moment, and of course the supply of fuel had run low; and none of the children happened to be about, to fetch more.

Keen did not try to delay Sparrow on her errand, but she followed lightly, saying, "It's been ages since I saw you. Where have you been keeping yourself?"

"Hither and yon," Sparrow answered. She could never be rude to Keen, or walk away from her, even knowing what Keen was married to, and what she thought of him. Keen did not know the truth of her husband. That much Sparrow was sure of. Whether for fear of Keen's father, who was a man of wealth and power among the elders, or because it simply amused him, Walker was as kind to his wife as he could be. That he had no other wife, nor gave Keen anyone to help her look after his tent, was a matter for mild scandal among the women, but Keen did not seem to mind. She had an air about her of enviable ease. Very little disconcerted her, and she never seemed to struggle with the tasks that gave Sparrow such fits of frustration. Keen, like Wolfcub, was good at everything she did.

Sparrow, whose only gift was to dream as a shaman dreams, found it impossible to hate her. Keen was too pleasing a presence and too undemanding a companion. She never seemed to want anything of Sparrow but her company. She was the only one like that; everyone else either ignored Sparrow altogether, or had need of her as a servant.

That had been so long before Keen was given to Walker; since they were children, when the lovely gold-haired child attached herself with inexplicable persistence to the small and sullen dark one. Keen saw no visions, but listened when Sparrow spoke of hers; and in turn she spoke of the things that mattered to a woman, small things of the tent, the women's gathering, and later on, her husband.

The world she lived in was sunlit, undarkened by shadows. She knew that Sparrow's visions were the same as Walker's, but she did not seem to understand that only Sparrow saw them; Walker took them and called them his own. Sparrow had tried more than once to make her see this, but she would not. "My husband is a great shaman," she said with gentle firmness, and no anger that Sparrow could discern. "He doesn't need to steal from you, beloved, even if he could want to."

After a while Sparrow had given it up. Keen was blind, willfully or otherwise. Maybe it was best for her. She was married to him, after all. Her honor was his honor. Her will must be obedient to his.

Today she was not thinking of him at all. She was full of Wolfcub and the boar, as everyone else seemed to be. "Do you believe what he did?" she asked in wonder. "Who'd have thought it? Not that I ever reckoned him a coward, but he's always been a quiet boy, more hunter than warrior. Who'd have expected that he'd take the great boar, and save the prince's life, too?"

"He says it was an accident," Sparrow said a little sullenly.

"He's too modest." They had come to the edge of the herds of cattle. As Sparrow stooped to gather the dried dung, Keen helped her, moving easily beside her, caught up in wonder at the feat. "And now he's off hunting again as if nothing had ever happened. That's so like him. Any other of the boys would hang about the camp for days, drinking *kumiss* and boasting."

"Even Linden?" Sparrow asked, trying to be casual, but she could feel the heat in her cheeks.

"Well," said Keen with a glance that saw too much, and laughed at it, "maybe not Linden. He'd only hang about for a day or two. Then he'd be off in search of another boar to conquer."

"Nobody seems to mind that it's not Linden who did it," Sparrow said. "I'm surprised."

Keen's face did not cloud over, nor did she act as if she knew what her husband had been doing. "Yes, people are a little surprised at that," she said, "but that's the gods' gift, clearly. He certainly isn't troubled by it."

"Linden has a generous spirit," Sparrow murmured.

Keen smiled. Her glance turned wicked. "Yes, and there's much else about him that's generous, too. But Wolfcub—did you see how he looked by the fire last night, with the king beside him? Wasn't he handsome?"

Yes, he had been. But Sparrow was not about to admit it. "He's all arms and legs and eyes. And his shoulders stick out like a bird's."

"Not so much, any more," Keen said. "Do you know what I heard? Fawn has been wandering about all day with a dreamy look on her face. She never looks like that after the king has shared her. Lark says she stops sometimes and smiles. Wolfcub must be a wonder in the sleeping-furs, says Lark."

"Lark is a chattering fool." Sparrow pitched a handful of dung into the basket with such force that half of it leaped back out again.

"Lark says," said Keen, not the least disconcerted by Sparrow's temper, "that when he comes back from this latest hunt, she means to see if he's as good as Fawn's smile says he is."

"And what will Lark's father say to that?"

Keen laughed. "Why, nothing, of course! Black Bear is much too busy keeping his sons in order, to notice what his daughter does."

"He'll notice when her belly swells, the way she carries on."

"Maybe not even then," said Keen. She straightened, stretched, smiled at the sky. When she looked about her again, she paused. "Sparrow, look. That's a horse. It's watching us."

Sparrow did not look. She could feel it on her skin. The white mare had appeared somehow among the herd of cattle. The wonder of it was, none of them challenged her. Even the bull did not approach her.

Of course he did not. She was a goddess. Now that Sparrow knew, she could see how the mare shone like clouds over the moon.

As if Keen had taken the thought from Sparrow's head, she said, "See how bright she is. Isn't she one of the horses who came to the herds—what, a hand of winters ago now? It's strange, the way she watches us. As if she could speak, if she had a mind."

"Horses don't talk," Sparrow said to the basket, which was nearly full. A handful or two and she would be done. She wanted to be done. But she dallied, scowling, refusing to look at the mare, who so clearly wanted her to look. She could not afford that betrayal. Not in sight of the camp. And certainly not in front of Walker's wife. Keen was the friend of her childhood, closer than a sister, but this was a secret she could not safely share.

Keen was more intent on the horse than on Sparrow, which was perhaps a merciful thing. "She's beautiful. Like the moon. Like a new snowfall. Do you think one of the boys will try to tame her?"

Sparrow's rage rose so swiftly and so strongly that she almost lost control of it. But somehow, by main strength, she held it down. She spoke tightly, but she did not scream. She did not rail at Keen for saying what was, after all, but an idle thing, and reasonable enough as far as Keen could know. "No male would be caught on the back of a mare," she said. "Even such a mare as that."

"Silly," Keen said. "What stallion ever had such eyes? She sees us, Sparrow. She's actually looking at us. I wonder what she's doing with the cattle?"

"Maybe she's never seen two women crouched in the grass before," Sparrow said. "And maybe we should go. If the men find out how close we've come to one of the horses, they'll not be pleased at all."

"No," Keen sighed. "They won't." She rose regretfully and walked away, not pausing until she was at the distance deemed proper for a woman whom necessity brought near the herds.

Sparrow left with considerably less regret but fully as much reluctance. She could feel the mare's eyes on her, the mind intent, willing her to come away, to ride, to be free. But she could not do that. She was a woman of the People. What she had done already, raising the mare, lingering with her, riding her, was sacrilege that, if discovered, would cost her her life.

Not that she cared for that. But she did care that Keen might be caught up in it. Keen must not know this of all Sparrow's secrets.

She walked away therefore, without ever looking at the mare. When she came level with Keen, Keen was standing, looking back, yearning in a way that Sparrow knew all too well. "I wish . . ." she said. "I wish we didn't have to . . ."

But Keen did not finish the thought. It was close to unthinkable as it was. She stiffened her shoulders and took the laden basket from Sparrow's fingers, and walked back quickly to the camp.

✢ ✢

Keen liked to tell Walker of her days' doings, if he came to her early enough and if he seemed in the mood to listen. Usually he was, or pretended to be. Maybe he simply enjoyed the sound of her voice prattling on as she fed him his dinner and tended his belongings and, more often than not, waited for him to be ready to bed her.

But she did not tell him of the white mare. Part was prudence: telling him would force her to confess how close she and Sparrow had come to a horse. The rest was—yes, was the desire to keep something to herself. The mare was magical. Keen was not one who had a gift for such things, but even a blind man could see what that creature was. And she had looked at them—had looked at her, with eyes as dark as deep water, and such an expression that even now she struggled to put a name to it. Intelligence, yes. Curiosity? Maybe. Interest, to be sure. The mare had noticed her and her companion. What that notice meant, what it would mean hereafter, she did not know, and she was not minded to ask her husband. Shaman he might be, but he was a man. He would see only the profanation, never the magic.

She kept the secret, therefore, and chattered of other things, things that she barely remembered even as she said them. Walker, perhaps fortunately, was preoccupied himself. For a while she thought he would not want her tonight, but as she bent her head and began to withdraw, he caught her hand. She stopped. He did not move at first, simply held her. His fingers were hot. They almost burned. She bit her lip but did not speak.

Suddenly he seemed to remember that she was there, and to realize that he had a deathgrip on her hand. He loosened it somewhat but did not let go. His eyes were dark in the lamplight, his face flat, empty of expression. But his rod was high and hard, rising from beneath his tunic.

He took her without tenderness, without appearing to be aware of her at all. Her body was stiff, unready; but she submitted as a wife should, and tried to please him, though she was dry inside, and he hurt her, driving at her, grinding his loins on hers.

He spent himself quickly, for a mercy, got up and straightened his tunic and wandered away as if in the grip of a vision. She lay aching, with a burning between her legs, and tears pricking her eyelids. Foolish tears. Sometimes he was like this. He was a shaman. If his gods possessed him, there was little he or anyone could do, except to submit.

Tomorrow he would be himself again, tender, solicitous, bringing her a balm for the burning, and making love to her all the more gently, to atone for the way the gods had taken them both. She had only to live until then, and tell herself that it would be so. It always had been. That was the price they both paid for the gift the gods had given him.

WOLFCUB HUNTED FOR three days before he found his father. Even at that, he was surprised to succeed so soon. When Aurochs went on one of his hunts, he could wander for whole moons, traveling as far as the forest in the north or all the way to the dark-haired tribes of the south, the southernmost of whom, he said, lived on the shores of a great water. "Greater than any river," he said, "or any lake on the steppe. They call it *sea,* and insist that it goes on forever. But I think it pours off the edge of the world."

Wolfcub did not know if he believed that or not. But Aurochs had not gone so far this time. He had tracked a lion to its lair, simply for the pleasure of having done it; then he had followed a herd of antelope that grazed toward the west, bringing down a fawn to feed himself, and leaving the bones for the wolves.

When Wolfcub came upon him, he was making camp by a spring, building a fire and roasting a haunch of antelope. He greeted his son with utter lack of surprise, as if they had only parted that morning, and tilted his head, granting Wolfcub leave to share his dinner.

Wolfcub sat by the fire as was polite, ate what he was given, and belched his thanks. He did not speak. That was for his father to do, if his father saw fit. Which Aurochs did not always do; Aurochs was not a man for chatter.

Tonight however, as the stars came out, Aurochs said in his rough sweet voice, "It will rain tomorrow."

Wolfcub nodded. He could smell it on the wind, though the sky was clear. "The grass will be glad. It's been a dry spring."

"Spring should be wetter, yes." Aurochs stretched out on the ground, propped on his elbow. He was a compact man for one of the People, not particularly tall, with wide shoulders and strong arms. The women thought him handsome. Then, of late, they giggled and told Wolfcub that he looked like his father.

Wolfcub did not think that he did, but the women only laughed when he said so. Aurochs did not look as if he had ever been awkward or gangling. Wolfcub was both, to a distressing degree. What Aurochs thought of this, Wolfcub did not know. He had never asked.

But in one thing they two were alike. They preferred to hunt alone. Other men hunted in packs and companies, but Aurochs had always said that for real hunting a man needed to be free of distraction. He had taught his son the rudiments of the art long ago, then left him to it.

Now Aurochs looked at his son, really looked, and said, "So. You killed the boar."

Wolfcub sat still by the flicker of the fire. All the accolades of the People, the prince's admiration, the king's honor and his gifts, together meant less than that long level stare and those few words.

He had to say what he had been saying since it happened: "It was an accident. I got my spear in him, then he fell on it."

Aurochs nodded. "That would be how it was. He needed a god's hand to finish him."

Even Sparrow had not understood that. She wanted it to be Wolfcub's honor and his doing. But Aurochs saw. He knew. He still looked on Wolfcub with what could only be approval and said, "It's as well you did it. Another might have taken too much of the credit."

"They gave me much too much," said Wolfcub.

"People do that," Aurochs said. "Did they try to follow you?"

"I slipped out before they knew," said Wolfcub.

Aurochs smiled at that, a flicker almost too quick to see. When it was gone, it was wholly gone. "You didn't track me down to tell me of that."

"No," Wolfcub said. "Or . . . not simply that, though it's part of it. I wasn't hunting boar. Linden was, he and the pack of boys who run at his heel. But Linden wouldn't have done it if he hadn't been put up to it."

Aurochs nodded. His brows had drawn together slightly. He waited for Wolfcub to go on.

Wolfcub meant to, but he needed to think for a bit, to get his thoughts in order. His father did not mind. Aurochs had a gift of silence. He would lie there all night if it suited him, sleep, wake, and keep on waiting for Wolfcub to say what was troubling him.

In the end he said it baldly, without easing up to it. "It was the young shaman. Walker. He dared Linden to bring him home a piglet, and sow's milk to cook it in. I heard him do it. I was going hunting on my own, but after that I went with Linden. I didn't know what I could do, but I wanted to be there. I suppose the gods were calling me to use my spear against the boar."

"And that troubles you?"

"No, not that. Walker. He's a shaman. He must have known what the boar would do."

"Any hunter would know that," Aurochs said. "Have you considered that the shaman foresaw what you would do, and sent the prince to lead you on?"

Wolfcub had thought of it. But that had not roused the quiver in his bones when he saw Walker with Linden. Walker had not been thinking about Wolfcub at all—Wolfcub was sure of it. "It was Linden he thought of," he said. "He wanted Linden to provoke the boar. I think he wanted Linden dead."

"Or Linden was meant to kill the boar," said Aurochs, "and not you. That could well be."

Wolfcub shook his head. "That's not what my bones say. My bones say the shaman is up to no good."

"Shamans usually are," Aurochs said dryly. "That's what they do. They brew trouble."

"Yes," Wolfcub said. "Yes, that's what my bones say. What if— what if he wants Linden dead? Or the king?"

Aurochs seemed not to find that thought disturbing, though it made Wolfcub's stomach feel cold and sick. "What, king-killing? What purpose would that serve?"

"It's a ninth year," Wolfcub said. "And it was a hard winter, and is a dry spring."

"Not so hard anybody died of it," said Aurochs, "and not so dry that we suffer unduly."

"But it's a ninth year," said Wolfcub, "and the king is no longer young."

"The king is not old, either, or diminished in strength." Aurochs shook his head. "You never liked that young man, even before he was a shaman. Not that I have any great regard for him, but I doubt he's strong enough yet, or bold enough, to try his hand at making and unmaking kings. If you had said that the old one, old Drinks-the-Wind, had done it . . . then I might believe. But that boy, for all his pretensions? I don't think so. In the next ninth year, or the next, be wary and more than wary—but not in this one."

Wolfcub set his lips together. Of course his father must be right.

And yet his bones said no, and no, and no again. Walker was very young to be what he was, and he was reckoned extraordinarily gifted. He might not care that he was too young or too weak to do such things. He had been working great magics since before he grew his beard.

Aurochs knew that. He was also a man grown, with grown sons. He could not see that a boy, which was all Walker must be to him, might not only think of king-killing, he might try to do it.

Sparrow would not be pleased, Wolfcub thought rather distractedly. But this much he could do for her—and for himself, and for Linden. He could say, "Maybe that is so. But there are rumblings in the tribe that my bones don't like. It is a ninth year. People do strange things in a ninth year, and so do the gods. Didn't they raise my spear to kill the boar? Who knows what they will do next?"

"And you think I can do something about it?"

Wolfcub looked into his father's face. Aurochs was indulging him—a rare enough thing that it caught him off guard. But his wits rallied. "I think a man of sense, a man whom everyone respects, might be useful if something odd happens."

"I suppose," mused Aurochs, "I could hunt closer to the camp for a while. And visit my wives and the rest of my sons. Maybe make more sons. Would that content you?"

Wolfcub flushed. "Does it matter what I think?"

"Clearly you seem to think so, since you came so far to ask me to come back."

Wolfcub bit his lip. "It was presumptuous. I'm sorry I did it. Sorry I—"

"Stop that," Aurochs said mildly, but the words had the force of a slap. "You never did it before. Mind you don't do it again. But this once, I'll humor you."

Wolfcub bent his head. He would never tell his father who had in truth wanted Aurochs to come back. Aurochs might not be angry and he might not be insulted, but he well might decide to continue his hunt after all. No man of any standing would do something because a woman wanted it—though if it was his wife, and she pressed hard enough, he would do it simply to win a little peace.

Sparrow would have known this when she sent Wolfcub to his father. Wolfcub sat and watched his father sleep, but the face he saw was quite different: dark round face with eyes too big for it, fixed on him with fierce intensity.

He sighed. It was as well, he sometimes thought, that a woman could not be a shaman—because Sparrow would have made a terribly strong and dangerous one. Stronger than Walker, even. Maybe stronger than her father. She had the will for it, and the sheer bloody-mindedness. Though he could not imagine that she would ever want to kill the king.

No, he thought. That was not so. She might, if she decided it was right and just, take the king's life with her own hand. But she would never dream of killing the king's son. Not Linden, whom she had followed about like a forlorn puppy since she was small. Linden was not, that Wolfcub knew, even aware of Sparrow's existence, but that had never mattered to Sparrow. Sparrow was in love with the king's empty-headed but undeniably pretty son.

And Wolfcub was a fool, very probably, for doing her bidding. He did not dislike Linden, at all, but the man was by no means worthy of Sparrow—king's son or no.

It was an odd world, Wolfcub reflected as he lay by the dying fire and closed his eyes. He could still see Sparrow's face. As he gazed at it, he saw again what he had seen when he left her: the white mare at her back, glowing like the moon. It meant something, something important. But before he could grasp it, he had fallen asleep.

10

THE MARE WAS never satisfied. She wanted Sparrow with her far more often than Sparrow could manage. And it was never safe to be there; if any of the men caught her among the horses, she would be charged with profanation.

The mare did not know this, or if she knew, she did not care. Sparrow was hers. She wanted Sparrow there, with her, on her back or serving her. She hated it when Sparrow stayed away, as she had to, sometimes for days. Sparrow began to be afraid that the mare would follow her into the camp, and horrify everyone by trying to storm her father's tent and carry her away. Sometimes Sparrow wished she would do it and get it over. But she never did.

The nights were the best. Sparrow could slip out then, eluding wakeful children and suspicious wives, and leave the camp, and find the mare grazing in starlight or moonlight. Horses did not sleep as much as humans did, by night or by day. The mare was glad to leave her grazing and take Sparrow on her back and carry her as far as they both had a mind to go. More than once they wandered almost till morning. Much more than once, Sparrow slept among the horses, nestled in grass under the stars, with the mare standing guard over her. She never slept as well as she slept then, though she had to rise in the dark before dawn, and hasten back to her father's tent before anyone knew she was gone.

When she was with the mare, she dreamed strong dreams, and sometimes terrible; but she never was afraid. The mare stood guard, a white and shining presence, warding her against the dark. She would wake and find that the world without was the same as the world within: the vault of stars, the breathing night, the white mare.

It was harder and harder to go back to the day's duties, the women's pettiness, the men strutting about or lying in their circles, boasting of the things they had done or meant to do, and fancying themselves lords of the world. The real world, the world Sparrow longed to live in, had nothing to do with them at all.

She had always been apart from them, captive's child that she was, suffered by her father to live but little regarded past that. Then the dreams had come, that should have belonged to a shaman. And now she belonged to the white mare.

She began to think things that shocked her, that should have been unthinkable. This was not her tribe. These were not her people. Everything she was, they forbade, because she was a woman. She should go. She should ride away, one of those long starlit nights, and not come back.

Leave the People? Leave the safety of the tents, the protection of the tribe, even as little as that had ever profited her? Go out alone, forever?

What of Keen? What of Wolfcub? What of Linden, who had never even noticed she was there, but her world was the brighter for that he was in it? How could she leave them? How could she live all alone in the world? No one did that and survived. Even the hunters who went out by themselves always came back. The exiles, the people sent away, all died within the year. Sometimes the People found their starved bodies by the track as they traveled from camp to camp, or hunters came on them far out on the steppe. People were like horses, like wolves. They lived in packs and herds. They did not live alone.

So then, the spirit in her said. *Find a tribe that is yours. Or make one.*

She silenced that dangerous voice, that seductive spirit, but it pursued her wherever she went. It woke her on the rare nights when she slept in the camp, or followed her when she went to the mare. It would not let her be.

She had no thought for what anyone would think of all this, till one morning she stumbled out of her father's tent, barely awake and still remembering a long ride under the moon. She had been sent to fetch water, but she had forgotten the waterskins. One of the wives pitched them after her, shrilling at her to be quick, and adding nastily, "That is, if you can walk, after all the riding you've been doing of nights."

Sparrow stopped as if she had been struck. She did not even know who had spoken; it could have been any of the older wives. Someone else laughed and said, "Whatever she's been riding, it must be a marvel—the smile on her face when she comes staggering home . . . ah, to be so young again!"

Sparrow did her utmost to still her hammering heart, to overcome the horror that held her rooted. They did not mean horses, or that kind of riding—or she would have been cast in front of the king and the priests, and beaten to death for profaning the herds.

They thought she had a lover.

She would have laughed if she had had any breath for it. She unlocked her stiff fingers, bent and picked up the waterskins, and made her way, not too awkwardly, down to the river.

✦ ✦

Keen heard what people were saying of Sparrow. At first she laughed and told them to stop talking nonsense. But they insisted. Even sensible people, such as Aurochs' senior wife, declared that it was true. The shaman's odd daughter was creeping out at night and running off who knew where, and coming back late or just before dawn, looking both hollow-eyed and deeply satisfied. What else could she be doing but trysting with a lover?

Certainly people did such things. Some of the unmarried women kept whole herds of young men, concealing them all from fathers and brothers, if never from the women. The young men were not always discreet; sometimes one would get to boasting, and the wrong people would hear, and the woman would pay with her freedom or even her life—or if she had an indulgent father, she would be given to the man who boasted of the conquest, and so end the scandal.

And yet . . . Sparrow? Keen would never have imagined that Sparrow would creep away to lie with a lover, unless that lover was Linden. And Linden, as everyone knew, was dancing the old dance with Greyling's red-haired daughter. She was a jealous sort, and wildly beautiful, and had let it be known that she expected her lover to offer half a dozen horses for her at the next gathering of tribes, and so make her an honorable wife. She would have flown into a rage if Linden had been lying with anyone else.

Not Linden, then, unless he was far more circumspect than Keen would have thought he could be. And not Wolfcub—he was gone on one of his long and solitary hunts. There was no one else among the young men that Keen could think of, who might have drawn Sparrow's eye, or been inclined toward Sparrow, either. One of the older men? Maybe; some of them might actually have eyes to see the beauty in that small dark woman, though Keen rather doubted it. And if any of them had wanted her, he could simply have asked her father for her, and had her for but a token price. Drinks-the-Wind was in no way attached to that one of his daughters.

Maybe Sparrow was going out to sleep under the stars, that was all, and finding rest by herself that she could not have among her kin. Sparrow had never been afraid of night spirits or the things that walked in the dark. Even when she was small, she had said, "The stars watch over me, and Mother Moon protects me. I'm safe in the night."

Keen should be content with that. But people were talking, and Sparrow was taking no notice at all. She had a look about her that warned Keen not to approach, and certainly not to demand an answer to the riddle. Keen had learned long ago to heed that look.

Keen had also learned how to circle round it. It was not easy. Walker came home every night of late, and wanted his dinner and her body. She was glad to give him both, but would have been content to see him go away again after, chasing his dreams; but he seemed to have decided that the dreams would come, or not, whether he lay in his own tent or on a hilltop under the stars.

On the night of the new moon, at last, Walker stayed away. His time was the dark of the moon, as Drinks-the-Wind's was the full; he worked his greatest magics then, and performed his strongest rites. And, more to the point, he fasted and denied himself his wife's body, the better to receive the gods' messages.

Keen did not like to be as glad as she was that he would not come to her for three days; perhaps longer if his visions were particularly strong. Time was when she hated every night they were apart, and yearned for him, and barely slept in her cold and solitary bed. But he had been odd of late, abstracted, short-tempered; he was inclined to take her and spend himself in her and turn away before she began to be satisfied.

Maybe the rite and the visions would calm his spirit and restore the husband she loved. And while they did that, she would see for herself what took Sparrow away from her father's tent every night.

Keen had to lie in wait, which she was better at than some of the men might have liked to know: she and Sparrow and Wolfcub had played at being hunters when they were small, and Keen remembered. She settled herself in shadows not far from the elder shaman's tent, so placed that she could see both the front and the back of it. The camp quieted about her. Some of the men were celebrating a successful hunt, noisily, off by the young men's place, but here was dark. The camp dogs sniffed about her for a while; she held still, and they went away. Nothing else troubled her but the small things that bit in the night; and she had rubbed herself with a salve that kept most of them away.

She waited long, so long that she was sure, after all, Sparrow would not go out. Her legs were cramped with sitting, and her back had begun to ache. The night chill crept into her bones.

Still she waited. Patience, Wolfcub had taught her, was a hunter's best virtue. "And just when you think the quarry will never come, it does. Then be ready, or it will escape."

At first she was barely aware of the flicker in back of the tent, but she was alert; she fixed on it. A shadow had crept out from beneath the painted leather wall, moving so swift and so soft that it was all but imperceptible. But Keen had sharp eyes in the dark.

She eased to her feet, taking great care not to groan or stumble, and followed the shadow.

It was quiet and it was quick, but it was not particularly wary. Maybe many nights' safety had lulled it. It never looked back, nor seemed to know that someone followed in its track.

It went straight out of the camp, over the long hill and out by a way Keen knew well enough. The herds were there, north of the camp and spreading along a lesser river that flowed to the great one: goats closest, then cattle, and out beyond them, ranging farthest, the horses. In this, the dark of the moon, the priests would be among the stallions, celebrating rites that no woman might see or speak of, but all the women knew of them.

But the priests were not among the mares, and it was to the mares that the shadow went. Far in among them, fearless and unmolested, to the farthest of them all. To the king-herd, the god-herd, the herd that belonged to the great lord of stallions himself.

Keen should not have followed, but by then her feet were bound to the track, and her spirit was fixed on the shadow that was, that must be, Sparrow. The horses moved about her, quiet, unalarmed, though a mare snorted warning when she passed too close to a sleeping foal.

Keen had never gone among the horses before. Some of the girl-children did it, she had heard, but she had always thought that was boasting. Anyone who profaned the horses so could not but be marked by it. Child and woman, she had kept the proper distance, never going closer than she needed in order to gather dung for the fire, and keeping out of the way when the young men rode whooping through the camp, or a horse escaped and ran among the women and children.

Now she was close enough to touch the sacred hides if she dared, threading her way through big soft-breathing bodies. Their warmth was clearly perceptible. Their smell was sharply familiar. Men brought it back with them from the herds, pungent and rather pleasant.

She was not afraid. She was past that. No lightning fell from the sky. No priest leaped out of the shadows to strike her down for her transgression.

She had lost her quarry. But her spirit knew where it had gone. Starlight and night wind told her, and a surety in her bones.

The white mares, the strange ones, glimmered under the stars. Their dark children moved among them, grazing or dozing or lying in the grass. One shadow was smaller than the rest, and moved differently. She saw it clear against a pale and shining shape, then caught her breath: it was *on* the horse, sitting on its back, turning its face to the stars. The white horse neither reared nor bolted in rage. It stood very still. Its head was up. It was watching Keen.

There was nowhere to hide. The horses had drawn away as if to expose her. She stood alone on the hilltop.

The white horse approached her. Sparrow sat on its back, easy as one of the men, which told Keen that this was far from the first time she had ridden the horse. Her face was a pale blur, its expression unreadable.

Then Sparrow did a strange thing. She held out a hand. Keen took it without thinking. The horse moved. Sparrow pulled. Keen had to do something or fall under the horse's hooves.

When the flurry was over, Keen sat, breathing hard, with aching ribs and hammering heart, behind Sparrow on the back of the—mare?

Mare. Of course it would be. The stallions were all away with the priests. She was broad and warm and terribly alive. And Keen was sitting on her, clinging for dear life to Sparrow's middle.

Sparrow pried her grip loose, but let her hold on less strangling-tight. The slight tensing in her body was all the warning Keen had before the mare began to move.

Later Keen would wonder if that forbidden ride had been, after all, a dream. A woman could dream of riding, though she could never do it, and though she must never tell the men. But to do it—that was beyond any woman's reach or daring.

It was as impossible as it was true. She was flying over the grass on the thin edge of panic, with Sparrow in front of her, as calm as if she did this every night—which surely was the truth. Neither of them had spoken a word, nor had the mare made a sound.

It was a terrible thing they did, a forbidden thing, a violation. It was beautiful. It was glorious.

Keen could not leap from the mare's back: she did not dare. That made her a coward, but so be it. Women did not have to be brave as men did. They merely had to be wives, and be obedient, and break no laws. It should not have been difficult. Except that she was here, and breaking one of the great laws of the People, because her friend had done it before her.

They did not ride long by the stars' turning, though to Keen it was forever. They stopped apart from the herds, with no other horse to be seen, and no human thing, only the steppe and the stars.

Keen slipped helplessly from the mare's back. Her knees buckled. She fell and lay in the grass. She was dizzy and sick. Her heart beat so hard, she must surely die.

And yet after a while she succumbed to a desperate calm. The mare stood over her. Sparrow sat on the white back, gazing down. Keen could not meet those shadowed eyes. "You should have taken a lover," she said, "as everyone thinks you've done. It's far less deadly than this."

"Will you tell them?"

"No!" The word had been startled out of Keen, but once it was spoken she did not try to call it back. "No, I won't. But someone will find out. I can't be the only one who's curious."

"You're the only one who cares enough to follow."

"I'm the first who's cared to follow." Keen sat up shakily. Her thighs ached and burned. The earth wanted to surge and swell like a horse's back. "Why?"

Sparrow did not play at stupidity. She answered the question as Keen had meant it. "I was given the gift."

"By the mare?"

Sparrow nodded.

"But—"

"Do you know," Sparrow asked, "who first rode a horse? Do you really know? The Grandmother told me before she died. It wasn't the prince. It was a woman—a girl. The Grandmother. The gift was hers first. Her brother took it from her. Now," said Sparrow, "Horse Goddess gives it again."

Keen shivered. The nature, even the gender of the divinity who dwelt among the horses was a mystery, a secret for the priests to keep. And maybe, she caught herself thinking, they kept it so because they did not want the women to know that it was a goddess, not a god. Female—a mare—not a male.

Keen did not want to think of it—to believe it, or understand it. Sparrow was fevered; she was trembling. And the words she spoke . . .

"When the priests find out what you have done," Keen said, "you'll pay a terrible price." Sparrow's face was set against her, dark eyes hard. Keen regarded it in a kind of despair. Still, she had to say it. "If you stop now, come back, live quietly and stay away from the horses, no one will know. I'll make sure no one finds out."

Of course Sparrow answered, "I can't do that. The gift is given. This time I won't let it be taken away."

"You may not have a choice."

"I never did," said Sparrow. She stroked the mare's neck. The mare slanted a narrow ear back at her and made a soft sound, not quite a snort. Sparrow smiled at it. That smile struck Keen's heart. It was a smile of pure love, and pure, blank implacability. "Yes, you chose me. No one can undo the choosing."

"The priests will do it," Keen said, "and the shamans."

"They can try." Sparrow slid from the mare's back. She stood above Keen, crowned with stars. "They are not the only ones who exact prices. Nor are they the rulers of this world. The gods will have what is theirs, regardless of what men may say."

"You're mad," Keen whispered.

"I may be," Sparrow said. "But if I am, so is this mare. And so is Horse Goddess." She held out her hand. "Come, up. Let's go home."

Keen let herself be pulled to her feet. Mercifully, Sparrow did not force her onto the mare's back. They walked instead, a remarkably little distance—for, however long they had ridden, they had come back just over the hill from the camp. The mare followed as far as the hill, but as they climbed it, she wheeled and snorted and leaped into a gallop. She was returning to her herd, Keen thought, as the women returned to theirs.

·········· 11 ··········

THE EARTH WAS empty of magic. The sky was silent. Even the voice of the wind was still.

Walker sat on a far hilltop, naked to the sky, empty with fasting. He was all open, all bare to the gods, but the gods had nothing to say to him. Not even a bird flew, to offer him an omen.

He had sat on that hilltop for a hand of days past the time of the new moon. He had sung till his voice was gone, danced till his feet were raw. He had called on the spirits one by one and each by name: the spirits of earth and air, the ghosts of his ancestors, the great ones

who walked in darkness and the greater ones who walked in the light.
Not one had answered his call.

Such silences had befallen him before. The spirits did as they
pleased, and magic was not a tamed thing. And yet, like Sparrow's
recent refusal to give him her visions, this had a tang of malice in it.
They knew what he needed. They were not inclined to give it.

One more full moon. Then, in the moon's dark, the ninth year
began. The People would gather some days' journey south of this
camp. They would sing and dance and worship the gods, make marriages, make alliances, and—if it went as he hoped—make a king.

For that, he needed a vision, an omen. The source of his visions
would give him nothing. Now, it seemed, the source of his omens
was equally contrary.

A small, small part of him whispered that perhaps the silence was
his answer. But he would not accept that. He was the great shaman,
the prophet, the seer of the People. He would have his omen. He
would have his vision, too. He would have everything. This was a
test, that was all. He would pass that test, and his power would be
all the greater for it.

He rose. Naked but for the sacred signs painted in ocher on brow
and breast, and the amulets plaited into his hair and wound about
his neck and arms and middle, he walked where his feet led him.
They took him over the hill and down a narrow valley to a broad flat
plain. It was full of horses. The herds had moved while he kept his
vigil, shifting east and somewhat north. They would advance soon,
he knew, toward the great grazing grounds where all the herds gathered in summer, the plain as wide as a world and well-watered with
rivers both great and small.

The herds knew it was time. Did they also know it was a ninth
year? Walker's feet took him to a hill that overlooked the plain, and
let him sit there as he had sat on that other hill. The herds grazed
below him. They kept to their own clans and tribes, with spaces between. The stallions paced, wary, defending their bands of mares.

There were a great number of foals this year, many and many
small gamboling shapes amid the larger, quieter ones. Last year's
foals, the yearlings with their rough coats and big bellies and raw
half-grown look, prowled the edges, much set upon by both the
mares and the roving bands of young stallions.

Walker saw the priests among the horses, naked men wearing the skulls and maned hides of stallions. The rite had begun, then, the invocation of the king stallion, bidding him lead them to the summer gathering. It was silent as yet, the men standing or crouching on the edges of the herds, watching as Walker watched. They would be looking to see if the king would give them a sign.

He grazed among his mares, oblivious to the men. One of the mares had foaled not long ago, perhaps even this morning. She grazed closest, keeping herself between the tiny stumbling foal and the king, but making it clear that she sought his protection.

She was one of the royal band, the strange ones, the white mares. The foal was dark as all that kind were. It wobbled about as newborns did, exploring this world into which its mother had brought it.

The king took no notice of the foal, but he did not drive off the mare. He was a glorious creature, golden dun, with a heavy mane and a tail that dragged the ground. The scars of battle, wars of both men and horses, were thick on him, and his back had begun to weaken with age, but he was the king, the lord of the world. Perhaps he fancied himself immortal.

The young stallions had moved in close to the royal mares, not so near as to seem presumptuous, but one of the mares on the edge was in her foal-heat, and wanton with it. Sometimes the king would allow a lesser stallion to cover such a mare, if it suited his whim. The young stallions knew it. Those in the lead flared their nostrils and arched their necks. Their rods were rampant, thick and long as a woman's arm. Those behind tumbled and nipped and intermittently fought. Too timid to press to the front, they squabbled among themselves, finding excuses to do battle: a choice bit of grass, a stinging fly, a fellow who came too close and must be driven back.

Of the stallions who led the band, two were known to contend for mastery. One was a dun, a son of the king. The other was young to stand so high. He had been born in the spring after the grey mares came to the herds; his dam had been in foal before the king ever saw her. He was dark, black indeed, but dappled silver. His mane was bright silver, and his tail streaming behind, bright as moon on snow. His beauty was very great, and well he knew it. He put Walker in mind of Linden.

He left the herd of his fellows. The mare was visibly apart from her own herd now, grazing with great nonchalance, but her tail was high. She had turned so that the wind wafted her scent toward the stallions. She was a wanton one, to be sure, even ignoring her foal who had wandered off with another of the mares and her rather older offspring.

The silvermaned stallion approached her delicately, lifting each foot and setting it down with mincing precision. He was at his most beautiful, neck arched, nostrils flared, tail curled over back.

When he was still a little distance from her, he began to dance. He lifted and floated over the grass. He halted, wheeled, curvetted. He snorted and launched himself into the air, kicking exuberantly. He came down in a lofty, prancing trot, circling her, showing her every side and facet of his beauty.

She had raised her head at his approach. Her ears flicked back, then pricked sharply forward. Her tail rose even higher, as her rump lowered. But when he moved toward it, she squealed and struck with vicious swiftness.

He retreated rapidly, snorting. The mare stood still. He approached with great caution, stretched his neck out as far as it would go, touched noses. She squealed and struck again, but coyly. He held his ground until she had quieted once more. Then, tentatively, he ventured to nibble her cheek.

She would squeal again, of course, and upbraid him for presumption, but permit successively greater liberties until she had allowed him to mount her. But the king had taken notice at last of the interloper. He abandoned his lady and her foal. He roared through the herd, ears flat, long yellow teeth bared.

The young stallion was a beauty, but—unlike Linden—he was no fool. He had known what price he might pay for so enticing a mare. As the king charged toward him, he set himself between the king and the mare, and braced.

The king was tall and broad. He was aging but strong. The silvermaned stallion was taller and suitably broad, but he was young. He had yet to reach his full strength. The few fights he had fought were small ones, or he would have boasted greater scars; and he had won none of them, else he would have ruled a band of mares.

The king had been king for nine years. He was wise, and crafty in battle. Just before he would have struck the young one with his body, he veered. The silvermaned stallion stumbled off balance. The king lunged. He caught the silvermane on the shoulder. The silvermane screamed and lashed with his teeth. He was supple, and he was quick. He was also, perhaps, lucky—or a god favored him. As the king drew back from the bleeding shoulder, rearing for a new assault, the silvermane's teeth closed in his throat. The silvermane gripped blindly and tore.

The king's trumpet of rage died to a gurgle. Blood sprayed. The silvermane held on, tenacious as a wolf on its prey. The king battered him with frantic hooves, but he eluded them. He thrust his weight against that massive body, teeth still sunk in its throat, and cast it to the ground.

It fell with force that Walker felt on his hill. The silvermane stood over the king. His mouth was bloody. He was eating of his enemy's flesh—ears flat back, lips wrinkled in disgust, but chewing and swallowing. He had, in the way of magic, devoured his rival. He had taken the power into himself.

So did a warrior do among men, in the madness of battle. So did a king of men do when he conquered an enemy. The silvermane stood over the fallen king of horses. The king was still alive: legs thrashing, head tossing, though his throat was bitten out. The silvermane reared on his hindlegs, poised, came crashing down, full on the king's skull.

⁜ ⁜

The king of stallions was dead. The new king trumpeted, pealing his victory. He danced about the fallen body, prancing and curvetting, but once he had crushed its skull, he did not violate it further.

The herds, even the king's herd, seemed strangely unmoved. The lesser stallions kept to their places, guarding their mares. The royal mares went on with their grazing, except the one whom the silvermane had won. She beat him off when he approached, would have none of him.

But he was young and proud and full of his triumph. He persevered. At last she suffered him to touch her, to nuzzle her, to offer her a mouthful of choicest grass and a single white flower. She ate the grass, spat out the flower. He nuzzled her nape. She curled her tail over her back, and staled in the grass as mares will, tormenting him with her scent.

Without warning he mounted her. She squealed, but softly, bracing to take the weight of him. He fumbled about, both fierce and awkward; then suddenly, with a grunt as if of surprise, found his target.

He bred her well, in the way of stallions, and long, which was

not common. When he was done, he slipped from her and nigh
fainted in the grass. She danced about him, eager still, calling to him,
beckoning, bidding him serve her again.

One of the other young stallions slipped close, hoping perhaps to
take advantage of his fellow's exhaustion. But the silvermane had a
little strength left. He lunged. The other fled in great disorder.

No one else undertook to challenge the new lord of the royal
herd. As the day went on, he bred such others of the mares as were
in season, and bred the first of them again, with strength that Walker,
watching, found remarkable. In that way he laid claim to all the
mares, and they accepted his right to rule them. None, even the old
mare who led them, troubled to drive him off. They did not mourn
their fallen king, nor resent the young interloper.

Walker had his sign. It was the greatest that he could have wished
for, and the surest. What he would do among the People, the gods
had done in the royal herd. The king was dead. The young king ruled.

This young king had no ally, no shaman to aid him—unless it
were Walker's presence, and his prayer for a sign, that had won him
his title. Yes, Walker thought. His prayer had done this. Just as it
would aid Linden—and among the People he could do far more, and
more strongly, than he had done among the horses. Come the ninth-
year feast, Linden would be king, mounted on the king stallion. Walker would make sure of it.

.... 12 ....

L ATE IN THE day on which the king stallion died and a young
upstart took his place, Wolfcub came back to the camp with
his father. The People were in great disarray. For such a thing
to happen so close to the gathering of tribes, and in a ninth
year besides, seemed to them a terrible omen. The king in particular
was grey with shock. The conquered king had been his companion,
his mount in war and on the march from camp to camp, and the
great sign and seal of his kingship. Now a stranger ruled the herds,

a stallion who did not know the king, nor was there time to tame him before the tribe must move.

Or so the king said. Certain of the young men declared, and none too quietly either, that a true man needed but a rope of braided hide, a morning's span, and his own courage to tame a stallion. They seemed not to understand or to care what a king was, or how a king stallion was made.

While the men strutted and came close to quarrelling, and the king sat in his circle with that white and stricken face, the priests flayed and gutted the carcass of the fallen stallion and brought it back in procession to the camp's center. The women hid themselves away lest their eyes profane the rite. Especially they must not see the great and broken head raised on a spear, with its torn throat and crushed skull, but royal still, and somehow terrible.

That night they ate the flesh of the stallion, cracked his bones and offered the sweet marrow to the gods, and set the king upon his hide. The hide on which the king had sat, the hide of the great sacrifice that came in the gathering of tribes, they wrapped about the broken bones and buried in a secret place, with the skull set on it, and words of power laid over it. Then they feasted till daybreak, all the men of the People, with a kind of grim abandon.

✦ ✦

Wolfcub had fretted at his father's slowness in coming back to the People. First it had rained in torrents, and they had waited out the day in such shelter as they could muster. Then they met a hunting party of the Black Rock People, allies and kin of their own tribe, and brewers of a sour but potent spirit from the wild barley. These hunters had pressed them to hunt a rogue lion that had been stalking their herds. Aurochs could hardly refuse, for his pride as a hunter and for generosity toward a tribe in need. The hunt was quick, which was a mercy, and the kill clean, with no men badly wounded, and the lion dead with Aurochs' spear in its heart. Then of course Aurochs must be feasted and praised in the Black Rock camp, given great gifts and offered the pick of the women, and for courtesy he had to accept it all, or do dishonor to the people and their king.

And all the while, Wolfcub fretted, twitching with urgency that grew as the days crawled past. No wonder, either, with what they came back to: a thing that had never happened before, a king conquered out of season and a young stallion raised in his place. Nor was it any of the lesser kings and herdmasters, but one of the wandering band of mareless stallions—such a young creature as Wolfcub himself was, without wife or wealth, rank or standing among his people.

"He'll fall," Spearhead said by the young men's fire, after the youngest men had eaten their small portion of the king's flesh and dived into a large skin of *kumiss*. "He had a stroke of luck, or the gods were in the mood for play. But once the older stallions get over the shock, they'll challenge him. One of them will bring him down and make himself king."

"That's what the old men say," said Linden. As the king's favored son, he could have sat in the king's circle, but he had chosen, for whatever reason, to settle among the men of his own age. Most of his usual companions lounged about, taking more than their share of the *kumiss*, but neither Linden nor any of the others made an effort to stop them.

Linden was in a splendid mood—one of the few who truly was. Nearly everyone else felt a bleakness in the heart of him, a cold knot of fear. This kingmaking was not natural. It was out of season, and the king who had risen was not the one who should have done it. But Linden was in high good humor, drinking rather lightly of the *kumiss* but conducting himself as if every drop of it had gone to his head.

"What if," he said, "he doesn't fall? What if the gods are with him, and he holds his place and rules as king? What will all the old men say then?"

"Why," said one of his followers out of the shadows, in a voice too slurred with drink to set a name to, "that they always knew he had it in him!"

Linden laughed. Others echoed him. But most of those about were somber. Spearhead said, "This is not a good thing. I heard someone wonder if it might be the work of an ill spirit or a sorcerer, to throw us into discord before the gathering. Not everyone is glad to call our king the king of kings."

"But any king may challenge," Linden pointed out, "and if he wins the fight, the power is his. Why would anyone enchant our king stallion to his death?"

"To weaken our king," Spearhead said. "To gain the upper hand."

"But a king who did that would do it at the gathering," said Linden. "Not here, at this odd time. No; I think the gods did it, or else it simply happened. Horses do what they will do. They care little enough for the wants of men."

Now that, thought Wolfcub, was manifestly true, and rather profound for Linden. Wolfcub had not drunk much *kumiss,* he did not think, but his head was light. He had an urge to say something, anything, that would shock everyone who could hear it. But the one thing he could think of, which was that he thought he knew who had done this thing, was more shocking even than he could bear to set in words.

He had seen Walker with the elder shaman, standing in the king's circle. Drinks-the-Wind looked as taken aback as the king, and as much at a loss. Walker wore a grim expression and precious little else—for he had been on the steppe, fasting and praying, when the stallions fought—but Wolfcub could see in him no shock. No horror. If he had not brought this about, he had welcomed it. Wolfcub was almost sure of that.

It was of a piece with his sending Linden to the old boar's kingdom and bidding him do insult to the boar and his wives. Walker had sent a message to any who could understand it. He had it in his mind to make a king. Who that king would be, Wolfcub was not absolutely certain. It well might be Linden. But if Linden proved weak, or failed, surely Walker had another prospect in mind—one who likewise was both handsome and biddable.

But there was none more handsome than Linden, and few less truly wise. Linden wanted to chatter of the stallions' battle, which Wolfcub doubted he had seen: it had played itself out far from the camp, in the heart of the herds. Even the priests had come too late to defend the king; they had seen only the ending, and the king's fall.

That did not silence Linden. "Can you imagine? A young stallion out of the roving band, challenging the king—and winning. They say he tore out the king's throat, cast him down and crushed his skull. Is that the work of mere luck, I ask you? Is that the act of a weakling or a half-grown colt?"

"Ah well," said Curlew, who sometimes followed Linden, but sometimes not, "you know who it is, don't you? It's one of the grey herd. An outlander. Who knows what gods live in them, or what powers even the young ones hold?"

Linden nodded. "Have you ever seen him? He's beautiful: all black, with silver dapples. His mane is white. He looks like the moon in a field of stars."

"Ah! A song!" hiccupped the drinker in the shadows.

"Well, and I'm no singer," Linden said, too modestly: he had a pleasant enough voice when he troubled to use it. "But you know what the priests say. The grey herd came on the wings of storm, from the gods' own country. This stallion is one of them. Maybe a god sired him. Maybe he was meant to be king."

"Maybe he's a jest of the gods," said Spearhead, but the rest were falling under Linden's spell. He did have a way about him, with that pretty face. Rather like the new king of stallions, Wolfcub thought.

He had seen the one they spoke of. It was a pretty creature, and full of itself, but he would not have wagered that it would do what it had done. In that much he could agree with Linden. The gods played a part in this somehow, for whatever purpose. Or Walker had made certain that they did.

✢ ✤

Aurochs heard Wolfcub out patiently, considering the head he must have had after a nightlong debauch with *kumiss*. He sat in his tent, waited on by the youngest and loveliest of his wives, but they had retreated when Wolfcub came. His mother came out instead from behind the women's curtain and sat demurely as a woman should, but he caught the sidelong flash of her smile. She would speak with Wolfcub afterward, that smile said, but let the proprieties be observed.

If Aurochs noticed, he did not acknowledge it—and that too was proper. While Wolfcub told him what the young men had been saying, he drank the potion that Wolfcub's mother brewed from herbs and willowbark, grimacing at its bitterness, but draining it manfully.

Wolfcub had his own cup, but he had put it aside after a sip. His head was not as bad as that, and he was intent on what he was saying. "I think Walker had something to do with this. And I think Linden is getting a thought into his head. He likes pretty things. The new king of stallions is very pretty indeed. Might not Linden begin to think that he would look most handsome on that back?"

"He may think it," Aurochs said, "but there's no talk of a new kingmaking among the People."

"There has to be," said Wolfcub. "The king rides the king stallion. If he won't, then—"

"Did anyone say he would not?"

Wolfcub frowned at the grass mat in front of his folded legs. "People heard what the king said. There's no time for a taming before we leave for the gathering."

"But," said Aurochs, "there will be ample time for one once we come to gathering."

Wolfcub looked up sharply. He did not need to be told what that meant. The king would tame the new king of stallions in front of all the gathered tribes. That would be a kingmaking indeed—affirming his own power and proving to the world that he was still, in the autumn of his years, both a man and a king.

Aurochs nodded at the comprehension in Wolfcub's eyes. "What, you didn't think of it yourself? It's the wise thing. Of course the young men don't see it. They're too impatient. They want it done now, in haste, to much lesser purpose."

"Yes," said Wolfcub slowly. "And suppose the shaman foresaw that—planned for it. Made sure it would happen. Then if there's an accident, or if the king fails in strength, he does it before all the tribes. And the one who steps to the fore soonest will be everything that the old king hoped to be."

"I think you impute far more evil to the young shaman than is actually in him," Aurochs said mildly, but it was a reprimand. "You've always disliked him. Don't let that color your thoughts of him now."

Wolfcub set his lips together. He could argue further, and he would have liked to, but his mother's glance stilled him. Willow, though no longer the lissome creature who had earned that name, had both the astringent wit and the strength of the willowbark that she brewed into her potions.

His father left not long after, seeking out the men's council, where they would no doubt consider and reconsider and consider again all that had happened on the day before. Wolfcub lingered as his mother wished. She served him bread and stewed antelope and a delicacy that she knew he loved: the gut of a pig stuffed almost to bursting with meat and herbs and wild grain, roasted on the fire. He savored its pungent sweetness, which she knew best how to make of all the women of the People.

When he lay back and belched nobly, she set a cup beside his hand. It held herbs steeped in water, much more pleasant than her potion, and mildly invigorating. As he sipped it, she sat on her heels nearby and said, "You'll not get the older men to believe Walker is conniving at anything more than the choosing of his next wife."

Wolfcub's brows went up. "Is he doing that?"

Willow shrugged. "He might be. It's been a year since he brought Keen into his tent. She's given him no son, nor showed signs of conceiving any. But that one . . . who knows? He's always been odd. He well might think that one wife is enough trouble, and leave it at that."

"Unless he can gain some advantage by taking a second. He might cast his eye on the daughter of another tribe. A king's daughter, maybe. If there is a kingmaking at the gathering, and he's seen to stand behind the new king, who knows what wealth he might win?"

"You," said Willow, "are surprisingly subtle for a young male. Who taught you to think like that?"

Wolfcub grinned at her. "Why, Mother! You did."

"Yes, it's very improper," she said, from her very proper and demure position, sitting on her heels, knees close together, hands folded in her lap. She had been pretty enough when she was young, people said, but had grown plain with age, a plump comfortable figure with hair dulled to plain earth-brown that had once been as ruddy as his own. But her eyes were lovely still, clear grey, and warm as they rested on him. He was her only son who had lived to manhood, and the last of her children to be among the People: the two daughters who had survived were both married to men of other tribes, marriages that brought honor and alliance to the family, but gave her no comfort of a daughter to share the tent.

Wolfcub supposed she doted on him more than was suitable. But somehow he could not think of her as a doting mother. She was too sharp in her wit, and too little inclined to indulge him when he was being a fool. She was a great deal like Sparrow.

"Do you believe me?" Wolfcub asked her. "Can you credit that he might be doing what I think he's doing? He's young, but he's always been clever. He has far more power than a man of his age is expected to have. If it's gone to his head, might he not think that he can make and break kings?"

"He might," Willow said.

"Yes," said Wolfcub. "And this is a ninth year. If he waits, it may be nine years again before he can gain so much power from a king-making. What young man ever could wait so long to take a thing he wants?"

"He could as easily do it in a year," said Willow. "Or two or three."

"But a ninth year, Mother. A year when the gods demand human flesh and human blood in their sacrifices; when the blood of bull or hound or stallion is not enough. What greater sacrifice than a king? And our king is no longer young."

Willow sighed. "You never liked him. No one ever likes shamans, even before the dreams come to them, or the spirits speak and claim them for their own. I remember Drinks-the-Wind before he was a shaman: what an arrogant young monster he was. His son is remarkably like him."

"But when Drinks-the-Wind became a shaman," Wolfcub said, "he learned to be wise, and to soften his tongue."

"He was older then than Walker is now," said Willow. "I always thought it was ill-advised to give that boy the rank and the power when he took his manhood. No matter how strong he was or how sure in his power, he should have been made to wait. Shamans are best made with the second coming of age, when a man's eldest child is grown. Not while he is still a child himself."

"Then you must see," Wolfcub said, "that Walker is capable of this—of making and breaking kings."

"Or trying to." She shook her head. "Who am I to judge? I'm a mere woman."

Wolfcub knew better than to laugh at the thought of his mother as a mere anything. She paid lip-service to every propriety. It was her weapon and her protection. Sparrow should learn it, he often thought, and maybe would, if she lived to his mother's age.

"And I," he said, "am a mere boy. The men won't hear me when I warn them. Even Father barely listens."

"He came back with you," said Willow. "He gave you that much credence. And he'll be watchful, which is what you need of him. If he thinks that others of the men should know, he'll see that they do. You've done all you should, and most of what you can."

"But it's not *enough!*"

"Nothing is ever enough, when one is young and male and knows no patience." Willow filled his empty cup again, this time with new milk sweetened with honey, and said, "Now drink, and get you gone. You've paced and snarled long enough. The sun's up and the wind's freshening. We'll be breaking camp within the day, if I'm not mistaken. Did you hear the Old Mare calling in the dawn?"

Wolfcub had heard nothing before sunup but the hammering in his own skull, but he did not say so. He drank his sweet milk and let himself be chased out into the sunlight, where he was one of the few men on his feet and almost clearheaded.

The rest would lie groaning abed till nightfall if they could, but his mother had heard true. The horses were calling to one another, shrill voices of stallions, deeper ones of mares. Whether the making of the new king had roused them, or it was simply time, the herds were beginning to move.

·········· 13 ··········

I T WAS NOT the Old Mare who woke the women with her pealing in the night, though the voice was very like hers: strong and deep and royally peremptory. It was the young mare, the one whom Sparrow knew better than to think of as her own. She was declaring to the world that she had, at last, found a stallion worthy of her. That he had been hanging about since he was a yearling, and that he had hitherto been less than the least of the foals in her estimation, mattered little to the mare. He had conquered the king whom she had never suffered to breed her. He could, in his turn, presume to court and then to mount her.

Their mating was a wild and triumphant thing. The stallion, who had taken remarkably few wounds in his battle for the kingship, came out of that union streaming blood. The mare was somewhat torn about the neck and shoulders, but never enough to concern her. She danced in the dawn, to the stallion's torment: she had drained him dry, so that he would not breed a mare again that day, nor for a while, Sparrow suspected.

She was there. She watched. In the confusion of the king stallion's passing and his funeral feast, she had managed to escape her duties and run away to the herds. She had to hide: the priests were on watch, such of them as lacked the rank or the boldness to officiate at the feast. They were waiting to see if one of the other stallions challenged the new king. But none had.

They had a skin of *kumiss* for the vigil, and a feast of their own, a young calf that they claimed as their portion. It was, she observed, one of the king's calves. She wondered if he would notice, or if he would care. The priests could take whatever they pleased, within reason, but mostly they left the king's belongings alone.

Walker had had nothing to do with the old stallion's fall. Sparrow hated to admit it—she would have been more than glad to blame him for it—but the gods had their own intentions. And the mares chose as they would, however subtly they might do it. They had decided, for reasons best known to themselves, that this young and rather callow if very pretty stallion was fit to be their king.

Still, it served Walker's purpose, and that she liked not at all. She had seen him come back from his days on the steppe, naked and painted and hung with amulets, handsome and knowing it, and not minding in the least if the women happened to notice and admire. It had been he and not Drinks-the-Wind who affirmed what the priests had come running to announce: that there was a new king among the herds. And it was he and not the elder shaman who stood with the priests while they roasted and divided the old stallion's carcass. Drinks-the-Wind came late from Lark's bed, where he had been joyfully making another child, and found himself relegated to the second place.

Sparrow could not tell even now what her father had thought of that. He wore his face as a mask at the best of times, and veiled his thoughts behind his heavy eyelids. He seemed to accept this usurpation of his authority.

Maybe the shaman, like the king, grew old. Maybe Walker had meddled somehow with his spirit. Dreams and true visions were not all a shaman knew. He learned the ways of magic, too, spells and poisons that needed little enough power for the working. Even as a child, Walker had sought out the wisewomen and the healers and the priests, flattering them till they told him their secrets: herbs and potions, workings and wishings both well and ill. Whatever he lacked as a true shaman, as a witch he was greatly gifted.

Sparrow did not like where that thought led her. She would have been glad of the mare's warm strength, but if she left the hollow in which she hid, the priests would see her. A woman in the herds now of all times would not be taken back to the camp for judgment. She would be cut down where she stood, for sacrilege.

And that was maddening. A woman could know what the mares knew, that the herds would move soon—perhaps as early as daybreak. The mare had called the new king to her to seal a pact of sorts, to bind him and command him. Already as she tormented him with his own exhaustion, the elder mares had begun to call their children together. The eldest of the grey herd, who would lead, grazed placidly beside her sleeping foal, but Sparrow could see the purpose growing in her. Her grazing had a pattern to it, a slow drift northward.

The mare, having had her fill of vexing the stallion, dropped her head and began to graze. Unlike the eldest, she cropped the grass quickly, sharply, with many liftings of the head, and a squeal as one of the lesser mares wandered too close. Her drifting too was northward, ahead of the eldest, till she had passed the rest of her herd and taken the place of guard. Then for a while she seemed to grow calmer, but her grazing was almost fierce, as if she must eat as much as she can, as quickly as she can, for strength on the journey.

By then the priests began to see what Sparrow had seen since before sunup: that the herds had begun, if slowly and subtly, to move. The grey herd's drift had borne it through the lesser herds. It was almost in the lead, and the others beginning, in casual fashion, to take the places they took on the march from grazing ground to grazing ground.

Sparrow escaped while the priests were intent on their discovery, slipping soft and swift through the grass. Not till she was nearly to the camp did she rise and compose herself and enter as if from the river, trusting to the confusion of breaking camp to conceal her.

The tumult was worse than usual, what with so many men still barely able to move, and everyone in such dismay over the old stallion's fall. Some of the women were indulging in shrieking and carrying on, which served no purpose whatever except to win them a beating from the nearest snarling male.

White Bird, of course, carried on in grand and splendid fashion, secure in the knowledge that her husband was in council with the king, and no other man would dare touch the elder shaman's wife. Even Mallard could not quell her. It seemed some idiot had tried to coax her yet again to accept her daughter, who was, for her age, quite a pretty thing. White Bird had come back to herself in most respects, except for that one. She was still thoroughly convinced that the child was a changeling, and someone was hiding her son somewhere, keeping him away from her.

As Sparrow approached her father's tent, White Bird burst out of it, half-naked and shrieking. A handful of women ran in pursuit, but White Bird was very quick on her feet. She was aiming, as far as Sparrow could see, for the king's circle. Her white breasts and streaming hair, and her ear-splitting shriek, cast everyone into confusion. Such of the men as could bear the sound of her voice stared hungrily at her body.

Sparrow brought her down quite simply, by catching her as she hurtled past and flinging them both to the ground. White Bird fell beneath her, the shriek cut off with the air that had abandoned her lungs. Sparrow was much the smaller in height, but compact and sturdy and stronger than she looked. White Bird was slender and tall, and like all the favorite wives who spent their days lying about and cherishing their beauty, had no strength worth the name.

Before White Bird could find breath to renew her clamor, Sparrow scrambled up and pulled her to her feet. Nothing happened to hand, to cover those exuberant breasts. Sparrow set her lips tight and dragged White Bird back through the briefly silent tents, and flung her through the flap of the one that belonged to her father. Who caught her, or whether anyone caught her at all, Sparrow did not care. Something in her had snapped, quite without warning. "The herds are moving," she said sharply. "Get ready to break camp."

People who had never heard her raise her voice before—perhaps who had never heard her speak at all—gaped at her with the same astonishment with which they had regarded White Bird. Before she lost patience and repeated herself, Mallard emerged from the tent and said in her dry calm voice, "Do as she says."

"But the men haven't—the king hasn't—" Lark began.

Mallard slapped her, abruptly and firmly. She stopped chattering for sheer white-faced shock. "The camp moves," said Mallard. "Get to it."

The women had never moved camp on their own before, that Sparrow had heard of. But the horses would leave, whether the People followed or no. If the king was not quick enough to see that, then let him follow when he could.

Maybe, if the camp had been in less disarray, more women than Lark would have protested, and the men would have understood what was happening. But one of them, staggering out of his wives' tent to find the camp breaking about him, bellowed, "You! You women! What are you hanging about for? The king says break camp. Break camp!"

One male voice invoking the king's name was all the People needed. Out of confusion they fell into a sort of order. People remembered their places and their duties. Some gathered belongings, others gathered and packed foodstuffs, still others readied the fire-baskets and put out the fires that had burned since the People made camp in the spring grazing grounds. Tents began to fall, one by one and then in companies. Men and boys mustered themselves to gather the herds of cattle; women and girls brought together the goats. Priests who had roistered in the camp ran to catch the horse-herds, some in as much disorder as White Bird had been in, but with somewhat less noise.

Sparrow had her place and her duties, packing the women's belongings, bringing down the shaman's tent and unlacing its joined hides and packing them to fit on the back of an ox. She had done such things since she was small, season after season in the long rolling of the years. Her hands moved of themselves, free of her will. That begged to depart her body altogether and ride the wind toward the herds, and accompany the mare in spirit as she could not in flesh. But caution, deep ingrained, and no little portion of fear, kept body and soul together. She wandered far enough in dream that often she despaired of coming back. She could not let herself do it in waking. That was a shaman's trick—and she could not be a shaman.

When the sun had begun its descent to the western horizon, the camp was gone and the People departing from it in a long shuffling column. Behind them lay the charred corpses of the campfires, and trampled earth, and a thin scatter of refuse. The steppe opened before them. This road they all knew, all but the babies born in the spring.

The women trudged afoot as they had since the dawn time. Those whose husbands had rank and wealth enough led oxen burdened down with tents and belongings. The rest bore their lives on their backs, and often the youngest child on top, drowsing contentedly as his mother plodded beneath him.

No man walked. They all rode on horses, riding alongside the column or ranging ahead of it. Those too old or infirm to ride were set on the backs of gentle geldings, with younger sons or grandsons to lead them. So were they raised above the lowliness of women and children, and permitted to travel at ease while the women labored, bound to the earth.

Girls learned early not to lament the unfairness of it. Sparrow, who had raced the wind on the mare's back, hated worse than she ever had, that she must plod in the dust while fools and braggarts of men knew the freedom of the air.

The herds led. The People followed. And a mare led the herds: a mare the color of the moon, who answered to no heart but her own, and to no power but the goddess inside her.

·········· 14 ··········

KEEN WAS AWAY from the camp when the stallions fought their battle. She had roused in the dawn of that strange day with a griping in her belly and a hammering in her head that told her it was time to go to the women's place, the hut of woven reeds where they went during their courses to purify themselves and to free the men from the pollution of their presence. It was early, or was it late? She had lost count of the days. Foolish of her who hoped so for a child, but there was so much else to think of, so many frets and worries, Walker's odd moods of late, and her days' duties.

Walker had not come back from his vigil. Keen was not sorry therefore to go away, particularly when she found the hut empty and swept, and no one in it to share her solitude. She was in the mood to be alone just then.

Some women were terribly ill in their courses. Keen never had been. She seldom needed the herbs that were stored in the hut, or the potion that soothed those who suffered most terribly. For her these few days in every moon's cycle were rather a pleasant pause.

This was not pleasant. By the time she came to the hut she was bent nearly double, fighting back the bile that rose and threatened to choke her. She barely had wit for the rites or prayers, even to invoke the spirit of the place and ask it to look kindly on her in her time of impurity.

She crawled into the herb-scented dimness. The sleeping-place was clean, though the grasses that bedded it were dry and a little dusty. She lay there, drawn into a knot about the red pain in her middle, and took what rest she could.

When morning came, her pain had passed from body into heart. These were not only her courses, after all, that racked her. With the blood that flowed out of her came life, a tiny thing, barely begun, and yet in its passing she knew what it had been. She had been carrying a child. And it was gone.

She did what was necessary. She cleansed herself, drank the bitter potion, said the words and prayers that were prescribed. She wept, and not a little. She let the hut conceal her and her grief, which was greater than ever such a thing deserved. Life was not life till it was born and named and given to the People. And yet it had been a beginning.

When she came out at last, the People were gone. The place by the river was empty. All the herds, the tents, the tribe itself, had departed.

She was not frightened. She knew where they had gone. It was sudden, but hardly unexpected.

And yet it was rather terrible to be alone, without the camp to be aware of, the tribe in its place, and everyone as they had been since they came here in the first of spring. No one had come looking for her or seemed to notice her absence, though the tent she had shared with Walker was gone with the rest. He must have taken it, or seen that it was taken.

He had not sent anyone to look for her, not even one of the children. Had he forgotten her? Or was he so angry to find her gone that he had not cared what became of her?

She had a few things with her, a little bread, a bit of cheese, a few strips of dried antelope. The way was clear, even if she had not known something of tracking. The whole of the People left a broad and unmistakable track.

She was numb still with the passing of the child that would have been, remote and somewhat ill. That perhaps shielded her from the shock of solitude. She went back to take down the hut and to retrieve what was in it, the herbs and the sacred things. It was nearly sundown when she finished, close enough to night that she reckoned it best to stay where she was. She took shelter in the reeds, made herself a bed there, curled and slept as best she could.

In the morning she set out on the track of the People. There was little enough to eat except what she had with her; they had stripped the land in their passing. She told herself she did not mind. Fasting was not so ill a thing. It cleared the mind and purified the spirit. She was almost happy, walking under the vault of heaven, lonely as the eagle that soared above her. So it must be when one of the hunters went out by himself. It was—refreshing, yes. In a way, it made the soul anew.

+ +

For much too long a while Sparrow did not know that Keen was absent from the People. She had more than enough to occupy her on the march, and in the evenings, when they made camp, she was much called upon for this and that. She did notice that Keen's tent was not in its accustomed place, but when she had a moment to wonder, or to think that perhaps she should look to see where it was, the moment passed too quickly. No doubt Keen was keeping to another part of the march, and camping at night with some friend or kinsman. People did that on the march from camp to camp. It was not at all uncommon.

Certainly she was not with Walker. He ran with the pack of the young men these days, with Linden and the rest. It was not obvious; mostly he seemed to ride by himself. But he was always near Linden, one way and another. In camp, as she discovered, he had taken to sleeping just beyond the circle of the young men. There were no women near them, nor might there be: they were always mounted, and at night they helped to guard the herds.

By the third day Sparrow could no longer deny it: Keen was gone. No one had seen her. Sparrow thought then to ask the children. Children knew everything and went everywhere. "Oh," they said, "she went to the women's place. She was sick."

"Her face was green," said one of the girlchildren. "I didn't know skin could be that color."

Sparrow's heart went cold at that. Ill, and gone to the women's place—and no one had noticed. No one had thought of her at all.

Sparrow was used to that. She welcomed it. But Keen was valued, for a woman. She had a husband of rank and standing. She should not have been forgotten.

Except that that husband was Walker, and Walker cared for nothing. He had no other wives or women to miss her; and her family, like Sparrow, no doubt had supposed that she was elsewhere among the People.

There was a way to go back to her, and quickly, but it would need great care and stealth, and the cover of night. Sparrow knew where in the herds the mare was—she always knew that. But the herds on the march were guarded and kept in close, for fear of hunters both animal and human. Sparrow had already resigned herself to separation from the mare while the march lasted.

But to find Keen again, she needed the mare.

It was a long wait from midday till sunset, and past it to dark. Sparrow was very quiet, kept her head low, and was careful not to attract any man's notice, least of all Walker's. Tonight of all nights, she did not want to confront him, or be taxed with his need for a vision.

But he seemed to have had a foreseeing of his own for once, or what he imagined to be such. He had been full of himself since the king of stallions died, not strutting or boasting as another young man would do, but he had taken a place among the elders. And they, perhaps out of astonishment, had allowed it.

Tonight, as he had done since the march began, he settled near Linden, not watching the prince, but Sparrow could feel his awareness, how it focused, fixed on the target. Whether he meant to kill Linden or make him a king, Sparrow did not know yet. Maybe Walker himself did not.

But that she must leave to Wolfcub. While she made camp for her father and his wives, she set aside quietly such things as she would need, hiding them in shadow. She did her duties, kept her head down, avoided drawing notice.

At last, and none too soon, it was full dark. The children had gone to sleep, all but a few who were determined to outlast their elders. The men sat in their circles, drinking or drowsing, or else went out to stand guard. The women finished the day's tasks and went at last and gratefully to their beds.

When the camp was as quiet as it would be, Sparrow retrieved the bundle that she had made, and slipped away.

✢ ✢

Wolfcub was out and about that night among those set on watch over the horses. He came there late, later perhaps than he should: he had delayed while the others went on ahead, first because he made

sure that Linden was safely bedded down in the middle of his following, and Walker was well apart from them for once; then because his
mother wanted a word with him. It was nothing terribly important.
She wanted mostly to see him and feed him cakes made from a honeycomb that one of the lesser wives had found on the march. He was
never averse to being spoiled, if there was honey in it.

He was still licking his fingers as he walked through the camp,
and there was a packet of cakes in his bag, still warm from the baking.
He was not looking for Sparrow, though as he passed Drinks-the-
Wind's portion of the camp he wondered if he might see her. Everyone there was asleep, rolled up in blankets or sheltered under
canopies.

He went on quickly and quietly as a hunter should, slipping past
the guards on the camp—with a small and secret smile that none of
them either saw or challenged him—and circling the herds. The
herdsmen stood guard at wide intervals, tall shadows afoot or seated
next to their grazing horses. Wolfcub had retrieved his stallion before
anyone saw him, slipped the bridle on and walked openly out to the
edge where his post was.

He passed Spearhead, who greeted him with a lift of the hand,
and Hemlock, who started up as if struck and would have sprung at
him if he had not stepped quickly aside. Hemlock growled as he saw
who it was, not at all gracious about his own failing. Wolfcub
shrugged. He and Hemlock were not friends, but neither were they
enemies. He went on without commentary, giving Hemlock time to
compose himself—and to wake enough to stand guard as he should.

Past Hemlock no one seemed to be on guard, though here was
the royal herd. The mares gleamed in the starlight; the new king
stood hipshot beyond them, with his mane like a fall of white water
and the rest of him a shadow on shadow. His head came up at Wolfcub's presence, but apart from a sharp snort of warning, he made no
move toward either Wolfcub or his stallion.

Wolfcub had in mind to set himself outside the royal herd, on a
low rise that he had marked on his way there. But as he made his
way toward it, something made him stop.

There was a shadow among the white shapes, too small for one
of the foals, too large for a wolf. It walked upright as no lion ever
did. Its gait, the way it flitted through the starlit grass . . .

He was a hunter. He could remember a track once he had seen
it, and name the deer that he had let pass a season before. His eye

was keen and his mind attuned to subtleties. He knew that shape, the way it moved—though it could not be here. It should not, ever, be here.

And yet he could not mistake it. Sparrow was in among the royal herd, slipping soft as a breeze through the sleeping or grazing mares and foals. And none of them, not one, not even the stallion, drew to the alert, or seemed to care that she was there.

While Wolfcub stood gaping, his mind wandered off on its own. Gossip in the camp, idle talk on the march. His sister Ember, her voice as clear as if she stood beside him: "They say Sparrow has a lover."

"No!" said his father's youngest wife, whose name was Swift. "Not that little brown bird. Who would want *her?*"

"Someone does," Ember said. "She creeps out every night and goes to him. Lark saw her. So did Arrow's wife."

"Oh," said Swift. "Arrow's wife—that whey-faced thing. She's just saying it so nobody will notice her running off to tumble in the grass with her favorite of the hour."

For a moment Wolfcub, listening, had thought they might wander off in pursuit of that riper scandal. But it seemed it was too ripe. Ember persisted. "It is true. Sparrow goes out all the time. Nobody knows who he is."

"I'm sure he's not boasting," Swift said with a toss of her head. "All the men would laugh at him and wonder why he couldn't find something better."

Wolfcub would have been happy to sweep down upon them then and throttle them both, but they were not his wives or his women, and he was not supposed to be listening to women's gossip. He went on about his business, but with a trouble in his heart.

Sparrow, creeping off to lie with a lover? Wolfcub had never thought of such a thing. And not because no one could want her. It was not like her.

But after he heard Ember and Swift at their gossiping, he had listened, and other women chattered of it, too: how Sparrow had a lover, but no one knew who he was. Certainly none of the men had admitted to it. Some thought it might be Wolfcub—but unless they were meeting in dream, that was not so.

He was not jealous. No, of course he was not. Why should he be? He could be outraged, to be sure, that she should sully her honor so; but he hated the darkness of that, and the wrongness.

Now he saw her among the horses, and a thought had risen in him. It was preposterous. It was much more appalling than that she was lying with a man in the nights, a man who had not taken her as his wife, nor gained her father's leave to do it. A woman's virtue was a valuable thing. A woman among the horses was a profanation.

And yet she was there, passing among them, aiming with purpose for one who stood on the far edge, some little distance from the stallion. It was one of the mares, a younger one, and beautiful—she was as fine a creature as Wolfcub had seen. He had noticed her before, with a horseman's eye, and the thought that here was a fine mother of stallions; but despite her ripe and suitable age, she seemed not to have bred or borne a foal.

As Keen had done before him, if he had known it, Wolfcub saw Sparrow meet and greet the mare. He was perhaps more shocked than Keen had been—a deep and heartfelt shock. And not, indeed, that a woman dared touch a horse, and more than touch it, mount on its back and turn it southward. No, though that was shock enough. Wolfcub had never imagined that Sparrow would keep such a secret— and more than that, that she would keep it from him.

Of course she would. He was her friend, closer than any of her brothers. But he was a man. How could she ever trust him with this? It was a terrible thing she did, forbidden on pain of death.

If he had been thinking clearly at all, he would have turned his back and gone to his post beyond the herd and set himself resolutely to forget what he had seen. Maybe he had dreamed it, after all. Maybe it was a trick of the starlight.

But he was not thinking clearly. He sprang onto his stallion's back, but quietly, crouching over the rough-maned neck, so that Sparrow would not see and take alarm. He waited so, till Sparrow was well on her way. Yes, she was headed to the south in a wide sweep round the herds and, he could suppose, the camp.

When he was sure of her path, he slackened rein. The stallion needed no more encouragement than that to set off in pursuit, but quietly, as quietly as he could, and as swiftly. He kept the mare in sight but did not close the gap, not till the herds and the camp were well past. Then and only then did he press for speed.

The mare was moving quickly, but Wolfcub came on at the gallop. She made no effort to increase her pace, nor did Sparrow urge her on. Wolfcub caught them just below the summit of a long hill, veered round them and pounded to a halt.

The mare stopped perforce. Sparrow's face was a pale blur in starlight, but he could sense no fear in her. "Truly," she said, "I do need to be more careful."

"You'll be killed for this," Wolfcub said. He was breathing hard, and not only because he had been riding at the gallop.

"I suppose I shall," Sparrow said serenely. "But not tonight, or you'd have killed me before you said a word."

That was true. Wolfcub was none too pleased to acknowledge it. "Why?" he demanded.

Sparrow did not answer. She rode past him to the hilltop, eluding him as easily as if he had been a breath of wind. He had his bow and his spear, for guarding the horses. He could, indeed should, have felled her as she rode away from him. She made no effort to protect her back, nor seemed to care that he was behind her.

He sent the dun after her. This time he could not catch the mare so easily, though she seemed to move without haste. He could only ride beside her in the wake of her silence.

"Tell me why," he said as they crested the hill and started down the other side.

"Keen," Sparrow said, startling him—he had expected no answer, and certainly not that one.

As he gaped, Sparrow sighed, audible over the thudding of hooves. "Keen is not with the People. No one's seen her since we left the spring camp."

Wolfcub did not want to be diverted from the fact of her transgression against the great law of the People. And yet there was no avoiding what she had said. "Keen is missing? But how—"

"Who would notice, if her husband didn't?"

That was bitterly true. Still, Wolfcub came back to the other thing, the terrible thing. "You can't be doing this. You can't—"

"I am doing it." Sparrow's voice was completely immovable. "I'll find her, if she's to be found. You go back. Watch Linden. Make sure Walker doesn't do something we'll all be sorry for."

"You trust me to go back? What if I bring the whole wrath of the People upon you?"

"You won't," she said with maddening certainty. "Now go. I'll bring Keen back. No one need ever know how I did it."

"I'll know."

"Yes."

He shook his head. "I can't do that. I can't. *You* go back. I'll fetch her, and we'll all be safe."

"Keen knows."

His mouth opened, then shut with a snap.

"I can't keep watch over Linden," she said with audible patience. "You can. What I can do, I am doing. Who taught me to hunt, after all? Who but you? Now go!"

He could not obey her. He would not. But his stallion was another matter. He stopped short as if he had struck a wall. Wolfcub, caught off guard, somersaulted over his head.

When the stars had stopped whirling overhead, Sparrow was long gone, and the white mare with her. Wolfcub snarled at his traitor of a horse. The dun did not look even faintly contrite. Nor would he go forward at all, for anything Wolfcub could do. He would go back, and happily, stretching into a long easy gallop, back to the herds and the herdsmen and a secret that Wolfcub would have given heart's blood not to keep.

15

KEEN HAD NEVER been alone before. Not truly—not all alone in the world, far from kin and friends. It was strange. It was frightening, but she refused to give in to fear.

On the third day the lion found her track. Lions of the plain were not given to stalking the children of men, unless they were old or mad or terribly hungry, but a woman alone, unarmed, afoot, was tempting quarry. Keen saw it first as she paused at the summit of a long hill, stopping to breathe and to strain her eyes, knowing she would see nothing, but hoping rather foolishly that she could see the dust of the People's passing. But they were long gone. It was when she turned back, slumping in despair, that she saw the tawny shape in the grass.

It made no effort to conceal itself. It sat at its evident ease, watching her. It was not hungry, not just then, or she would never have known it was there till it fell upon her. It was curious, maybe. It wanted to see where she was going and what she would do, lone frail creature that she was.

Keen was going to die. This was the shape of her death.

She was oddly calm, contemplating it. It helped that she was so empty; the wind blew through her, and sang in the bones of her skull. This must be what shamans knew, who fasted and purged themselves so that they might walk between the worlds. But she was very much in the world, this and no other. She saw no spirits, heard no voices in the wind. Unless the lion was a spirit—which could well be. Else why was it letting her live?

When she had rested, she went on. The lion followed, keeping its distance. She never forgot that it was there, but she kept her eyes fixed ahead of her. She would not glance fearfully back. When it attacked, if it attacked, she would not turn to face it. She would let it bring her down as it did the gazelle, headlong and all at once. There would be less pain then, and less terror.

All that day she walked in the track of the People, and the lion walked in the track that she left. She began to believe that it was a spirit, or a god's messenger. Though what it came to tell her, she could not imagine. Maybe she would know when it killed her.

She walked for a while after the sun had set, not because she was afraid, but because her feet were in the habit of walking. She was as light as air. Maybe the lion would not need to bring her down: maybe her spirit would slip free of its own accord and leave her body for the lion to eat. Maybe that was what it waited for.

Starlight bathed her. Moonlight washed over her. She did not know if she slept. Maybe she had no need of sleep.

Out of the moonlight, over the silvered grass, came a white shape. Keen saw it with utter lack of surprise. She was in the gods' country now, surely, on the far side of the sky. And there was Horse Goddess with her servant riding on her back there as in the lesser world, come to take Keen home.

Keen held out her arms. As she had on that night outside of the spring camp, Sparrow drew her up to the mare's back. Keen did not cling so tightly now. She was dead. What harm could come to her? She rode almost at ease away from the lion, toward the moon and the tracks of the stars.

✦ ✦

When the People broke camp in the morning, Sparrow was not among them. Wolfcub had slept somewhat in the night, once he was relieved of his place in the guard. He was fresh enough come daylight, in body, though his heart was deeply troubled.

He had decided before he slept to let be; to make himself forget what he had seen, and to hope that Sparrow came back safe and with Keen, equally safe, beside her—afoot, and not riding on the white mare. But once he was awake and had broken his fast and mounted to ride, he kept his stallion to a walk as the People moved on past. Some of the men called greetings. No one seemed curious. The women he avoided, and they avoided him, for he was mounted on a horse.

But the gods were not content to let him be. Just as the last of the People passed, as he prepared to turn back through the ashes of the camp, one whom he should have been watching for came up beside him.

Walker the shaman had not spoken to him since he slew the boar; indeed had never had much use for him, as young as he was and as little use as he seemed to be. But a boarslayer was a different creature than a mere lone hunter.

"A fair morning to you," Walker said with what many might have taken for good cheer. But Wolfcub saw how cold his eyes were. "Will you go hunting, then, and bring us back a fine kill for the pot?"

"I might," Wolfcub said, making no great effort to be pleasant. "Why? Do you want another boar?"

Walker laughed. It was a lovely sound. No doubt he practiced it in secret. "Are you minded to slay one?"

"Not likely," said Wolfcub.

"That's wise," Walker said. He rode forward. His horse was a handsome creature but evil-tempered, as he himself was. It jostled Wolfcub's stallion—by accident, maybe; or maybe not.

When the flurry had settled, Wolfcub was riding beside Walker, and there was no sensible way to escape. Walker went on as if there had been no interruption. "Boarslaying is a mighty thing and a great honor, but it's best done sparingly."

"I would be the last one to contest that," Wolfcub said.

Walker smiled. "They say you have a level head and few pretensions. And yet you slew a boar."

"I did what was necessary," Wolfcub said. "And now, if you will pardon me, I must go hunting."

"Oh, yes," said Walker maganimously. "Yes, go, go."

As if, thought Wolfcub, he thought anyone needed his leave to go where he would. Wolfcub escaped, a little desperately perhaps, but very glad to be free of that presence.

Out of wariness, or perhaps even fear, he let Walker see him go off eastward, and not south where he wanted to go. Then, again warily, before he went out of sight, he turned north. Only when he was far from the march and well out of its view did he turn back southward. Foolish maybe, if the shaman had the eyes of a raven or a falcon and could see where he went; but surely Walker would not trouble with that.

✦ ✦

Wolfcub hunted, chiefly because the gods set prey in his path: a brace of fat geese. With a soft grey body slung on either side of his horse's withers, Wolfcub continued southward for a good while. He was not at all displeased to be away from the People so soon after he had come back. They all said he was odd in his predilection for solitude. Odd or no, he preferred to be alone.

He followed the beaten track, the grass trampled down and scattered here and there with the refuse of a tribe on the march. Somewhat before noon he came to last night's camp. Nothing stirred there but a flock of birds squabbling over the People's leavings, and a thin and mangy jackal that slunk off with its tail between its legs.

He found them soon after that: Sparrow afoot, Keen on the mare's back, walking doggedly northward. Sparrow was as she always was, compact and complete within herself. Keen looked as if she had come back from the dead.

They paused as Wolfcub drew near. He had a greeting ready, as calmly casual as Sparrow's expression while she waited, but he never uttered it. Keen sighed just as he came level, and slid bonelessly to the ground.

Wolfcub sprang from his stallion's back. Sparrow was there already, cradling Keen's head in her lap. "She won't eat," Sparrow said. "She's ill—she lost a baby back there, I think; she won't say. Her spirit keeps trying to wander away from her body."

"Ai," said Wolfcub: a soft sound of dismay. Sparrow's eye caught his. It was dark and steady. In it he found what he needed to do.

They did it together. They settled Keen as best they could, built a fire, plucked and cleaned the geese and spitted them and set them over the fire, and heated water in Wolfcub's traveling-pot. Sparrow cast herbs in it, that she took from Keen, who did not revive to challenge her.

While the geese roasted and the water boiled, Wolfcub sat with Sparrow and stared at Keen. "Will she die?" he asked.

Sparrow lifted a shoulder in a shrug. "The gods know. She lost too much blood. Then she walked so far before I found her. She had meat with her, and a little bread. She hadn't touched it. She's spirit-lost, I think."

Wolfcub shivered. Sparrow could be calm about it—she was a shaman's daughter. But such things were strange to him, and frightening.

Sparrow touched his hand. It was a rarity, and it made him shiver in a very different way: one that she seemed unaware of. She never had seen him as he saw her. He was like a brother, he supposed, male but not a man—not someone she looked on with desire. Whereas he, when he looked at her . . .

He reined himself in, sternly. Her hand still rested on his. "I can try," she said, "to bring her back."

"That's shaman's work," he said, too hastily. He was not thinking. He was trying very hard not to think of her touch, or the way her dark lashes brushed her cheeks when she blinked, or the sweet round shape of her in the shabby deerskin tunic.

She bridled at his words, withdrawing her hand, half-turning away. "Yes. I should wait, shouldn't I? Till we can bring her back to the People. So that a shaman can find her spirit where it's wandered, and bring it back to her body."

Of course she should. But as Keen lay by the fire, white as milk, thinner and frailer than he could ever remember her being, Wolfcub knew what Sparrow surely knew. She might not live so long.

"You can do it," Wolfcub said. "Can't you?"

"A woman cannot be a shaman," Sparrow said, stiff and cold.

Wolfcub snorted. "Oh, come. When did that ever stop you?"

She was angry, but she must remember as well as he the games they had played when they were children: games in which she did things that the Grandmother taught her, which he had learned afterward were shaman-things, things of magic and power. Such things as she still did, but without telling him. Riding the white mare. Hunting and finding Keen where no one else had thought or known to go.

"If I do this," she said abruptly, taking him by surprise, "you have to help me. Hold my hands. Keep part of me in the world. Can you do that?"

He nodded. His spirit was a little lost itself, maybe, here on the wide plain under a cloud-tossed sky. The white mare stood near, grazing quietly, and the ugly little stallion not far from her. What that meant—what it said of Sparrow—Wolfcub could not tell yet. He was not sure he wanted to.

They were out of the world in their way, far from the People. Sparrow turned back toward him and took his hands in her warm firm ones. He was always surprised to find her so solid and so strong for a woman. "Watch over me," she said. And with that, she went away.

+ +

Sparrow had been thinking since soon after she found Keen that she would have to do this—this thing that shamans did. Keen's pallor, her remoteness, the way her soul wandered, frightened Sparrow; and more so as she understood what it meant. She had tried to speed the pace, to bring Keen back to the People, to Drinks-the-Wind who knew best how to bring back a lost spirit, but Keen could not travel so quickly. Her body was too fragile.

Wolfcub's coming was Horse Goddess' own gift, and utterly like him. He would never know, because Sparrow would not tell him, how glad she was to see him and how welcome his presence was. She would have been happier not to burden him with the secret of the mare, but that was betrayed already, and had been when she left to find Keen. Horse Goddess wanted it. She made that clear.

Now Sparrow sat opposite him in the savory odor of roasting geese, hand linked to hand. He was quiet and strong, clear-eyed and very still, just as she needed him to be. His familiar face, the peak of ruddy brown hair on his forehead, the way his brows arched over his grey eyes, held her to the world as strongly as his hands, as the soft hiss of his breathing, as the warmth of his body and its familiar musky scent.

But she had to walk where spirits walked, or Keen would go away and not come back. Balanced between his hands' strength and his eyes' clarity, she stepped—outward.

The Grandmother had taught her this long ago. She had thought it a great game then to slip in and out of the body's bindings; to ride the wind at night or to soar on falcon's wings by daylight. After the Grandmother died, when her courses came, it became terribly, wonderfully easy to slip free, particularly when the moon's blood flowed.

But she had clung to the flesh of late, out of wariness and for fear that someone would catch her in it. Then the mare had claimed her, and that took all the soul and spirit she had, and left none for spirit-walking.

It was still easy. So simple, like the release of a breath: gathering the threads of her spirit, winding them into a shape like a bird or a spear, and casting it forth. For a little while she hovered in the air between the two bodies, one empty, one bright with living presence.

As she paused there, her eye drifted toward the one who lay beyond, the pale shell wrapped in something other than sleep. A thin thread of spirit coiled within it, but it was no more solid than spidersilk.

She touched it. It uncoiled, shrinking away from her. She sank down into the shadows inside it.

This country she knew. It was like the world without, a wide and rolling plain threaded with rivers and vaulted with sky. It edges were dark, the deep shade of forests. Far away on its horizon rose the jagged teeth of mountains. But where the living world was green and gold, blue and white, grey and brown and red, this was all grey, like rain, or like pale shadows.

The sky boiled with clouds. Things flew there, shapes like her own, like birds, like insects, like arrows shot from the bow. Those were spirits, the Grandmother had told her. So too was the land alive with creatures, guides and servants, shamans on journeys, witches, sorcerers. Some were dead, but most were the living, or spirits bound to earth or air. The dead, the great ones, the ancestors and the gods, lived in their own country beyond the horizon. Sparrow had walked there, too, but today she would not do that; not, please the gods, while Keen's body clung to life.

Amid so vast a country, so full of beings coming to and going, small wonder Keen was lost. She was no shaman, nor greatly gifted in matters of the spirit. And yet somehow, when the thing that had not been a child yet slipped out of her, too much of her had gone with it. Her spirit had tried to follow, and been caught in this country between, this grey and shadowed place.

Sparrow had kept a grip on the thread that was Keen's life. Now she followed it, as thin and nigh invisible as it was. She traced it through the shadowed country, across the featureless plain beneath the starless sky. It stretched almost too taut—as if it would break.

A shape grew out of air beside her. The mare was a white light in this grey place, a splendor of divinity amid the flittings of lesser spirits. Her light put the shadows to flight. As she had the first time Sparrow rode her, she bade Sparrow rode on her back, and carried her swifter than Sparrow could ever go alone.

Sparrow clung to the shining white mane and slitted her eyes against the bite of wind. On the mare's back she had her own shape and substance, and her own strength, too, which was greater than she might have imagined.

She needed it for that ride along the thread of Keen's life. It went far, very far, on and on till without the mare's presence Sparrow herself might have begun to diminish and fade into a shadow.

Then at last near the heart of that plain she found what she looked for: the shadow of a shadow, a dim and flickering thing that even as she cast her eyes on it, began to fade. The mare's light gave it a little more substance, but not enough. Sparrow swooped upon it, and caught it. It was like catching at a spider's web, so fragile and so easily broken. And yet somehow she closed her fingers about it. She drew it up.

As it came, as it touched the shimmer of the mare's light, it deepened into a greater solidity. The thing in her hand was an arm, and a body dangling from it, too thin, too pale, and all but lifeless, but it wore Keen's face. Sparrow held to it, letting it fall face-first over the mare's withers. The mare stood fast under it. She wheeled in a long curve and sped back the way she had come.

+ +

Wolfcub did not know how long he held Sparrow's hands. It was not so very long: the geese were still roasting, the water simmering, steeping the green astringent herbs. Sparrow gasped, quivered, gripped his hands so tight he set his lips against the pain. Just as suddenly, she broke free, half-falling, stooping over Keen.

Keen had not roused. But her breast rose and fell strongly. Her cheeks were no longer quite so pale. She looked alive as she had not before: as if she slept, not as if she slid into a long slow death.

"She'll live," Sparrow said. Her voice had a flat sound to it, as if she had emptied herself of all emotion.

"But will she wake?" Wolfcub asked—foolishly perhaps, but he had to know.

Sparrow nodded, though the movement almost felled her. "I need to sleep," she said. "Feed her some of the broth with goose-fat stirred in it. Wake me when the sun goes down."

She did not wait for Wolfcub to answer. She dropped down beside Keen. When he touched her, she did not stir. She was deep asleep, deeper even than Keen.

He sighed faintly. He had a great deal to ponder, but he was not ready yet to do that. Sparrow and the mare. Sparrow doing such a thing as shamans did—and with ease and grace and swiftness that he had not seen even in the great ones. He had eyes to see, and a spirit that perceived more than some. He had followed her a little way. He had seen where she went and how she went there.

If a woman could not be a shaman, then gods knew what Sparrow was. Something greater than a shaman, maybe. Just as a woman could not ride a horse—and this mare carried Sparrow willingly. This mare who was, his heart knew, more than simple earthly creature. Much more.

It was all too much to take in. He settled for meddling with their dinner, drawing off the fat as Sparrow bade him and stirring it into the broth of herbs, and feeding it sip by tiny sip to Keen. At first she took it passively, but all at once she seemed to wake; she struggled, tossing her head, spitting out the mouthful of broth that he had dribbled into her.

She was alive, awake, open-eyed and glaring. A glare from gentle Keen bemused him perhaps beyond wisdom. He could only stare at it till she came to herself a little, looked about and softened slowly. "Where—what—"

Her voice was rusty, but to his ears incalculably sweet. "We'll catch the People tomorrow, I expect. Here, eat a little meat. You need to find your strength again."

Keen looked as if she would have argued, but women learned early to heed a man's voice—and Wolfcub's had deepened gratifyingly in the past season. She gave way to it with little of her usual grace, let him feed her a mouthful, then two, before she turned her face away.

He did not press her. She had eaten enough for one who had

been fasting. The sleep that took her then was good sleep, strong sleep, sleep that healed. She would live, as Sparrow had said. He thought she might even gain back the heart and spirit that burned so low in her still.

·········· 16 ··········

KEEN CAME BACK to the People on foot, walking arm in arm with Sparrow. The mare was nowhere that any of them need see. Wolfcub had been prevailed upon with difficulty to hunt elsewhere and return later. Sparrow might not have insisted on that, but Keen had roused from her long black dream to the conviction that it were best he not be seen with the two women. Even if he walked—she would not hear of it.

She doubted that he understood. Sparrow did, perhaps: she let the two of them settle it while she bade farewell to the white mare. The mare was not happy, either. Her ears were flat and her tail flicked restlessly. But she went as Wolfcub did, because she was not given a choice.

The People were camped two days' march from the plain of gathering, in a place where they had camped for time out of mind. The priests and shamans had already begun to prepare for the rites which they would oversee. The young men practiced with weapons and in the dance. The elders held council.

The two women slipped into this camp with all its bustle and confusion, and dared to hope that if they had been missed, it would have mattered little to anyone where they were gone. That indeed seemed true for Sparrow. As soon as she appeared near Drinks-the-Wind's tent, one of the wives was shrilling at her, bidding her do something or other, and not so much as a greeting or a by-your-leave.

Keen escaped under cover of Sparrow's preoccupation. She was not as strong as she wanted Sparrow and Wolfcub to think, but she had the strength to find her tent and belongings in a heap with the rest of the baggage. She set up the tent in its usual place in the camp, alone, though people paused to stare, and one or two tried to offer a hand. But she wanted none.

At this time of day Walker was always out and about with the men or sitting in the elders' circle. She was free, then, to rest; and in a little while she would go out, and see what there was to eat. By sunset, when Walker was likely to come in search of her, everything would be as it had been since they were married. She spent a little time imagining what she would say to him, and what he would reply. She hoped he would not be angry; surely he would have worried, though he had trusted others to go looking for her.

⁕ ⁕

Walker did not come back that night, nor did she see him in the morning. When they broke camp, she packed up the tent and its belongings as always and loaded it all on the back of the dun ox that her father's wives had given her at her wedding. She was weak still: she had to pause more than once to breathe.

The second time she did that, the bundle she was lifting flew out of her hands. Wolfcub flung the rest of them onto the ox's back, bound them with skill that left her staring, and walked away before she could muster a word.

Of course he would do that. A man who lowered himself to such a task, and for another man's wife, trod the thin edge of propriety. His silence let people pretend they had not seen it. His departure freed them of any need to disapprove.

Keen found that her eyes had pricked with tears. She blinked them away quickly. She was being a fool, as she had been since she let herself be lost on the plain. She had to be strong, to be herself again.

On the march she often took her place near her father's wives and some of her sisters, but today she found it simplest to fall in behind Aurochs the hunter's women and youngest children. Aurochs was out hunting again as he nearly always was. His senior wife, who happened to be Wolfcub's mother, walked alongside Keen, leading her own ox and carrying on an easy and altogether undemanding conversation. Hunting, of course. Men in general. The best way to cook the neck of a deer, with which some of the other wives took issue. Gossip here and there, of things that Keen had cared about once and would again, maybe, but she was still too frail in spirit.

Something in Willow's expression, some tilt of the glance, told Keen that this was not happenstance. Wolfcub had asked his mother to look after her. Keen's resentment was sharp as she understood that, but she lacked the strength to be contentious. After a while she could even smile a little, thinking of that young man and his meddling. Wolfcub was like that, after all. Not like Sparrow, who was inclined to let things be, or else to rush in headlong and cause a great deal more trouble than if she had kept away.

Friendship, thought Keen. Her eyes were pricking again. She gripped the ox's lead tighter and trudged on steadily, the women's gait from the dawn time, one foot in front of the other, pace after pace, measuring the broad earth in the length of her stride.

✦ ✦

The People were among the first to come to the plain of the gathering. Only a handful of tribes were there already: Red Deer, Dun Cow, Cliff Lion that was nigh as great as the White Stone tribe, and would have been glad to be greater. White Stone, as the largest tribe, the king-tribe, had the best camping place, the long rise above the great river, with a lesser river flowing along the foot of it to merge with the greater one beyond. They had clean water unsullied, and the best grazing for their herds. From the hilltop they could look down on the rest of the tribes as they came in one by one, and at night see the campfires spread along the river like a field of stars.

Their camp guarded the great circle on the hill's summit with its stone of sacrifice, and lay closest to the field where the dancers gathered. They were the guardians of the sacred places. Their priests were highest in rank, their shamans known to be strongest and most skilled in magic.

Of course there was envy. And it was a ninth year. Everyone spoke of it. The sacrifice, which in lesser years was but threefold, Hound and Bull and Stallion, this year would be ninefold. And some of the tribes that held still to the older ways would gather to choose one of their young men, an unblemished youth, a warrior and a dancer, for the great sacrifice.

Time was when he would have been offered as king, but now even these tribes chose kings as the White Stone did, though the taming of the king of stallions. The young warrior that they chose would go as messenger for all the people of the plain, all the tribes who bowed before Skyfather and rode on the back of the horse-god, bearing their greetings and prayers to the gods beyond the sky.

But people were whispering. Everyone knew that the king of the White Stone stallions was dead, and that a new king had risen—and the king of the White Stone People had not yet tamed him.

"*Yet,*" said an elder of the Cliff Lion as Wolfcub was passing by. "What if that is never? It takes a young man to tame a stallion."

"Or an old one with skill and craft," one of his companions said. "It's a young stallion, hardly more than a colt. It shouldn't tax the king too greatly."

Wolfcub's step faltered. At that, some of the elders of the Cliff Lion had laughed, but it was a low sound, like a growl. There was danger in it.

None of them spoke aloud what they must be thinking. If the king of the White Stone was not strong enough to keep his place, another king might think to claim it for himself.

Wolfcub wondered if Walker had thought of that. In all his plans and scheming, he might only have considered his own tribe. But the other tribes might have somewhat to say of such a king as Linden.

✦ ✦

"As the kings of the lesser herds did?"

Sparrow was scraping hides when Wolfcub found her, kneeling on a great pale bullhide and attacking it with a scraper of hardened bone. It was a vigorous task, particularly in the heat of the day. Her face was crimson, her hair escaping its plait to cling wetly to her cheeks. Wolfcub could not at all escape noticing how the neck of her worn tunic drooped over her round breasts, or how the thin leather clung to them.

He tore his eyes away and focused his mind on her words, which were sharp, clear, and measured in strokes of the scraper. "The king stallions all bowed to the mares' choice. How do you know the kings of men won't do the same?"

"Men are men," Wolfcub said, "and they don't listen to women."

Her eyes flashed up at that, but she kept her temper in check. "Men listen to shamans."

"One young shaman, however powerful?"

"All the shamans of the tribes, even Drinks-the-Wind, if my brother has his way."

"You don't know this."

She bent to her scraping. The hide gleamed with her labor. It

would be a fine tunic, from the quality and thinness, for her father
or one of his wives.

"You don't know it," Wolfcub repeated. "Do you?"

She did not answer. She never did, if she decided that she had
said enough.

He hissed in annoyance and left her kneeling there. He had been
going hunting, but now he was minded to hunt men. She had made
sure of that. He could not go his own way, not until he had proved
to himself that she was wrong.

Shamans in camp kept to themselves except during festivals, when
they gathered to work magic and to cast omens for the tribe. Shamans
at the gathering, which was one long festival, made camp by the
sacred places, and therefore in or very near the camp of the White
Stone People. It always surprised Wolfcub to see how many of them
there were. The People had Drinks-the-Wind and Walker Between
the Worlds, and Drinks-the-Wind had a handful of apprentices. Each
of the other tribes had a shaman, rarely two. Two full shamans in one
tribe was a great thing, though it was only to be expected of the
White Stone People. They were great in magic, everyone knew, and
much blessed of the gods.

Or so Wolfcub had been told. He wanted no magic but what
aided him in the hunt, or—he could admit it—what was between
man and woman. Shamans were strange creatures. All of them, as he
saw them together in their circle, bore some deformity, some oddity
of shape or form, that marked them as belonging to the gods: a
twisted leg, an eye born blind, a blood-red stain marring the face.
Only the White Stone shamans lacked that—and yet, might not their
beauty be a strangeness of its own?

Their circle was not openly forbidden, but people avoided it.
There was always someone sitting in it, sometimes one or two or
three, shaking a bone rattle or muttering to himself or staring at the
fire. The rest came and went from the great tent that was pitched on
the edge of the stone circle. Scents wafted out of it, drones of chants,
a sense that raised the hackles on Wolfcub's neck.

He could not go in there. He would not enter the circle. There
was no way to discover what Sparrow wanted him to know. He
mused briefly and a little wildly on asking Walker outright: "Are you
plotting to cast down the king and raise another?" But Wolfcub was
never so much a fool.

He turned his back on the shamans' circle and let his feet lead him through the camp, past a circle of dancers and a circle of warriors and a gathering of women by the little river, who blushed and hid their faces and giggled when he went by. Women had been doing that ever since he came to the gathering. At first he had looked to see if his leggings had slipped to bare his secret parts, or if he had some mark or stain on his coat, but he was in as good order as ever. The women were being women, that was all.

Past the Cliff Lion and the Dun Cow, the Tall Grass People had come in just this morning and made camp in their wonted place. Tall Grass came from farther south than most, near the country of the little dark people, and many of them were smaller and darker than the run of the tribes.

Wolfcub had a hunting-companion or two among the Tall Grass men. As he was thinking of seeking them out and hearing what they could tell of the world to the south, his eye found a very tall, very fair figure among the shorter, swarthier ones. He slowed his advance, slipping without thought into a gathering of men, glad for once that he was not as tall or as pale as some.

They greeted him with reserve in the way of the Tall Grass, but there was warmth in it. Someone handed him a bit of dried meat; he offered in return one of his mother's honeycakes. That, shared out, was well received.

And all the while he observed the courtesies, he was aware of the tall man nearby, sitting with the king and a man even paler than he, white as a bone indeed, who was the Tall Grass shaman. Walker was not saying anything that Wolfcub could take exception to. But his presence there, the way he leaned toward his brother shaman, made Wolfcub uneasy.

It was foolish. Sparrow's fears made him see trouble where there was none. Walker was observing the courtesies, that was all, just as Wolfcub was doing; as men did all through the tribes, and women, too. That was what gathering was.

And yet when Walker bade farewell to the king and the shaman, Wolfcub lingered only a little longer. He did not want to follow the shaman and be seen. But he took note of where Walker went. He was visiting the tribes one by one, with seeming casualness, and in each one, paying his respects to its king and its shaman.

Drinks-the-Wind was doing no such thing. He had not been seen since the People came to the gathering. He was in the shamans' tent, performing great rites and preparing for the sacrifices. So should Walker have done, but he chose to be out and about.

At least he had let Linden be. Linden was doing much the same as Walker, but of him it was expected, even required. He was a king's son of the White Stone; he should be leading the dances and the games.

He was also one of those who guarded the horses. Which was nothing to wonder at, but after Wolfcub left the Tall Grass camp, he wandered by the herds. And there was Linden sitting on the back of his pretty gold-and-red stallion, surrounded by an even larger pack of young hellions than usual, watching the new king court a mare.

The mare was not particularly inclined to oblige her suitor, but he was persistent. He was not well endowed with wits, Wolfcub reckoned, but of beauty he had more than enough. He was prettier even than Linden's stallion—and that, surely, was what so enraptured Linden.

Wolfcub might have been able to escape Walker's notice, but his cousins and kinsmen about Linden marked him before he could fade into the grass. They called to him with glee that had a fair ration of *kumiss* in it, and would not hear of his leaving them. Linden, shaken out of his contemplation of the silvermaned stallion, favored Wolfcub with his most dazzling smile, a welcome so pure and so perfectly warm that Wolfcub could only sigh and give way to it.

Wolfcub stood beside Linden's stallion, where the crowd of them insisted that he be. Linden bent down from the horse's back and laid an arm about Wolfcub's shoulders and said, "Look at him now. What do you think?"

Wolfcub thought that the new king was terribly pretty, terribly young, and terribly foolish. But he could hardly say that to the king's very image and likeness among men. He said instead, "He's not going to breed that mare today, unless she has a change of heart."

Linden laughed. "And I'll wager he wins her over."

"A wager, a wager!" some idiot sang out. "And what will you lay on it?"

"Why," said Linden, "what's it worth? A fine bridle, and a skin of *kumiss*."

They were all staring at Wolfcub now, waiting for him to take the wager. He sighed faintly. "A well-tanned deerhide," he said, "and a skin of *kumiss*."

They cheered at that, and no doubt thought him a great good fellow. Wolfcub wondered why they made him feel so old. He was the same age as they, but his spirit was never so light.

While he reflected on that, the stallion approached the mare with clear intent to mount her. She squealed in rage and planted both hind feet squarely between his legs. He groaned. She threatened with a restless heel. He slunk off, head and tail low, walking, Wolfcub would have sworn, considerably more spraddle-legged than he had before.

Linden had roared with the rest at the stallion's discomfiture. He paid his wager handsomely, and applauded when Wolfcub passed the skin of *kumiss* round. He was altogether undismayed to have lost his wager.

He was also, Wolfcub noticed, fixed still, if subtly, on the stallion. That lord of horses recovered soon enough, though he kept his distance from the mares. And Linden watched him steadily, perhaps not even aware that he had done it.

························ 17 ························

WHEN ALL THE tribes of the plain had gathered by the river near the sacred place, three days before the ninefold sacrifice began, the king of the White Stone People went out to tame the new king of stallions. He had prepared himself with fasting and honed himself in the dance, leaping and whirling and stamping by firelight, naked and painted with signs of power. Then he had gone into his tent and prepared himself in another way, lying with the chosen of his women—it was Fawn, the women said to one another, and certain of his other women had not taken it well at all.

Women could not watch this rite of taming the stallion. They were kept in the tents as they would be for the sacrifices, shut away lest their eyes and their presence pollute the rite.

But Sparrow could not stay away from it. She would far rather have gone out onto the open plain than confined herself in close and reeking dimness with women who did nothing but bicker among themselves, play endless games of toss-the-bones, and drink far more *kumiss* than their men would have been pleased to know of. Indeed she would have done that as she had in years past. But in the morning when the women were ordered into the tents, she woke from a dream of the mare. The mare was calling her urgently, demanding her presence at once.

She tried to resist it. She banked the fire in front of her father's tent. She herded the youngest children within. She gathered such oddments as they all might need for confinement.

But the calling would not stop for that. And when she tried to enter the tent, her body turned instead and slipped away, concealing itself as best it could till it had passed the camp and found the safety of the plain.

The mare was waiting for her, pawing with impatience. Sparrow could not tell her that any woman's presence at this rite would profane it. The mare cared nothing for men's laws. Sparrow would come. That was her will.

Sparrow went, because Horse Goddess would not have it otherwise. She was allowed at least to go in hunter's wise, and to conceal herself in the tall grasses above the field of the trial. It was a hollow in the earth like the print of a vast hoof, somewhat steep-sided, smooth and almost level within. The men were gathered there, all those of the White Stone and as many of the other tribes as were minded to come. They perched on the hillside and stood or crouched on the edges of the circle. They were utterly, preternaturally still.

The priests had brought the silvermaned king to the circle. He was not at all pleased to have been roped and bound and dragged apart from his mares. But the priests were many and their ropes were strong. In the end he submitted.

The king of the White Stone People stood near the eastward edge of the circle, the morning side, waiting for the stallion to cease his fighting of the ropes. He was stripped to the waist, baring strong shoulders and corded arms, and a rich array of scars amid the king-marks swirling on breast and back. He was barefoot, his leggings plain, no weapon on him. In his hand he held a rope of braided hide.

The stallion stood quiet for a long moment. He might have erupted again, but the mare snorted gently behind Sparrow. Sparrow tensed to dive for cover, but no one seemed to have heard, except the stallion. He lifted his head and flared his nostrils but held still.

In the silence Sparrow scanned as many faces as she could see. There were the priests in their masks of featureless horsehide. There was a cluster of shamans, and her father tall among them, with his flowing beard and his heavy white braids. Her brother she did not see.

No—there. Not far from the king, standing beside Linden, arms folded, wearing no expression at all. Linden was oblivious to the shaman's presence. He was intent not on the king but on the stallion. Sparrow wondered that people did not remark on the yearning in his eyes.

But the silvermaned stallion belonged to his father. He had to stand unmoving while the king gestured to the priests. They hesitated for a breath's span, but his command was clear. They slipped the ropes that bound the stallion, all but one, which the last of the priests handed, with a bow of his mane-crowned head, to the king.

The stallion had not moved while he was freed. Nor did he move when he felt a new hand on the rope. He was alert but quiet, ears flicking nervously, soft black nostrils fluttering.

The king approached him slowly. That at least the stallion could bear: he had had men about him since he was a foal, and a woman, too. Sparrow had gentled him when he was small, and taught him to seek the touch of a hand.

So he did now, to the manifest awe of those who watched. He approached the king delicately, one step, two; he lowered his nose into the king's hand. The king ventured to touch his head, his ears. He shied only a little.

Was the king relieved? Sparrow could not tell. Swiftly but carefully he fashioned his rope into a bridle and slipped it over the stallion's head. The stallion tensed but steadied. The king stroked along his neck and shoulders, back and flanks. He barely quivered.

With sudden decision, the king sprang onto the stallion's back.

Sparrow tasted blood. She had bitten her tongue—it hurt appallingly. But better that than a cry of outrage. Fool! Had he no patience?

The stallion stood stunned under that imposing weight. The king clamped legs about his barrel. Fool, again; fool and thrice fool. The stallion, appalled, went up.

Straight up, lunging for the sky. There could be no thought in that lovely head but to be rid of the clutching, clamping thing. When it hauled at his head, forcing it about, driving him down to the earth, he flung up his heels in revolt.

Still the king clung to his back. He bucked furiously. The king only laughed.

Sparrow did not see exactly what it was that sent the stallion into another paroxysm of revolt. The king was riding more lightly now. The stallion was growing calm again, beginning—she thought—to accept this burden on his back. He was not evil of mind or spirit; he quite lacked the wits to lull his rider into complacency and then fling him off.

And yet from almost-quiet he burst into sudden, spinning, bucking fury. The king's laughter rang out anew. Round the edges of the circle men began to cheer, stamping their feet, clapping their hands in salute.

Maybe that was more than the stallion could bear. Maybe something stung him. A bee—a dart? His bucking gained a frantic edge. He twisted, flinging himself up, then down, over and over.

The king held on. But he was tiring. Maybe there was more to it; maybe someone had laid a wishing on him. One moment he was riding well enough, holding fast to mane and sides. The next, he spun through the air.

He seemed to hang there for a long, long while, many counts of breath, many beats of the heart. Then slowly, oh so slowly, he fell.

Sparrow saw how he would go. He should have gathered himself, drawn into a knot, rolled free. But he fell limply, all sprawl. His head struck the earth first.

People were still clapping and chanting, as if their eyes had run far ahead of their bodies. Sparrow heard no sound of body striking ground. Nonetheless she could have sworn before the gods that she heard the soft, distinct snap of his neck.

⊹ ⊹

Silence, when at last it fell, was profoundly blessed. The stallion had fled still bucking to the far side of the circle, as far from—yes, as far from Walker and as near to the mare as he might go. There perhaps he would have regained his wonted calm; but the men there, no less fools than the king, broke the bonds of the circle to surge toward him. He veered snorting and plunged back the way he had come.

The king lay where he had fallen. He was limp, a broken thing. The priests ran to him, and some of the shamans. First to reach him was Drinks-the-Wind, his old friend and battle-brother. Even from a distance Sparrow could see her father's face, how still it was, how starkly white—nigh as white as the fall of his beard.

The stallion, mad now with all the people closing in on him, bolted straight for the king and the kneeling shaman. None of all these men, horsemen though they claimed to be, had the wits to understand that if they had kept their places, the stallion would have settled to grazing well away from the fallen king.

A lone figure darted out from the crowd. Its yellow plaits streamed behind as it ran. Linden, by luck or fate or the gift of the gods, caught the stallion's rein as it whipped past, sprang, got a grip on mane, flew onto the stallion's back.

He was mad, but so was the stallion—mad with running, not with bucking and plunging. And Linden let him do it. He did not clamp or clutch as the king had. He sat as quietly as a man could on the back of a horse bolting wildly in a ceaseless circle, darting aside from men who stumbled into his path, and no thought in his head but to run and run and run. Linden gripped mane and loosened rein, crouched down and let him run himself out.

It had dawned on the crowding men, slowly but inevitably, what Linden was doing—what he had done. They drew back out of his way. They settled in their old places, more or less, in their old silence. They watched.

The priests and the shamans too had seen it, first in avoiding the stallion's flying hooves, then in marking who rode on his back. All but Drinks-the-Wind, who was intent on the fallen king. He did what he could. He straightened the tumbled limbs, and the head awry on the broken neck. He closed the staring eyes. He sang a death-song over the body, while the stallion, the kingslayer, galloped round the circle.

Nine times the stallion ran that great circle. Sparrow counted. Then at last near the fallen king, he pounded to a halt. That was Linden's hand on the rein and his weight on the young back, breaking through the fog of fear and speed. The stallion stood breathing hard, foam on his neck and between his hindlegs, but he was far from spent: he could still raise his head and snort at the dead thing in front of him.

Linden gentled him with a hand, stroking his sweat-streaming shoulder. It was a gesture altogether without thought, a horseman's gesture. The stallion settled somewhat to it, and consented to walk a slow and much smaller circle, till his breathing quieted and the sweat began to dry on his neck.

Linden, alone of all of them, did not seem to know what he had done. He had calmed a frightened horse, that was all, and taught him to carry a rider, so that he would not imagine that he could cast off any man who sat on his back. There were tears streaming down Linden's face, grief for the king his father—but no thought, Sparrow was sure, of the consequence of his fine horsemanship. The king of stallions had cast off and killed the king of men. The king's heir, his favorite son, had mounted the stallion and tamed him, and rode him as horses were to be ridden, as both lord and servant.

The king was dead. The king lived, mounted on the back of the silvermaned stallion.

Sparrow looked beyond Linden to the place where Walker had been standing. Where he still stood, scrupulously out of the way, and for a while forgotten. He was smiling with great satisfaction. There was no sign about him of a dart, but Sparrow did not expect to find one. A shaman's tunic was capacious and full of secrets.

But Sparrow knew. It was as clear in him as if he had shouted it to the sky. Walker had the king he wanted. The rest, he was certain, would follow.

18

THE KING OF the White Stone People was dead. The new king rode into the gathering on the back of the young king of stallions, and the priests paced behind, bearing the old king on a bier of spears and warcloaks. Word had come to the camp already, as swift as such things always were. The women streamed out of the tents, wailing and rending their garments. Camp dogs barked and snarled, shrieking as they did battle with one another, or as men kicked or beat them out of the way.

The noise was indescribable. It brought Keen out of Aurochs' tent where she had been invited to spend the day with Willow and the lesser wives. It rent a cry out of her as if her body were not her own, a long shrilling lament that went on and on without her willing it. They were all doing it, all possessed by the grief and shock of a king's death.

But even as the wailing poured from lungs and throat, her eyes marked Linden on the stallion's back, and Walker close behind him. Everyone else was fixed on the king or on the old shaman who walked beside him. But Walker, no. Walker looked like a father whose son has tamed his first stallion.

There was no evident evil in it, no malice, only joyful pride. Yet Keen's shoulders tightened. She had never looked at her husband so before—as if he were a stranger. And one, moreover, whom she did not particularly like or trust.

Was this how Sparrow saw her brother? Sparrow had no love at all for Walker, Keen knew that. Keen had never understood why, until now. And for no reason, either, nor for any provocation. Walker had done nothing to her. He had not even seen her since she came back to the People.

Maybe that was why. She was healed inside, but there were scars. She wanted, needed, his warmth, his touch to assure her that she was beautiful, his kisses to remind her that she was cherished. She needed—maybe not to make another child, not so soon, but to know that she could. That they would together, and this time, gods willing, it would live.

But he had never even noticed that she was missing, nor come to look for her, nor cared to discover what had become of her. And Aurochs' young wife Teasel had muttered just now, before the clamor brought them out, that it was little wonder Keen had not seen him; he was always in the Tall Grass camp, ingratiating himself with its shaman and exchanging heated glances with the shaman's red-haired daughter. Keen would have wanted to know more—would have demanded it—but then the kings had come back, the living and the dead, and everything was lost in that.

A king could not be buried at once as a simple man could, still less thrust into the ground and forgotten like a woman. Because this one had died so close to the great sacrifices, he was laid on his bier before the altar-stone in the sacred place, with guards to keep off the vultures, and priests and shamans wreathing him about with prayer and chanting and pungent smoke. His sons were among the guards, and some among the priests, all gathered as was proper for their father's farewell.

All but Linden. He was taken away into a place so secret that the women were not allowed to speak of it, though they all knew somewhat of it. It was an old tomb, the grave of a king so ancient his name was long since lost, who some thought might even have been a god. The young king must go down into the earth, into the heart of the tomb, and there lie in the dark, and lay himself open to gods and visions. Three days he would lie there, and at moonrise of the third, come forth as if born into the world again. Then he would be made a king before the tribes.

It was a great thing, everyone reckoned, that Linden would come out of the tomb on the morning before the first sacrifice. It was an omen. It foretold mighty things for him as king, that he had taken his place in so sacred a season, before the whole of the gathered people.

The women had much to do to prepare for what would be a greater feast than they had reckoned on. Hunters went out far and wide to bring back meat for the feast. It had to be skinned, cleaned, readied for the fires or the spits or the cookpots. Young girls and women free of other duties were kept busy all day long gathering dung to feed the fires and seeking out herbs and roots, greens and the seeds of the wild grasses; fishing in the river; and hunting the honeycomb.

Only the king's women did no such thing. They secluded themselves in the tent that had been his, making his funeral garments and preparing for their own fate. The wives would go into the tomb with him. The concubines would go to the new king.

No one was allowed to visit them or to console them. "They're afraid we'll talk sense into them," Sparrow said as she and Keen and some of the other young women went berry-gathering, the day before the king's burial.

Keen was not exactly shocked. Sparrow always said such things, though she was usually more careful as to where she said them. "Sometimes," Keen said to her, pausing in stripping a bramble of its sweet red burden, "I think you'd argue with a god if he said something you didn't agree with."

"I probably would," Sparrow said willingly. She had filled a basket already and was beginning on the other. Her mood was odd, almost too bright. She even hummed to herself as she worked—and Sparrow never did that.

Keen eyed her narrowly. "You're up to something."

Sparrow's expression was pure innocence. "I am not."

"You can't go in there," Keen said with a flash of alarm. "You can't convince the king's wives to rebel. The priests would kill you, if the rest of the men didn't find you first."

"What makes you think I would do that?"

"I know you," Keen said. And she did; she was afraid, suddenly, for this odd creature whom she called friend. "Just because you can—because of the mare—doesn't mean—"

"I fail to see," said Sparrow, "why the new king can't take the old king's wives. Surely they'll serve him better alive, bearing sons to his heir, than dead and buried in his tomb."

"They go with him," Keen said, a little breathless with the shock of Sparrow's daring. "They serve him on his journey into the sky. They wait on him when he becomes a god-ancestor."

"Such a life," said Sparrow. "Condemned to servitude forever."

"The gods have ordained—" Keen began.

But Sparrow was not listening. Sparrow was lost in her world again, the world that, Keen often thought, touched on this one even less than the shadow-plain did. Sparrow did not see as other people saw. She had her mother's eyes. Stranger-eyes, witch-eyes.

Keen gathered sweet red berries in silence, apart from Sparrow as from the other women. They had heard nothing of what passed between Sparrow and Keen. They were laughing, singing, trading jests and gossip as Keen had known how to do once. Before she went into the women's house. Before she was lost on the shadow-plain.

She made an effort. She laughed at a jest. She widened her eyes at a scandal. No one rebuked her for the pretense. To them she was as she had always been.

It was comforting, almost. It made her forget Sparrow for a while. Then when she remembered, the place beside her was empty. Sparrow and her brimming baskets were gone.

+ +

Sparrow was sorry that she had shocked Keen. Keen had known her all their lives, and yet was still distressingly easy to discomfort. When she turned away from Sparrow to indulge in the others' silliness, Sparrow sighed a little, but without anger. No one thought as she thought; that she had understood long ago.

No one but a man. Sparrow considered that as she brought her baskets back to her father's tent. Tomorrow the king would go to his tomb, and a dozen women with him. None of them deserved to be shut up in the dark without escape, to die of hunger and thirst, for it was forbidden to shed the blood of women in a holy place.

Men never questioned that. Of course they would not. They would reckon it more than fair that twelve women died to provide one man with a harem in the gods' country.

Still, what could she do? No one would listen to her. Wolfcub might, if she could find him—he was hunting, most likely, as all the young men were, bringing down game for the cookpots—but he was too young to have much voice among the men, even with his new title of boarslayer.

She might have given it up, not happily but perforce, if when she came to her father's tent her father had not been there. That was unexpected. He had been keeping vigil over the king's body, and would, she had thought, till the king went to his burial. But there was Drinks-the-Wind, sitting in front of his tent, refusing food and drink but accepting a few moments' rest with his head in White Bird's lap.

"He was taken ill," Mallard said when Sparrow emptied her baskets into the much larger basket that would, when the women had all come back, be full of sweet berries. "Some of the men carried him here. He'll go back, he insists, as soon as he's permitted."

Sparrow considered him from this safe distance. He was pale but he did not look terribly ill. "Do you think someone slipped him something?"

She had not known she spoke aloud till Mallard's brows went up. "Do you? Why would someone do that?"

Sparrow shrugged. "There's a new king now. This was the old one's friend. Someone might think the old king should have a shaman to keep him company among the gods, along with his wives."

Mallard, like Keen, was accustomed to Sparrow's oddities, but she did not indulge them as Keen did. "Hush, child, and get you to the river. We need water for the stewpots."

No one listened. But Drinks-the-Wind was awake, and by chance his eye had fallen on her. It was alert enough, though very tired. Sparrow let it draw her until she stood over him.

She seldom came so close to her father. His wives and favored daughters waited on him in the tent. She was little better than a servant. Sometimes she wondered if he even remembered who she was.

He did seem to know her now, or at least to recognize her for one of the women who belonged to him. "I heard you," he said. "What makes you think someone is doing this to me?"

"You were strong enough," said Sparrow, "until the king of stallions died. Do you trust everything you eat and drink? Are you certain no one has laid a wishing on you?"

He did not look as if she had frightened him. Neither, she thought, did he believe her. "You are a suspicious creature," he said.

I saw the old king fall. But she could not say that. She had seen what the silvermaned stallion did—and that was no natural eruption. Something had stung him. She would wager it was not a bee; that it was a work of man's hands. A man. Walker.

She could not say so. No more could she prove it. She only knew in her heart.

Aloud she said, "Things change when the king changes. What if the new king were to take the old king's wives? Wouldn't that serve the tribe better than burying them in a tomb?"

"They serve the king," Drinks-the-Wind said, much as Keen had, and with the same blind innocence. Strange to see that in a shaman. But age had crept up on him. His power was waning. She could feel it seeping out of him like slow tears.

"They serve the king," Sparrow agreed. "Why not the young king, then? Why not give the old one carven images, with magic on them to make them live among the gods?"

Those of Drinks-the-Wind's wives who stood about gave way to various displays of horror. But none of them would speak in his presence, not without his leave.

There was no anger in the eyes that fixed on Sparrow's face, as if Drinks-the-Wind needed to remind himself of what she looked like. There was no understanding, either. A man saying such things, a shaman, would have been heeded. He would have been granted the strength of his vision. But Sparrow was a woman, and of no account.

"You are an interesting child," Drinks-the-Wind said a little faintly. He was tired. She watched sleep creep up on him, with White Bird to guide it: holding his head in her lap, stroking his brow and his hollowed cheeks. White Bird did not find Sparrow interesting. Indeed, from the glances she cast, she would rather have said appalling.

Sparrow left without waiting to be dismissed, not caring where she went, either, or how she came there. She was not in despair over the king's wives—not truly. But the rest of it, her father's weariness, the old king's fall, Walker's smile that he had not perhaps meant anyone to see, those were all things that she could not well shrug away. Walker had made a king. And he had done it without any of Sparrow's visions.

Someone else might have imagined fondly that he had found the gift at last. But Sparrow knew he had not. Her bones could tell. Walker was as blind as ever to magic. All the visions he had, she had given him. There was nothing in her now, no word or sign of a kingmaking. And yet Walker was making a king.

·············· **19** ··············

RINKS-THE-WIND would not listen to Sparrow. The other shamans would laugh at her, if they allowed her near them at all. But there was one who knew what she was. One who would hear what she had to say.

She had not wanted to do this. She would have avoided it if she could. The rest of the world could do little to her, to harm her or to touch her spirit. But Walker—Walker had stolen her visions.

It should not matter what men did, even to the king's women. None of them was a friend. None had ever shown Sparrow a kindness, or acknowledged her existence at all. They were like Linden: beautiful, remote, and unconcerned with the existence of the shaman's ill-favored daughter.

Still this was a thing that Sparrow had in mind to do. It was goddess-born, she supposed. Most of what she did and said these days came from some aspect of the mare. She was not a slave or a blind voice—she was still herself, clear down to the bone—but the mare's presence in her heart made her do things, say things, that she would never have ventured before. This was what it was to be a priest, she thought, though a woman could no more be a priest than she could be a shaman.

This gathering, this sacred place, this ninth-year feast and immi-nence of the great sacrifice, made Horse Goddess' presence all the stronger. It burned in Sparrow's spirit. It possessed her and gave her courage, so that she could seek out the one she both feared and despised.

Walker had gone to the secret place, to the old king's tomb. Sparrow was not supposed to know where it was or what it was; but she did not care just now for men's laws. Horse Goddess was in her, driving her.

No one could go into the tomb with Linden. He must endure the ordeal alone. But the shaman stood guard at the entrance, that door into the dark, warded with a standing stone. Cold breathed out of it, the chill of death, old roots and old stone and darkness that had ruled since the dawn of the world.

Sparrow shuddered at the sight and the sense of it. She hated to think of Linden shut up in that terrible place: sun-bright, lighthearted Linden with his ready smile and his easy manner. He was no great marvel of wit. He had no notable strength of will. All there was to him was beauty and a kind of sweetness, and a child's love of pretty things.

"You should never have made him be king," Sparrow said to Walker.

He started half out of his skin—deeply and profoundly satisfying to watch. She had not made any great effort to be quiet as she came, but he was sitting in the shadow of the doorway, eyes shut, asleep or close to it. Sparrow doubted that he had been gathering his powers or dreaming deep dreams. He only did that, or pretended to, where he thought anyone could see.

She had been rather surprised to find him alone. Other shamans should have been there, and priests of the Stallion. But there was only Walker.

He scrambled up at the sound of her voice, startled, taken off balance, so that for a moment she could see the man beneath the masks he wore. He was a small man, shallow of spirit, but subtle— yes, he was that—and deep in malice.

That helped her to say what she had come to say. "This was not well done of you," she said.

He recovered quickly enough, when all was considered. He stood to his full height as he always did, to dwarf her in spirit as well as in body. But her spirit was riding on the mare, high as the stars and almost as fearless. She met his glare full on, as she never had before— and that, too, took him aback.

Maybe he spoke more quickly than he should, then, and with less thought. "You think I did all this?"

"I know you did. What was it? A dart in the stallion's rump?"

Walker flushed. She had never seen him do that before. It was gratifying. "The gods did it," he said.

"By your hand," she said. "And now that poor boy is buried in the earth. What if he comes forth mad, or dies of terror?"

"Linden?" Walker laughed, a sharp sound, short and mirthless. "It takes intelligence to go mad in the dark. That, and imagination. He has neither. He's lying there, I can assure you, in a fair passion of boredom, or sleeping the days away, waiting till I bring him out."

"And will you give him a vision if that's so? Tell him what to say to the elders and the shamans?"

"If such is laid on me," Walker said.

Sparrow drew a breath, careful not to let him see it. "I have one for you, and maybe for him, too. But I'll not give it to you unless you promise me something."

She had never done that before; never set a price on her visions. He had simply taken them, or she had simply refused to let them be taken. This surprised him, but he was steady now, on ground he knew well. He looked her in the eyes and said, "You will give it to me. You have no choice."

"But I do," said Sparrow. He was trying to ensorcel her, fixing her with that cold pale stare, flat as a snake's. But there was no power in it. "I'll bargain with you, brother. My vision in return for a favor."

He bridled. "What favor could you ask of me?"

"This," she said. "Give the king's wives to Linden. Send carved images into the grave with him, enchanted to come alive in the gods' country and be his servants there."

Walker gaped. Then he burst into laughter—genuine this time, and incredulous. "You want me to— What in the world made you think of that?"

"Visions," she said. Which was true, in its way.

"Preposterous," said Walker.

"Are you saying you cannot do it? You lack the power?"

"I lack nothing!" he shot back before he could have thought.

"Then it's a simple thing, a matter of no effort. Do it and I'll give you a vision for the new king."

"It is not simple," he said. "It is—" He broke off. His eyes narrowed. "There's more to it, isn't there? You want to be the king's wife."

She felt the heat rush to her cheeks. She did not blush as her fairer-skinned kin did, but the burning was no less for that. "I have no desire to be his wife," she said. "This is the price of the vision. The gods have said so."

"The gods, is it?" Walker did not believe her, but neither, from his expression, did he dare to disbelieve. "They're not asking an easy thing, with but a day to do it. All the priests and shamans, the elders, the kings, the people, will be outraged."

"Are you not the greatest shaman of them all? Have you no power to do this one and only thing?"

She had him. He could resist for a little longer, but she had pricked his pride. All at once, with very ill grace, he surrendered. "I'll do what I can. Now give me the vision."

"Swear that you will do it," she said. "Swear on the standing stone."

That made him stiffen. But he laid his hand on the stone and swore before the gods to pay the price that she demanded.

Then she gave him what she had come to give. "Here is my vision," she said. "I see the place of the stallion's taming. I see the king fall, and the young king rise. He mounts on the back of the stallion and springs into the sky. The stars dance about him. The night wind sings of his glory. Daughters of the gods bow before him and give him gifts of flowers, cups of sunlight, and sweet honeycomb. 'Live,' they bid him. 'Live a thousand years.'"

Walker's eyes had closed as she spoke, as if her words took shape in his mind. Great joy dawned in his face. Just as she had expected— as she had bargained for.

She did not tell him the rest of it. That was hers. How the white mare came and took the stallion away, and the gods' daughters followed. Then the stars went out one by one, except for the last, the greatest, nigh as bright and nigh as large as the moon. It was the white mare again, wrapped in light. Her shadow fell over Linden. In it he shrank and diminished till he was no larger than a child. Then the mare gave birth to a new flock of stars, more even than had been before, and brighter, crowding the sky.

Sparrow had given her brother a promise of the young king's glory. The rest—how Horse Goddess would humble him—she kept to herself. It was a mystery, both high and sacred. Walker would only sully it.

Walker was content. She left him rapt in contemplation of the vision, slipped away and was gone before he roused to her absence.

····· **20** ·····

THE OLD KING could not be laid in his tomb until the young king had come out into the light. For three days the men of the White Stone had prepared the tomb out on the plain, raising it high with heaped stones and facing it toward the sunrise.

Now it was done, all but the laying of the body in it. They waited, all the people, for the young king to come.

Wolfcub had come back from the hunt to find a message waiting for him. The young king asked—did not command; asked—that the boarslayer be his companion at the kingmaking. There were nine of them for a ninth year, picked men of the People, all young, all strong, all tested in battle. The rest were as Wolfcub would have expected, Linden's followers from his childhood.

Wolfcub wondered who had been rejected and would plague him with resentment later. But he did not speak of that. His father's pride, his mother's pleasure in the honor paid him—however dry the wit with which she said so—kept him silent. He could be glad. Yes, he could. To rise up in the morning before it was full light, and know what the day would make him: a king's companion. To put on the weapons that had come with the message, the beautiful new coat with its embroideries of shells and beads, the leggings of white doeskin as soft as a woman's cheek. To have his hair plaited with feathers and stones, his sparse young beard cut to be less ragged, and signs of power painted on his cheeks and brow—it was wonderful. It was splendid.

That was the word his mother used of him. *Splendid*. She stood back in the flock of the lesser wives. They were all staring, and the youngest were giggling behind their hands. He flushed at that, fought down an urge to scrape off the paint and shed the coat and run away from their mockery.

But they were not mocking him. Not even his mother, whose tongue could flay a bull's hide. Her smile was pure pleasure. "Child," she said, "you've grown up well."

"Beautiful," said one of the others. He did not look to see who it was. He was too preoccupied with the thing that had struck him, that he had not seen before. His mother was so small. Or—was he grown so tall?

"You are a handsome thing," she said, "after all. Who'd have thought it?" She brushed at his coat, which was perfectly clean and had not a wrinkle in it, and fussed with his braids till she was satisfied, then thrust him out with little ceremony into the first pale glimmers of sunlight.

People stared at him as he walked through the camp toward the place where he had been told to go, where he could see the others waiting with horses and a company of priests. He held himself straight, though he would have liked to turn hunter, sink down and seek shadows and pass unnoticed. A king's companion should not do that. He walked in the light, with pride and in such beauty as he had—however great or little that might be.

The women seemed to think he had a fair store of it. It had never mattered before, but with the rest, it made him stand taller.

The others were all gathered when he came there, Spearhead coming next to last and just ahead of him. Boys had caught and readied their horses for them, brushing even Wolfcub's dun to such sheen as he ever had, and working the tangles out of the rough black mane. He was nearly handsome in his slabsided way, and very full of himself, too. Two of a kind, they were—Wolfcub could almost hear Sparrow's voice saying it. He grinned and slapped the stallion's neck and swung astride.

None of them was finding it easy to mourn the fallen king. He had been both high and remote, closer to gods than to the hearts of the young men. This new king whom they went to greet—he was their friend, their kinsman, and their battle-brother.

They milled about for a bit without direction, while the priests sat quiet and faceless on their horses. Wolfcub took his pattern from that; he kept his mount still and waited.

A priest came toward them on foot from among the herds. He led the king of stallions, brushed and scrubbed until he gleamed, in a fine braided bridle, with a soft doeskin flung over his back. The priest led him up to Wolfcub and held out the rein.

Wolfcub took it blindly. This was the great honor, the one the others had been vying for: to take the stallion to his king. He caught Bullcalf's scowl and Spearhead's shrug. None of them contested the choice. "Boarslayer," someone said, almost too soft to hear. It was both title and explanation.

They formed in ranks then, priests ahead and behind, the pack of companions in the middle, and Wolfcub the last of them, leading the silvermaned stallion. He was skittish but not unreasonably so; Wolfcub gentled him with soft words, drawing the stallion's head toward his knee. His own horse, sensible beast that he was, flattened an ear but offered no other threat. The stallion took comfort from that, maybe. He followed docilely enough.

It was not a long way to the holy place, but they took it slowly, in processional. The priests chanted as they rode. One of them had a drum on which he beat, stroke and stroke.

Walker Between the Worlds waited for them in the shadow of the barrow, with a handful of shamans for escort. And it was an escort, just as the companions would escort the new king. Walker stood tallest of them all, with his winter beauty and his arrogant lift of the head, which he had from his father. He was shaman born of a race of shamans, wielder of powers beyond the reach of simple men, and well he knew it.

The silvermaned stallion snorted wetly at him. Wolfcub bit his lip. Horses cared little for men's pretensions to power.

Walker did not seem to understand that the stallion had been expressing an opinion. He was deep in the importance of his position, opening the door into the underworld, letting in the sun, and calling out in a splendid and carrying voice: "Come forth! Come forth and be reborn."

There was a long, breathless pause. In it, the companions glanced at one another. Some of them had begun to be afraid. What if Linden was dead? What if he had gone mad? Or worse—what if the gods had rejected him?

A scrabbling broke the silence: the sound of a footstep on rough and sloping ground. A figure strode out of the darkness into the dazzle of morning light. He stood squinting through tears of pain, erect and still under the sky, finding his balance and his vision.

Walker took his hands. He peered at the shaman. He did not

look mad, and he was certainly not dead. He smiled, and that was purely Linden. "Walker," he said. His voice was rough with dryness, or perhaps disuse. "Is it time?"

Walker nodded. "It is time. What did you see?"

Linden frowned. Whatever his days in the dark had done for him, they had not granted him any quickness of wit. "I saw dark," he said. "I smelled dust and old stone. The king is down there still. He lies on the stone. His bed—it was flowers. Long dead and gone to dust, but I smelled the ghosts of them. They were the only ghosts that came to me. Do you know what I thought, Walker? I thought, that's no king. That's a woman. They laid her to rest in a bank of flowers."

One of the companions snorted as if to stifle laughter. No one else dared move or speak. Wolfcub wondered if any of them began to regret this lovely idiot who would, by the gods' will, be their king.

Walker betrayed neither anger nor dismay. He answered gravely, as if Linden had been speaking sense. "My lord, that is an odd vision. Most odd indeed. And did you dream?"

"I think so," Linden said. "The air was full of flowers. There was a woman. She looked like the old people, little and dark, but very beautiful. She came to me and we did what man and woman do. She never spoke. When she left me . . . she turned into a mare. A white mare. Then—" He faltered.

"Then?" Walker prompted him.

His brows knit; he shook his head. "I don't remember. It seems the flowers all turned to arrows. And there—there were women riding on horses. They had bows and spears. I woke up then, because it was so preposterous. I didn't want to dream it any more."

Walker would have been glad not to hear it, either, Wolfcub thought. But he mastered himself before he spoke. "This dream is most strange—but much of it, surely, is no more than a dream. I see nothing in it that bodes ill for you. Indeed," he said, and his voice swelled richly and filled with deep music, "while you were communing with the gods, they came to me in this outer place and showed me wonders: a field of stars, and all of them singing your name. Great and glorious king, they called you, lord of warriors, mightiest of the People. They foretold for you a great kingship and a glorious reign."

That was far more to the taste of those who listened. Linden most of all—he drew up taller as Walker spoke, and his eyes shone. "Truly? Truly you saw that?"

"As truly," Walker said, "as I am a shaman."

"The king's shaman." Linden freed his hands from Walker's to rest them on the shaman's shoulders. "Walk with me. Stand beside me while I lay my father to his rest. Be my guide and my guardian. Will you do that? Will you serve me as the gods allow?"

"As the gods allow," said Walker, "I will be your shaman."

Linden's joy was as bright as the sun, and as free of guile. He would not have heard what Wolfcub had: that Walker would be his shaman, but he said nothing of service. "Splendid! Oh, splendid. But first," he said, sobering as much as he ever could, "we have to bury my father."

Walker inclined his head—acquiescing, it might have seemed. But to Wolfcub's eye, it seemed almost as if he granted his leave; as if he allowed the king to command him.

+ +

As the young king had been brought forth in the morning, so was the old king laid to rest in the evening. The sun was setting as Linden came with his companions and his shaman to the sacred circle within the White Stone camp, where the priests and all the people and the elder shaman waited for him.

He was beautiful, riding on his black-and-silver stallion, with his bright hair gleaming and his fine open face all pale with grief. He mourned his father, however little it seemed to matter to anyone else that the old king was dead. He slipped from the stallion's back to kneel by the bier, taking no apparent notice of the reek of death that the priests' efforts had failed to keep at bay. He murmured a few words—far too faint for Sparrow to hear, crowded back among the women. It was miracle enough that she could see him: and that was by virtue of a convenient stone, and no men nearby to tower over her.

He bade farewell to his father and commended the old king's spirit to the gods. After a while he rose. At that signal, priests of the Stallion lifted the bier on bare strong shoulders, their faceless masks and tall maned crests making them seem like creatures out of the otherworld, spirits come to walk among men.

They all went to the place of burial, a long winding march, all but the young king on foot, treading earth as the people of the plain had done since the dawn time. Women wailed and beat their breasts. The more extravagant rent garments and tore hair, whirling and spinning as they shrieked. The men walked silent, their faces schooled to stillness. A warrior might weep with decorous sorrow or roar in rage, but this shrilling clamor was a women's thing. The death-music, it was called. It opened the gate of the world and granted the dead admittance to the far bright country. The louder, the more deafening it was, the swifter the gate opened and the greater his welcome.

Sparrow shrieked with the rest of them, a shrill ululation that tore her throat at first, but after a while poured out of her without effort, a throbbing of pure high sound. Some of the other women were doing the same. Then others, and others, coming into harmony, matching tone and rhythm to—why, Sparrow's; and that was matched to the beating of blood in her veins.

All voices gathered into one voice, one great ringing peal at the gate of the gods' country. It carried them to the burial place, to the open maw of the barrow, and the silent and stunned-looking priests and shamans. There had never been a death-cry like that one. There might never be again.

All at once, as the people reached the barrow, the cry abandoned Sparrow, left her alone and silent and rather cold in the deepening dusk. Her ears were ringing. She could barely hear the drum that began to beat, or the priests' chanting, late and rather feeble, as if the death-cry had left them reft of strength for their own part of the rite.

She was half out of herself, and not minded to return altogether to her body. In this state she saw, oh, so clearly. The stars were great blooming flowers in the deep blue of the sky. The people were shadows with pale blurred faces. The torches that kindled among them and about the barrow were dim and red, like embers. Only the stallion, of all that stood on that earth, seemed real. His coat was night sky flecked with stars. His mane and tail were a fall of moonlight. Horse Goddess was not in him, but he was her child. Her blessing washed him in light.

Sparrow watched the priests lay the king in his tomb, settle his weapons about him and his belongings and the provisions for his journey to his tent beyond the stars. They brought in a fine bay stallion, one of the sons of the fallen king of stallions, and sacrificed him to the king's spirit, laid the body at his feet and the head above him.

Then the women came, all his wives and concubines. They were dressed in their best tunics, with their most precious ornaments, their long hair flowing free and crowned with flowers. They bowed before their husband—stumbling, many of them, as if drugged with grief or a shaman's potion. Their faces in torchlight were blank. None uttered a sound.

They lay in the barrow, composed as if for sleep. And the priests and all the men of the People raised the barrow over them, closing them within, still living, still breathing, drugged nigh senseless but alive.

·············· 21 ··············

NOT ONE OF the old king's women was left in the outer world. All of them had gone to the tomb with him, every one, wife and concubine. Sparrow, trapped far back among the people, dazed and stumbling with the aftermath of her strange song and stranger trance, could say nothing, do nothing, prevent nothing. She was a woman of no account, the lowest of the People. Only a newborn girlchild was less than she.

Walker had done this. He might protest that it was no decision of his: the priests and shamans had decided it, taking no notice of any bargain that he struck with a woman. But Walker was the great shaman, the young king's favorite. One word of his would have changed the law and set the women free.

Sparrow found a name for the thing that swelled inside her. Anger. No, more than anger. Rage.

It was not only hers. Horse Goddess had spoken through her. It had been the goddess' will that this change be made. And the shaman had not only disregarded it, he had made certain that every royal woman died in her husband's tomb, not only the wives. It was a message, and clear—as clear as the sky full of stars, and the voices of priests and warriors singing the king to his rest, and the night wind across the plain.

Sparrow went away with the other women, silent as they all were, and left the men to complete the rite alone. When they came back to camp, she did not speak to anyone. She crawled into a corner of her father's tent, pulled one of the sleeping-furs over her head, and vanished into darkness.

✦ ✦

Wolfcub had been startled to see all the king's women led into his tomb. Even Fawn, for whom he grieved, and the redheaded woman whom Linden had tumbled on the night Wolfcub slew the boar— every one of them. It seemed excessive. But none of the priests raised an objection. The shamans watched without expression. Drinks-the-Wind looked shrunken and old, leaning on the shoulder of one of his sons.

It was not Walker who did that filial duty. Walker stood beside Linden, gleaming with satisfaction, and watched the old king's burial as if he had wrought the whole of it. Very probably, thought Wolfcub, he had. Walker's star was rising fast, overwhelming the elder shaman's. Drinks-the-Wind was wholly in his power, or else cared too little to stop him.

Wolfcub stood on Linden's other side. He could not protect the king if Walker chose to stab him with a knife, but Wolfcub did not expect the shaman to do that. Linden was too perfect a tool in Walker's hand.

While the rite and the burial stretched toward a grey dawn, Wolfcub studied the men about him, the priests, the shamans, the king's companions. As he would in a hunt, he considered paths, discarded some, and came to a clearer sense of what he could do, or would. He did not waste time in recalling that he was young and had little by way of either wealth or power among the People. He was the boarslayer, the king's companion. That should be enough.

When at last the old king was closed up in his barrow with his escort of wives and concubines, Linden rode nine times round the barrow, mounted on the stallion who had killed his father. He sang the final song, the departing-song, which entrusted the king's body to the earth and his spirit to the gods. Then in the grey light before sunrise, he led them all to the camp, to sleep as they could before the sacrifices began, the great rite and festival of the ninth year.

✦ ✦

For all those nine days Wolfcub kept his counsel, performed the rites as he was asked, and kept watch over the young king. Thrice they sacrificed the Hound, thrice the Bull, and thrice the Stallion. Nine times they feasted, till even the lustiest of them was heavy and sated. Nine nights they danced and drank and sang.

There were women, too. Unmarried women whose fathers and kin were oblivious or willfully ignorant, even a few married women who dared defy their husbands, haunted the shadows about the circles of the dance, and lured dancers away to celebrate the festival in the most pleasant wise. There would be children born in the spring, hasty marriages made and wives protesting that their husbands must have forgotten in the fog of *kumiss*—of course they had coupled together in the festival. Offspring of this rite whose secret was known were called the gods' children. It profited them little enough, granted them no power or magic, but they seemed more blessed with good fortune than some.

Wolfcub was much sought after. His place near the king, the legend of the boar, and this new face that he seemed to have grown into without knowing it, made the women come seeking him. He lay with one or two: a girl of the Dun Cow who was as sleek as an eel and as noisy as a heifer in heat, and a woman of the Tall Grass people who lay with him silently but sang to him after, a sweet wandering song that maybe had magic in it. It did not weaken him, whatever it was. It sent him back to his king's side refreshed and alert for any threat to the king's life or spirit.

He never saw Sparrow. She was not one to go hunting young men in shadows, and she was not among the women who served the men in the feasts. There was never quite time to go in search of her.

The tenth day was a day of great quiet and, in no few instances, roaring indisposition. Wolfcub woke in the king's tent, which was now Linden's, and concluded that he was not as badly off as most. He had drunk relatively little, and eaten not much more than he needed. He would live.

It was full morning already when he emerged from the tent. The women were out and about as always, tending fires, baking bread, looking after children. For the most part they ignored him as he went to the trenches to relieve himself. There was no other man in sight, there or in the camp, except for a figure or two snoring in the shade of a tent.

Wolfcub did not return at once to the king's tent. He went to his father's instead. Aurochs, as he had had hoped, was up and eating a bite of breakfast, washing it down with Willow's potion. They both greeted Wolfcub with a smile, and Willow fed him as she had his father.

Wolfcub fully intended to speak his mind to them. But somehow he could not do it. He ate, drank, spoke of small things. He basked for a while in their pride. He reflected that Willow was wise and Aurochs one of the elders, when he chose to be.

But when he had spent an hour with them, he left with the words unsaid. This was not a thing for the elders, or for his mother, either, though she might argue otherwise.

Some of the other companions were awake when he came back to the king's tent. Linden was in the inner room, but it was clear what he was doing: whoever the woman was that he had taken to bed with him, she made no secret of her pleasure in his company.

Wolfcub had to wait an annoying while before he could speak to Spearhead, whom he had settled on as best for the purpose. Spearhead, fortunately, was more or less awake and aware, and not too prostrate with the aftermath of the feast. A dose of Willow's potion restored him most of the way to himself. When he went out to the trenches, Wolfcub went with him.

As Wolfcub had hoped, there was no one there. They did their business together, then as Spearhead turned to go back into the camp, Wolfcub said, "Walk with me for a bit. I'm all fuzzy-headed with camp smoke and *kumiss.*"

Spearhead shrugged and consented. He was not a particularly amiable man, but he was shrewd and he was not afraid to speak his mind. He was also, Wolfcub thought, fiercely loyal to Linden, though he would have denied it if anyone had asked.

They followed the track past the trenches, up over a low hill and down toward the herds of cattle. The camp was not visible from there, nor was there anyone in sight but a boy who watched over the cows. His eyes went wide when he saw who walked on the edge of his herd, but he did not trouble them with his presence.

They halted on the outer edge of the herd. Spearhead squatted in the grass, marked out a bare spot, produced a handful of bones. He held them up with an inquiring look. Wolfcub nodded.

They played at cast-the-bones, quietly, for no wager but the pleasure of winning. After a while Spearhead said, "Now then. Tell me what's bothering you."

Wolfcub raised a brow. "You think I'm troubled?"

"I know you are. You've been as twitchy as a bitch with pups. What is it? Afraid Linden can't be the king he needs to be?"

"Are you?"

Spearhead shrugged. "He's not the brightest star in the heavens. I'm not sure he's suited to ruling anything greater than his own flock of women. As to whether he can be king enough for the purpose . . . who knows? If he picks his advisors well enough, it won't matter that he's not much more than a pretty face."

"He is more than that," Wolfcub said. "Not a great deal more, but his heart is good. He wants to do well by his people."

"And you're not sure he can."

"I'm not sure he'll be allowed to." Wolfcub drew a breath. In it, he cast the bones. He clapped his hands. "Victory!"

"I'll top that," Spearhead said, and did. He left the bones lying where they were, looked Wolfcub in the face and said, "It's the shaman, isn't it?"

"Which?"

Spearhead spat. "Don't play the fool, wolfling. You know which. He's been hovering over Linden like a vulture since the day we met the boar."

Wolfcub nodded. "I think," he said, "it wasn't accident that the old king died."

"I know it wasn't," said Spearhead. "I looked after the stallion when Linden was done with him. He had a thorn in his rump and another in his neck. Whatever was on them was long gone and he was himself again, but someone put them in him. Someone maybe with a blowgun and a quick hand."

"It might not have been Walker," Wolfcub said. He was being cautious. His heart was beating hard. When he chose Spearhead to confide in, he had never imagined that this of all the king's companions would have stumbled on what he needed most to know. The gods' hand was in that, surely.

"Maybe it wasn't the shaman," said Spearhead, "but I'll wager it was someone in his power. He's got the hunger. He wants to rule."

"A shaman can't be king," Wolfcub pointed out.

"No, and should he want to be? There's more pure power in what that one is than in anything Linden can hope to be. He's making and breaking kings. I wonder, what will he find to do after this?"

Wolfcub shivered. "I'm not sure I want to know."

"And you're afraid you do."

"Yes." Wolfcub scooped up the bones and cast them moodily. They fell into a pattern that they seldom fell into. That pattern, in the game, was called War. He stared at it. War was not a thing to be afraid of. Young men loved it. And yet when he looked at the fall of the bones, he saw darkness, and Walker's white and pitiless face.

"He's going to do something," Wolfcub said, "that maybe no one's dared before. Or he'll hark back to something that the old people did, that was too terrible or too wasteful to keep."

"Or both." Spearhead scattered the bones with a sweep of his hand. "It's not really what he'll do, is it? It's how he'll elect to do it. He loves himself too much and the People too little. And he's a great deal more powerful than wise."

That was so like something Willow would say that Wolfcub loosed a snort of laughter. "Make a pact with me," he said. "We'll keep Linden as safe as we can. We'll protect the People if that's possible. And if we can, we'll pull Walker's fangs."

"And how," Spearhead inquired, "do you intend to do that?"

"I don't know," Wolfcub said. "The gods will show us a way."

"Unless he's tricked the gods into feeding his power, too."

"Then," said Wolfcub, "we'll let them know what he's done— and stand back from their wrath."

"Oh, they'll be angry," Spearhead agreed. "They will indeed." He gathered the bones and tipped them into their pouch and tucked it back in his belt. "Well then. I'll play this game. Do we tell anyone else?"

Wolfcub shook his head. "Not unless there's someone you can trust."

"I trust most of the companions," Spearhead said, "to be loyal to the king, to fight as well for him as they can, and to be completely incapable of keeping a secret as great as this. Even if they believe it— and most of them probably would—they're inclined to chatter to whoever will listen. Best they not know what creeps in the shadows."

"Yes," said Wolfcub in something like relief. "Yes, best they not know."

They clasped hands over it, a clasp that turned into a test of strength, and then a contest, and at last a wrestling match that fetched them up laughing against the feet of a placid cow. Wolfcub had won, but Spearhead had given him a fair fight.

He sprang up under the cow's nose, held out a hand, pulled Spearhead to his feet. Side by side they went back to the camp.

K EEN SAW THE two young men walking back from the herds, grass-stained and rumpled and content with themselves and their world. It was a moment before she recognized one of them as Wolfcub. By the gods, he had changed. His hair was sleek, no longer as untidy as a winter field. His shoulders were broad, his arms and legs matched to the length of his body. And his face—no wonder all the girls were giggling over him. Who would have imagined that Wolfcub would be a handsome man?

He was a man of consequence, too. He stood beside the new king. No doubt, now the sacrifices were over, his mother would set about finding him a wife and a tent of his own. This was the time for it: the time after the festival, when the gods were propitiated and, in such years as this one, kings were made and unmade. The gathering would go on for another round of the moon, confirming alliances, settling feuds, and making marriages within and among the tribes.

That was on her mind of late. A year ago, Walker had brought gifts to her father's tent, bargained for and won her. She had been too happy to speak. Beautiful Walker, Walker the shaman, wonderful and powerful, had chosen her of all the women in the tribes. He had taken her into the tent that her father and his father combined to give them, full of all needful things, and discovered with great joy what she had kept for him. She had not, like others of the women, given her maidenhood to strangers during the sacrifices. She had waited and been patient, in spite of temptation.

It had hurt. There was blood. She wept a little, but he dried her tears and kissed her and told her she was beautiful, and promised her that the next time would be better. And so it had been. And each time after, better yet, till she knew no greater joy than his coming to her in the evening after a long day's labors.

He had not come to her since the People left the spring camp. She kept his tent, prepared dinners for him that he never came to taste, made certain that she was clean and dressed becomingly. He would come back, now the festival was over and the king was made. It was his tent she lived in and his possessions she looked after, among them no small quantity of things that a shaman needed for his magics.

As Wolfcub and his companion strolled back arm in arm from wherever they had been, Keen was coming up herself from the river with a basket of fish and a harvest of green herbs. Walker loved fish rubbed and stuffed with herbs and baked in clay. It had taken her most of the morning to catch the fish—she had had to go far up the river to find an eddy with life in it, with so many people camped by the river and fishing in it. Then she had tarried to dig up the clay and to gather the herbs.

It was nearly noon when she came to the camp. Her heart was lighter than it had been in a long while. Today, surely, Walker would remember her and come to her. She would prepare the fish and bury it in embers, then she would tidy the tent, and after that she would spend a leisurely while making herself beautiful for her husband. Her best tunic, her best ornaments, yes. She would wash her hair and scent it with some of the herbs that she had set aside in preparing the fish.

What would come of that woke a flutter in her middle. Much of it was excitement. Some was fear. She was going to make another child, if she could at all. She had asked old Mallard, the elder shaman's wife, for something to help make sure of it. Mallard had twitted her, of course, but almost gently, and given her a clay pot full of something eye-wateringly pungent. "Put a little of that in a cup of *kumiss*," she said, "and drink it just before you go in to him. Then say a prayer to Earth Mother and to the Lady of Birthings, and let them bless you as you lie with him."

Keen could do that, and gladly. It was better by far than some things she had heard of, spells and incantations that required ghastly substances and arduous rites.

She smiled at the thought as she rounded the camp and approached her husband's tent. There were a number of people about, more than usual; but this was the gathering. Sometimes everyone happened to be in the same place at the same time.

They were, she realized, crowding about her husband's tent. Her heart leaped. He had come back—he was receiving guests. She had seen such a crowd about Drinks-the-Wind, people begging him for his wisdom or asking for spells or simply paying their respects. Walker was the king's shaman now. Of course the crowds would come to him.

The people who came to Drinks-the-Wind were nearly always men. These were all women. They were, what was more, women of the Tall Grass, and none of White Stone or any other tribe. They came and went with great intentness of purpose. Those coming carried bundles and baskets. Those departing looked as if they were going to fetch more.

A few women of the White Stone stood about, staring and offering commentary. When they caught sight of Keen, they flushed and made themselves scarce.

Keen found that puzzling, but she was not apprehensive. There was a perfectly good explanation. Of course there was. She held her head high, firmed her grip on her basket, and walked to the tent as she well should, as one who had every right to do so. One or two of the strangers seemed not to like that very well—but that was no concern of Keen's.

The tent was not small, in fact it had been overlarge for Keen and Walker and their possessions. As Keen slipped into it, she nearly barked her skin on a basket. The tent was bursting with baskets, boxes, and bundles. They were heaped by the flap and mounded by the tent-wall. The partition that divided the outer room from the inner, women's portion, which Keen kept fastened out of the way— she had never needed it—was down and fluttering with presence beyond.

Keen was beginning to be angry. Whatever invasion this was, it came without her leave. She flung back the partition and stood face to face with what, at first, seemed another great crowd of women.

It was only a few, she realized once her sight had cleared. Three very young women or girls, a somewhat older woman, and one who must have been both wife and mother: she was plump, her ruddy hair was shot with grey, and she conducted herself like the mistress of a wealthy man's tent. It was she who faced Keen with arched brow and expression of disdain. "And who may you be?" she inquired.

Keen stiffened. That should have been hers to say. This was her tent. But habits of grace, hard-learned and sternly kept, overwhelmed her temper. She answered civilly, "I am the shaman's wife. How may I serve you?"

The Tall Grass woman looked her up and down. She was not

prepossessing, she knew. There was mud in her hem and her feet. Her hair was caught back in a rough plait, and she carried a basket like a servant. She held her head high and recalled who she was, whose daughter and whose wife.

The interloper tightened thin lips and sighed. "You're pretty enough," she said. In her accent, which was broader and softer than the White Stone dialect, it sounded lazy and faintly insulting. "I suppose he'll keep you, one way and another."

Keen's jaw set till it ached. "My name is Keen-Wind-in-the-Grasses. I am the daughter of Flint, king's brother, elder of the first clan of the White Stone. My mother was a shaman's daughter. Her brother is a great hunter of the People. I was wedded in gathering to Walker Between the Worlds, shaman of the White Stone People. This is my tent. I welcome you to it, and I offer you hospitality, with all such grace as custom requires. Is it my husband you wish to see? If so, you would do best to seek him out in the king's circle. He will linger there till evening."

"Ah," said the Tall Grass woman. "You're a proud one. It might serve you well to seek him out yourself. He's taken a new wife, and spoken no word of the old one."

Keen held herself still by effort of will. This woman with her rough tongue and her bold eyes must not—must not—see her tremble. She managed the faint hint of a smile. "Indeed? Oh, that man! He never said you'd be arriving so soon. Since it's customary for marriages to be made at the full moon, and it's not even the new moon yet, I had thought . . ." She trailed off sweetly, lifted her chin, and shrugged as her mother had taught her, both to charm and to show off the excellence of her neck and shoulders and breasts. She made a little dance of it, which in turn showed off her white hands— somewhat smudged now, but of lovely shape, with long fingers. "Ah well, it's done, and I'd be greatly remiss to send you away. Come, is this the lady? Come here, child, I won't bite."

There could be little mistaking which was the bride-to-be: she was slender, her hair was a glorious deep red, and her eyes were as green as young grass; but she had her mother's round face and somewhat prominent teeth. She was more than lovely, but time would bring her to her mother's looks, or Keen was no judge.

She met Keen's stare as if she had only now deigned to notice that there was a stranger in the tent. Her mother was rude and forthright. She was haughty. Here, thought Keen, was one who reckoned herself fit to lie with a king. Was she perhaps a little disgruntled to have been given to a shaman?

Certainly she was not pleased with the tent. "This is your tent, you say? It's barely adequate for one. I'll require another, and larger. See to it."

Keen's smile had a distinct edge. "Oh," she said, "but that would be an insult! Your father will wish, of course, to provide you with all necessities, among them a tent of appropriate size and grandeur. At least," she said, "that is the custom of the White Stone. Among your people, then, it is the senior wife who provides?"

"I am to be senior wife," the girl said with more than a hint of petulance. "I was promised. He never mentioned you. They said he had a woman in his tent, but of course he would; every man requires a servant."

"I am his wife," Keen said as gently as she could, "and senior by virtue of his having married me first. Come, are these your servants? Let us send one to your father and inform him that there has been, perhaps, a little confusion. I'm sure he'll be delighted to enlarge this tent which my father and my husband's father combined to give us at our wedding. In the meantime, if you will, I'll borrow the rest of your servants, and see that your belongings are arranged as conveniently as possible. I'll send one when we're done, to fetch you from your father's tent."

The girl was speechless. Her mother bridled. "Are you sending us away? How dare you!"

"Oh, no," Keen said. "No, of course not! But wouldn't your lovely daughter be better served at home, while we ready the tent for her here? I beg your forgiveness; I was not warned that you would come so soon. By tomorrow, or the next day at the latest, all will be ready for her, in as much comfort as she could desire."

"I'm not going anywhere," the girl snapped. "I came to be senior wife here. I *will* be senior wife here."

"Such confusion," Keen sighed. "You—girl with the brown braids. Take your mistress home, if you please, then come back to me. If you and your sister can bring the rest of the tent, then do it."

For a stretching moment Keen knew that her will was not strong enough; that these invaders would refuse. She had no strength and no assistance to cast them out bodily.

But the mother gave way, with no grace and nothing resembling politeness, but it was a surrender. She swept her daughter with her in a grand exit, trailing servants.

Keen yearned to collapse in tears, but she could not do that. She called back the servants, all but the one whom she had ordered to bear the message to the girl's father, and was deeply relieved that they obeyed her. She set them to work at once, shifting all their mistress' possessions to as small a corner as possible, and heaping in front of the tent those that overflowed the corner. The girl's father would provide shelter for them, or not; that was not Keen's concern.

Keen knew what anger was. She had a temper, though her mother had taught her to master it long ago. But she had never felt what she felt now.

This was rage. More than rage—wrath. It had no reason in it. It had nothing to do with sense. It was born of Walker's neglect and her own grief and illness. It was larger than she was, and far stronger.

She would go to her father. Her mother had died in the winter, and she was not close to the other wives. Flint was old and his mind tended to wander, but he was still a very rich man, and very clever in adding to his wealth through trading and favors and, rather often, wagers on this or that. He was fond of Keen and proud of his son-in-law. He would not be the least bit pleased to hear of this invader.

The Tall Grass servants were doing well enough. Keen laid on them the terror of her husband's reputation, the mighty curses that a shaman could lay on those who stole from him or so much as looked at his belongings. When they were suitably round-eyed and appalled, she left them to finish what they had begun, and went to find her father.

✦ ✦

Flint, by good fortune, was sitting in front of his tent while two of his youngest wives combed and plaited his hair. He had been drinking deep of the wild berry wine that his eldest surviving wife was renowned for, and was wrapped in warm good humor. He greeted Keen with delight, pressing a cup of wine on her till she took it to avoid offending him.

He watched her closely, so that she had to drink a sip or two. Then, content, he sat back against the knees of his plump fair wife, while the dark one wove a string of beads into one of his plaits. He was a vain man. He never left his tent before he was properly dressed, his beard combed, his thinning hair plaited.

He smiled at Keen and said, "Daughter, you're as lovely as ever I remember. Where have you been keeping yourself? Is your husband treating you well?"

Keen's anger, at least, burned away the tears. She was able to return his smile, to shrug and say, "Well enough. He's been kind to me, as husbands go."

"Good," said Flint. "Good, good. And how's that new wife of his turning out to be? I hear tell, she refused every man of her own tribe and most of the tribes round about, till her father threatened to give her to the next man who walked into the camp."

Keen sat still. She felt as if she had taken a blow to the middle. When she looked for air, there was none.

At length she managed to find her voice. "You—knew that he was—"

"Of course," said Flint. "He's been courting the girl since he came to the gathering. I'll wager he got her to accept him—he's got a honeyed tongue on him, that lad, and a smile to go with it."

Keen stared at the cup in her hand. With a sudden motion, she lifted it to her lips and drank it down. The wine was gaggingly sweet, and strong enough to dizzy her. "The women haven't talked about it at all," she said from somewhere remote and cold.

"Oh, they know, they know," her father said with a sweep of the hand that sent his cup flying. Wine splashed Keen's skirt. She ignored it. He, oblivious, said to her, "I suppose they keep their tongues leashed when there's a senior wife about. How does it feel to be that at last? Has the girl's father given you a nice big tent?"

Keen regarded him in despair. He did not understand at all. Whatever hope she had had that he might prevail on Walker to send that insolent child back to her father, vanished as Flint babbled on. Not only did he think that she had known of this; he too obviously saw it as a good thing.

"It's time," he said, "that you had someone to wait on you and look after the tent and do the things that servants do. Not that I blamed you overmuch for not wanting servants when I tried to give them to you—a first wife wants her man to herself for a while—but a year of that should be enough for any woman. Maybe once the girl's had proper training, she'll give you time to make a baby or two, eh?" He winked and nudged her in the ribs, nearly falling over with the rush of wine to his head.

Keen steadied him without speaking. If she tried to say anything, she would scream.

He staggered up, leaning heavily on her. He grunted, belched richly, and patted her head. "You're a good child," he said. "Now I'd best go and celebrate the bridegroom. Don't forget: senior wife lays out the bridal bed. A few flowers, a charm or two, he'll do his duty for the nine days and then come back to you—I'll lay wagers on it. That's a pretty girl, they say, but nothing like my yellow-headed darling."

She set her teeth at his clumsy stroking of her hair, stood still and let him weave off in the direction of the Tall Grass camp, without ever speaking the words that she had come to say.

················ **23** ················

K EEN WENT BACK to the tent that had been hers, but which now, by the laws of marriage, she must share with another woman. It was much improved, the stranger's belongings removed or shifted out of the way. She sent the servants home to their mistress, retrieved the fish that she had all but forgotten, and set numbly to cleaning and stuffing and baking them. They would spoil if she left them; baked, they would keep a little while at least, and she could give most of them away.

She did not trouble to make herself beautiful. What point? He was not coming tonight. He would be lying about in the Tall Grass camp, being charming to his new wife's kinsmen.

The fish were done just at sunset. Keen dug them out of the fire and broke the clay that had baked hard over them, and emptied them into a basket. Their scent, so rich and savory, made her stomach churn. She had no appetite at all. The wine that her father had made her drink was heavy in her middle, weighing down her spirit.

She covered the basket and laid it aside where camp dogs and children could not get at it. Moving slowly, without thinking much past the task at hand, she banked the fire and spread her sleeping-furs and lay down. She had always slept in the outer room, in the man's place—beside Walker when he was there, alone when he was not. He had never objected, indeed had said once that it was convenient; they could lie together all night long if they chose.

She had left the flap tied open to let in such breeze as there was. It was a still night, and warm. After a while she slipped out of her tunic and folded it and laid it under her head. The fire without died slowly, sinking to embers. She sank with it into a half-drowse.

Her heart was heavy, as it had been when her mother died: a blackness, an emptiness, as if she had lost something precious. Yet all she had done, if custom were true, was to gain a new pair of hands in the tent and in her husband's service—and since this was a wealthy woman, a whole flock of servants, too. She should be glad, not so deeply angry that she could see no way out of it.

A shadow came between her eyes and the dying fire. A small part of her heart leaped. She knew that shape, oh, yes: slender, tall, but wide enough in the shoulder, moving with grace that not so long ago had caught her breath in her throat.

It still could, if she let it. Walker slipped into the tent as he had so many times before, paused to let his eyes come clear in the dimness, moved toward her. Her body must have glimmered, to guide him; or he heard the sound of her breathing.

He did not greet her or speak to her. He lay down beside her, hand reaching for her breast. It drew taut at his touch. Her belly fluttered. Her secret place ached with wanting him.

And yet her heart was cold. He stroked her and fondled her, and her body roused as it always had, quick as a horse to its master's touch. When he rose over her, she opened to him and took him inside her. They danced the dance, treading the familiar steps, knowing each other's rhythms and cadences.

When they had come to the end, he did not leave her as he usually did. He held her in his arms, a rare thing, and one she would have much prized only a day before.

She lay still, not speaking. Her breathing quieted. The ache in her secret place had eased a little, but not so very much. As if, she thought, the dance of flesh on flesh was not enough. It needed something else. Something—

"My love," Walker said in his beautiful voice. "My wife."

She did not respond. This was unlike him, too, even as he had been when he first took her to wife.

"I hear," he said, "that you sent Blossom away."

Was that the girl's name, then? Blossom? Keen would have called her Ice, or Pickerel, or something equally chilly and sharp.

"I am sorry she came so soon," he said, seeming undismayed by her silence. He stroked her as she spoke, cupping her breast, kneading it. She had never liked that. She had never told him so. Nor did she tell him now, though he went on and on. "Her tribe's custom is somewhat different from ours. The new wife comes at her own discretion, and takes the husband's tent for her own."

"And if he already has a wife?"

She spoke so low, for a moment she did not think he heard. Then he answered, "The senior wife comes when she chooses."

"I am senior wife."

She felt how he stiffened. His hand tightened on her breast. It hurt. She set her teeth and endured. "My love," he said in a tone she had never heard him use in this place before, though she had heard it often when he spoke before the People. "My sweet and golden lady. You are first wife and will always be. But her father is shaman of the Tall Grass people. She has always expected to be chief wife in her husband's tent."

"My father," said Keen, "is king's brother of the White Stone people."

"The old king's brother," Walker said. "That day is past, my love. Flint is an old man. His powers have waned. Blossom's father is in the prime of his life, at the height of his strength. The Tall Grass king is his sister's son. His brother is the hunter of the tribe. He offers a great alliance, and great gifts not only to me but to our new king and to the People. So you see," said Walker as if there were nothing more reasonable, "if his daughter requires that she be chief wife, then she will be. It need matter little to you. All the burdensome things you did, her servants will do. Keeping the tent, scraping the hides, cooking the meals—all done for you now. You can be free to do as you please. I've asked her to be kind to you, to be your friend. Haven't you always wanted a friend?"

Keen had to struggle to breathe slowly, to be calm. There was so much to answer that she chose to answer only the last: "I have friends."

"But not a sister-wife, a woman to share the tent and divide the tasks. You're angry now, I can tell—you're jealous. Don't be. I've love enough for both of you."

Or for none. For some reason, Keen heard that in Sparrow's voice. She was seeing Walker again as Sparrow must see him: cold, cruel, blind to anything but his own wishes. And yet her father, who was neither cold nor cruel, had been just as blind.

"What," she said, "if I had done the same? If I'd gone out, found another husband, made him lord of this tent—would you be willing to accept it?"

"Of course not!" he said at once. "That's outrageous. A woman belongs to one man, and one man only."

"And yet," she said, "you take away my rank, you cast down my father's honor, you order me to step aside for a stranger. You would never permit it if I were to do the same."

"Because," said Walker, still with that air of preeminent reason, "a woman does not do such things. She is made to serve one man, as men are made to rule many women. That is the gods' law." He rose over her. His face was a pale glimmer, with shadowed eyes. Her hands, clenched by her sides, remembered the strong clean planes of it, the softness of his young man's beard, the way his lips would set a kiss in her palm as it passed by.

She put that memory aside. He, like her father, spoke perfect sense, sense as the People had known it for time out of mind. Men did not share wives, unless they were kings; and then they chose who would lie with their women. Women shared husbands. That was the way of it. And if the first wife was not so highly ranked as one who came after, she stepped aside as she was bidden, because that was a woman's lot.

Keen had never minded that she was a woman. Sparrow complained constantly, condemning this unfairness or that—never wishing she could be a man, certainly not, but just as certainly declaring that a woman should be able to do all that a man could. Sparrow was odd and outspoken, and was going to suffer terribly if she was not careful.

Keen had never minded, either, that as a child she could do so much more than she could do as a woman. Once her courses came, she was content to put on the long tunic and put up her hair and wait to be given to a husband. Keeping his tent, warming his bed, bearing his children when they came—she had taken joy in all of that.

Even when she thought of sharing with other wives: well, and every woman did, sooner or later.

Sooner had come, and before she expected it. Walker was only doing what was best for his fortunes, and no doubt for the People. She should be schooling herself to accept it.

And she could not. This was not right. The way he had done it, without a word to her—coming to her after it was done and breeding her like a heifer and thinking that that would be enough to soften her heart.

It was being alone that had done it, waking from her blood-red dream to find all the People gone and herself forgotten. And Walker had never come to her, not once, until tonight. It did not matter that there were reasons for it, reasons that would seem important to a man. Keen was not a man. She had lost a child. Her heart had needed him to make it whole, and he had been finding himself a new wife.

She was a very selfish, small-minded, unreasonable person. She knew that. She could not make herself care.

Walker took her silence, maybe, for acquiescence. He stooped to kiss her. If he felt the cold passivity of her lips, he did not speak of it. He fondled her breast again, a touch that made her flinch inside, then rose. His voice came down from far above her. "There, my love, I know; it's always difficult the first time, even knowing what the gods have willed for us. You'll come to love her. She'll be your sister and your friend. You'll see."

Keen said nothing, which in the end was her only refuge. He seemed to have expected it. He turned and slipped out, striding away into the night.

When he was well gone, Keen rose in her own turn. She found and shook out her tunic and put it on. She gathered a few things, finding them by touch in the dark, and tied them into a bundle. With that in hand, she slipped out as he had, and went where her feet saw fit to take her.

PARROW HAD AVOIDED going to the women's house for a handful of months now. She had found that if she gathered up certain things and put on a certain air and walked out without stealth, she could gain herself a handful of days with the mare, and never be missed at all.

It should have been even easier in gathering, with so many tribes and so many houses, and women wandering from one to the next as it pleased them. But when Sparrow woke on the sixth day of the sacrifices to the familiar ache and ruddy flow, sought the basket with the necessities, and slipped out, she found herself accosted by no less than White Bird, her father's odd but undeniably lovely wife.

White Bird had never had any use for Sparrow. But this morning, for some reason best known to herself, she held up her own basket and said brightly, "You, too? Come, we'll share the days together!"

Sparrow barely restrained herself from glancing about to see if Walker was watching. How would he know to thwart her so? The gods well might, but them she could not see, not with her daytime eyes.

There was no help for it. She had to go to the hut that the White Stone women had raised. It was set upstream of the camp on the little river, well out of sight and sound of the sacred places. There were two other women sitting outside of it, one of the White Stone, one of the Red Deer who had been born to the White Stone. She was a tireless gossip, and she knew every scandal.

She was chattering when Sparrow and White Bird came, and she did not stop chattering, day or night. By the third day, they knew the arrangement of each and every basket in her husband's tent, what was in it and how much, where each wife slept and on what kind of fur, how many children they had, what their names were, and precisely how large and of what shape was the organ of the man who had sired them all. "Or most of them," said Magpie, "if you're charitable."

Sparrow thought she might go mad. She wanted to be away from here, free on the plain, riding the mare—and maybe watching over Linden from afar, though that would not be easy. Yet she was trapped by her body and her kinswomen. When Magpie was not chattering, White Bird was babbling of the spells she would cast and the songs she would sing, so that next month she would not be in the women's house, she would be growing a son in her belly.

The third woman, Redwing, at least was quiet. From what little she said, her husband was thinking of sending her back to her father for her failure to bear him a son, though she had given him four daughters. He had refused to name all of them, every one—as he refused to name the daughters his other wives gave him. And none of them had given him a son.

Sparrow tried to imagine a woman whose arms were so empty, who had carried and birthed four children, and each one had been taken away to be given to the wolves. White Bird, whose daughter was growing up lusty and strong and completely unacknowledged by her mother, would not hear Redwing's story. She ran straight over it with her sweet breathless voice. "I shall bear a son in the spring. You'll see. It's all prepared. As soon as I leave this place, I'll start the spells."

Redwing shut her mouth and did not open it again. Magpie began to chatter anew. Sparrow shut her eyes and prayed for an end to it.

She endured it for close on four days. Redwing left late on the third, no doubt with enormous relief. As if Redwing's silence had served to quench the full spate of her chatter, Magpie redoubled her efforts to deafen her companions.

By dawn of the fourth day, Sparrow had had enough. She was not done with her courses. She did not care. Magpie was chattering in her sleep. White Bird was babbling, it seemed, to herself. Sparrow simply walked away.

Magpie slept on undisturbed. White Bird might be awake, but her eyes in the firelight were blank. Neither of them called Sparrow back.

She stretched her stride. When she was out of sight of the hut, under paling stars, she stretched her whole body from toes to fingertips, reaching for the sky, then swaying, dipping, whirling, dancing through the tall grass.

She stumbled and went sprawling. The thing that had caught her was no stone: it was soft, and it grunted. She snapped into a knot and rolled away from it, flinging herself to her feet.

It was no wild sow or sleeping wolf. It was a human figure in a woman's long tunic, with long hair streaming over its shoulders. Even in the grey light of morning, it was as bright as sunlight.

"Keen!" said Sparrow, astonished. "What are you doing out here?"

"The same thing you are, I suppose," Keen said. "What did you run away from?"

She spoke lightly, but something in her tone made Sparrow drop to her knees and seize that rounded chin, peering into the face.

Keen twisted free. "I'm not hurt. I . . . just had to get away."

"From what? What did he do to you? Tell me!"

Keen did not look as if she wanted to, but Sparrow had always had the stronger will. She got it out as if through clenched teeth. "Nothing. Nothing with his fist. But—he took another wife."

"I heard," Sparrow said flatly.

"You heard? And you never told me?"

"I couldn't," Sparrow said, taken aback by the flash of Keen's eyes. Keen, angry? Keen was the most even-tempered creature in the world. "I was in the women's house. One of the others there knew every scandal. She made sure we did, too. We heard all about the shaman's daughter of the Tall Grass, and the White Stone shaman. So it's true? He's making her senior wife?"

Keen nodded. "Her father is more useful to him than mine, you see. So he sets her over me. I'm to be glad of it, since it gives me a friend in the tent, and brings me a flock of servants to do everything I used to do. It sets me free, he says. Free—indeed. Free to walk away."

Sparrow could not give way to temper. Not yet. Her mind had to be clear. "Free to walk where? Back to your father?"

"No," said Keen. "He tells me to be glad of it. It's easier for me, you see. I can sit back and let someone else rule the household."

Sparrow sat on her heels. Keen's calm was brittle to breaking. Sparrow had never seen her like this. As if—

"Are you sure he never touched you?"

"Of course I'm sure!" Keen shook herself. "Please. I'm sorry. It's just—he didn't tell me. Until—until last night, he hadn't been near me since spring camp. He—he never—he never looked to see if I was gone!"

Sparrow could not bear to see her cry. She folded arms about Keen, held her and rocked her while she wept herself out. It took a long while.

How strange, Sparrow thought as she felt her shoulder growing wet through the worn leather. Years of Walker's cruelties had done little to shake her; they were nothing that she took pleasure in, but neither did they break her spirit. A few days of them had shocked Keen to the marrow.

Ah, but he had been kind to Keen. No doubt he had told her he loved her. He was probably still saying it, even as he supplanted her with a newer, wealthier wife. It would never occur to him that what he did might wound her to the heart. It was convenient. It served his purposes. Of course Keen would accept it.

Sparrow did not like to understand her brother so well. All men, from what she could see, thought such thoughts. Women were cattle, to be bought and sold without regard for what they might think of it. But Walker had a way about him. If he had been as heedless as any other man, it would not have mattered; but he lied. He made one think he had a heart.

As Keen wept, the morning brightened about them. The sun rose in a sky heavy with haze. The day would be hot, searingly so. Sparrow had a day or two before she was looked for. Walker likely would not go hunting his wife, with a new wife to keep him occupied.

She dried Keen's tears and smoothed the hair back from that lovely face—it even wept beautifully, blushing rose rather than going all to blotches. "Listen to me," she said. "We'll go away for a day or two, you and I. We'll take the mare and ride till we're tired of riding. Then we'll camp and rest, and never mind the world beyond us. If you want to go on after that, we will. Or we'll go back, and we'll find a place for you. You won't be a servant to that child from the Tall Grass, not ever. Not unless you truly want to."

Keen shook her head. She was a gentle creature, but when she made up her mind, it was firmly made up. "I won't share a tent with her. Everybody tells me I'll learn to be a sister to her—but she'll be sister as Walker is your brother. As—as you always told me he was."

"They're well matched, then," Sparrow said. "He might even let you go. If when we go back, we speak to the king, catch him when Walker is busy being married—Linden has a soft heart. He'll give you your freedom, I'm sure he will. Maybe," she said with swelling heart, "maybe he'll even take you for himself. The king can do that. He can take you in and honor you and treat you with respect."

"Linden . . ." Keen made the word a sigh. "He is pretty. And yes, he's kind, and he's a fine lover, they say. I could do worse than that."

"Much worse," Sparrow said. "He's the king."

"So he is," said Keen. "I'd forgotten. It's so much to keep in mind—kings dying, kings rising up. Stallions fighting. There will be a war, I suppose. There's always a war when the men make themselves a new king."

"That won't matter to us," Sparrow said.

"It should," said Keen. "People die."

"People won't die."

"Promise?"

Sparrow opened her mouth, but the words did not come out. She had been saying whatever came into her head, to comfort Keen. But this—Keen was not asking only for comfort. Keen wanted something more.

Keen wanted surety. And Sparrow could not give her that. Sparrow was a shaman. She was not supposed to be, but she was. If she promised that no one would die, she would have to keep that promise—and she could not.

Keen understood her silence. The tears were all gone, which was as well. She stiffened. Sparrow let her go. She stood, smoothing her skirt, combing her hair with her fingers. "I want to go away," she said. "We can do that. The rest . . . if it will be, it will be."

Sparrow was content with that, if Keen was.

✦ ✦

Sparrow's captivity in the women's house and Keen's flight from her husband's tent had taken them to the far side of the gathering from the horse-herds, though the herds of cattle—and their herdsmen—were nearby. They had to crouch low and pretend to be wind in the grass, Sparrow with the ease of practice, Keen mimicking her name. She was not as sturdy as Sparrow. She had to stop more often, and rub legs and back that ached with moving so slowly and so unnaturally. It had been a long while since she ran wild with Sparrow and Wolfcub, and he taught them both to hunt as his father had taught him.

They made a broad circle round the cattle and skirted the outermost edge of the camp. It was a clear run there till they came on the horses. Once the swell of the ground hid them from the camp, Sparrow straightened and gestured to Keen to stand erect, and sped through the grass. Keen trailed her, but not too far.

Sparrow was giddy with freedom. Her anger at Walker was deep and lasting, but she set it aside till she could use it, like a new-made weapon. For the moment she gave herself up to speed, and to looking out for Keen, to be sure she did not stumble or fall behind.

The mare was waiting. Sparrow could feel her impatience. In what seemed a very long time but by the sun was brief enough, they ascended the last hill and looked down on the horse-herds.

Sparrow dropped to the grass before the summit and crawled the rest of the way in concealment. Keen was in no wise unwilling to do the same. When they had reached the top, she lay on her face while Sparrow scanned the herds. She was breathing hard, and shaking with exhaustion.

Foolish creature, why had she not said anything? Sparrow bit her tongue on the rebuke. Keen was one of the bravest people she knew, and one of the least inclined to complain. She would go until she dropped, like a good horse. It was Sparrow's fault; she should have seen that Keen was pressing the limits of her strength, and slowed down. But she had been too eager to come to the mare.

Keen was recovering as they paused. Sparrow searched the herds below for signs of priests or herdsmen. There did not appear to be any. By ancient custom, no one waged war during the gathering, nor did tribes raid one another. There was nothing to watch for but wolves and lions, and those tended to be lazy in the summer's heat.

The herds were quiet, grazing in their clans and tribes. The royal herd kept the far edge as always, with the mare on guard as she so often was. She knew Sparrow was there. She grazed, but watchfully, with an air that bade Sparrow be quick—she had somewhat in mind, and she needed Sparrow for it.

Sparrow waited a little while even so. But no human figure stirred, nor did a dog lope along the edges, questing for invaders or stragglers. These might have been wild herds for all the evidence she found of men's presence.

At last, when Keen's breathing had quieted and the mare had begun to stamp with impatience, Sparrow rose from the grass and trotted down the hill.

L INDEN HAD MADE a very pretty king for the nine days' sacrifices. He astonished people, perhaps, by drinking in moderation, dancing all the dances with tireless grace, and seeing to it that every tribe's fire saw him at it for at least a little while. Whatever his failings of wit or wisdom, he had a gift for winning people's hearts.

On the second day after the sacrifices, Linden was called upon to be king over the gathered tribes. He had to sit in the king's circle and hear petitions, settle disputes, and pass judgment on those who had broken this law or that during the time of sacrifice. This clearly was much less to his taste. He had learned to sit still, all hunters did, but Wolfcub saw the hint of fidget in the way he sat, in the flicker of his eyes toward the circle's edge. But for Walker, who sat at his right hand and advised him frequently and very softly, he might have simply stood up and walked away. But Walker would not allow that.

Linden did not have a gift for judgment, or much patience either. Wolfcub watched with interest as the morning stretched. Linden had been called out before the sun was well risen, dressed and combed and set in the circle with barely a bite to eat or a drop to drink. The old king had done as much—held audiences in the morning before the day's heat rose too high—but Linden had never been at his best in the morning. He was a creature of the evening, a dancer about fires and a lover of women. In the mornings, he best preferred to sleep.

At first Wolfcub thought Walker had done this to test the young king, to prove his fitness or lack thereof. But as the sun rose higher, Wolfcub began to think that Walker had not thought such a thing at all. He had brought his puppet out to do his bidding. It had never occurred to him that the puppet might object.

When the sun poised between sunrise and noon, Linden rose abruptly. One petitioner had gone. Another was coming forward, dragging a much disheveled woman who was perhaps his wife. Linden took no notice. He smiled charmingly, inclined his head to them all, and said to the petitioner, "Take her home, good man. Do with her as you see fit. I," he said sweetly, "have duties elsewhere."

The woman shrieked and began to babble, begging the king's mercy. The king turned away, still smiling, and said to his companions, "Come, we're going hunting."

It was a terrible insult to both Walker and the elders, and no less to the petitioners still remaining. Wolfcub and Spearhead exchanged glances and, after an instant, shrugs. Linden was king. He could do as he pleased. And it was pleasant to see Walker struck speechless.

Linden was not quite done in the circle. He spoke again to the elders and petitioners. "After this, audience will begin midway between noon and sunset, and continue till dark. I'm much more awake then, and much more likely to give you a fair hearing. For now, good morning; and may the gods keep you."

He left them with that, walking lightly, taking visible joy in his freedom. The clamor of outrage that broke out behind him was muted somewhat by his promise of a later audience. Still, that clamor captured Walker as he moved to follow, and held him fast.

Linden's smile grew sly. He waited till he was out of earshot; then he laughed, deep and long. His companions had to hold him up or he would have rolled on the ground. When he could speak again, which was some little time, he said, "Did you see the shaman's face? Oh! Oh, gods! Like a clubbed ox."

Some of the companions laughed with him. Wolfcub did not, nor did Spearhead.

Linden noticed. He put aside his mirth, not easily, and patted each on the shoulder. "There, there, my elders. I won't do this every day. But by the gods, hauling me out at the crack of dawn and making me listen to all that before I'd even had a cup of *kumiss*—it's ungodly. I couldn't stand for it. I'll be a good king tomorrow. Today I'll hunt. Or swim or fish, or whatever else I can do that's not either in the camp or concerned with being a king."

Few of them could contest that. They had been hauled out, too, to stand behind the king; and without even his grace of being the one everyone looked to. It was crashingly dull to stand guard for hour upon hour while people droned on and on. The beaten woman might have been a diversion, but Linden's hunt was a better one.

"He'll probably kill the woman," Spearhead said as they strode toward the horse-herds. "I know that man—he's one of the Dun Cow People. He's given to killing wives when they cross his temper."

"Then she shouldn't have done it," said Linden. He shook his head. "Women. I'm supposed to take a wife when the marrying starts. Wives, if some of the old men have anything to say about it. One from each tribe, they're telling me. Can you believe it? I don't remember that my father did any such thing."

"Probably," drawled Curlew, "because he already had a tentful of wives when they made him king. I remember he married one or two."

"He always married somebody at gathering," Linden said. "They want me to do it all at once. Something to do with sending all my father's women to the tomb with him—that was a noble gesture, but nobody asked me if I wanted it."

"Truly?" said Wolfcub. "Nobody did?"

"Not a soul," said Linden. "They try to tell me it was the old shaman who commanded it, but he's been shut in the shamans' tent, talking to nobody. He's willing himself to death, I suppose. That would be like him. No—it was Walker. I'd lay wagers on it."

"No gamble there," Spearhead said. "My brother, the one who's an apprentice—he tells me the old man's refusing food and drink."

Linden nodded. "Yes, I can believe it. He loved my father. They were battle-brothers, did you know? The shaman was older, but with being a shaman and all that goes into it, he rode to his first battle when my father rode to his. They fought together then and always. It was like having a second right hand, my father said."

"Drinks-the-Wind is left-handed," Curlew said.

"Yes, and they'd ride side by side, and a spear on either side, and no one could stand against them."

That was an old song, and none of Linden's making, but the companions seemed to find it stirring. Wolfcub was almost reluctant to break into their mood, but he had a thought, and he had to speak it. "What if it's not the shaman who's willing himself to death? There are poisons that work slowly, and spells that eat away at a man's spirit."

Eyes rolled at that. But Linden said, "No. No, I don't think that's so. Drinks-the-Wind is old. He was losing his powers before all this even began. Now, without his battle-brother, what's left for him?

He'll walk across and be with my father again. They'll travel the gods' country as they traveled this one."

Wolfcub set his lips together, carefully. He might have tried to persuade Linden, but this was not the time or the place. He walked on instead, and the conversation turned to other things.

+ +

They did not approach the horse-herds by stealth. There was no need; they were not raiders or lovers on tryst. But they quieted as they drew nearer, and stepped more softly, so as not to alarm the mares or the skittish foals.

The riding stallions ran in their own herd, all but the king's stallion, who as lord of the royal mares kept his own place and eminence. This morning they had claimed a fertile field near the river, at somewhat of a distance from the rest, but still closer to the camp than the royal herd. The companions paused there first to catch and bridle their own mounts, while Linden looked rather longingly at his former stallion, the pretty sorrel with the mane as fair as his own. But his new horse was much prettier.

He caught Wolfcub watching him. His face brightened; he clapped his hands. "Boarslayer! Here, I've a gift for you. Take this horse. I insist!"

Wolfcub swallowed a groan. The horse was pretty, oh indeed, and tractable, and not too slow in a gallop. But for heart and sheer intelligence, he was not even the beginning of a match for Wolfcub's ugly little dun.

There was little Wolfcub could do but put on a smile and accept the gift. He could have sworn his dun sneered—and when the beast turned his back and dropped manure almost in the sorrel's face, it was as clear as words. Wolfcub sighed and bridled the sorrel and sprang astride, as one by one the others did the same. All but Linden. Wolfcub offered him a hand. He grinned and swung up behind Wolfcub.

They rode out of the field, over a low ridge and onto the windy plain. Horse-herds dotted it. The royal herd was impossible to miss, with its white mares and its silvermaned stallion. They were farthest out as always. The stallion stood on the edge. One white mare wandered away from him.

There were riders on her back, one behind the other as Linden rode behind Wolfcub. Wolfcub knew at once and incontestably who those riders must be. He had no clear thought, only a kind of resignation. Of course it would have to happen this way.

Of the others, not many could see as far or as clear as Wolfcub. He dared to hope that either they would not see the mare leaving the herd, or would not understand that the figures on her back were women.

But Curlew, too, was farsighted—and Linden was watching his stallion. The stallion moved away from the rest of the mares, calling to the one who was departing. She took no notice. He tossed his head and stamped, and galloped after her.

Linden's cry had no words in it. But words came soon enough. "Raiders! Thieves! After them!"

The companions needed no urging. Wolfcub's gift horse, burdened with two men, could not rise to a gallop. Wolfcub could not say he regretted it, but Linden was wild to go after his stallion. Wolfcub slipped to the ground and left Linden to it—and prayed, not at all wisely, that two women on a lone but sturdy mare could escape, and that the companions could catch the stallion and so be diverted from his apparent thieves. They were not stealing him at all, a blind man should have been able to see that. He was following the mare.

Wolfcub did not linger long afoot. His ugly little dun had been trailing after them, aggravated by Wolfcub's desertion but determined not to be left behind. He had to punish Wolfcub with a coy dance, but after he had led a merry chase, he let himself be stopped and bridled with a bit of spare leather. The dun was already moving as Wolfcub caught mane; he let the movement carry him onto the narrow familiar back.

✢ ✢

The king and his companions were swift, but the mare was the wind made flesh, even with her double burden. After a while an even more terrible thing happened: the king stallion came up level with the mare, and the rider in front sprang onto his back. The other continued on the mare, who ran even faster now that she had only one rider to carry.

Wolfcub had never seen Linden so angry. He even strung his pretty bow as he rode, and tried to shoot an arrow from it; but his aim was not the best, even if the bow could have shot so far.

The mare and her companion were broadening the distance

between them. Their riders were lighter and they were faster. However furiously the king and his men thundered in their wake, they thundered farther and farther behind.

Linden was in a red rage. He would have followed them beyond the world's end, if his horse could have done it. But the sorrel was neither fast nor particularly strong, and Linden was a big man, heavy for such a beast to carry. He faltered for all that his rider could do. At last he caught his foot on a stone and tumbled headlong, sending Linden flying.

For Wolfcub who was close behind him, it was a terrible thing to see his young king fall as the old one had done.

But Linden was more fortunate, or quicker in his reactions: he tucked and rolled and fetched up winded but alive against a hummock of grass. His mount was alive, too, but as he struggled to his feet, one leg hung broken. He stood three-legged, lovely head hanging, as the men crowded about his rider, pulling him up, fretting over him, determining that he had no more than a gathering of bruises. The wild rage had been struck clean out of him, but in its place was a colder, deadlier thing.

He would not let anyone else give his poor sorrel the mercy-stroke. He did it himself with his flint knife, holding the head in his arms, thrusting the keen grey blade into the great vein of the neck as he had done in the sacrifices of the Stallion.

The sorrel died gently, sinking down as the blood drained out of him, slipping into the long sleep. Linden stayed with him till he no longer breathed, watching over him, his face white and still.

Their quarry by now was long gone. Linden did not rebuke his companions for failing to follow. He slipped the bridle from the sorrel's head and stepped away from the body. "May the god of horses protect your bones," he said.

Then he faced his companions. Some looked down abashed. Others looked everywhere but at the king. All but Wolfcub, who looked Linden in the face, and Spearhead, who was likewise lacking in proper submission. "You go," Linden said to them. "Bring them back to me—alive, thieves and horses. The thieves' lives are mine, do you understand? Bring them back!"

"I understand," Wolfcub said. Spearhead nodded.

"Go," said Linden. Nor was there any choice but to obey.

PART TWO
SPARROW AND KESTREL

OLFCUB AND SPEARHEAD rode swiftly away from the
king, but once they were out of his sight, they slowed
to a more sensible pace. Wolfcub's heart and throat
were both clenched tight. Of all the ways he had expected Sparrow's rebellion to end, this was not one he had thought
of. Riding away on the white mare, yes—that he could credit. But
taking the king of stallions was madness. With the mare alone she
might have escaped; it was only a mare, even if one of the royal herd.
But the king stallion was the heart of all that the People were. He
summoned them to their wanderings. He ordained their pauses and
their camps. He made and then carried their king.

Sparrow had taken the kingship away from the People. She could
not, if she tried, have made more certain that she was hunted down
and killed.

And he was her hunter. He who loved her, though she had never
known or cared. The friend of her childhood, and her ally of late
against her brother the shaman. She had bidden him look after Linden—and now, in doing that, he had to submit her to the grim justice
of the People.

He would far rather have done it alone. But Spearhead was a quiet
companion, not given to chatter or to unnecessary galloping about.
His plain, practical bay strode along easily beside Wolfcub's homely
dun. After a while he spoke, but it was to the point. "We'll not catch
them by running after them."

"No," said Wolfcub, forcing the word through his constricted
throat. "No, we won't. We'll have to be hunters, and they the deer."

"The king is not going to like it if we take too long."

"We'll take as long as it takes," Wolfcub said through set teeth.

Spearhead nodded, then shook his head and sighed. "The king

stolen from the gathering itself—and by a woman. Who'd ever have imagined it?"

Wolfcub raised a brow. "A woman? Are you mad?"

"Don't play the fool," Spearhead said. "I saw the shape of her, if no one else did."

Wolfcub sighed. "So," he admitted, "did I."

Spearhead glanced sidelong at him. "Tell me what you know of her."

"Should I know anything?"

"It's the shaman's daughter, isn't it? The little dark one? She's a witchy creature. I crossed her once, I forget for what. Her tongue has an edge like a fresh-knapped blade."

"So. You recognized her?"

"So did you. I've seen you talking to her. And the other one—don't tell me that's who it seems to be."

Wolfcub set his lips together.

"That can't be Walker's wife. Can it?"

Wolfcub shrugged.

"Well," Spearhead said, "and well. She wasn't happy with his taking a new wife, was she? Is that why they both did it, do you think? For spite?"

"It's a very great and terrible thing to do for spite."

"It is that," said Spearhead, "if you have a man's wits. Women—who knows what they think? Or how? Or even if they do?"

"They do think," Wolfcub said, snapping it.

"Ah," Spearhead said, as if he had suddenly understood something—but what, Wolfcub could not guess.

Nor would he ask. He pressed his dun to move a little ahead of the bay, and set himself to following the women's track more closely. They had stopped running straight and had begun to weave a little, not for weakness, he did not think, but maybe in some hope of throwing off pursuit. Sparrow at least should have known better, if she suspected that Wolfcub would go after her.

She might expect that he would stay with Linden, and that whoever hunted her would be less skilled and much less likely to understand her mind. Not that Wolfcub claimed anything of the sort, but he had known her since she was a child. He knew what she was likely to do, given choices.

He could let her throw him off the scent. It would be easy. A day, two, three—follow a false trail, lose the true one altogether, go back and face Linden's wrath. But Sparrow would be safe.

He could not do that. He had given his word to her that he would look after Linden; and Linden was his king. For the king's sake, and for the sake of the People, he must bring back the king of stallions. Or the People would have no strength, and the gods would forsake them.

He followed the women's track therefore, grimly, with none of his wonted pleasure in his skill. Of the People, only one man was the better tracker, and that one was his father.

Spearhead was not too unskilled at it, either. He found a place where their quarry had paused to drink from a little stream and to graze the horses. "They'll be wanting to eat," he said. "Would women know how to hunt?"

"These would," Wolfcub said. "And they can fish, if they make for the river that runs south of here."

"We'll catch them soon enough," Spearhead said. "Two women, even if they can hunt—how strong can they be?"

"Stronger than you might think," Wolfcub said. He mounted his dun and left Spearhead standing there, following the trail down the stream and then across it. Yes, it seemed they were making for the river. If they forded that, they left the lands that were common to the tribes of the plain. He knew somewhat of what was beyond: a plain not so broad and somewhat greener, broken by forests of trees, outriders of great forests to the south.

This was the country from which Sparrow's mother had come. That tribe was gone, her mother the last of it, but others lived here and there, small dark people who as often as not took shelter in the forests. Some of them had horses and some were riders, but how many or what skill they had, Wolfcub did not know. He had never thought to ask his friends of the Tall Grass, whose lands ran along the river. They raided the green country and intermarried with the dark women.

Ah well, he thought. He would learn soon enough, if Sparrow did as he thought she would. She would look for refuge among the dark people. If they did not kill her, they might even welcome her—until the People came against her with the full force of war.

Maybe she would come to her senses. Maybe she would let the stallion go. Maybe—if he could persuade her to give him the stallion, he could go back and leave her where she was, and convince Linden not to pursue his vengeance.

He could do that. Yes. It was not dishonorable. She had not meant to steal the stallion, he was sure of it. The pretty idiot had been following the mare.

With a somewhat lighter heart, he went on, keeping a pace that was steady but not grueling. When the trail wove and doubled back, he went straight. He might even catch them before they reached the river. That would be well; he could take back the stallion and send them across the river. Exile was a terrible thing, more terrible than death to most of the People—Linden might even accept that as a proper punishment.

And Wolfcub might be deluding himself. But it kept him going when he would have preferred to stop and howl at the moon. It gave him something to hope for.

+ +

Sparrow had never expected the king stallion to follow when she took the mare and ran. That was a mad enough thing, but the mare was wild to go—pulling at her spirit, robbing her of will or sense. The mare was a goddess. She cared nothing and less than nothing for the men who saw her with her chosen one.

Then when she had got Sparrow on her back, the idiot stallion had insisted on going with her. By the time Sparrow understood that the mare could not carry two and still escape pursuit, Sparrow had also understood what her only choice must be. The mare showed her the way to it: let the stallion come up beside her, and leaned just so. It was oh so easy to catch the flying silver mane and let the force of their speed pull her across.

The king of stallions did not rebel at her touch or cast her off in outrage. His little lean ears flicked back. He snorted a little as if her weight surprised him. She was much lighter than the man who had been riding him, and rather less inclined to pinch. The flow of his gait, the turn of his ear, spoke of his pleasure. He even danced a little when the mare slowed to breathe, tossing his mane. He was a lighter spirit than the mare, more frivolous.

But he was determined to stay with the mare. When they paused by the stream to drink, to let the horses graze, and to eat berries from a bramble that grew up over the stream, Sparrow tried to send him away. He paid no attention to spoken dismissals. Slaps made him trot off a step or two, then drop his head to graze. When she picked up a stone, a large white figure interposed itself. The mare grazed placidly between her and the stallion, nor would she move: if Sparrow stepped aside, she was there, quiet but firm. Sparrow was not to chase the stallion away.

"You do know," Sparrow said to her, "since you are a goddess, that his being here is going to get us all killed."

The mare ignored her. So did the stallion. Keen, who might have paid attention, was lying on the grass by the stream, asleep or close to it.

In sudden concern, Sparrow dropped beside her, peering into her face, feeling her forehead. She roused at that, blinking up at Sparrow's face. "Sparrow? Is it morning?" Before Sparrow could answer, she shook herself, sitting up, taking in the horses and the stream and the wide stretch of the plain.

She shuddered, clasping arms about her middle. "We've done it this time, haven't we? We've done the one thing no one will ever forgive us for."

"I'm afraid so," Sparrow said. "I'm sorry you got caught up in it."

Keen stared at her. "Caught? I caused it! If I hadn't convinced you to run away—"

"I was running away before I saw you," Sparrow said. She sighed and let herself sink down beside Keen. It felt suddenly wonderful not to be standing or sitting, to be letting Mother Earth hold her. "We're meant to do this. It's Horse Goddess. She wants—for whatever reason, she wants us here, and the stallion."

"Gods are difficult," Keen said. She yawned. "Oh, I'm tired. But we can't stay here, unless you think we're meant to die before we've been gone half a day."

"I'm not sure we're meant to die at all." Sparrow rose reluctantly, groaning—her muscles had stiffened already. What Keen must be feeling, she did not like to imagine. But Keen said nothing.

They mounted again, Keen with Sparrow's help, and went on as quickly as the horses would consent to go. The mare led, carrying Keen. The stallion followed. Sparrow found his gaits easier than the mare's, smoother and softer. She could let herself drowse on his back as men did on the march, erect or else lying on his neck. He was tolerant of it, for so young a creature, and a stallion besides. Small wonder that Horse Goddess cherished him: he was biddable, as a mare reckoned a male should be, but strong enough when strength was required of him.

The mare led them on past sunset, then at last let them rest, hidden in a hollow. There was grass enough for the horses, but the women had only water in the skins that each had brought and filled at the stream, and a few berries, and a bit of dried meat from Keen's store. Tomorrow, Sparrow thought, they should camp earlier, and she would set snares. Provided that they were not caught. Provided that they lived to see another sunset.

· · · · · · · ·   27   · · · · · · · ·

CLOUD WAS ENTIRELY out of patience. Whatever god of mischief had invented both yearling colts and half-grown girls, he all too clearly had intended them to drive Cloud mad. When they were both together—the colts besetting the mares till the mares were thirsty for their blood, and the girls egging the colts on for the delight of seeing the mares' rage—they were enough to drive the herdsman to distraction.

He could set the dogs to herding the colts back where they belonged, but the girls were more elusive. They scattered when he rode at them, then simply ran back together when he was past, jeering and making ghastly faces.

All at once they scattered and stayed scattered. He greeted his mother with relief that he hoped was not too desperate. She, mounted on her strong grey mare, watched the children's flight with lifted brow. "I wonder," she said, "how the lot of them would take to a good birch switch?"

"I should love to discover," Cloud said feelingly.

Storm laughed. She was a comfortable woman to look at, deep of breast and hip, and gifted with ample flesh even in a lean winter. In summer she needed her mare's strength, but she rode well always, as light on the mare's back as a girl.

She looked over the horse-herd with a discerning eye, and nodded approval. "They've done well this summer," she said. "So many new foals—and so strong. Horse Goddess willing, most of them will last out the winter."

"I think so," Cloud said, not sorry to be diverted from the pranks of impudent girlchildren. "With as many calves as we've had, too, we'll do well in winter camp. And if the women do their part . . ."

"Wicked child," Storm said, but without censure. "If the women do their part with *you,* do you mean?"

"Or with anyone else," he said. He coaxed a tangle out of his mare's mane, until she grew tired of his fussing and went back to her grazing. "I should like us to be richer. More numerous, too. We're not what we were in the dawn time, but we can be a great people again. Why not? We have horses, and they prosper with us. We can fight if we have to. If we would raid across the river—"

Storm's frown stilled his tongue before it ran on further. "If we are ever ready to make war," she said, stern as she seldom was with him, "that will not be this year, or even next. We're richer than we were, but we're still a poor people. Our way is the hare's way, close to the ground, swift and wary—not the way of the horse running proud over the plain."

"But we should be horses," Cloud said. "We're Grey Horse People. Not Slinking Hare or Cowering Mouse."

"War is a boy's dream," Storm said. "What, did I misremember it? Did we never make you a man at the midsummer feast? And my heir, too?"

He flushed. "Maybe you should have chosen one of your sisters' daughters after all. Not your only son, who knows no better than to wish his people great again."

She was not to be swayed by such force. She regarded him calmly, with the same expression she wore when people were obstreperous in a gathering of the tribe. In that way she reminded him, without a word spoken, that he might be prince-heir, but she was queen of the Grey Horse People, strongest of all her mother's children, and gifted with both queenship and powerful magic.

Cloud was not a shaman, nor would he be. He was not born to the power. One of his cousins apprenticed to his mother—and indeed most people had expected that she would choose her sister's daughter Rain to be queen after her, and not name her son instead. They two were born on the same day, of sisters who were twinborn. They were bound from before birth, and fated to rule side by side, shaman and king.

Or so Storm and the elders had said when Cloud was given the horsehide cloak and the herdsman's staff. It was of little moment out among the horses, with Storm disinclined to indulge his dreaming. When he was king, it would be different. While he was heir, he would do as she bade him.

It was not an easy discipline. She brushed his cheek with her hand, ruffling the curly beard. "Child," she said, "in your day you will be a king of notable wisdom. But until then, indulge me. Teach yourself to be patient."

"Patience is not a young man's virtue," he said, but less sullenly than he might. It was difficult to stay in a temper with her smiling at him, daring him to see the humor in it. With a snarl that was at most halfhearted, he bowed to her will.

+ +

Cloud camped with the herd that night, because the women who would have been the night guards were occupied with one of their sisters: she was birthing her first child. Cloud did not mind. It was a fine evening, clear and not too terribly warm. At sunset he settled in the camping place on a hill that overlooked the grazing grounds, and ate the dinner that his mother had brought him.

The sky darkened as he ate, and the stars came out. There was a thin new moon, delicate as a young girl's cheek. The hounds, whom he had sent to circle the herd, to be sure that nothing threatened the foals, came back to lie panting at his feet.

Not long after full dark, the dogs' heads came up. Cloud had been drowsing, part of him alert for signs of trouble among the horses. He snapped awake.

A figure came toward him in the thin moonlight, glimmering white, seeming to float above the silvered grass. It seemed a goddess made flesh, and wonderful flesh, too: round and sweet, full-breasted and deep-hipped, clothed only in long black hair.

She bent over him. Her broad nipples were dark in firelight and moonlight, her face hidden in the shadows of her hair. She smelled of grass and smoke and horses, warm woman and sweet herbs, and over them all the scent of flowers. She had crowned herself with them, petals hardly softer than her skin.

Cloud wore only leggings against the night's warmth. She unfastened the clout that covered his member, laughing softly as it sprang free, rampant in the moonlight. Her warm hand grasped it and guided it inside her, where she was warm to burning.

She rode him as if he had been one of the stallions, the tall bay whom she favored most, with his beautiful red-brown coat and his waving black mane. Her fingers tangled in Cloud's hair, which was as thick as the stallion's and as black, and curled with abandon. Her lips brushed his, teasing, tormenting, as she held him just short of release.

He could not bear it. He would break; he would scream. She grasped him with sudden and startling strength, rolled onto her back and pulled him over her, and then at last had mercy.

He sank down gasping beside her. He was streaming with sweat. She licked a runnel of it from his shoulder. "Don't fall asleep yet," she said. "I'm not done with you."

He opened his mouth, indignant. She laid her hand over it. "Hush. Look at the moon. Isn't she lovely tonight?"

The moon was exquisite. So was she. He ran his hand over her breasts, down to the faint curve of her belly.

She smiled and rested her hand over his, freeing him to speak if he would. Which after a while he did. "It's well?"

"Very well," she said in a tone of deep contentment. "And will be till spring."

He sighed. When she said such things, she comforted him greatly. She was not an ordinary woman wishing for the best. She was a shaman. If she said it would be well, so it would.

He had no such gifts, and yet he could swear that he felt something there. A warmth beyond her body's warmth, a presence apart from her own.

She arched under his hand, shifting it till it rested much lower. She rocked gently, almost lazily, and with an expression of pure wickedness.

"Insatiable," he said. "And wanton. Did you actually come from camp like this?"

"Will you be shocked if I say yes?"

"Nothing you do can shock me."

Her brow arched. She looked remarkably like the queen, just then. "Truly? Then it seems I have work to do."

"Not tonight," he said. Her rocking quickened. He matched it. She spasmed against his hand, locking about it, till with a sigh she subsided. He reclaimed his hand. She stretched along the length of him, head on his shoulder, and toyed with his manly organ. It was too early for that to revive, though it would have been glad to try.

She was all but asleep, he thought, till she said, "Cloud."

"Rain," he said, naming her as she had named him.

"Cloud," she said again, "Horse Goddess lives in the moon. Remember that."

She was asleep after all, and dreaming. Her voice had that sound to it. "I'll remember," he said to her.

"And remember," she said, still in her dream, "that the moon can come down to earth. A woman rides her. A man pursues her. He thinks he can destroy her. But no man can harm a goddess."

"That, too," he said, "I'll remember."

And he would. When Rain spoke so, she spoke true.

28

WOLFCUB STOOD ON the bank of the river that marked the southernmost border of the tribes' lands. The ford to which he had come was much marked with prints of wild deer and boar and antelope and the beasts that preyed on them, even the vast deep tracks of a herd of aurochs. There were tracks of horses, too, a wild herd that he had seen not long before, winding up a hill in search of better grazing.

But amid all the rest, he had found what he looked for: two horses of good size and rounder hoof than was common in this country, each carrying the weight of a woman. His quarry had come this way, had paused to drink, then forded the river.

He had tracked them from quarter moon to quarter moon. Tonight it began again to swell to the full. Spearhead was still with him, no longer contemptuous of women's strength, or of their hunting skill either. Wolfcub, who had taught these two everything his father had taught him, often caught himself regretting it. They had been apt pupils—delighting him then, defeating him now. And they were mounted on faster horses.

He squatted on his heels and dipped a handful of water, then another, quenching his thirst. Within arm's reach was the place where Sparrow had done the same. He brushed his finger over her tidy print, broader than Keen's but smaller. A glimmer of her presence came with it, a memory of her face—and memory, too, of a round brown breast, glimpsed once when he caught her swimming near spring camp. She had caught him watching her, had made no move to hide, but finished coming out of the water. It was he who had averted his eyes and fled before he saw more than a flash of breasts and belly and thighs.

He sighed. Spearhead crouched beside him and drank as he had done, but seemed not to see the print. He had seen the horses' marks, and the droppings that they had left, which was good tracking in its own right. "Do we go on?" he asked.

Wolfcub wet his hands again and laved his face. He tilted his head back, letting water run from his beard down his neck, cooling his breast. "Do you want to go back?"

"Not without the stallion," Spearhead said.

Wolfcub nodded. "Bad enough that we've taken this long. If we come back empty-handed, what do you wager we'll do worse than be booted out of the companions?"

"We'll find ourselves marching afoot and waiting on the women." Spearhead spoke dispassionately. He was not one to shrink from the truth. "Or more likely we'll go as escort for these horsethieves when they're sent to the gods' tribunal."

"You don't think Linden's anger would have cooled?"

Spearhead snorted. "Even if his could—and the way he thinks of that horse, it's not anything I'd lay wagers on—the People wouldn't let him. That's their strength running away southward, stolen by a pair of women."

"Stolen by a white mare." They had had that argument before. Spearhead shook his head, but for once did not try to contend that a mare could not steal a stallion. Stallions stole mares—and human folk stole horses.

Wolfcub thrust himself to his feet and stretched, groaning a little. He had run afoul of a lion—fortunately a young one, and solitary—hunting the same herd of deer. The marks of its claws were healing. The claws themselves hung about his neck, all but a pair that he had insisted Spearhead take, and the lionskin was the dun's new saddlecloth. Spearhead, who had brought down a fine doe before he realized that Wolfcub was entangled with a lion, had come in time to weaken the lion with a well-aimed arrow. Wolfcub had dispatched it then with his spear. And now he was lionkiller as well as boarslayer, which was surely the gods' jest.

He did not want to cross the river. He wanted to go home, crawl into his father's tent, rest his head in his mother's lap, and sleep till the world passed away. Kings and shamans, death and revenge, boars, lions, mares, stallions, women whom the gods drove mad—all gone. All vanished.

But he was bound. He had to go. He called his stallion. The dun came a little reluctantly: he had found a patch of sweet grass. He brought a trailing mouthful with him, and finished it as Wolfcub mounted and turned him toward the river.

✦ ✦

Sparrow's great worry on the long flight, that Keen would sicken and fail, proved entirely misplaced. The longer they rode, the farther away from the People they went, the straighter Keen sat on the mare's back, and the clearer her eyes became. The shadow that had been on her was still there, but it had sunk deep. She was close to her old self again, the bright and laughing child who had run as wild as a boy until her courses came. She had decided to be a woman then, a creature of long skirts and lowered eyes, and nothing that Sparrow could do would shift her.

They forded the river amid a herd of antelope, who jostled one another but did not flee the horses—strange thing, for these beasts must have known the terror of men on horseback. But it seemed they recognized the mare for what she was, and had no fear of her companions.

Past the river, they rode for a while up a long slope to a broad green level, then down into a rolling country where, for the first time, they saw little thickets of trees marking the courses of streams. Trees were not a thing the People knew a great deal of. There were few on the plain, and none that a woman was allowed to approach, for like horses they were sacred to the men's gods.

Keen would not go past the first small wood, not until she had entered it and stood in light that was all strange: dappled green and gold, and bounded with the trunks of trees. She looked like a tree herself, slender and tall, arms raised over her head, swaying in the wind that blew off the open country.

She was quite outrageously beautiful. Sparrow smiled to see her. Even if she died for what she had done, she would die knowing that, for at least a while, Keen had been happy.

But when they rode on, Keen's face was somber, her gaze turned inward. It was some while before she said what burdened her mind. "Do you think anyone's followed us this far?"

Sparrow stroked the stallion's neck. He arched it under her touch, and leaned into it as she rubbed the spot he loved best. He was neither goddess nor soul's self, but she had grown greatly fond of him as he carried her uncomplaining day after day. It never troubled him that he had abandoned kingship and power to be a lone mare's servant.

But men never let go so easily. "They'll think we stole the king," Sparrow said. "I hope they followed one of our false tracks, or lost us in the herds that have so obligingly crossed our path. But if any one of them is hunter enough to see through all that . . ."

"Wolfcub," Keen said.

Sparrow's lips tightened. "Yes."

"He wouldn't, would he? He'd have to kill us."

"Yes."

Keen shivered. But she kept her chin up. Her voice was firm. "Wolfcub would never do that. Even for king or shaman."

"For king or shaman he would do it," Sparrow said. "His honor wouldn't let him do otherwise."

Keen shook her head. "I don't believe it."

Sparrow shrugged. Keen could believe or disbelieve. It did not change the truth.

She had been dreaming of Wolfcub. It was odd, because such dreams had the clarity of true dreams, but she knew they could not be. In some of the dreams, he was hunting her. That was true—her spirit knew it. He and another man, taller than he and thinner, with a brown beard. But the other dreams, the ones that were even clearer, must be some jest of the gods.

In those dreams, there was no hunt, no revenge, no killing. The two of them were doing quiet things, ordinary for the most part: sitting by a fire sharing a bowl of something savory, or walking along a river-bank, or riding side by side, she on the mare, he on his ugly little dun. Always in those dreams, she was deeply, utterly content. She would wake from them with warmth in her heart that lingered even after she remembered where she was and how she had come there.

And then there was the dream she had had last night. It began much like the others: the fire, the bowl. It was venison, she remembered, stewed with herbs and roots. The taste of it came to her even in memory.

But after they had eaten it, he had risen and held out his hand. And she, in the dream, had taken it. They had gone into a tent that reminded her vaguely of his father's and somewhat of the king's. There he had turned to her, and the look in his eyes was unmistakable. Nor was her dream-self astonished. Wolfcub who in waking had treated her always like a sister, never as a woman, in the dream was all passionate, and all lover.

She had seen him naked. Of course she had. Somehow, in this place of her dream, he was different. He was older, yes, than he had been the last time she saw him as bare as a peeled wand, leaping into the river amid a crowd of naked boys. His body fit itself. It was lean but graceful, the lines of it carved clean, like the lines of his face. It was a man's body, strong and eager.

And she was eager for him, a warmth between her legs and in her heart that she had not known before. It was she who closed the space between them, took him in her arms and drew him down into heaped furs. Her dream-self knew very well what to do there, though her waking self had never lain with a man in that way. No man had wanted her, nor had she wanted any of them.

Except Linden; and she had always known that he was not for her. This man she lay with in dream was not Linden, and yet he was beloved. And beautiful—oh, he was that. Not like Linden, all sunlight and ruddy good humor, but a longer, leaner, more deliciously dangerous beauty. Strange to think of her childhood friend so, and yet he was. He walked like a young lion, and he was strong, with effortless strength.

When she woke, her body was thrumming, as if she had indeed taken a lover in the night. But there was no one about except Keen, curled tight like a little child, sound asleep; and the horses standing nose to tail. Wolfcub was far away. She doubted very much that he dreamed of her, except as a memory of grief.

✦ ✦

Wolfcub dreamed of Sparrow as he lay in camp on the far side of the river. It was not the first time he had done so, nor did he expect it to be the last. In dreams she knew what she was to him, and she was glad. She loved him as he doubted she ever would in waking. And if he had to kill her in order to take back the stallion . . .

Even dreaming, he could not set that thought aside. He turned his dream aside instead, and let it wander where it would, if only it was away from her.

The night had not cooled more than a little. Morning brought with it a breathless heat, the sun hanging motionless in a pallid sky. Even the buzzing gnats were sluggish, and the horses had no speed in them. They plodded through dry and hissing grass. There were trees—they tracked the women to a thicket and out again, and onward across the rolling green country.

The heat rose with the day. At noon they paused in the shade of a wood, though flies tormented them. There was water from a stream, and relief for a while from the sun. Wolfcub was tempted to stay, but he did not like the look of the sky. He would rather be out in the open if it turned as ugly as he feared. Clouds had begun to heap overhead, one atop the other, white as curds, but as they thickened, they darkened. The horizon to the south was blue-black.

The storm struck midway between noon and sunset. Even as long as he had been waiting for it, when it came, it came with appalling suddenness. One moment they trudged onward in the searing sunlight. The next, the world was black and roaring, and shot with lightnings.

They flung themselves from their horses, covering with their bodies whatever they could, and weapons most of all. The skies opened. Thunder pealed. Lightning smote the earth again and again. The gods' wrath buffeted them. The rain nigh drowned them. Hail battered them, stinging unprotected skin.

At last the lightning strode away, and the thunder rolled with it. Rain fell still, but more gently, soaking the parched earth.

Wolfcub rose to his knees. He was shivering—his tunic was dry underneath him, but his back and shoulders were bare. He pulled on the tunic and looked about. The horses stood close by, drenched, heads hanging, waiting out the rain. Spearhead lay as he had, arms over head. Wolfcub reached over and shook him lightly. "Here," he said, "it's over. Let's go on while we've got the cool to travel in."

Spearhead did not move. His shoulder was cold, but so was Wolfcub's—wet with rain. With still heart, Wolfcub turned him onto his back.

The lightning must have struck him even as he went down from his horse's back. His breast was black over the heart, his face set in a rictus of astonishment. Wolfcub could not close the staring eyes, any more than he could lower the lifted arms. The whole body was locked, rigid.

He drew back carefully and wiped his hands on his leggings, over and over. His mind was empty of thought. His belly felt hollow and yet oddly tight.

He spoke in a clear voice, not loud but meant to carry. "Whichever of the gods you are that struck him, and whatever he did to earn your spite, he did not deserve this."

No reply came from earth or sky. Even the thunder was quiet, though it had been rumbling just before. The sky was clear overhead, pale and rain-washed blue. It promised serenity that he had not known since he left the place of the gathering. Now, maybe, he would never know it again.

He buried Spearhead where he had fallen, taking the rest of the day and much of the night to dig the grave and raise the cairn—for he had to go back to the stream in the wood to find stones, and come and go many times before he had enough to cover the grave. Then in wan moonlight he spoke and sang the words that granted rest to the spirit so abruptly ripped from its body. A shaman would have known a dance, too, that would bind it surely, but Wolfcub was only a hunter.

He did what he could. He hoped it would be enough. As morning came again, though he was hollow-eyed with exhaustion, he mounted his dun and led the bay, and left the dead to his long sleep.

A LL THE WAY through the plains, Sparrow and Keen had met no one. The tribes were gathered in the sacred place. Any exiles or wanderers kept well away from them as they kept away from any possible camps. But beyond the river, where the tribes looked to a different gathering, they began to see signs of people's passing: ashes of campfires, dung and trampled grass where herds had grazed, and more than once, a thread of smoke on the horizon that marked the camp of a tribe.

Keen wanted to find a camp and trade such little as they had for things that people in tribes were likely to have: cheese, bread, tanned leather to mend her tunic which by now was very worn. But Sparrow, whose tunic had been worn to begin with, had become as wary and skittish as a wild creature. She looked like one, too, with her face thinned with long travel and short commons, and her tunic worn through in places, baring glimpses of warm cream-brown skin. Her eyes were darker than ever, wide and maybe a little mad.

Keen tried to reason with her. "We've outrun anyone who might have pursued us. And I doubt people here would know what horse you're riding. Your mother came from this country, didn't she? Maybe they'll think you're one of them."

"When I speak," Sparrow said, "they'll know I'm not. I talk like a blond horseman."

"And I am one," Keen said. "Come, you know what people say— the tribes here are anything but warlike. They welcome guests, and they're generous to strangers. You told me that yourself. Maybe one of the tribes will offer us a refuge."

Sparrow shook her head. Her face was set, her will locked tight. "We can't trust anyone. Not anyone."

"Then where are we going?" Keen demanded. She was not losing her temper, no, not that, but she was somewhat less patient than she might have been. "What will we do? Go on and on till we fall down and die? Or come to the edge of the world and fling ourselves off? What are we traveling to?"

"Safety," Sparrow said.

"But where is safety, if not with these tribes?"

"Out there," said Sparrow, sweeping her hand toward the south. "Far away from here. Too far for anyone to follow."

"That may never be far enough," Keen said, "as long as we have the king with us."

Sparrow shook her head. And that was that, for a while—days of burning heat, nights of breathless stillness, broken by storms of awesome ferocity. The first one nigh drowned them both, but they emerged none the worse for wear. After that they knew to find such shelter as they could when the sky grew dark and the wind began to blow, and wait and pray while the lightning marched about them. It never touched them or harmed them, nor did it come close enough to be a danger. The gods were angry, but not, it seemed, with them.

And that was preposterous after what they had done; but Keen, though no shaman, could feel it. Horse Goddess protected them. The mare wanted them alive and in her company, for whatever purpose, just as she wanted the stallion.

Keen had had a great deal of time to think while she learned to ride the mare. At first it took her mind off the pain in her legs and buttocks, the tormented muscles, the skin rubbed raw in her tenderest places. Then as the pain faded and the rawness turned to calluses, she whiled the long hours in thought.

Here she was, riding on the back of a horse—and not any horse; Horse Goddess herself, as Sparrow declared and she believed. She was a woman, and Horse Goddess not only did not care; she was not profaned by Keen's presence. She wanted it, or at least tolerated it.

What if the men were wrong about other things, too? If women could ride without danger to horses' spirits, what else could they do that the men insisted were against the gods' laws? Maybe those were not the laws of gods but the laws of men.

And why would that be? Why would men do such things? Because—maybe because they were afraid of women's power?

That was a frightening thought, and yet oddly exhilarating. It made her heart beat hard and her hands go cold. A woman could have power, real power, shaman's power. Sparrow did. Sparrow said the Grandmother had, too; and Keen had heard from other women, though in whispers, that the Grandmother had been stronger than any shaman.

What if she had been?

One night as they waited for their dinner of roast rabbit to be done, Sparrow told her again the story of Horse Goddess' first gift— the story that was true, not the one that men told. Of the girl, not the prince, who first sat on the back of a horse. After so many days of riding and learning and thinking, Keen knew deep in her bones that it was the truth. A man had not been the first to take the gift. It had been a woman, and a very young one at that.

"Why?" she asked Sparrow. "Why did the men do that?"

Sparrow shrugged. "Why do men do anything? Because they want it all, all the power, all the glory."

"Do you think," Keen asked, "that they do it because they're afraid?"

"What, of women?"

Keen nodded.

Sparrow did not laugh at her. "I suppose they might be. We're smaller and weaker, and we don't like to fight. But we do one thing that no man can ever do: we give them sons. Without us, there would be no men."

"I think they resent us for that," Keen said. She realized as she said it that her hand was resting on her belly. It was no rounder than it had ever been. And yet, as she paused, she tried to reckon days and nights and phases of the moon. How long had it been? Surely—

Surely not. But Sparrow had had her courses once already, and she had just been finishing them when they ran away from the gathering. Keen had not had hers since spring camp. When she lay with Walker—when had that been?

Long enough. More than that, as she counted days. Angry though she had been and still was, and as little pleasure as she had taken, if it had given her what she hoped, she did not care in the slightest.

She was still angry with Walker. Her anger had set deep, as much a part of her now as the breath in her lungs or the heart in her breast.

Did he even remember her? He must have married his strident Blossom—even the shock of the king stallion's vanishment would hardly be likely to turn him aside from a course once he had chosen it. He might elect to expunge Keen from his memory and the memory of the People, such a crime as she had committed, not only to steal the king stallion but to run away from Walker the shaman.

Still she missed him. The husband he had been before he went all cold, the lover who had come so willingly to her bed, was still bright in her memory. His touch, his kiss, the smell and taste of him, kept catching her unawares. Sometimes she found herself weeping, as if to mourn the dead.

But she did not turn back, even if she could have hoped to be accepted into the People again. This country was calling her: its green rolling hills, its many rivers, above all its trees.

She loved trees. She had always found them magical somehow, the ones on the steppe that she was not allowed to touch, and tales of forests had captivated her since she was small. When she saw them growing together in their green stillness, touched the cool smooth boles and smelled the smell of earth and leaves, her heart had sighed and for a while forgotten its sorrows.

Sparrow would not stop for every copse and thicket, but as often as Keen could persuade her, they paused to rest where there were trees, or camped there for a night.

It was near one such thicket that they first met an inhabitant of this country. They were intending to camp, for it was close to sunset. As they approached the trees, the stallion snorted and shied, casting Sparrow ignominiously on the ground. Sparrow was up at once, before Keen could even stop the mare and fling herself down, but she was taking no notice of either the horse or her companion. She reached for what Keen had taken for an old broken tree-stump, and pulled it to gnarled and ancient but incontestably human feet.

Whether it was man or woman, Keen at first could not tell. It had thin wisps of white hair on chin and lip, but not enough to call a beard; and its body beneath colorless tatters was so old that all suggestion of shape was pared away. The eyes were the youngest thing about it: dark eyes only faintly clouded with age, fixing Sparrow with a glare as keen as her own. "You," it said in a voice too light maybe for a man's, but rather deep for a woman's, "are an exceedingly rude child."

It spoke the language of the traders who came and went across the plains and the green lands, a mingling of words from many tribes and places. Nearly everyone knew a little of it, for convenience, and because sometimes it was difficult to understand the dialect of a tribe from far away.

Sparrow bristled at the stranger's words. "And are you polite, to have startled my horse so that he threw me?"

"I think you were lazy and unwatchful, and he took advantage of it." The stranger peered at the stallion, who had got over his startlement and lowered his head to graze. "He's a pretty one. You should ride him better."

"I would, if it weren't for lurkers in the grass."

"Lions lurk in the grass," said the odd stranger. She—Keen decided to call it she, whether it was or no; she was oddly like Wolfcub's mother Willow—slipped free of Sparrow's grip and straightened her garb of tatters. "I'll be your guest tonight, so that you can make up for your rudeness. I have a fondness for rabbit stewed in herbs from this thicket. Make sure you cook it till it's tender, and—"

"We have no pot for stewing rabbit in," Sparrow said, "and no rabbit to cook, either. If you want one, catch one for yourself."

The old woman shook her head and clucked her tongue. "Shame, child, shame. Where's your respect for your elders?"

Sparrow opened her mouth. Keen intervened before she said anything more unfortunate than she already had. "We should be pleased to share our camp with you," she said, "and our dinner, too. Do you have a pot that we may borrow? We've snares, if there are rabbits to be had."

The stranger clapped her gnarled old hands with glee. "Now *there's* a child with manners! Yes, yes, I have a pot, and snares, too. You'll find them under the trees; and if I know my craft, they've caught a brace or three of fine plump rabbits."

Keen smiled and bowed as she would have done to an elder of the People. "Then I'll go and look, since you've been so generous. With the loan of your pot and a few fine herbs, we'll have as good a dinner as we've had on this journey."

+ +

It was a fine dinner indeed, even with Sparrow sulking on the edge of it. Half a dozen plump rabbits hung in snares among the trees. The greenery on which they had been feeding was sweet and wonderful to the taste, and flavored their flesh even before Keen cut it up and filled the pot which waited in a pleasant clearing. That was more than a night's camp: there was a shelter of laced branches, a firepit lined with stones, and a small flock of goats penned near the shelter. The goats gave them milk to drink and cheese to nibble on while the pot simmered.

The stranger did not offer them her name. Keen did not ask, and Sparrow had relegated herself to sullen silence. As to why she lived alone, far from any tribe—she made no secret of that. "I was shaman of a clan down by the river. Horsemen came and killed them all or carried them away. I was spirit-walking far from the people, or I would have died with them. I was a strong shaman, but young, and the horsemen were terrible."

"Horsemen like me?" Keen asked. She was not afraid; there was no hostility in the old woman's eyes. Only sadness.

The old woman shrugged a little. "Not as tall as you, or as fair. But close enough. As soon as they learned that one can ride a horse as well as eat it, they were hot to conquer the world."

"But they didn't."

"Winter came," the old shaman said, "and come spring they were too busy fighting one another to trouble this side of the river. Not that they failed to come back, but by then our tribes were wary. It was harder for them to slaughter and pillage and ride away."

"And your people learned to ride horses, too?"

The shaman laughed, not the dry cackle one would expect, but a warm ripple of sound. "My child, we've been riding horses since the dawn time. We just never made a great rite of it, and we certainly never used it to make war. Horse Goddess is pleased to carry us where feet are too slow or tire too soon."

"I don't believe you," Sparrow said from the other side of the fire. "We were given the gift first. No one else had it before us."

"No one on your side of the river," said the shaman. "This is a different world, child. Is that why you're so angry? Because it won't shape itself exactly as you want it?"

"I am not angry," Sparrow snapped.

"Of course you're not. You've done a terrible thing and expect to die for it, and you don't know what to do about it. Except run— but running is very wearing. Eventually you have to stop."

"How do you know what I've done?"

"How does a shaman know anything?" The old woman bent toward the stewpot and dipped a fingerful—without flinching, either, though the stew was bubbling heartily. She tasted, frowned, added a handful of herbs and stirred the pot. When she sat back, they were both watching her, and neither was inclined to speak. She laughed at them. "Children! You look so guilty. Yes, I know what you did, or think you did. I'm sure your people think so, too. They've twisted the world so completely, seeing it all through men's eyes. But in the end they'll understand. It's not the stallion who matters, however pretty he may be. It's the mare."

"They'll kill us first," Sparrow said.

"Not if you're wise," said the shaman. "You'll stay here a while and learn what I have to teach you. Then I'll send you elsewhere."

"And if I won't go?"

"You'll go," the old woman said, "because the mare will go in spite of you, and you're bound to her. You think you know what that is, but you've barely begun to understand. That's what I'll teach you."

"I don't want to be taught."

"So you think," the old woman said.

30

LONE IN THAT strange country, riding his dun and leading Spearhead's bay, Wolfcub knew that he had lost the trail. The storm had swept it away. He could only continue in the direction in which he had been going before, somewhat slowly, much delayed by storms and their aftermath: flooded rivers, falls of mud or stone, lightning that seemed aimed at him like spears in battle.

Maybe it was doing exactly that. Maybe the gods had had enough of his hunt and were determined to drive him back. They had killed his companion. He did not intend to be killed likewise; but he had to go on. His king had bound him to it.

His mother, and Sparrow certainly, would have observed that he was being bullheaded. He supposed he was. A day or two after Spearhead died, he acknowledged to himself what had been evident for a while: the wounds of the lion's claws were not healing as they should.

The effort of digging Spearhead's grave and heaping the cairn had burst Spearhead's careful stitching. The deeper wounds had opened and bled anew, bled clean as he had thought, but now they had begun to fester.

He did what he could. It was not much, alone, with the worst of them raking round to his back where he could not reach without opening the wounds further. If he had had *kumiss* he could have made a poultice with it, but the last of that was long gone. Down by one of the myriad little rivers he found willows, stripped their bark and steeped it for a gaggingly bitter tea, which helped somewhat. But he had no wherewithal to brew a stronger potion.

He had to go on. The women had been riding south. He had no reason to suppose that they would turn aside from that course, unless something turned them—and he had found no sign of them in the wrack of storm or tumbling in the swollen rivers.

As best he could in pain and fever, he continued his hunt. By now it might be a hunt for the edge of the world, unless he had the great good fortune to pick up their trail. But so many storms, so close and so evidently directed at him, scoured the land clean day by day.

He lost the horses in one even more terrible than that which had slain Spearhead. They had been struggling along the bank of yet another river—this country was one great tangle of them—when the storm struck. The earth gave way beneath them. They tumbled and slid, buffeted by wind and rain. Wolfcub caught at a trailing root as the bay disappeared from beneath him, and held on for grim life, though it made his torn back and sides scream with pain. Even in the storm's darkness, in the pouring rain, he could watch the river take the horses: the bay limp and broken even as the water took him, the dun alive, struggling, but overwhelmed in the turbulent water.

As always, the storm ended in peace, soft light and kiss of rain that washed the mud from Wolfcub's face and body. He longed to let go, to let the river take him, but he was a coward. He could not simply die.

He made his halting way to firmer ground, then followed the river till he found the dun's body. The bay he never found. The river must have kept him.

Maybe, with the sacrifice of a good hunter and two strong stallions, the gods at last were appeased. Or else they reckoned that Wolfcub would never find his quarry now, alone as he was, afoot, and stripped of all his weapons but a flint knife. The rest had been with the bay. The dun had been carrying a waterskin, and the skin of the lion that Wolfcub had slain. He would have left that, but it was a blanket and a cloak as well as an empty brag. He would need it if he survived till winter.

Strange to think of that in this hot still weather. But leaves were turning in the copses, little by little. The days were shorter, the air very slightly different. Summer was passing.

With only a knife he could not hunt larger game, but he could set snares for rabbits and squirrels. And the wild grains were ripening. He had little strength and no tools to grind them into flour, but he could eat the sweet kernels, as he could harvest fruits from trees and brambles. He could keep himself alive while he must, if the fever would only let him be, and the wounds finish draining and begin again to heal. They were hot to the touch and more painful than he would ever have admitted if he had not been alone, but they had not shown yet the red streaks that warned of death's coming. As long as he did not see those, he told himself, he could go on. He could hope to see the end of the hunt.

+ +

It was a strong storm season—the strongest that anyone could re-member, even the Grandfather, who was so old he could remember when most of the horses had been duns and bays. Now of course they were nearly all greys, Horse Goddess' children as people called them, because like her they were the color of the moon.

Storm had been born in such a season. It was her time of greatest power, and she was deeply attuned to it. Before the first storm came, she had taken the people from their summer camp to one better protected, farther south, close to a river but not so close that its flooding would harm men or beasts. The rise of a hill sheltered it, and there was good grazing along the slopes. When the strongest storms struck, they struck the far side of the hill; the people's tents and shelters were safe, and set up high enough that if the hard rain fell, it ran down away from them into the river.

It was a good camp, even with the storms. The river was rich in fish, and the hunting was much better than it had been round about the summer camp. There were apple trees near the river, and a stand of beeches, with nuts just coming ripe.

There was no need to hunt far afield. Deer came to the beech-wood, and there was a boar with a harem of wives. They were shy as pigs went, and not inclined to challenge passersby, as long as they were left to their rooting and feeding, and as long as no one ventured too near the boar's lair. Some of the more headstrong boys wanted to try their hand at pig-killing, but while there was ample and less dangerous game, Storm forbade them to touch the boar or his tribe.

Cloud was thinking of this as he made his way through the beech-wood. He had heard the pigs not long before, feeding on the rich mast. He was hunting deer, but today, for whatever reason, he had found no sign less than a day old. There had been no storm the day before to drive them off; indeed it had been some days since the wild winds blew. Nor was there any other tribe within reach, or any party of hunters that he knew of. The nearest, the Stag, waited out storm season three days' ride from the Grey Horse camp. Sometimes men or women of the Stag came to visit kin or lovers, but none of them would be inclined to drive the deer away.

Close to the wood's edge he found wolfsign, tracks and dung and the half-buried carcass of a fawn. A pack had come through this morning, brought down the fawn and eaten it, then set off in pursuit of the doe and her twin yearlings. He sighed and shrugged. So: the rest of the deer had gone into hiding. Wise deer.

And maybe his mother's tent would be content to dine on fish and waterfowl, since the wolves had laid claim to venison. He was not even slightly tempted to try for roast pig—not against his mother's prohibition.

The sky was clear as he left the wood. No storm today, either; and that was well enough. He preferred not to be hunting and fishing along the river when the storm-gods walked.

He trotted easily through the tall grass, bow in hand, quiver bouncing comfortably between his shoulderblades. It was warm, but a light breeze blew, cooling the sweat on his breast and cheeks. Maybe, after he had done his fishing, he would swim in the river. That would be pleasant.

He saw the body somewhat before he came to the water, lying on the bank as if it had been cast there in a flood. But it was not wet, and the river ran quiet. It lay on its face, a long lean man's body in much-worn leggings and boots worn through in the soles. Cloud could see what had likely killed him: great oozing wounds in back and sides, buzzing with flies. They rose in a furious swarm as he turned the stranger onto his back.

This was no tribesman of this country. The long face with its sharp curve of nose, the hair dark with oil and dirt but still ruddy brown, and the sparse beard, were unmistakably foreign. He wore as armlets the tusks of a boar who must have been divinely huge, and on a string about his neck hung the claws of a lion—maybe the same lion that had killed him.

If that was the lion, it had died for its sins. The man was lying on a lionskin. He did not, for all of that, look terribly warlike. His only weapon was a knife of flint with a bone haft carved in the shape of a leaping wolf. His wounds circled round his ribs. Cloud saw what might be the white of bone.

The man stirred. Cloud jumped like a deer.

The stranger stirred again, feebly, murmuring something in a language Cloud did not know. His eyes opened. They were clear grey, like rain. They had a remarkable effect on his face. Without them it was rather plain, long-jawed and thin-lipped. With them, it had an odd and striking beauty.

He did not seem to see Cloud, or to recognize him as human. Though his shoulder had been cool when Cloud touched it, his forehead burned with fever. He spoke again, more loudly this time, to someone who appeared to be standing behind Cloud.

"Stranger," Cloud said in the language that traders used, "you are welcome to Grey Horse lands. Can you stand? Or shall I carry you?"

The stranger blinked. He peered at Cloud. He did not, as Cloud had half feared, turn hostile and spring on him with the knife. That would have been hardly surprising if he was what Cloud thought he was; but he was too ill or too sensible to do such a thing. He spoke in traders' patois, slowly, with a thick burring accent, but Cloud could understand him. "Grey Horse? Are you—am I dead?"

"Not quite yet," Cloud said. "I can't tend you here—I've nothing to tend you with. I'll have to take you back to camp. Can you walk?"

The stranger nodded. It seemed to make him dizzy. His eyes closed; his face tightened. With an effort he sat up. With a greater effort, and with Cloud's aid, he pulled himself to his feet. He stood easily a head taller than Cloud, even doubled over with the pain of his wounds.

He walked four steps. The fifth would have flung him flat on his face again, if Cloud had not caught him. With a faint sigh, Cloud heaved him over his shoulders. He was light for his size, at least, and

Cloud was strong. And he did not struggle, which was fortunate. He was still alive: his breath hissed in Cloud's ear, fast and shallow.

Just as he would have done to bring back the body of a stag, Cloud steadied himself under the long limp weight, and made his way home.

+ +

Storm was waiting for him. She had not spoken to him this morning or sent him on that particular hunt, but she greeted him calmly and regarded his burden without surprise. It was Rain, happening past, who said what Cloud had braced himself for: "Fool of a man. What use have we for manflesh?"

Cloud glowered at her. She had the grace to look down, though she refused to blush.

Storm sent her in haste to fetch certain things from the stores. People had gathered, curious, to see what Cloud had brought back from his hunt. Storm sent some of them on errands, too, and scattered the rest with a word.

Some of those sent away returned quickly with a tent, which they raised beside the queen's, rolling and binding the sides so that it was no more, for the moment, than a canopy. In that fashion it sheltered the stranger from the sun but let in ample light.

Cloud was no shaman, but his mother had taught him what she knew of healing. He had a gift for it that Storm said was a kind of magic. But wounds like these, old and suppurating, were not anything he was delighted to contend with.

Storm helped him settle the stranger on a clean hide, raising her brows at the stained and bloodied lionskin that had wrapped him, folding it and handing it to one of the men who hung about. "Clean this," she said. He was none too happy to be dismissed, but he went obediently. People always obeyed Storm when she was in this mood.

Cloud and Storm together relieved the stranger of his leggings and took off his necklace and his armlets, laying them aside. By the time he was naked, warm water had come, and the wherewithal to bathe him and dry him. While Storm washed his hair, Cloud studied the wounds. Now that they were clean, they were if anything uglier than before.

"Cautery?"

Cloud glanced over his shoulder. Rain stood just behind him with a basket in her hands. Cloud took it from her. Salves and potions would not be enough for this. But to burn away the diseased flesh . . .

Maybe he would need to do that. But there was a thing he could do first. It would not be pretty. He would have to pray that the stranger did not wake and run shrieking from it.

His mother had known. Some of the wilder children, at her behest, had brought what he needed from the refuse-heaps, white and wriggling and hungry for carrion. Flinching a little with revulsion, Cloud spread maggots like a poultice over the worst of the wounds, those that had begun to blacken on the edges. The others he treated with a less revolting salve, leaving them all open, as unlovely as they were.

It seemed precious little to do, but when he thought of other, more seemly things—bandages, bindings, poultices of mud or herbs or dung—the gift in him, that his mother called his magic, turned away in refusal. This if anything would bring the stranger back to life.

"And pray he doesn't make us regret it," Cloud muttered.

Rain's brows went up. "Why? Did he try to kill you before he fell over?"

"No," Cloud said. "Not at all. He seemed a very polite sort, for a man near dead. But if he is what he looks like—"

"That is a horseman from beyond the river," said Storm. She said it perfectly calmly. "Are his eyes blue?"

"Grey," said Cloud, "like rain"—just as Rain burst out, "How can a man have blue eyes?"

"Or grey?" Storm slapped her lightly. "Don't be foolish, child. Horsemen are sun-people. Their hair is as often yellow as not, or sunset red. Their eyes are sky-colored, or the color of rain."

"This one's hair is brown, but almost red," Rain said. "Like a hawk's tail."

"Sparrowhawk," Storm said.

"Kestrel," said Rain. "I shall call him Kestrel."

"He probably already has a name," Cloud pointed out.

She tossed her head. "And I'll wager that name is Kestrel. Doesn't he look like one? Such a lovely beaky face, and that ruddy hair."

Cloud sighed. When Rain took it into her head to name something, nothing would possibly do but that name, forever after. He had only escaped that headstrong magic of hers because his mother had named him when he was small, and refused to allow Rain to change it.

This man, this Kestrel, whatever he had been before, was going to wake and find himself made new, with a new name and, Cloud prayed to the gods of healing, new strength. And, alas, new scars; but there was no helping that. They were not on his face, at least, or on a limb, to weaken the use of it.

There was nothing now but to wait and watch, to pour gruel and potions into him, and to take care that he neither shifted nor took harm from lying so long on his side. They took watches through the night and the day thereafter, the three of them and their kin, and anyone else who came under Storm's stern eye.

He did not die at once, as Cloud had feared he would. He still could die, and quickly; but for that night at least, he would live.

·········· **31** ··········

WOLFCUB SWAM IN and out of a black dream. Somewhere in it he paused in sunlight by the rushing of a river and looked up into the face of a stranger. It was a man, dressed much as he himself was, but unmistakably foreign: short but broad in the shoulders, with warm brown skin and a pelt of curly hair. The man spoke to him, and it seemed he understood, but he could not afterward remember what they had said.

The sunlight went away, but the man was somehow present, still with him in the dark. Then there were other people, women shorter and if anything broader than the man, with curling black hair and round lovely faces—women, indeed, like Sparrow. But she was nowhere in his dream. Nowhere at all.

He woke with a start. It was his dream again, the sunlight, the man with his curling beard and his broad black-furred chest. But this time Wolfcub could have sworn he was awake. A great lassitude was on him, and pain like a hand clenched tight about his ribs. He stared at the man, who stared back with calm dark eyes. They were rather wonderful eyes, like Sparrow's: clear and penetrating, with a light in them that he had always thought must be the spark of magic.

"Am I alive?" Wolfcub asked, searching for the words in trader-tongue.

It was not what he had meant to say, nor did it make any sense, but the stranger did not seem to think him odd for saying it. He answered, "You do seem to be. Do you feel dead?"

"I feel . . ." Wolfcub tried to move, but his breath caught. No; he was not ready for that yet. "I feel as if a lion mauled me and left me for dead."

"Actually," said the stranger, "I think you killed the lion."

Wolfcub could not sigh, either. It made his ribs cry for mercy. "I suppose I did. It's not what I set out to do. I was hunting something safer."

The stranger laughed: sharply, as if it had been startled out of him. "By the Mother Goddess! You don't talk like a wild raider of the steppe at all. Are you a foundling, then? A wanderer from some country we've never heard of?"

"I'm a hunter of the White Stone People," Wolfcub said, some-what cautiously. "I come from north of the river. If that makes me a wild raider of the steppe—yes, I am that. Will you kill me for it?"

"We'd have done that already, if we were going to," said an al-together new voice. It belonged to a woman, and a young, proud, delightfully forward one, too. She was as dark as the man, with the same curling hair and round face, and she was dressed just as he was, in embroidered leggings and necklace of colored stones. Her breasts were round and full, the nipples dark and very large.

Just as Wolfcub reflected on how like Sparrow she was, it dawned on him that his leggings were nowhere near him, nor was there any covering on him at all. She could see very clearly what he thought of her: for all the weakness that beset him, one part of him was able and willing to rise for her. Not as high as it might, or as proud as it could, but high enough to be properly mortifying.

She smiled with profound sweetness. "I thank you," she said. "And a fair morning to you, man of the White Stone People. I have decided that you are Kestrel—the hawk with the ruddy tail, the spar-rowhawk. Tell me that your people call you that, too."

"I can't," he said. "They call me the Wolfcub." And the boar-slayer and no doubt, if he ever came home, the lionkiller. But he did not say that.

That astonishing creature shook her head firmly. "You are not a wolf, nor his cub either. Not you. You are a swift creature of the air—a falcon. A Kestrel."

He found that he was gaping. He shut his mouth.

The man, who had listened with an air of high amusement, said in the silence, "You'd do as well to give in now as later, stranger. Once Rain names a thing, that thing stays named. Regardless of what it called itself before."

"But I am not—" Wolfcub began. But he broke off. Not because he had surrendered—because a movement had caught his eye, something flitting past against the sunlight. A shape like—a falcon?

A small falcon, but very swift. It swooped over him—into the place in which he lay, which seemed to be a tent without walls but with a roof of tanned leather—and came to rest just above him, where two poles joined to hold up the roof. It tilted its head at him, and fixed him with a wild yellow eye.

He shivered as a man must when he faces a god, or a god's messenger. But he was not willing to give up the name his father had given him. Not though it was a child's name, and he was a man. He had kept it when he took his manhood, because no other name was given him, nor did one come to him.

Because he had waited for this?

"See," said the woman named Rain. "You are Kestrel. There is the face of your spirit. Isn't it a handsome one? Be swift, as he is. Be fair. Be made new in this world."

He shivered again. When he tried to think of himself as Wolfcub, his mind blurred. But he was not Kestrel yet. He was no one.

Strong hands took his. They were not the woman's, which somewhat surprised him. The man said, "There. It's a lot for your strength. Sleep now, and grow strong. When you wake, you'll truly be made new."

"Or dead," he said—Wolfcub, Kestrel, whoever he was.

"Not dead," the man said firmly. In his way he was as forthright as the woman, and as determined that the world should go as he wished it. "Now sleep."

+ +

Kestrel slept—not like the dead; he was alive, and by Earth Mother would stay so. Cloud glared at Rain. "And no thanks to you, either," he said. "What did you do that for? Couldn't you see he was too weak to carry a new name?"

"He's stronger than you think," Rain said, unrepentant. "And isn't he beautiful? Those eyes—they're marvelous. And so," she added wickedly, "is a certain other part of him."

Cloud was not about to deny that. But he said, "You embarrassed him horribly."

"Didn't I? He's such a modest creature—who'd have thought it? He makes me think of the Long River boys: so shy and yet so sweet. They're wonderfully bold in the inner tent, once you get them there. I wonder . . . ?"

"That," said Cloud, "you'll not be finding out tonight, or for a fair number of nights after. He's a long road still to ride before he's strong again."

"I'll help him," Rain said.

"Not *that* way."

"Not," said Rain, "until he's ready. No."

Cloud eyed her in mistrust, but she was all limpid sincerity. There was little he could do but sigh and hope she meant it.

✢ ✢

The man who had been Wolfcub, who was now named Kestrel, slept and woke and slept again, a blur of waking and dream. When he was awake, people fed him and made him drink—water sometimes, but more often mixtures of strange tastes, pungent and sweet, bitter and salt. The man was often there; Kestrel learned that his name was Cloud. The woman, Rain, who declared herself to be a shaman, came and went. And sometimes there were others, small dark people like the rest. None of those would speak to him; they averted eyes and did whatever was necessary and left.

They were keeping him drugged, he understood early on, but he lacked the will to fight it. It was to help him heal, Cloud said. Cloud was the healer, and also a prince of the tribe—not its king, but king-heir.

The king never came. A woman did, one very like Rain, but not her mother; Rain addressed her as "aunt." She was Cloud's mother, and she was a woman of great presence and clear strength. Like Rain she had no modesty as women of the tribes knew it; sometimes she wore a tunic as a woman should, but equally often she appeared in leggings or in a kilt of fine white leather embroidered with swirling signs. There were like signs circling her breasts and her ample belly, like—king-marks?

She was the king. She was also the shaman of the tribe, and Rain was her apprentice. Cloud was her heir.

It was most strange. Women and men walked freely together here. There seemed to be nothing that either did not do. He saw women coming in from the hunt, and men tending children—though none made shift to nurse an infant.

Sparrow would love these people. Women rode horses, too, sturdy grey horses with remarkable grace in movement, such horses as Kestrel had seen in the royal herd of his own people. But none of those greys was Sparrow's mare, nor was there any sign of her, any suggestion at all that these people knew of her.

And why he should think there might be, he could not imagine. He had long since lost her trail. He was not even sure where he was, except that he was south of the river—far south of it, if he could trust his memory. Sometimes he thought he truly had died and was gone among the gods—and such gods, too, these dark lively people who seemed to laugh as easily as they spoke.

They were mortal enough. Someone died while he lay mending, a very old man, who seemed to have been much revered. That night one of the half-grown boys stayed with him, sullenly, while everyone else took the body and wrapped it in a horsehide and carried it away. Whatever rite they practiced, however they entrusted their dead to the gods, he was not to see. The next day they came back, walking quietly, and returned to the business of living.

As indeed should he. Their potions were growing weaker as he grew stronger. The day came when he happened to be left alone for a few moments in a changing of the guard. He had been measuring a tentpole for some days, judging its strength.

It was strong enough for him to pull himself up. He was barely strong enough to do that, or to stand gasping and with his sight growing dark, till he had to let go or pull the tent down with him.

When he could see again, he looked up at Cloud, who stood as tall as a hill above him. "Good," Cloud said. "You did it yourself. I was pondering ways to force you."

Kestrel blinked. He was stupid with exhaustion, but Cloud pulled him up. He already knew how strong that short broad man was; stronger by far than Kestrel. Nor would he let Kestrel rest till he had walked, on his feet though leaning on Cloud's wide shoulders, back to his too-familiar bed.

After that Kestrel was to get up whenever he could, and if he lay too long, Cloud or Rain or even the queen would come to drag him up and make him walk. First about the tent, then to the fire and back, and thereafter by greater distances until he had circled the whole camp and begun to explore the fields and woods about it.

Summer had passed while he lay healing. Autumn had come: warm red-golden days, crisp chill nights. As soon as he was up and walking, he was given garments to wear, made to his measure for he was taller and narrower than people here: leggings, tunic, and his lionskin cleaned and much more adeptly tanned than he had managed to do on the hunt. It was a beautiful thing now, supple and tawny-gold. He had his necklace back, too, and his armlets that he had taken from the boar.

He did not fancy himself overmuch, though he was well and properly clothed. He had lost flesh terribly in his sickness. His side and back were deeply scarred. Cloud gave him an ointment to soften the scars and keep him from stiffening on that side.

He would have been gladder of that if Rain had not been so eager to help him. He had come to understand that she was, if not Cloud's wife, then his woman. They slept in the queen's tent, close to the wall of the one in which Kestrel lay, and there was no mistaking what they did together.

And yet she was terribly free of herself with Kestrel. That she ran about half-naked seemed to be common and accepted for women of these people, but none of the others made herself so evident to Kestrel as this one did. If she was feeding him or pouring a potion for him, she always found a way to brush his arm with her breast, or to stand so close that he could not move without touching her. She loved to touch him: combing and plaiting his hair while he was still too weak to do it, brushing his cheek with her fingers, resting her hand on his shoulder or his arm. More than once she slid her hand down his arm till her fingers were wound with his, easily, as a child will, but those eyes were no child's.

The ointment was a difficulty. He could salve his ribs well enough, but his back was hard to reach, between tightness and old pain. If Cloud was about, Kestrel could ask him to help, but Cloud never seemed to be nearby when Kestrel needed him. Rain, on the other hand, never seemed to be elsewhere. She loved to find him struggling with the sweetly pungent stuff, snatch it from his hand and work it into his back and sides with skilled fingers.

They were very skilled, and adept at working strongly but without pain. But they tended to stray. They wandered up along his shoulders, which was not so bad; but they also wandered down and round until, if he was not deeply wary, they had found his rod. It of course by then was defiantly erect. It did not care that she was another man's woman.

But his spirit did, and his good sense. He always found a way to shift away from her, to elude her hand; but one day when the apples were full ripe in the wood near the hill, she would not let him escape. When he turned to remonstrate, she had rid herself of her leggings, and knelt boldly naked. His movement, by his accident and her design, brought him up against her body.

She laughed, rich and warm, and gripped him tight before he could recoil. His rod was trapped between them, escaped from its leggings—her doing, too. Deftly and utterly wickedly, she mounted him where he knelt.

His heart thudded in horror. But his rod was wild with delight. She was hot inside, hot and sweet, clasping him like a wonderful strong hand. She knew very well what to do and how to do it. She bore him back and down, driving him deep inside her, with a gasp and a shudder of pure animal pleasure.

He could only be glad, with the last fading glimmer of sense, that they had long since lowered the walls of this tent which they had given him. He was not forced to couple in full view of the camp. But anyone who passed by could hear—for he was grimly mute, but she was making no secret of it at all.

All the while his mind babbled in terror, his body took everything she gave and returned it joyfully. He had no power to resist her. She was a shaman. Whatever she wished for, she had.

She did not take him and use him and abandon him as a man might a woman. When she had brought him to a roar of release, she held him inside her for as long as his slackening member would stay there, then sat astride him still, rocking gently, regarding him with enormous contentment. "You," she said, "are a beautiful man. You don't really know that, do you? So many men do. But you don't believe it."

He was in no condition to banter with her, or indeed to speak at all. She did not seem to mind. She brushed her breasts across his breast, sliding down the length of him. "Smooth," she said. "Like a boy. Except here." She had it in her hand again, but gently, as if it were a bird lifted from the nest. "And here." Her fingers raked his beard, lightly, combing it smooth. "Are all of you so lightly furred?"

That, too, he could not answer. He was wondering when Cloud would come, and how the prince-heir would kill him. Cloud seemed a mild-mannered man, but Kestrel had seen him come back from a hunt with the hide and meat of a bear. Cloud was as strong as that bear, and deadly skilled with bow and spear.

While he lay speechless, Rain explored his body. She was like a child with a new toy, searching out all its secrets. She found the mark on his shoulder like a tiny splayed hand. She kissed that—irresistibly, she said. She loved the freckling on his arms and legs and across his shoulders, and over his nose, too: sun-kisses, she called them. She measured his limp hands against hers, marveling at how narrow they were, and yet so long, and strong enough when he was not frozen with fear of what her man would do to him.

When she took his hand and laid it over her breast, then at last he found his voice, if not his strength. "No," he said.

She widened her eyes.

"No. I can't do that. Your husband—"

"I don't have a husband," said Rain.

"Your man, then. Your—"

"*My* man? Can one person own another?"

"Cloud," Kestrel said in desperation. "Whatever he is. The man you lie with at night. What will he do when he finds us? Geld me? Kill me?"

She stared in flat astonishment. "Why in the world would he want to do that?"

"Because you belong to him. Because—"

"I do not belong to him. He does not belong to me." She paused. Her eyes narrowed. Her head tilted. "Are you telling me that one of you would kill another for lying with a woman?"

"For lying with someone else's woman. It's great dishonor."

She shook her head, amazed. "What savages you all must be! And do women kill women for the same cause?"

"Of course not," said Kestrel. "A man may have several women. They share him."

"But men don't share a woman?"

"Only," said Kestrel, "if it's a king's woman, and the king offers her as a gift. But Cloud, who will be king, has not—"

"You *give* women? As gifts?"

Now he was astonished. Her light mood had vanished. Her eyes were blazing. She pulled away from him, recoiling, as if he had said something that made her terribly angry. She snatched up her leggings where she had cast them, but did not even trouble to put them on before she had stalked out of the tent.

+ +

Kestrel was still lying there when Cloud slipped through the half-open flap. He scrambled up, seeking about wildly for something, anything, that might serve as a weapon. But there was nothing in reach, nor anything that he could come to before Cloud stood in front of him.

The prince-heir did not seem angry. He was, as far as Kestrel could tell, amused. "Gods," he said, "what a temper you've thrown my clan-sister into! I haven't seen her so angry in days."

Kestrel's teeth clenched. Some men smiled before they killed. If this was one—

"What did you say to her?" Cloud asked with every appearance of honest curiosity.

Kestrel answered truthfully, because he was mad perhaps, or because he did not care if he lived or died. "I told her that kings among my people give women as gifts."

"Do they?"

"Don't they do that here?"

Cloud shook his head. He was not angry, but he was not delighted, either. "And I suppose you said something of her being that gift."

"Not—exactly," Kestrel said.

"Ai," said Cloud, half amused, half dismayed. "No wonder she was in a rage. We don't give or trade people here, plainsman. Only cattle and food, and things made by hands."

"But women—"

"Women are the living incarnation of Earth Mother, as men are of Skyfather. Do you give away the earth under your feet? Do you value it so little?"

Kestrel had long since begun to see where Sparrow got her strange notions and odd sense of fairness in the world. "But why is

Rain so angry?" he asked, since Cloud did not seem immediately ready to kill him.

"She chose you to lie with her," Cloud said. "She reckoned you worthy. Some women will lie with any man, but a shaman chooses only the best and the most beautiful. Her magic depends on it. And you let her know you thought of her as chattel—a thing to be traded, like a heifer or a shell necklace."

Kestrel's mouth was open. He shut it. "You knew—she—"

"She's been talking about it since she first laid eyes on you. She wanted to do it days ago, but I wouldn't let her. You needed to be stronger first."

"But she is—your—"

"She is my clan-sister. We can make a child together, but we can't marry. When she takes a husband, she'll take one from another clan. She was thinking of taking you, but I don't think that's wise. You're too different. And," said that astonishing man, "I think your heart beats for another woman than Rain."

Kestrel could think of nothing at all to say. He was in a world unlike any he had known—except for the glimpses Sparrow had shown him. To say his heart beat for her . . .

"I hunt that woman," he said in a flat, hard voice. "When I find her I am bound to kill her. As for your shaman—I am sorry I offended her. I never meant to. Will you tell her that for me?"

"I can try," Cloud said. He crouched down by Kestrel's side and inspected the scars, calmly, as if it was no matter at all that they had lain with the same woman.

Kestrel looked him in the eyes. "Aren't you even slightly jealous?"

Cloud stared back, dark eyes quiet. "I suppose I could be. I'm good enough to look at, but you are beautiful. All the women want you. But when they've had their fill of you, they'll come back to me, because you may be splendid and foreign and therefore alluring, but I will be king."

"What if one of them doesn't come back? What if that one is Rain?"

"I would be sorry for that," Cloud said. "But even if she never lay with me again, we'd always be bound: she as shaman, I as king. Nothing will ever change that."

Kestrel lowered his eyes. Cloud's quiet voice, his serene mind, put Kestrel to shame. Such a hunter he was, who could not keep his own temper in check.

"There now," said Cloud, in the same tone he used with the children. "You come from far away, where people are different. Understanding is hard. You'll learn."

"And if I don't want to?"

"Then you don't." Cloud rose. "Come out into the sunlight. You've been too long in the dark."

That was true. Kestrel staggered up, stiff, gasping as he stretched the scars over his ribs. He was still astonished that this man knew what he had done and seemed not to care in the slightest; still faintly convinced that he would be killed for it. But Cloud treated him exactly as before, with quiet courtesy and a warmth that, if he let it, could be friendship.

It did not matter what Cloud said. Kestrel would never understand these people.

.... **32** ....

S PARROW TOOK TO calling the shaman Old Woman, since she offered no name of her own. "That will do well enough," she said when Sparrow first called her that, in defiance and in some expectation of a rebuke. But Old Woman seemed pleased.

She made no effort to hold the women prisoner, or to compel them to stay. She simply expected them to do it. She was a shaman. She knew what Sparrow had to admit: that her wisdom was beyond price, and Sparrow was hungry for it.

She did not seem to teach anything. She set the women to cleaning the shelter, sweeping out old rubbish and molding grass mats and flea-infested furs. Then they were to weave new mats, and tan the pelts that were stretched on racks of lath and sinew, and make new furs to sleep in. They were also to make themselves coats out of deerhide tanned most finely; and no matter that Sparrow did not expect to be there when the snow came. "You'll need it," Old Woman said of the coat that Sparrow had begun sullenly to piece together.

Sparrow was better at cutting and piecing than Keen. Keen was much better at fine work: embroidery of shell and bone and stone beads, which she would do while she listened to Old Woman telling stories; or else she wove fine grass mats and lovely tight baskets. Her hands were always busy.

Sparrow hewed wood and drew water with the skill of long practice, made a fair stew and a very good honeycake, and laid snares and hunted for the pot, or brought fish from the river. She was learning no magic, and few mysteries. In the evenings Old Woman told stories, such stories as the Grandmother had been used to tell, of Earth Mother and Skyfather and the myriad gods. When she spoke of ancestors, it struck Sparrow that these might be ancestors of her own— or of her people at least. Her mother had come from this country.

And yet she did not feel as if she had come home. This was a pause on a journey, forced upon her by the shaman's will. When she had had enough of it, she would leave. For the moment she stayed, and waited to learn something she could use.

At night Old Woman slept in the shelter, but the young women elected to sleep outside unless it was raining. They had grown accustomed to the stars overhead, and Keen loved to lie under woven branches, counting stars through the leaves. Keen was happier here than Sparrow was, by far. She liked Old Woman, and Old Woman was gentle with her as she never was with Sparrow.

As the days passed, Sparrow began to notice something else about Keen. It was not only the green face in the mornings and the reluctance to break her fast till midday, when she roused to blooming health, or even the slight rounding of her belly. Sparrow could *see*. She could look at her friend as if she were made of clear water, and in the middle of her, a little silver fish. The fish grew from day to day, till it had the appearance of a human child, tiny and soft but unmistakable.

One morning as Sparrow ate honeycake with good appetite and Keen had excused herself from a half-drunk cup of herb-tea and run off to the privy, Old Woman said, "You begin to learn."

Sparrow raised her brows. "Oh? And what am I learning?"

"Not manners, certainly," said Old Woman. "But you begin to see."

"Do you know what I'm seeing?"

"No two people see alike," Old Woman said. She took the last honeycake, which Sparrow had been eyeing, and ate it with considerable relish. Then she said, "I have to go away. I'll be gone three days, maybe four. You two will stay here and look after the goats. Have the shelter clean when I come back, and hunt a fat doe for me to dine on."

"Where are you going?" Sparrow demanded.

Old Woman smiled and rose and took up a bag that had been lying beside the shelter, reached into the woven branches that made the wall and slipped out a staff of polished wood, and left without another word.

Sparrow thought of pursuing her, but Old Woman would never answer a question she did not wish to answer. She might even be expecting Sparrow to follow her wherever she was going; something in her glance suggested it.

For that, and for no better reason, Sparrow stayed and did as she was told. It was peaceful without Old Woman about, though Keen professed to miss her stories. Keen did not ask where Old Woman had gone. She sat in the sunlight for most of the day, making a deerskin coat into a thing of beauty, while Sparrow tidied the camp and filled the stewpot with squirrel and young rabbit. Then Sparrow could lie in the sun, too, but with idle hands.

She watched Keen for a while, rapt as always at the way the other-sight saw her. It came to her that she might see other things so, as well. Goats were a lesser light, with a glint of wickedness. Birds in the trees were small bright sparks. Something larger and darker slipped through the wood, skirting the camp. Wolf, she thought. It woke no fear in her. It was autumn, when wolves were well fed. It was not winter yet, when, fierce in their hunger, they might bring down the weak of the People.

Smaller creatures fell silent as the wolf passed. Even the birds went still. All but one, a swift bird with a ruddy tail and blue-grey wings. A sparrowhawk, a kestrel, had come to hunt birds in the trees beyond the camp. Sparrow watched it idly, until her sight shifted again, and she saw it with the eyes of the spirit. It shone like the sun at noon, both beautiful and terrible.

For a moment. Then it was a swift grey-and-ruddy bird again, hunting lesser birds and bringing back its prey to its nest.

Her spirit took wing, not as a falcon, no, but as a small brown bird, the sparrow of her name. It was quick in flight, and could fly high, right up to heaven, and from there look down on Earth Mother's breast.

The lands south of the river were quiet. She saw camps of tribes,

herds both wild and tamed, a pride of lions stalking a herd of antelope, and a pack of wolves loping after the red deer. Here and there
people walked or rode, hunters, herdsmen, a trader with his laden
ox. Or—her? The trader was a woman, stripped to the waist in the
day's heat, with heavy breasts and broad belly.

Beyond the river was much the same. The tribes had returned to
their lands, to late-summer camps and hunting runs. She did not see
great crowds of them gathered near the river, nor was there any war
rising against the southward tribes. One raiding party slunk toward a
camp in the west of the world, wild young men with their eyes on
the camp's horses.

White Stone camp she did not see. Where it should have been
was shadow and confusion. A storm walked across the plain, veiling
the People in rain and blinding her with lightning. That was not
Walker's doing—he had no such power. But the gods were not inclined to let her spy on her father's people.

They sent her back to her body, a force like a hand closing about
her and carrying her away from the storm and the tribe. If she was
to know what they had done to win back their king of stallions, the
gods would reveal it in their good time.

She had not found Old Woman, either. She might have walked
right out of the world for all the sign Sparrow found of her. There
was a way, Sparrow thought, but she did not know it, nor did it
suggest itself to her. Veils that the gods had raised, she might not
presume to shift aside, but Old Woman was no god.

She came back into her body with a faint but penetrating shock,
as if she had fallen a little distance and struck earth abruptly. She lay
getting her breath back, and pondered veils and darkness, concealment and revelation, and the ways in which a shaman might provoke
an apprentice to learn in spite of herself.

Sparrow was not this shaman's apprentice, whatever Old Woman
might think. She sprang to her feet. She had to get out, away. She
needed to be on the mare's back under open sky, where her heart
was whole and her spirit strong.

✢ ✢

When Sparrow leaped up so suddenly, she startled Keen into stab-
bing her finger with the bone needle. Keen sat sucking her finger,
shaking her head as Sparrow found the mare beyond the goats' pen,
mounted her and rode off.

The stallion stayed, which was rather surprising. He liked the goats. They would play with him, he outside, they in their pen, leaping on their hindlegs and shaking their horns. Those horns were a threat, but he seemed not to mind, nor indeed did they: sometimes Keen saw a goat leaning against the wall of the pen, and the stallion stretching his elegant neck over, chewing happily on a horn.

When the mare left with Sparrow on her back, he called after her but did not follow. He had sweet fodder that Sparrow had cut that morning high up on the hill, and shade, and water to drink. He was as content as stallion could be.

"Pretty, isn't he?"

Keen started again. This time, fortunately, her needle was out of the way, her mind distracted by the stallion. She stared at Old Woman. "You didn't go away at all!"

"Wise child," Old Woman said. She sat in her customary place just outside the shelter, emptied her pouch of apples, and tossed one to Keen. Keen caught it without thinking. Old Woman cut up another with a flint knife, till it was small enough and soft enough for her few teeth.

Keen, whose teeth were strong, bit into the apple. It was ripe and sweet, an early delight; come full autumn, Old Woman had promised her, there would be a whole thicket of them.

It was none too pleasant to think of full autumn, because after it came winter, but in the warmth of late-summer sunlight, Keen could not trouble herself with it overmuch. She ventured to say, "You're teaching Sparrow. Would I be presumptuous to ask what she's supposed to be learning?"

"Presumptuous enough," Old Woman said, "but worthy of an answer nonetheless. She's learning to see the world for herself. And to cultivate manners."

"Not magic?"

"Manners are magic," Old Woman said. "They smooth the way for people in the world, and put an end to wars—or even prevent them from starting."

"Men don't want to prevent wars," Keen said.

"Men on the plains," said Old Woman. "They're different here."

"Really? I haven't met any."

Old Woman laughed. "And you would like to. They'd flock to you like flies to honey, with your sunlight hair and your sweet ways."

Keen flushed. She had not been thinking of that at all—oh no.

And yet Old Woman saw so clearly. Had she seen when Keen lacked wits to see?

Keen had a husband. He had treated her badly, but he had not put her aside, that she knew of. He most likely would not, either, if he found her. He would kill her first.

She was not afraid of it, not really, sitting here in the sunlight with Old Woman smiling at her. It was something that could happen, but not today, nor yet tomorrow.

And she had something else to think of. Someone else. This time she knew there was life growing inside her. She could feel it if she stopped and thought. It felt strong and bright and somehow joyous. That joy warmed her and made her happy, even in this strange country, far away from her kin.

Old Woman could always tell what she was thinking—and never failed to be amused by the way her mind kept wandering. "It's the baby," she said. "It makes you silly. But when it's born, you'll find a new father for the next one, yes you will. A handsome man and kind. He'll love you as you deserve."

Keen did not say that she deserved nothing. She had said that before, and Old Woman had rebuked her smartly for it. "You deserve everything a good woman deserves," she had said. And that was all she would hear of it, so that Keen learned to keep her modesty to herself.

Old Woman was teaching her, too, maybe even more subtly than she taught Sparrow. Keen could feel herself growing stronger in the spirit. Maybe she was braver, though that might be too fond a wishing.

Out of that bravery, if it existed, she asked, "Who are the people in this country? What are they like? Are they all like you?"

"They're like themselves," Old Woman answered.

"Are there any nearby?"

"Ah," Old Woman said wickedly. "You do want a man. How badly do you want one?"

"I don't—" Keen stopped. She did *not* want a man. But to see a tribe of these little dark people—to know what they were like— that, she wanted.

She sighed. "It's not wise, is it? We're strangers. I look like an enemy. People won't welcome me."

"You look like sunlight in a dark place," Old Woman said. "People will be delighted to welcome you. But not yet. You're not ready."

"Ready?"

"To face that world." Old Woman rose. She was agile when she wished to be, light on her feet like a much younger woman. "Remember, child: I didn't come back. I'll be returning from my great journey in three days, or maybe four."

She winked broadly. Keen smiled in spite of herself. That smile lingered even after Old Woman had gone, as she took up her needle again and threaded beads and went back to work on the coat that she was embroidering for Sparrow.

·········· 33 ··········

W HEN OLD WOMAN came back, Sparrow was away from camp again, sitting on a hill while the mare grazed nearby. She had been flying in the spirit, following the kestrel, shaping herself to its shape: handsome sharp-beaked face, swift wings. It had struck her that this hawk was a hunter of sparrows, and that for Sparrow to hunt the kestrel was an oddity to make a god smile.

She was smiling at it as she returned to her body, a smile that lingered in spite of itself—even as she saw who stood in front of her, leaning on a staff. To the eyes of the spirit Old Woman was invisible.

"Tell me how you do that," Sparrow said.

"What, walk the country?" Old Woman was not going to give her anything—unless she begged. And she would not beg.

Sparrow set her lips together. If Old Woman wanted to talk, Old Woman could talk. She would not trouble herself.

Old Woman stood without speaking, leaning on that length of smooth-rubbed wood. It had no ornament. The top of it was a burl, the base of the branch from which it had come, maybe, or the roots of the sapling it had been. It was much worn, with a sheen on it that spoke of long use.

It was a walking stick, a prop for her age, but there was something more to it. Sparrow reached to touch it. It did not writhe and turn into a serpent and bite her. It was wood, that was all, warmer than stone, denser than bone. Old Woman had grounded it in the earth. It was long since parted from its roots, and yet it still remembered. It was still, in a fashion, alive.

"Looking for magic?" Old Woman asked her.

"Is there anything to look for?"

"Answer a question with a question," Old Woman said. "Very good; you'll be a great shaman among certain of the tribes."

"Not my father's tribe," Sparrow said.

"Probably not," said Old Woman. "Though once the real shaman is dead and his apprentices weakened with fear, who's to say that some of them might not grow wise?"

Sparrow stiffened. "The real shaman? My father's still alive?"

"For a while," Old Woman said. "Until the dark of the year. Quite possibly longer, but his strength burns low."

"How do you know that? How do you know him?"

"Why," said Old Woman, "the same way I know you. I know."

"Does he know you?"

Old Woman grinned, baring her few blackened teeth. "Do you think he does?"

"I think," said Sparrow, "that even if he knew you existed, he wouldn't believe you."

"There," Old Woman said. "You see?"

What there was to see, Sparrow could not exactly determine. Old Woman was like this: odd, elliptical, infuriating. She was less like a shaman than like a trickster: one of those rare personages, quite hopelessly mad, who appeared sometimes among the tribes. The last one she had seen was a huge man, rampantly male, with a great brown beard and a pelt like a bear, who minced about in a fine deerskin tunic and insisted that he be called Flower of Perfect Beauty. He spoke prophecies, it was said, but so much of what he said was nonsense that there was no telling what was true and what was mad rambling.

Sparrow had found him pitiable and rather disgusting, with his crown of wilted flowers and his grease-encrusted beard. Old Woman was nothing of the sort. But she had that antic spirit, and that refusal to be bound by plain human reason.

"Child," said Old Woman, "as long as you think you know what you know, you will know nothing."

Sparrow stared at her.

"Empty yourself," Old Woman said. "Be a reed in the wind. Be the word the gods speak."

"How do I do that?"

"Beyond knowledge," Old Woman said, "you know."

+ +

Sparrow was ready to leave then: take the mare and the stallion and such belongings as they had, and go. But Keen would not budge. "I want to stay here," she said. "There's food, shelter. There's hope of living through the winter."

"It's months yet till the snow comes," Sparrow said. "We'll find a place—a place where people are sane."

"Old Woman is very sane," Keen said. "Saner than anybody."

"Old Woman is mad."

But Keen would not listen. She had finished one coat and was well embarked on the other. Sparrow jabbed a finger at it. "When that is done, we go."

"When Old Woman is ready for us to go, we go."

Sparrow had never seen that quiet strength in Keen before, that placid refusal to be moved. It was the baby making her stubborn, thought Sparrow. She wanted to stay in a place that she reckoned safe, even if a madwoman lived in it.

Old Woman had not spoken to her since those strange words on the hilltop. She was back in her place, doing what little she did now that she had two sturdy young women to keep the camp for her. For the most part she sat like a lizard on a rock, blinking in the sun. No doubt, Sparrow thought nastily, she was emptying herself—knowing nothing, seeing nothing, perceiving nothing.

She had been a shaman once. Her tribe had died. Now she was a solitary fool, witless and wandering, who had found two greater fools to look after her.

Not for long. Sparrow might wish it were summer still, but the days were growing short. The leaves were changing in the wood. The nights were not so warm now, the stars not so close. They were retreating to their winter eminence, to the cold heights.

Keen began to wax like the moon, her belly swelling, it seemed, overnight. There was no doubt now that she was carrying a child. She had that habit of bearing women, of resting her hand on the place where the child was, as if to assure herself that yes, it was there, growing inside her.

Because Keen would not go, they stayed. Sparrow hunted farther and farther afield, avoiding Old Woman and the camaraderie of the camp: the friendship between Keen and the shaman that felt, too often, as if they conspired against her.

There had been no tribes within a day's ride, but as winter drew in, Sparrow found signs that one of them was camped not so far away. Some of its hunters took a doe from a herd that she had been watching. She followed their track for a while, but her courage failed. She turned back. She did not want to meet these people, though they might be like her: small, dark, headstrong.

The chill rain of autumn fell on her as she rode toward Old Woman's camp. It was not yet edged with ice as it would be later, but summer's warmth was long gone from it. She was glad of the coat she was wearing, that she had made and Keen made beautiful, and of the bit of fire that she had thought to bring with her in a pot. Dark would fall far too soon for her to return tonight. She would camp in a place she had marked before, a hollow in a hillside like a shallow cave, where there was room enough for her and for the mare. She had water to drink, a brace of rabbits to eat. She was not at all displeased to be kept by the storm from going—not home, no. Back to the camp.

The mare might have been glad, too. She was in foal, not hugely as yet but she was as aware as Keen was of the life growing in her. Mares in foal, like some women with child, had no use whatever for males—and the stallion vexed her sometimes as thoroughly as Old Woman vexed Sparrow.

The cave was warm once Sparrow had lit a fire in it, and fragrant with the scent of roasting rabbit. The mare grazed for a while in the rain, then came in to be dry. Sparrow rubbed the rain out of her pale coat with the goatskin that had lain over the mare's back, spread the goatskin by the fire to dry, and fed the mare an apple from her bag. The mare would have been delighted to eat all that Sparrow had brought, but Sparrow pushed her questing nose away. "No, you don't! Those are for me."

The mare snorted in disgust, but forbore to press harder.

Sparrow ate her dinner and one of her apples, gave the mare another and put the rest away for the morning. The night was wet and cold, but she was as warm as she needed to be, out of the wind, with a fire and the mare and a full belly. She was content.

But something was niggling at her. She lay down to sleep on heaped grass, with the mare nibbling the edges, but sleep eluded her.

Empty yourself. Old Woman's voice, soft as wind in branches. *Be a reed in the wind. Be the word, but never the god who speaks it.*

Somehow, in this place, that made her think of Walker: his pride, his cruel spirit. His conviction beyond any doubt in his heart that despite lack of either gifts or vision, he was a shaman.

What was he doing without her? Was he inventing visions? How long would he succeed in that before he trapped himself in the web of his own lies?

Perhaps a very long time. Walker was clever. He knew how to make men listen to him. He was very, very skilled in forming alliances and playing on the trust—and mistrust—of princes.

Walker was full of so many things. Pride, insolence, surety of his own right to rule. All that he lacked was magic—the thing that made a shaman.

What was magic, then? Was that what Old Woman meant? Not emptiness, but emptying. Clearing the spirit. Letting it be like water in the sun: transparent, yet full of light.

Sparrow did not want Old Woman to make sense. But if she gave way to temper and to her dislike of that odd creature, she was no better than her brother. Of the two, she much preferred Old Woman. Old Woman might be mad, and she was certainly strange, but she was a shaman in truth. She was so full of magic, she had emptied herself clean away.

Sparrow sat up, hugging her knees. She was shivering, though the fire burned well and the mare's warmth was close by her. That was fear. Fear of what she had just understood.

She could not let go of her self. That self, proud and stubborn and headstrong though it was, was all that she had ever had, until the mare. If she let it go, what was left?

The mare sighed vastly and groaned and folded her legs, till she lay down beside the fire. She seemed so much smaller then, curled like a foal, with her nose tucked in her tail. And yet she was all that she had ever been, living goddess, queen of horses, powerful and holy.

Sparrow was no less terrified for knowing that. She gave herself into the mare's charge every time she mounted and rode. The mare had brought her here, had brought the stallion, had set in motion things that were barely even begun. War—it would be war, not before winter, but certainly before summer came again. The tribes would cross the river in search of the lost king.

And the mare willed it. She kept the stallion by her when she could have sent him back. She wanted this war, for reasons that Sparrow did not understand.

Sparrow was thinking too much, circling wildly, shying from the thing in the center. The emptiness. The singing silence.

If she touched it, she would be changed. How much or how little, she did not know.

She had done no less in answering the mare's call. This was ordained; had been since she was born. She could run away from it, but it would follow her. She could refuse it, but it would force itself upon her. She had no more will in this than a young stallion in the taming. She was caught, bound. The more she fought, the tighter her bonds became.

Empty yourself. So she did when her spirit flew free of her body; but something must fly free from the spirit itself. Self. Awareness. Resistance.

Be.

Simply be.

Clear water in a pool. Still, untroubled. Empty, and yet full of light.

White light. Light like the moon, the mare's light. Pure stillness, and pure essence. Knowledge beyond knowledge. Knowing as horses knew, deep in the bone, and not all on the surface as humans were.

Not working magic. *Being* magic. Becoming the visions, living them, reflecting them as water reflects the sky.

What she had seen before as shadows and fragments came all clear, all distinct, myriad and beautiful as the embroideries of her coat. They *were* the embroideries, thick over back and breast and sleeves, running along the hems, dancing among the fastenings. Keen, no shaman and yet as empty of self as shaman ever need be, had given living substance to all of Sparrow's foreseeings.

Wonder was a pure thing, untainted with self. So was love for that quiet woman, so unassuming and so modest, who had come so far and stayed with such contentment. She was the gods' vessel, too, Earth Mother's child, as Sparrow belonged to Horse Goddess.

Consciousness grew out of this, knowledge as deep as the blood, set strong in the bone. Sparrow lay curled tight against the mare's back, wrapped in her warmth, comforted by her smell, which was part sweet grass and part horsehide and part living earth. The mare slept as horses sleep, brief but very deep. Sparrow slid effortlessly into her dream. It was a simple dream, a horse dream: moonlight on snow and swift hooves flying, keen air in the lungs and keen joy in the heart, and no end to it ever, until she woke to the living world again.

·············· 34 ··············

OLD WOMAN DID not mock Sparrow with what should have been self-evident far sooner if Sparrow had been less intent on her own pride and her lack of manners. But neither was she inclined to praise Sparrow for what was, as she pointed out, the simplest and most essential beginning of true power.

"Shamans are shadows dancing on a tent-wall," she said. "They awe people with their tricks. But true power has nothing to do with chants and spells. True power *is*."

"I'll never understand it," Sparrow said.

"No need to understand," said Old Woman. "Just be."

And that was the hardest thing for Sparrow to do. Keen did it as she breathed, that simply, that easily. Sparrow was a restless creature, always up, always about, always doing this or that. To stop doing, to sit, to let be, was an art beyond her skill.

"So learn," said Old Woman, no more sympathetic than she had ever been.

Old Woman never taught lessons as such, nor did she undertake to teach Sparrow spells or rituals. As far as Sparrow could tell, her teaching consisted chiefly of exasperating her pupil into discovering certain things for herself. It was a strangely erratic method, nothing at all like the Grandmother's meticulous and daily lessons.

"You had those as a child," Old Woman said when Sparrow taxed her with it. "I won't call you a shaman yet, but you're rather more than a child."

"But how will I know when I'm a shaman?"

"You'll know."

Sparrow went away as frustrated as always. What she had discovered in the cave, she had thought would reveal everything; but when she woke fully, she was much the same as before. She understood a little more, that was all. She saw somewhat more clearly. She had learned to read the signs embroidered on her coat and Keen's, though what they meant was still for the most part dark to her.

One day between autumn and winter, the last truly warm day, Old Woman stopped Sparrow as she prepared to go out hunting. "Not today," she said.

Sparrow considered disobedience, but she was too curious. Old Woman had a pot in her hand, and a bundle.

"Strip," she said.

Sparrow stared at her.

"Take off your clothes," Old Woman said.

Sparrow's jaw set. Whatever this was, she wanted nothing of it.

Old Woman sighed in sorely taxed patience. She did not do anything, say anything, but before Sparrow knew what was happening, she was taking off her tunic and her leggings and standing naked in the sun. It was warm, but not as warm as that. She shivered.

Old Woman took no notice. She led Sparrow to her favored place outside the shelter, where she had spread a finely tanned hide. At first Sparrow thought it was cowhide, but the shape was subtly different.

When she lay on it, she knew. It was horsehide. She shuddered in her skin. Foolish—but she was enough of the People to know that only kings sat on horsehide, or lay on it as she was doing.

For an instant, with that sacred thing pressed against her bare skin, she was the horse, the fine grey mare whose hide this had been.

Pain brought her back to herself. The pot was dye, deep blue. The bundle held needles. Old Woman had pricked Sparrow's breast and set a drop of blue dye there.

Sparrow still had no power to resist. She lay, gritting her teeth till they ached, while Old Woman pricked swirling signs in her skin. They wound round her breasts and down her belly, spiraling above the thick black hair of her sex.

With the pain, as it went on, came not outrage but the same strange sensation that she had known in the cave—but greater. These signs, each one marked in tiny drops of blood, were like the opening of eyes to see. Breasts that in their time would swell with the milk of life, belly that would grow great with children, dark tangle of curls that guarded the opening of the womb—where a man would go, and set the seed that would grow into a living creature.

Old Woman took most of the day about it, working tirelessly, exactly, never wavering, never wandering astray. Sparrow surprised herself by sleeping a little, but mostly she lay in a kind of dream, open to the sun and the wind and the voice of Mother Earth beneath her.

As the sun sank low, Old Woman pricked the last intricate spiral. Sparrow's body stung, and yet it was not so much pain as a tingling, an awareness of something new, something powerful. She could move at last. She sat up gingerly, trying not to touch skin on skin. Old Woman put away the needles and lidded the pot, stood up and walked away without a word.

Sparrow had expected that. In any case she was not particularly minded to talk to anyone. She felt strange. She looked strange.

She still did not feel like a shaman. Only the painful beginning of one.

✦ ✦

Sparrow rode out the morning after Old Woman set the shaman-marks on her, put on her coat with flinching care, took the mare and went away. Old Woman did not seem dismayed, nor did the stallion, who was grazing high up on the hill. He lifted his head and called to the mare. The mare ignored him. He went back to cropping the sunburned grass.

"She'll be gone a while," Old Woman said. "And so will we. Come, child. We're going walking."

"Would you rather ride?" Keen asked, mindful of Old Woman's long labor the day before. She looked tired this morning, Keen thought; thin and a little transparent, though her voice was as strong as ever.

Old Woman shook her head. "We'll walk. Unless you're too tired?"

Keen almost laughed. Her belly was swelling, she could swear, from moment to moment, but she was as strong as she had ever been. She put on her coat, for the wind was brisk, and plaited her hair tightly, and took up the basket that Old Woman had filled with an interesting assortment of things. Old Woman had her own burden: a filled waterskin and a smaller basket, the contents of which Keen did not see.

So laden, in bright sun but, with wind, far colder than it had been the day before, they walked out of the camp. They followed the stream that watered the foot of the hill, until it led to a larger river, and then one still larger. This guided them for a goodly distance.

It was somewhat past noon when Keen saw what they must be going to: the smoke of campfires, and sounds so familiar her heart ached. Cattle lowing, a horse's whinny, human voices both deep and shrill.

There was a camp in the bend of the river, tents and branch shelters spread across a broad level. The herds grazed up and down the river, spotted cattle and flocks of goats, and not so very far from the camp itself, a herd of horses.

Keen regarded them in astonishment. There were duns and blacks and bays, but most of them were greys, like the royal herd of the People. Just like: sturdy, solid-footed horses with surprisingly elegant heads, and eyes that would meet hers if they caught her staring. Their stallion was the largest horse she had ever seen, a great white creature like a mountain of cloud.

She was glad then that they had left the king stallion at home with the goats. Royal he might be, but he was young, and by no means ready to challenge a stallion of such size and strength.

As they approached the camp itself, children came as children would in every camp, shouting greetings, calling to their elders that there were visitors—or so she supposed; she did not understand their language. They were small dark people as she had expected, with black curly hair and bright black eyes. Their elders were much the same, the women plump and full-breasted, with broad hips; the tallest men not even as tall as Keen, but thrice as broad, with heavy shoulders and thick black curly beards.

They all stared at her. To them she must have looked like a young birch-tree, tall and narrow and pale.

A woman strode toward them from among the rest, not the tallest or the broadest but easily the most imposing. Her greeting was in trader-tongue, her smile warm, welcoming Keen as well as Old Woman to the camp of the Grey Horse People.

It seemed she was, of all things, a king. A king who was a woman. Remarkable. Her tent was not particularly large; this was not a rich tribe. But it was comfortable and its appointments were of good quality, and the food and drink she offered were excellent. Children served them, dark-haired boys and bold-eyed girls, looking as if they were sore tempted to giggle when Keen looked at them. She must seem very strange, with her yellow hair and her blue eyes. One or two of them managed to touch her hair, trying to be unobtrusive, but she could hardly be unaware of them.

They made her smile. She had missed seeing children; how much, she had not known till she came here. Indeed it was like rain on dry land to see people again, even strangers with dark eyes and round brown faces. They all looked like Sparrow, after all.

Old Woman and the king spoke in trader-tongue, out of courtesy, Keen was sure. It seemed mostly to be talk of small things, the doings of the tribe, the weather, the state of the hunting. Keen ate roast venison and stewed roots and bread finer than any she had had before, and drank warm milk laced with honey, and listened in a kind of white contentment.

The tent's front was rolled up to let the light in and to let people passing by see who sat with the king. Many people did pass, too, with open curiosity. One came in, a young woman who sat and dipped from the pot and joined in the conversation as if she had every right to do that. Her name was Rain, Keen gathered. She was close kin to the king, and of high position—a shaman, or something like it. Keen was fascinated to notice that she was with child, round and rich like the moon, but she walked about as freely as a man, and made no effort to conceal herself in a tent.

Not long after Rain came, a man joined them. Like Rain, he acted as if he belonged there. He was young, perhaps no older than Rain, though it was not easy at first to tell: his beard was thick, and made him seem a man of some years. But his eyes were youthful, and the cheeks above the black curls. Keen tried to see the face under them, the broad cheeks and square jaw. It was Rain's face, strengthened into a man's, she decided: not outrageously beautiful but distinctly good to look on, and warmed by those bright dark eyes.

He had caught her staring. She flushed and looked away, but she could not help herself: she glanced quickly back. He was smiling at her. There was no mockery in it, only warmth.

All sense and courtesy would have bidden her lower her eyes and keep them there, but his smile was irresistible. She had returned it before she thought.

He left the others, who went on talking as if he had not done anything remarkable, and came to sit beside her. She could not shift away without seeming terribly rude. He at least did not press too close. A man of the People, seeing such a bold stare as hers, would have been either terribly offended or unsuitably attracted; and she had not meant to do it at all.

He certainly was not offended. He did not try to rape her where she sat, or to kiss her either; in fact he offered nothing improper except his presence. "A fair day to you," he said in a lovely deep voice. It turned the trader-tongue to rolling music.

"And to you," she murmured, almost too late for politeness. Her cheeks were hot. Except for Wolfcub and her father, and Walker after he chose her for his wife, she had spoken to few men, and never in such circumstances. Would he be thinking that she was a wild woman, free for the taking?

"My name is Cloud," he said. "Old Woman calls you Keen-Wind-in-the-Grasses. Yes? That's a lovely name."

"I thank you," she said, more faintly even than before.

There was a silence. It was terribly uncomfortable. Keen wished she could leave, but he sat between her and the tentflap. She would have to climb over him to escape.

Then he said, "It must be terribly dull to sit here listening to gossip of people you've never met. Would you like to see the camp?"

Keen started to shake her head, to decline, but Old Woman said heartily, "Yes! You go, child. Cloud will bring you back when it's time."

They were all smiling and nodding, as if it were nothing improper at all for a man to play host to a woman not his wife. Cloud had risen and drawn her to her feet before she could say a word, holding her cold hand in his warm strong one, and leading her out like a child.

When they were in the sun, Keen slipped her hand from his, as politely as she could. He did not seem offended. In a cloud of curious children, they walked through the camp.

It was a small tribe, and not rich, but it had enough to eat this season. No one was sick. The animals were in good flesh, the young ones lively, and there were a good number of them, cattle and goats and horses. Even the camp dogs were not remarkably ribby, and more than a few of them seemed to have places beside fires or near tents.

It was a warm place, Keen thought, like the man who led her through it. He was the king's heir; not that he said so, but the way people spoke to him, and the air he had of pride in these people and of concern for their welfare, told her clearly what he was. They paused more than once to meet this person or that: a woman weaving grass

mats, a man making a pot of rolled clay. They were all gravely courteous.

And none seemed surprised to see her, though her bright hair
made them stare. Keen might not have dared to ask, but Cloud was
a comfortable companion—almost too much so. Before she had
thought, she said, "Everybody seems to know who I am."

Cloud smiled. She rebuked her heart for leaping when he did
that; he had a wonderful smile, that lit his whole face and sank deep
in his eyes. "We all know about Old Woman's guests. Everyone is
delighted to meet you finally. It's been a struggle to keep the children
from running off and doing it themselves."

"I would wager," Keen said, "that some of them have been spying
on us for days."

"A few of them have," he admitted. "So you knew?"

She shook her head. "It's what I would be tempted to do."

He laughed. It was infectious: Keen found herself smiling. He
blinked as if dazzled. "You should smile more often," he said.

She bit her lips and looked away.

"There," he said in quick regret. "I've insulted you."

She should have kept quiet and found a way to escape, but he
was so contrite and so troubled that she said, "You haven't insulted
me. It's only—I don't know how to talk to a man. We don't learn,
you see. I had a friend, he was like a brother, but when I grew up
and married, we weren't supposed to be friends any longer."

"That is sad," Cloud said.

"It is the way it is."

"Not here." He slanted a glance at her. "How horrified would
you be if I told you that you are beautiful?"

She must have been blushing scarlet: her cheeks were afire. "A
man never tells a woman such a thing! Unless—"

"Unless?" he asked when she did not go on.

"Unless he has . . . intentions."

"Wicked ones? Kindly ones?"

"Wanton ones."

"Well," he said, "I do. But only if you share them."

"Oh!" It was a gasp, trying hard not to be laughter. She was not
supposed to laugh at such terribly wicked words. And yet the way he
said them, the brightness of his eyes under the strong black brows,
the smile just revealing itself through his handsome curly beard, made
her want to do and say things that were absolutely improper.

And she a married woman with a child in her belly. Men were not supposed to see such things, but he would have to be blind not to mark the shape of her. Did it not matter to him?

He was certainly aware of his own attractions. Those were considerable. He walked like a stallion, light and proud, and with the same conviction that the world was made for his pleasure. And, even more, that he was made for women's pleasure.

She had not met a man like him before. Among the People, men were either properly restrained or given to falling on women without regard for honor or civility. A man who looked on a woman with frank desire, but did not leap on her immediately thereafter, was unheard of. And for him to say as much—outrageous.

Worse, she did not turn her back on him and stalk away. She stayed, there on the edge of that alien camp, and let him admire her. She knew she was beautiful, she had always been told so. Her hair was yellow, her eyes deep blue; her face was pleasing to men's eyes.

But these eyes were more direct than any that had ever rested on her, even her husband's. Walker had looked at her often, but never entirely seemed to see her. She was a face to him, a form, a pair of eyes. This man saw beneath them. His warmth touched her heart.

"You will always be welcome here," he said in that soft deep voice. "Remember."

"Honorably welcome? And not only because you want me in your bed?"

That was breathtakingly bold and awesomely rude, and it seemed to come from someone else altogether; but that was her voice speaking. He only smiled. "In all honor," he said, "though if you were to invite me to your bed, I would never refuse."

······· 35 ·······

ESTREL KNEW HE was healed when he went out to hunt the morning after Rain lay with him, and the hunt kept him out through the night and into the next day; and when he came back, he had been gone three days and the people of the Grey Horse were beginning to fret. But he had a fine buck to show for it, a pack of doeskin laden with dried meat of the doe, enough to feed the whole of the king's family for a fair few days.

"We thought you'd gone away completely," Rain said. She accosted him soon after he came back, as he had both expected and dreaded. He had devoted the days to his hunt, but in the nights he had reflected long on her, and on Cloud who was her lover but not her husband, and on the ways of men and women among these strange people.

Yes, he had thought of walking on and on till there was no hope of returning to the Grey Horse. But he owed them something for the saving of his life. And he owed Rain—something. Or she owed him. He went back, and faced her unflinching, even though she might be angry.

She did not seem to be that. She was glad, oh yes, and she had fretted: there was a hint of strain about her eyes. It eased as she looked at him. In front of anyone who could see, there by her mother's tent, she stood high and high, on very tiptoe, and drew his head down and kissed him.

It was quick, no more than a brush of lips, but it shook him almost to his knees. "Next time," she said, "don't walk away like that. Tell someone where you've gone."

"The king knew," he said. "I saw her when I went out. She gave me her blessing."

That took Rain aback. Kestrel's pleasure in her startlement was not altogether praiseworthy, but it was rare enough, and striking enough, that he did not care.

"She never told *me!*" she said in considerable pique.

"Should she have?"

"Oh!" she said. "You're as bad as she is."

He grinned. "I thank you," he said.

She hissed at him, wheeled and stalked away.

Kestrel sighed when she was gone, suddenly as weak in the knees as if he had just risen from his bed. He was glad to seek the refuge of his tent, and find no woman there, but clean furs waiting, and bread and goat-cheese and a skin of *kumiss.* He ate well and drank sparingly, contemplated the furs, decided to rest but not sleep. He was not tired. The hunt had been good, the air clean. He was himself again, no weakness left; or none that mattered. It would be a while before his side stretched as it should, or the stitch of pain left his ribs.

He was well enough. He stripped out of the clothes he had worn since he left, wrapped himself in his lionskin, and set to taking his hair out of its plaits and combing it. It was simple labor, empty of thought, close to sleep but not yet over the edge of it.

In the middle of it he gained an audience. Children here were given to going wherever they pleased. Their elders did little to quell them. They could even wander into great rites and high holy things, if they were quiet and did not interrupt with questions. Nor did it matter if they were male or female; they were all treated alike.

These were three who were given to following him about. The eldest was a girl, and of the royal clan, though whether she was Rain's sister or Storm's daughter, Kestrel had not yet determined. The other two were boys, much shyer and quieter than the girl, and overwhelmingly in awe of the stranger from far away.

Time was when he would have undertaken to drive them out, but that, he had learned, only brought them creeping back as soon as he relaxed his guard. He sighed therefore and endured, and went on with what he was doing.

After a while the girl said, "Will you teach us to hunt?"

Kestrel blinked. Not because the question was startling; because, as tired as he was, it had taken him back to another place and another tribe. A young and solitary Wolfcub was stalking shadows through the tall grass, hunting them down and killing them with the bow his father had given him. He was not very good at it, at all, but he was inordinately proud of such skill as he had.

Until a clear voice said, "You couldn't hit the side of a hill if it stopped and waited for you."

He whipped about. He had never heard that voice before, but he recognized the owner of it: the shaman's dark-eyed daughter, the one whose mother had been a captive from a long way away. She did not play with the other children. Wolfcub had thought it might be because she was different, but maybe it was for the same reason he kept mostly to himself: he simply preferred his own company.

He faced her as a man was supposed to face a woman, standing tall and glaring down at her. He did rather well, he thought, until she laughed at him. That made him forget dignity and snap, "I suppose *you* know how to shoot a bow."

"Not a bit," she said. "You could teach me. Then when I'm better than you, I'll show you how to do it."

The logic of that was perfectly preposterous. And even if it had made sense, Wolfcub resorted to the fundamental truth. "You won't ever be better than me. You're a girl."

"What does that have to do with it?"

"Everything!"

She snorted. "Show me how to shoot. Then I'll show you."

Because she was so stubborn, and so determined that she was right, he did teach her. And she did surpass him. Worse: another child wandered into one of their lessons, picked up the bow while they were squabbling over the fletching of an arrow, fitted one of the disputed arrows to the string, and put it neatly through the target they had both been missing by a notable distance. That was Keen, escaped from her doting mother, drawn by the sound of their voices to discover that she had a better eye and a greater gift for the bow than either of them. In the end she taught them both, though without seeming to understand what she was doing. She simply knew: how to stand, how to nock, how to release.

Wolfcub, grown into the man called Kestrel, wondered if any of these children would prove as gifted as Keen had been. Likely not. But he would not refuse to teach them either. "Tomorrow," he said. "Today I'm tired. I need to rest."

"You can sleep," the girl said. "We'll watch."

"You could go away," he suggested, "and come back in the morning."

"We'd rather stay here," she said. "Do you want us to be quiet? We'll be quiet. Or we could sing. Skimmer loves to sing. Don't you, Skimmer?"

The shyer of the boys ducked his head and mumbled into his tunic. The girl understood him, apparently. She glowered at him. "Of course he won't laugh! Sing him the song your mother taught you, the one about the trees."

Kestrel sighed and resigned himself to being entertained. He could lie down for that, at least, and be comfortable. The child did have a lovely voice, such as some boys had before they grew into men: clear, true, and piercingly sweet. The song was in the language of the tribe, which he was learning, a little, but not enough to understand more than that it was about a hunter in a wood. There was a lion, or maybe a bear, and nightfall, and sleep; but beyond that, he could not tell. Maybe the hunter sang the bear to sleep, then slept himself.

Kestrel was not quite ready to follow, though he closed his eyes and let himself drift. The song ended. The children conversed quietly in the way of children here. Some of it he caught. Tomorrow's hunt, and what they would learn. The venison they would eat for dinner tonight—and maybe tomorrow night, too, if they became mighty hunters. Visitors who had come while Kestrel was away, very important people, a shaman or great worker of magic and, it seemed, the shaman's apprentice. They were much enthralled with that one. He was too close to sleep then to listen harder, or to wonder why. It was nothing that mattered to him.

36

WINTER CAME SOMEWHAT more gently here than it did north of the river. The rolling green country and the thickets of trees broke the wind, and the rain was a little softer. But when the cold and the snow came, they came fast and hard.

They bound Sparrow to Old Woman's camp, where all had been made ready for them. There was ample food stored in the shelter, fodder for the horses and goats until they could go out again to forage, and the shelter itself was made larger with Keen's and Sparrow's labor, till it held the three of them in comfort, and the horses, too.

Old Woman at first seemed much as she always had. But as the cold went on and the snow deepened with storm after storm, even to Sparrow's less than loving eye it seemed that she was not as strong as she had been. She slept longer, rose later, spoke less.

So too did Keen, but Keen was swelling with the child; in her it was strength. In Old Woman it was a clear fading. Sparrow had seen it before. The old could die at any time of the year, but winter was most bitter for them. The Grandmother had died in winter, in much the same way, though it seemed she had gone much more slowly. Old Woman was like a dry stick in the fire, flaring swiftly into ash.

She did not slow or stop her odd oblique teaching for that. The brief stormridden days and long cold nights were made for turning the spirit inward. Sparrow traveled far within, and far without as well, riding the winds of the world. Sometimes Old Woman flew near her, a presence sensed but not seen. Her spirit was growing stronger as her body weakened. Death for her would be triumphant, a soaring into light.

She was eager for it. She had lived a long, long time; had outlived a tribe, and lived past the deaths of any who had been born the year she was born. She was ready to cast off the outworn skin and fly free.

But she did not go. She clung to life and breath, as little as that was. Keen particularly, but Sparrow too, made her as comfortable as they could, kept her wrapped in furs, kept the fire burning well and tried to tempt her with warm herb-possets and goat's milk laced with honey. What she would not eat, which was most of it, Sparrow forced on Keen—"For the baby," she said when Keen resisted. Keen would obey then, though not willingly.

The dark of the year came upon them. That year was a Great Year: when new moon and longest night were one and the same. Even without priests to count the days and reckon the moon's phases, she knew when it came. It was in her blood and bone, deep as the breath she drew.

With the moon's waning, Old Woman waned, too. Night by night she sank lower. The night before the new moon, she seemed nearly to have stopped breathing, but when the sun rose, she revived a little. Enough to say to Sparrow who was stirring the last of the honeycomb into the milk that she had taken from one of the she-goats a few moments before: "You, rude child. Come here."

Sparrow was startled enough at the sound of that voice, faint and fading as it was, to do as it bade her. Old Woman's eyes were almost as bright as ever, seeing far too clearly through all her pretensions. "I never did teach you manners," Old Woman said. "But that's no matter now. I'll die tonight, in the moon's dark. Be sure you stay awake and watch me go. And when I'm gone, there is that which you must do."

Sparrow frowned. "Do you think I'll fall asleep, then?"

"You'll be tempted. Don't give in to it. You have to watch. And then you have to do as I tell you. Do it exactly. Do you understand?"

"Tell me what it is," Sparrow said.

Old Woman told her. Sparrow listened in horror. When the dry and dying voice had gone silent, she said, "I can't do that."

"You can. Because you must."

"But—"

"I don't matter, child. Not any longer. You need this. Therefore you will do it."

"*Why* do I need it?"

"Always the questions," Old Woman sighed. "Always 'Why?' Child, when it's done, you will know."

"You said that of my being a shaman. When I was one, I would know. But I never have!"

"Yes," Old Woman said. And with that, maddeningly, she slipped back into her long dream. Nothing that Sparrow did or said could rouse her.

+ +

Keen wanted to stay. But Old Woman had made it clear: she was not to be part of this thing that had been laid on Sparrow. It was a mild day, for winter; the sun was almost warm. She took the stallion as Old Woman had instructed, and rode off eastward. There was a tribe camped at only a little distance, Old Woman said. The people there would welcome her and look after her.

Sparrow did not like that any better than Keen did. "You'd entrust her to strangers?" she had demanded of Old Woman.

"Not strangers," Old Woman said. "They know me, and know of my guests. She'll be more than safe with them."

Sparrow had to accept that, as Keen did, because Old Woman was firm. It was to be done just so. Neither of them was given a choice.

Therefore, in the morning, Keen rode away. The stallion carried her gladly, with understanding of his duty. Sparrow would have preferred that the mare do that, too; but the mare must stay. She was part of the rite that loomed ahead of Sparrow.

There were preparations. Sparrow made them. They did not take long enough; the day still stretched interminable. Old Woman lay like a banked fire, the life in her sinking low.

At long last the sun set. It was a mild night for winter, but with an edge of frost. The stars were high and very far away. By their cold faint light, Sparrow lifted Old Woman in her arms, finding her as light as a bundle of sticks, and carried her out of the shelter.

The mare was waiting, a white glimmer in the starlight. Sparrow laid Old Woman over the white back and held her there. The mare stepped softly under that fragile weight, picking her way through the snow, climbing to the summit of the hill.

It was a low hill, but the stars had granted it some of their lofty height. The world seemed to spread beneath it, a pattern of signs and images like the embroidery of Sparrow's coat. She stood beside the mare on the hilltop and eased Old Woman's limp light body down. It was alive, but the life clung to it by a thread. She laid it gently in the snow. It was beyond cold and beyond fear. She, who was neither, still was taken somewhat out of herself. Such cold and fear as she felt were remote, and therefore bearable.

She was the mare's chosen, Horse Goddess' child. She was high priestess of a rite that had not been seen in the world before, a new rite, terrible and holy. There in the dark of the moon, under the winter stars, she sang the words that came to her, words as high and cold and sweet as the stars' own singing. She called on Horse Goddess and Earth Mother and the gods of death and rebirth. She invoked the mare, and the life that swelled within the mare. And finally, kneeling in the snow, she bowed low before the old woman, the shaman of the lost tribe, the firstmother of this new order that was made flesh in her.

She bowed in deep respect, and in admiration, too; and if not in love, then in more esteem than she had ever thought to feel for that rough-spoken, ungentle creature. For they were very like—as like as kin, whatever the truth of that might have been. They had, in their way, been as grandmother and granddaughter. What the Grandmother had begun, Old Woman had completed.

So it was done. She drew the knife that Old Woman had bidden her take, long and wicked, with a strange black blade and a haft of polished bone. Singing, wordless now, a long, high keen, she performed the sacrifice. She severed the thread that bound spirit to body.

The body lay still and cold. The spirit soared up, matching the note of her song, swelling it, till it rang in the sky.

The silence that fell thereafter was enormous, and bore still a memory of sound. In it, with steady hand, she took the heart from the still breast and the liver from the belly. She offered them up to the gods. In their name, and by Old Woman's firm command, she ate of each: heart for knowledge, liver for spirit. They were warm and rich with blood—richer than she would ever have expected.

In blood was life. It drained out over the snow, black in starlight. She bowed low again, with the taste of blood in her mouth. Old Woman's command had been strict. She had no choice but to follow it. As if the body had been the carcass of a deer, she gutted and flayed it, stripped flesh from bones, and made a great offering of the flesh. She set it in fire that she had prepared on the hilltop, a tall pyre of cured wood that Old Woman had set aside in a hidden place, lit it from the hearthfire, so that it blazed up to heaven.

But the bones she kept, polishing them till they were white and clean. In bright firelight she buried them in the grave that she had dug that day, laying them with care as if they had been the bones of a king. She covered them with the hide of a white mare, a mighty thing and holy: first of the white mares that had been in the world, foaled when Old Woman was young, in the grim spring after her people were destroyed. She had been Old Woman's hope and her salvation. She had died at a great age, in the herd of her children and grandchildren, all of them greys as she was, sires and dams of greys, a whole royal race from whom Sparrow's own mare had sprung.

And now her hide covered Old Woman's bones. They needed no other shroud, and no greater treasure.

But the globe of the skull, Sparrow did not bury. When she had raised the cairn over Old Woman's bones, that remnant lay waiting, unburned and unburied. Grey dawn shone on it. The fire had died to embers and ash.

Sparrow bowed to the corpse of the fire, and deeper to the cairn in which lay the bones, but deepest of all to the skull, the clean white bone still faintly tinged with the rose-sheen of blood. She took it up in her hands, turned and carried it down from the hill, as the sun rose full in her eyes.

✦ ✦

She made a cup of the skull, as men did with the heads of their enemies. Three days she labored over it. She scoured it and polished it. She inlaid it with stones as Old Woman had instructed her, such stones as she had not seen before, blue as the summer sky. With the black knife she carved a winding spiral pattern, the same as that which wove round about her breasts and belly, and colored it with soot from the bonfire and with red ocher that was almost as bright as blood.

And all the while she did this, Old Woman's spirit watched, hovering above her, offering acid commentary. It was no more gentle than it had been in life, and no more complimentary, either. And yet, perhaps because it was freed of the flesh, it could not deceive Sparrow as it had done before. She could sense its approval, however grudging and however well hidden. Old Woman was pleased, though she loathed to admit it.

On the third day the cup was complete, or as much so as Sparrow could make it. It was a beautiful thing, a terrible beauty, like the rite that had made it. When she lifted it in her hands, she could feel the power pooling in it. Sunlight poured into it like water, filling it, brimming over.

She carried the cup to the stream that ran through Old Woman's camp. The water was icy cold and very swift. It filled the cup quickly, mingling with the sunlight. Sparrow, kneeling by the bank, lifted it up to sun and sky—and yes, to Old Woman's spirit that hovered still—then lowered it to her lips and drank.

It was like drinking winter, pure and cold, and yet sun's warmth was woven in it. It turned her blood to ice and then to fire. It pooled in her belly. There in her center, the rite was complete: heart and liver, blood and bone.

With a sigh that seemed half exasperation, Old Woman's spirit took wing at last, arrowing into the sun. And yet it left a part of itself behind, as a bird might: a feather of living light. It drifted gently down into the cup, and there rested, melting and flowing, till it had vanished into the cleansed and polished surface.

The cup was alive in her hands. She could feel the warmth in it, the presence that would not leave it now, not till the cup itself was broken and its fragments ground to powder.

Which will happen, said a voice in her mind, a voice very like Old Woman's, *when you die yourself, and your successor makes of your skull a new cup.*

But that would not be soon, if she survived the war that was coming. She set the thought aside, and the cup, too, wrapping it in soft doeskin and concealing it among the belongings in the shelter. Old Woman's shelter—hers now, if she chose to stay. Or she could go. She was free. She was, by every rite, a shaman.

"I still don't *know* that I am one," she said.

Somewhere perhaps, Old Woman ground her few teeth in frustration. But Sparrow could not lie to herself, or to Old Woman either.

The power that was in her, that she had drunk from the cup, still needed something to be whole. Time, maybe. Wisdom. Patience. Patience above all, one of the many virtues which Sparrow signally lacked.

·········· **37** ··········

KEEN RODE INTO the camp of the Grey Horse People on the back of a black-and-silver stallion who had been a king once and perhaps would be a king again. There were people waiting for her: Storm, Rain, and Cloud standing behind them. At sight of him, all without her willing it, her heart leaped.

They welcomed her warmly, handed the stallion to eager children for tending, took her to Storm's tent and fed her and made much of her. For all her worry and her grief, her fear for Sparrow and her sorrow that Old Woman was dying and she could not be there, she felt as if she had come home.

It was a strange feeling, because it was so unexpected. These were not her people. They looked nothing like her. She did not speak their language, though they were pleased enough to speak the trader-tongue that they had in common. And yet they were honestly glad to see her, and clearly happy to be entrusted with the care of her. She had never been so welcome among her own kin. The People reserved such effusions for sons, never for daughters.

She tried, guiltily, not to be content, nor to be comfortable. Sparrow would be neither, keeping the deathwatch over Old Woman, and then doing what must be done thereafter. Exactly what that was, she did not know. She did not want to know. But it could not be anything easy or pleasant. Great magic never was. She was—had been—a shaman's wife. She knew.

But it was warm here, in the heart as in the body. No one asked where Old Woman was. They knew. They grieved for her; she had been a great shaman of this country, much admired and even loved. But it was her time. If she did not go, she would defy the gods; and that would be a great ill thing.

Keen had no duties here. Tomorrow she would ask to be given somewhat to do. Today she was content to rest, and to stitch at the swaddling she was making for the baby. The camp's life went on around her, preparing for the rite that would greet the sunset: the ritual and sacrifice of the dark of the year. It was not as great as among her people—this was a poor tribe, and focused too on sun and earth, so that the rites of spring and fall and the brief night of midsummer were greater to them than this. But they had their priests and their procession, their fire built high against the dark, and their sacrifice, a black goat offered to the spirits of night and the world below.

Or so Cloud told her, sitting by her in the long and wonderfully mild afternoon. "Aren't you a priest?" she asked him. "Shouldn't you be preparing?"

"Oh, no," he said. "This is a women's rite. I offer the Bull at midsummer, and dance with Earth Mother's daughter in the spring. Autumn is for the old men, and winter for the women who are elders, and for my mother, who is queen and shaman."

"And your clan-sister?"

He nodded. "I'm not needed at all, nor am I wanted. Time was when as male and heir both, I would have been kept in my tent, lest my presence bring ill luck to the rite."

"Truly?" Keen asked, surprised. "That's how it is for women among the People, for all the great sacrifices."

"*All* of them?"

"We weaken them, you see. Because our spirits are so feeble."

He snorted like a startled horse. "That is outrageous! And you believe it?"

"It's the gods' command."

"Not our gods." He shook his head. "Women are strong. To bear and give birth to a child—there's no battle more terrible, and no courage greater. To call you weak . . . what, are your men blind?"

"We are weak," Keen said. "We can't fight as well, run as fast. We're not brave, or strong in battle."

He did a terribly improper thing: he laid his finger on her lips. It was warm and very light. "Hush," he said as if to a child. "Don't say such things. Don't believe them."

"They are true."

"Not here," he said.

She sat still. He had reclaimed his hand, to her deep and alto-gether unwilling regret. She would not touch him in turn. She refused. Though her fingers yearned to discover if his beard was as crisp as it looked, or if it was soft. Though her body would have loved to lean toward him, to rest in his warmth.

She had never felt such things for a man before. Walker had aroused her, had made her eager for his touch. But she had never wanted so simply to be near him, to be there because he was there. Walker came to take her as a man takes a woman, and she had submitted gladly to the taking.

She wanted to take this man. To be bold as a man was. To go to him and take him in her arms and love him. Even with the child between—the child that her husband had set in her.

It was terrible, this wanting. It tormented her. It made her loins ache, and set the child to stirring restlessly, protesting the tightness in her middle.

She was both glad and sorry when a child came with a message from Cloud's mother, bidding him go on some errand that had to do with the sacrifice. He seemed to regret the need to go; but he could hardly disobey his queen.

The child who had fetched him lingered, perhaps on the queen's orders. It was a girlchild, very bold in her expression, with a pair of smaller, male shadows. She amused herself for a while in watching Keen stitch at her baby-clothes. But soon, bored, she wandered off, followed by one of the boys. The other lingered, hanging back as if he worked up the courage to do something.

All at once, and quickly, he did it: he touched the long bright plait that hung over her shoulder. He horrified himself with his bravery. In the light of her smile, like a startled rabbit, he ducked and spun and fled.

She was still smiling when the currents of the camp, which had been more or less aimless, gathered and focused. She thought, as she watched, that perhaps the rite had begun, though it was well before sunset.

But it was nothing of the sort. It was an arrival in camp, a hunting-party coming back with wherewithal for the night's feast. Keen did not need to go out to see what they had brought: they came toward the queen's tent, bearing two nobly antlered stags and a young bear. It was a splendid hunt, she could see, and a great omen for the rite.

The hunters laughed and sang, and some danced, beating on drums and shaking rattles. It was an oddly bright music for the dark of the year, but fitting in its way. It suited the pale sunlight and the almost-warmth of the day, and helped a little to hold back the dark.

The center of the dance, the lord of hunters, came last into her sight as she sat by the tentflap. She had been expecting some great black-bearded bear of a man. But the one who strode long-legged among the shorter, darker, thicker tribesmen and—yes—women, was as lean as a yearling wolf. His hair was ruddy brown, his beard sparse, nothing like the thick black beards of even the young men.

He was so familiar that at first she did not know him at all. He belonged in another world, that had nothing to do with this one.

And yet even her shock could not long evade the truth. Her lips moved, shaping his name. *Wolfcub.*

He had not seen her. He was in the sunlight, she in the tent's dimness. People crowded about him, as she remembered they had been doing among the People: solitary Wolfcub, as he grew into a man, had become a man whom people yearned to follow.

He was more comfortable with it here than he had been in that other place. He was older, too, and thin as a sharpened blade. Pain had etched his face, so that if she had not known how young he was, she might have thought him a man full grown.

People were calling to him, and he was answering. They did not call him Wolfcub. They called him something—Kestrel?

Yes, they had named him after the sparrowhawk. Her heart paused a beat at that, and knew a small, cold stab of something quite like fear.

It did not have to mean anything. And yet, what was he doing here? How had he come here, and why, if he was not hunting Sparrow and the silvermaned stallion?

He must be alone. She had seen no others of the People anywhere.

Then maybe he had come because he could not bear to be parted from Sparrow. Sparrow did not know, or even guess, what she was to this man; but he loved her with all his heart. Keen had always known it. She had been jealous of it when she was younger, because Wolfcub loved her, but not as he loved Sparrow. She was his dear friend and his heart's sister. Sparrow was his heart and soul.

Yes, that was why he was here. Keen was sure of it. He was a great tracker. He had followed Sparrow, but had elected not to show himself to her. Probably he was wise. Sparrow would be very angry if she knew that he had left Linden, and his honor among the People, to run in her wake.

But it was utterly like him. Wolfcub was so named because he went where he would, and often alone.

Keen sat quietly in the queen's tent. He was coming toward it, or trying to; people kept stopping him. They wanted to talk to him, smile at him, touch him. She saw how he was about it: a little uncomfortable, and not greatly inclined to seek it, but gracious enough if there was no escaping it. He would, she thought, have made a rather presentable king. Kings were solitary, too, after all; set apart from their people.

He would have been appalled to hear her say that. She smiled at the thought.

It was her smile that he must have seen first as he stooped to come into the tent. For an instant she wondered if she had indeed said what she was thinking: for he regarded her in pure horror. But she had not said a word.

When she did speak, it was warmly, in some hope of reassuring him. "Wolfcub," she said. "Oh, I'm glad to see you well!"

"Keen," he said with no warmth at all. But that he knew her name, he might have been a stranger. "How did you come here?"

"I was sent," she said—biting her tongue on the first answer that came to her: *I rode.* A woman did not, must not ride. Not if she would remain among the People.

"And—the other?"

"You don't know?"

He went stark white. "She's dead." She thought his knees might buckle, he looked so suddenly feeble; but though he swayed, he stayed on his feet.

"Not dead," Keen hastened to assure him. "No, she's very much alive. But—"

He wheeled. Keen had seen the woman coming: the young shaman, whose name, she recalled, was Rain. He must have heard her. He flung his words in her face. "You knew!"

Rain did not seem dismayed, even before the blaze of his anger. "Knew what?" she asked, reasonably enough in Keen's estimation.

"You knew about this!" He stabbed his hand toward Keen.

Rain lifted a brow. "What, that Old Woman had guests? Everybody's known that since summer. I thought you knew."

"You never told me *who* those guests were."

"Should I have?"

He sucked in breath as if to bellow at her.

She spoke calmly through that sharp, furious hiss. "Kestrel, my dear and headlong beloved, while I can gather that this woman is someone you know, I can hardly have been expected to have foreknowledge of that. I'm a shaman, not a god."

"You knew," he said, "that there were two women from north of the river in this country. Surely, if you had been thinking—"

"When I troubled to think about it at all," she said, "I thought that you knew already, and it was no matter to you."

"I don't believe you."

She shrugged. She was calmer than Keen would have been in the face of such breathtaking rudeness. "Then don't believe it. Don't tell me, either, why you're so completely out of your head over this. I don't think I care to know."

Keen watched her turn and stalk away. Wolfcub, or Kestrel as he seemed to be now, refused. He glared at Keen instead.

"I think," she said mildly, "that you have a story to tell. Why not sit here and drink some of this goat's milk—the honey in it is very good—and tell me how you came to this country."

He was not listening. Nor, clearly, was he in any mood to be reasonable. "She's not dead? Then where is she?"

Keen had to pause for a moment, to remember what they had been speaking of before Rain appeared. "Sparrow is with Old Woman."

Kestrel stared blindly at her. "With the shaman? Tonight? That must mean—"

"Kestrel!" That caught his attention, at least. "You can't go running after her. Not now."

"Why not?"

"Because," Keen said, "you are not a shaman, and she is."

"But she can't be—"

"In this country she can."

For some reason that stopped him, and brought him somewhat to himself. "This country . . ." He rubbed hands over his face, raking them down his cheeks. "Oh, gods. Oh unmerciful gods."

He was gone before she could call him back, whirling, running away from her. She could not think what to do, except that it would not be wise to follow him. She stayed therefore, with her stitching forgotten in her lap, and thoughts waking in her that she did not want, no, not at all.

38

KESTREL HAD NOT been kind to Keen, or even polite. Nor should it have mattered, after what she had done; but he was all in a roil. He ran blindly through the camp, ignoring people who called after him, and children and dogs who followed till their elders called them back. He had no goal in mind, but his feet bore him toward the horse-herd.

And there he was, that black-and-silver beauty, tethered at the end of a line of young stallions, well apart from the king stallion and his mares. As many greys as there were in this herd, he was not strikingly unusual, but his silver-dappled black coat and his bright mane were difficult to mistake.

Keen must have ridden him to the Grey Horse camp. A woman, and neither royal nor shaman, riding that of all horses. He looked and acted like any other young male of his kind, grazing in his portion of the line, glaring down the bay on his left and flinching before the elder grey on his right. He was no king here, nor did he presume to be.

Kestrel did not approach him or touch him. There was a stone near the stallions' line, swept clean of snow. Kestrel sat on it with his knees drawn up, knotted tight within himself.

Here he sat in the dark of the year. His hunt had ended: the quarry had come to him, easily, unwarily, and all unlooked for. He could take the stallion now, simply lead him away, and make his long way back to the People.

He could do that. The Grey Horse People had given him a horse, a tall speckled grey with a dark mane. He could take that horse and lead the stallion and go. He doubted that anyone would pursue him. As for the command that had been laid on him, to bring back the thieves alive, he would hope that Linden had forgotten. Or he would tell the truth, that the women were in exile and would not come back. It should be enough, even for Linden.

So simple an ending; so tidy. Who but a god could have arranged it?

And yet he could not move. The stone was chill under him, the sun's warmth fading as it sank into night. His scars ached, straining over his ribs.

The stallion paid no heed to him at all. Horses, like gods, cared little for men's frets and follies. Kestrel wondered a little wildly if he remembered that he had been a king, or regretted that he had left it. Most likely he did not. He seemed happy enough here.

Kestrel would wait. He would endure the night and the day of festival. Then if Sparrow did not come, he would go to her. He would see her before he left—if only to assure his king that yes, he had found her; she had been alive. Then he would go.

Maybe the gods were laughing at the delusions of a simple mortal. Maybe this was as they willed. He was not a shaman. He did not know. He could only do what he reckoned best, however poor a best that was.

⁂

Kestrel did not go seeking Sparrow after the rite and the feast. He did not even see the rite. He stayed with the horses through the long chill night; and come morning, he paid the price he should have expected: a fever that lodged itself in his misused ribs. It was a sharp fever, but short. And it was Keen who nursed him through it, because the Grey Horse People were preoccupied with their festival.

Cloud would have left the feasting to look after him, but Keen convinced him that she could manage. Kestrel, slipping in and out of dream, saw how they looked at one another, they two, and thought that he should say something, or do something. But his head hurt too much, and his ribs were not happy at all.

He was only abed for two days—long enough to drive him wild with boredom, but not long enough to destroy all his strength. By the second day, Keen had discovered his scars, and come close to weeping over them. "Oh! You poor thing. No wonder you're all bones. What was it? Lion?"

He nodded. "More of my foolishness. I really should be wiser."

She laughed a little as she bathed him in warm water scented with herbs. It was a healer's potion: it made Kestrel's skin tingle. "You always say that. You're proud of yourself, admit it. These scars are as noble as any man could hope to live with."

"And not die of?" He shifted slightly on the heaped furs. It dawned on him dimly that he was naked and alone in a tent with a woman of quite remarkable beauty. But this was Keen, whom he loved as a sister. She seemed altogether oblivious to him, except as an object to be cleaned and tended.

She was also and rather obviously with child. Walker's, he supposed. It could hardly have been anyone else's. She bore the burden well, in a deep contentment that he had seen more often in mares than in women. It strengthened her beauty, made it both richer and softer. Small wonder that Cloud looked on her as he did; any man would, who was not her all-but-brother.

"You don't want to tell me, do you?" she said. "How you came here. You always did hate to tell stories."

Yes, he did; and this story was not one he wanted to think of. But he was weak with fever, and he was tired; he could not lie to her. "I came to find the stallion," he said, "and take him back."

She was not shocked or afraid. She nodded. "I thought that might be it. And will you do it?"

"The king commanded me."

"Then I suppose you should," she said. "If you can."

His brows drew together. "If I can? Will these people stop me?"

"Oh, no," she said. "But Horse Goddess might."

"Horse Goddess? Why would she do that?"

"He belongs to her," said Keen. "She brought him here. She wants him for something—I don't know what. Certainly not the thing that stallions do: she was in foal already when we left. But I don't think she'll let him go."

"She has to," Kestrel said. "If I don't take him back, the king will come for him."

"You think so?"

"I know so," Kestrel said.

"Then why didn't he come before? He had most of the summer, and the autumn. He never came."

That was a question Kestrel had asked himself. But he thought he had an answer. "He would have had to be king, more than ever with his stallion gone, and settle the tribes. By the time he could have done that, it would have been too late. But come spring, if I don't bring the stallion back, he'll come here. The shamans will show him the way."

Keen regarded him gravely. Her expression put him in mind of men's estimation of women's intelligence, or the lack thereof. But Keen was by no means weak in the wits. Behind that lovely face and those blue and dreaming eyes was a sharp mind and a clear perception. "Maybe Horse Goddess wants that," she said. "Maybe he's supposed to come here."

"And bring war?"

She shivered, but she nodded. "I don't know why the gods do anything. But I don't think Horse Goddess will let you take her stallion away."

"I have to try," he said. "These people are brave enough, and fight well when they have to, but they're a small tribe, and not rich. They can't hope to stand against all the gathered peoples. Even if the People come alone—they'll be hideously outnumbered."

"Maybe Horse Goddess will protect them," Keen said.

"Or maybe not." Kestrel tried to rise. "Now do you see why I have to go?"

"You'll go nowhere now," she said, pushing him gently back down again. "And yes, I see. I saw it to begin with. But I don't think Horse Goddess will."

✦ ✦

Sparrow rode into the camp on the fourth day after the dark of the moon. She came in by the same way that Keen had come, riding on the white mare. This time Kestrel was there to see, and to mark how the people were at her coming: silent, still, bowing as she rode past. She seemed unaware of them. Her eyes were dark, fixed as if blind.

But she could see. She saw Storm standing in the camp's heart, and Rain, and Cloud beside Keen. All of them she saw, and knew. But Kestrel she seemed not to see at all.

The mare halted in front of the queen. Sparrow slid from her back, holding up the thing that she had been carrying in her hands: a skull-cup such as warriors made, as richly and intricately ornamented as a king's. Storm sank down before it, to the ground, and everyone else followed—even, after a moment, Keen. But Kestrel stayed on his feet. He had not known the one whose skull this must be. He had not acknowledged her power, if such she had ever had.

It was an empty defiance. No one seemed to notice it. Sparrow spoke in a clear and carrying voice, simply but with clear strength of will. "Your Old Woman is dead. She bade me come to you, and give you her farewell. Her spirit watches over you. Her voice intercedes with the gods for you. She speaks as one of your ancestors, though she came from another kin and tribe. That is the love she bore you, and the care she took for you."

People wept, hearing that. They grieved as for one of their own. But Kestrel's heart was cold.

He had seen Sparrow. Now he could go. Indeed, he should, while she and the mare were occupied; but he stood still.

What she had done was beyond forgiveness—even if it was not she but the mare who had done it. She had taken the kingship away from the People. He was bound by honor and duty to bring her back to the king for that, and to see her suffer whatever penalty the king should exact. Probably the king would put her to death. If Kestrel had been king, he would have done it.

She had become a stranger, a violator of the laws of gods and men. She stood among these people who looked so much like her, and spoke to them in the voice of a shaman, and they bowed to her power. What she had done to gain that cup she held in her hands, and the power that both filled it and shone out of her, he did not want to imagine.

And yet she was still Sparrow. He looked at her and tried to be cold, tried to hate her; and he could only hate himself, because after all they had both done, he still loved her. He would always love her. Even if—or when—he had to kill her for what she had done to the People.

He turned and walked away from her and from the people about her. He went to the horses. He sat where he had sat on the night of the moon's dark, knotted as he had been then, and resolved that this time, when the sun went down, he would be sensible and find a warm place to sleep. Maybe that would not be in this camp, if she was in it. He had to leave—he could not stay. Because if he stayed, he would have to invoke his duty, seize her and carry her off and bring her to his king.

She found him there. It did not take much finding, to be sure. The mare had come in among the herd, cowing the queen mare with teeth and heels, and driving back the great white mountain of a stallion. And, having done that, she established herself near the young king, to the visible dismay of the other stallions tethered along the line. She fostered that dismay. She took pleasure in it, Kestrel was sure.

Sparrow came and sat on the rock beside him, not touching, but close enough that he could feel her warmth. She said, "If you try to take him, the mare will stop you."

"That's what Keen said," he said. He was amazed at how calm he managed to sound. "I told her it really would be better if I took him. Otherwise he'll bring the People down on this country."

"Yes," said Sparrow.

He glanced at her. He was older, people said he looked it, and certainly he felt it. She had changed, too, though maybe more subtly. She had not grown taller as he had. Her face was much the same. But her eyes were different. Shaman's eyes. They were dark and very deep, and had seen beyond the world.

"You're not afraid," he said.

"Would it help anyone if I were?"

"It might help these people."

She shook her head. "Horse Goddess will do whatever she pleases."

"Keen said that, too."

"Keen understands." Sparrow clasped her knees and laid her chin on them. "I suppose we're under some dire sentence. Is it death?"

His teeth clicked together. He always did forget just how direct Sparrow could be. "I was to bring you back alive."

"So my brother can kill me."

"No. Linden. Linden commanded me."

That startled her. His heart stabbed at the hurt in her face. All this time, all this power and wisdom, and she still yearned after that pretty fool.

She did not try to deny what he had said, at least. That was Sparrow: unflinching in the face of the truth. "He did love that horse," she said slowly. "He must have been very, very angry."

"The word I would use," said Kestrel, "is wrath."

"Ah." She sighed. "Yes, I suppose it would be that. We couldn't have done anything much worse than we did."

"I can't think of anything," Kestrel said dryly.

"And he sent you. That was cruel."

"He wouldn't have known," Kestrel said.

"I suppose not," said Sparrow. "You can't do it, you know. Take the stallion, or take me. The goddess won't allow it."

"The goddess? Not you?"

"I would go," she said, "if I could. I'm not particularly afraid to die—and I might not. But the goddess forbids. We're to stay here." She slanted a glance under those straight black brows. "You know that. You can hear her, too."

"I can't—"

But that was not true. Kestrel did not hear the goddess, nothing so clear or so direct. He knew, that was all. He looked at the mare, and she was going nowhere, nor was the stallion, nor was Sparrow.

As for him, whom the shaman here had named the Sparrowhawk . . . he had failed of his hunting. He should go back and take the punishment that he had earned.

"No," said Sparrow as if he had spoken aloud. "You'll stay."

"I can't."

She reached across the narrow space that was between them, and took his hand. "You will."

He stared at his long thin hand in her small round one. His fingers were cold. Hers were warm. He said, "You're playing me like a flute. Stop it."

She did not let go his hand. "I will play a whole night's dance on you, if that's what's necessary. I won't let you go back. They'll kill you."

"I don't think Linden will," he said.

"It's not Linden I'm thinking of." She raised his hand to her cheek. It turned of its own accord, fitting its palm to that soft curve. "She brought you here, you know. The goddess. She tested you; she tempered you with pain. She wants you here for what will come."

"And if I won't stay?"

"You, she won't stop. But I will."

"Can you?"

She closed the space between them, linking hands behind his neck. "Ask me now," she said.

She did not mean it. She did it because she knew what was in his heart—not because she shared any part of it.

He knew that, and he felt himself falling. Honor, duty, loyalty to his king—what had any of them been, from the beginning, but obedience to her wish? She had asked him to look after Linden. He had done that. Now he was here, and she asked him to do another thing, a terrible thing, to abandon the king whom he had served at her will. All at her will, because he had no power to resist her.

He groaned and willed himself to pull away. Of course he could not. His arms, raised to thrust her off, folded about her, drawing her closer.

He had dreamed of this. But in the dreams, she had loved him as he loved her. That was not so in this waking world. She was saving his life, that was all—that was how she would reckon it.

And he could not make it matter. She was in his arms, willingly, consciously, as he had always prayed she might be. He would hold her for as long as she would allow it, for the memory; so that when she went back to being herself again, he would have this to feed his dreams.

················ 39 ················

S PARROW HAD NEVER intended to do what she did. To keep him in this country, yes; to bind him here where he would be safe, at least until the People came to take back their king of stallions. But to do it this way . . . no, she had not meant or expected that she would do such a thing.

He was grown so splendid. When she saw him standing among the Grey Horse People, so much taller than any of them, and so light and proud in carriage, her heart had thudded wildly and then settled to a distressing flutter. She had had all she could do to say what she must say, to be as properly dignified as she should be before the queen and the people. It was worse for that, at sight of him, she had known exactly why he was here. She had seen it in him, in images like the embroidery of her coat: the command that bound him, the long hunt, the storms, the lion, all the tests the goddess had forced him to endure. She had seen the woman Rain, too, doing with him what a woman does with a man.

She had seen much too much. And rather sooner than was strictly polite, she had escaped the queen and the people and gone looking for him. When she found him sitting all alone and knotted in misery, her heart had run on without her, had spoken for her, acted for her, brought her into this embrace.

She did not yearn for him as she had yearned—in a way still yearned—for Linden. He was more beautiful than Linden, because his beauty was less perfect. His face was long and rather austere, not a face made for lightness or laughter. His body was lean and panther-lithe and very strong, with a way about it that made her breath catch. The way he moved, his light smooth stride, the way his head turned just so, that steady gaze of his from under lowered eyelids—she had known them since they were children, but she had never truly seen them.

She could not help it. She had to touch; to hold him fast. He was a little repelled, a little horrified. She could see it in his face. And yet she could not stop herself.

This must be what drove women to lie with men. Sparrow had thought she wanted to lie with Linden, but when she came to the point of imagining it, she could not. She could easily imagine lying with this man. Oh, easily indeed.

This man. Her friend, her better-than-brother. This king's companion who had been set on her trail like a hunting hound, whom honor and duty bound to capture her and carry her back to her death.

That was a torment in him. She, foolish heart, held him all the closer for knowing that, and tried to kiss the pain away. But that was not wise—no, not wise at all.

Men, so incited, could be as fierce as stallions. That, everyone knew. What Sparrow had not known—what she had never expected—was that a woman could be fiercer.

She should stop. She must stop. He was not struggling, which surprised her. But he must be frozen with shock.

Until she met his eyes, and saw what made her cry out. "You, too. *You, too!*"

They tumbled from the stone onto grass all sere and dry with winter, where the sun had melted such snow as the wind had not scoured away. It was surprisingly soft, and surprisingly warm. Not that Sparrow cared—the fire in her was enough to warm a world.

He stared at her, struck dumb perhaps by the sight of a woman naked in the winter sunlight. Then he touched her as she stooped above her, tracing the spiral that Old Woman had drawn round about her breast. She gasped. His touch woke—something. Not desire only. It was as if, under his hand, the power grew stronger. And as he traced each intricate and interwoven swirl, it gained in strength, till she was like to burst with it.

She would burst, unless she did the last thing, the thing that all this had led to. But she could not do it—she would not—if he was not willing. If he did not understand.

She stopped his hand as it came to rest above the thicket of her sex, where the spirals came to their completion. She held it there, cool against the fire of her body. "Do you love me?" she asked him.

He regarded her in—despair? "With all my heart," he said.

Her own heart leaped. "Is that truth? Do you swear it?"

"By Earth Mother's womb," he said, "it is the truth."

And then he said, "Do you love me?"

And she understood. As clear as his vision was, this he could not see. He could not pierce the defenses she had raised about her heart.

He thought she hesitated. His despair deepened. "It doesn't matter," he said. "Whatever you can give—"

She silenced him with her finger on his lips. "Don't say that. Don't think it! How can you doubt that I love you?"

"As a sister," he said. "As a friend."

"Surely," she said. "And more."

"Not more," he said. "Don't lie to me. I'm glad of what I can have."

"*I* am not," she snapped, "if that's all you think I'm capable of giving you."

There: her temper startled him out of his silliness. Not altogether, maybe, but enough that he began to believe her. The joy that woke in him then, however tentative, however uncertain that it dared exist, so brightened his beauty that she blinked, dazzled. Austere, had she been thinking? Stern, and little given to laughter? Not this man who lay in the winter grass. He was as light as air, and as golden-bright as the sun.

She took him so, as a man might take a woman: with both passion and gentleness. She was braced for the pain. What she had not expected—what she had not been prepared for—was the sheer white pleasure.

She almost fled the shock of it. But he held her fast. He took her as, just now, she had taken him. He was strong, and skilled enough that she widened her eyes. He seemed, now it was much too late to escape, to have given himself up to it; to have let the joy overcome all his misgivings.

No wonder they called it a dance. When it was danced so, as equal and equal, it was like the dance of warriors about the royal fire: bound and yet apart, vying in strength, vying in skill, but matched, so that neither could be victor, and neither be vanquished. They hung poised on the piercing edge of pleasure, until, with a swift, sure stroke, he lifted them up and ever up.

She had thought she knew. She had imagined. But to *know* . . .

And to know all of it. What she was. What he was. What they had done, they two, in a place of power, under the eyes of mare and stallion.

Old Woman had not told her. Old Woman had never told her anything that she was to learn for herself. It was not only the learning in the heart, the signs drawn on the body, the sacrifice made and consumed as the goddess required, that made the shaman; that completed the rite. It was this.

She laughed as she lay exhausted, with him a heavy, limp weight in her arms. She could feel him slipping free of her, shrinking and softening. Her laughter roused him, and offended him more than a little—he half-pulled away, relieving her at least of his weight. But she held him before he could escape entirely. "Was I *that* bad?" he demanded of her.

That only made her laugh the harder, and made him all the more ridiculously offended. It was a long while before she could master her voice enough to say, "Stop that! I'm not laughing at you. I'm laughing at *me*."

He did not believe her: he glowered through a tangle of loosened hair. She smoothed it out of his face. "You men," she said. "Everything is always to do with you. Can't you imagine for a moment that I might be laughing because I am a raging fool?"

"Why? For this?" There was a growl in it, but he was listening.

"For thinking that, without this, I knew everything there was to know."

"Why, didn't you?"

She slapped him lightly, but without anger. Then she kissed him, because she could not help herself. That might have led to other things, but he was only a man; he could not go on and on as a woman could.

She forgave him. She was dizzy, as she had been when she first rode the mare: as if all her life had been leading to this, and she had never known it or begun to imagine it.

He was coming out of his sullenness, a little. And more, as she traced his body in kisses, until, all unwillingly, he began to laugh. Then it was well. It was very well indeed.

40

THEY LIVED IN the camp of the Grey Horse that winter, at the queen's urging and by Old Woman's own wish. Sparrow had inherited Old Woman's belongings, her goats, and her shelter, too, though that lay empty through the winter. She was rather surprised on taking stock, to discover that by the measure of the Grey Horse People she was a woman of substance.

She owned a tent of respectable size, she discovered on exploring the shelter, and a remarkable number of comforts to fill it, even such treasures as a nest of clay bowls and a lidded pot painted with spirals like those limned on her skin. There were baskets of fine weaving, stores of herbs and potions, cured hides and furs, knives of flint and hardened bone and, folded well away, that strange black stone which took so deadly an edge. There was a great store of beads and shells, some strung into necklaces and armlets, most laid away in small baskets or scraps of hide. She even found things that she had no names for: odd gleaming stones, sun-colored or moon-colored, strangely heavy and cold in the hand. Sun's tears and moon's tears, she reckoned those; and the small dark stone, heavy and potent, that made her arm ache to hold it, must be the heart of the night.

Those she put away as she had found them, wrapped tight and hidden in a basket of more ordinary stones. What they were, what powers they had, she did not know; but someday perhaps she would.

She traded a pair of she-goats, each with twin kids, for an ox to carry it all back to the Grey Horse camp. The ox was well laden. She had wealth to share, hides and furs enough to give away, and ample herbs and simples for the work of healer and shaman. She would not be a useless burden on these people, any more than Kestrel would with his hunter's skills, and Keen with her needle and her gift for calming fretful children.

Sparrow had never dreamed that she would be either rich or a shaman. And here she was both. At first she fretted. With her presence, this small and none too powerful tribe boasted three shamans. North of the river, that would have been as difficult as asking a herd to accept three stallions, or three queen mares.

But Storm said when she murmured of retreating to Old Woman's camp, "My spirit is not so weak that it needs to fear a rival. Only grant that in matters pertaining to the tribe, my word rules yours. In all other things, you may rule me if you choose. Or we will consult, and settle matters between us."

Sparrow could agree to that. But there was still Rain to consider. Rain was younger and famously headstrong, and it was clear that she had been enjoying Kestrel's attentions before Sparrow came to displace her. She kept well apart, was not among the curious and the welcoming when Sparrow raised her tent on the camp's eastern edge, and did not share the daymeal with her mother and her brother and the guests. First she had gone off hunting, then she had disappeared with a man rather well known for his prowess with the women.

But after the long mild spell ended and the colds and storms of winter closed in once more, Rain could not wander so far afield. Sparrow ran her to ground one chill grey morning, found her in her mother's tent drinking warm goat's milk and playing a game of bones with Cloud. Keen was there, and one or two children; she was teaching them to string beads on a hair from a horse's tail and embroider them on a scrap of doeskin.

Sparrow sat on her heels to watch the game of bones. Rain played like a man, with a fierce edge of temper. Cloud was calmer, wiser. He had won a handsome handful of shells and beads, and was proceeding to win another.

He was doing it for Keen, Sparrow thought. When he cast a good hand, he glanced at her. She seemed oblivious to him, but when he was not looking at her, she darted her own brief glances. Sparrow wondered if they even knew what they were doing, or how strong the bond between them had become. It was like a rope of braided hide. She could see it if she shifted her eyes, see how it grew stronger the less notice they seemed to take of one another.

But she had not come to watch those two grow together in spirit while their bodies remained decorously and perpetually apart. She turned her attention on Rain.

Rain was a shaman. There was no mistaking it. She had the gift. But she was lacking in discipline. She was not calm and focused within herself as Storm was, or as Sparrow had learned to be. She tried to shift the cast of the bones to favor her cause, but she only succeeded in casting the figure called the Oxtail, which lost to every figure but itself. He in response cast War, and so won the round.

When the bones came back to her, she flung them down in a temper, leaped up and stalked out of the tent. Sparrow rose quietly and followed her.

She did not run away as Sparrow had half thought she might. Sparrow caught her near the tent in which, Sparrow recalled, her lover of the season lived with his mother and sisters. "He's not there," Sparrow said. "He went riding with some of his cousins. They were going to meet a hunting party from—was it the Boar?"

"Yes," Rain said more politely than Sparrow might have expected. "I left my bow here. I'm going to find them."

That was true, Sparrow supposed. "They went east, toward the beech-wood."

Rain stopped in front of the tent, and turned to face her. "I suppose you just know that."

"Don't you?" Sparrow asked, not trying to be provoking, but not forbearing from it, either.

"I'm not the shaman you are," Rain said. "Nor will I be. Old Woman told me that. I'm strong, and I'll do well for my people. But you were made for this whole country."

"Does that trouble you?"

Rain frowned. She did not seem troubled. Thoughtful, yes. Jealous? A little, maybe. "I think," she said, "that you'll have greater glory, but I'll have much greater peace of mind. I used to dream of being the one—I won't deny it. But now I know I'm not, I'm rather glad."

"Then you're going to be able to endure my being here?"

"I'm glad you're not living in my mother's tent," Rain said. "As for your being in the camp, no, that doesn't matter to me. There's room for both of us."

"Is there?"

"Why, are you going to challenge me?" Rain shook her head. "You're not that foolish."

"Maybe. But you might challenge me."

"What for? To see myself beaten soundly and put in my place? I think not. Although," Rain said with a flash of dark eyes, "if you're speaking of the Sparrowhawk, that's a different thing."

Sparrow eyed her belly, which was visibly rounded with the baby, and eyed the tent, in which she spent rather riotous nights with the handsome Horn.

Rain tossed her head. "What, you've never heard of two men sharing a woman? But you wouldn't, would you? North of the river, women share a man, but never the opposite."

"Maybe Horn would consent to that," Sparrow said, "but I doubt that Kestrel will."

"And if he would, would you let him?"

"He can go where he pleases," Sparrow said. "He's not my prisoner."

"So generous," sighed Rain. She sobered suddenly however, looked Sparrow in the eyes and said, "I won't squeal and kick at you like a rival mare. I'm content with what I am here, and with what I have. Maybe I want that lovely man—but if I do, I'll win him fairly. That much I promise you."

Sparrow decided to accept it. It was not what she had been looking for, but it would do.

✢ ✢

It was a long winter, and hard. The Grey Horse People did not suffer too badly. Only three children died, and two of them had been sickly in the autumn. None of the elders died; no one starved, though by the first thaw of spring, the hunting was as thin as the hunters.

Sparrow did not care at all for cold or hunger. She had all the warmth she needed, and all the sustenance. Kestrel kept his tent and she kept hers, but neither slept alone. Sometimes they slept in her tent, sometimes in his.

The first time, the night after they first came together, it was Sparrow who went to him, creeping out in the firelit dark and the frosty stars, and slipping into his tent, and finding him awake. She did not speak. His arms were as eager as hers, his body as urgent. This time there was no pain when he entered her, no hindrance; she was open and ready, as a woman is, taking him deep and holding him. And without pain, the pleasure was even greater—so much so that she cried out in astonishment, then buried her face in his shoulder, mortified.

He laughed at that, stroked her and held her until she would lift her head again. "Now everyone will know what a great bull of the plains I am," he said.

He did not blush when he said it, either. Something had opened inside of him, some gate of the heart that had been locked shut. In coming to him as she had, she had done much better than she knew. She had made him happy. She had made him hers.

They were lovely, those long icy nights, wrapped in each other's arms, whispering of anything and everything, laughing as often as they spoke, and taking one another with fierce delight. He loved to trace the shaman-signs drawn in her skin, to feel the tingle of power as it woke and grew strong. She let free a little of it to soothe the terrible deep scars in his side and back, the marks of the lion's claws. He lost himself in the thick dark curls of her hair. She freed his ruddy mane from its plaits, smoothing it and combing it till it hung waist-long, then binding it up again, as only a lover could do.

She was beautiful to him. He *was* beautiful, but she who to most eyes was rather ordinary, in his sight was as splendid as Keen. "You shine," he said to her, "like sun on clear water."

"That's the magic," she said. And, in wonder: "You can see it?"

He nodded.

"Wonderful," she said, brushing his brow with her hand, feeling the soft flutter of eyelids under her palm. "So few can see. Even some who call themselves shamans—they're blind to the light."

"But it's so clear," he said. "How can they not see it?"

"They don't have the eyes. But you," she said, "do." And such beautiful clear grey eyes, in so very handsome a face. She could never get enough of it. Many nights, long after he had fallen asleep, she would lie awake by whatever light there was—moonlight, firelight, starlight—and simply gaze at him. He was so very familiar, and yet he was all new, all wonderful, as if he had been a stranger.

By the deep heart of winter, she knew what their loving had made. It was very early; she had barely missed her courses. And yet she was a shaman. She felt it inside her, the tiny spark, growing as the days lengthened.

She did not tell him as soon as she knew. It was so early, and he was a man of the People; he might be odd about it, or be terribly silly and solicitous as some of the young men of the Grey Horse were inclined to be. Here, the office of father mattered less than the office of clan-brother—as Cloud was to Rain. But they did know how babies began, and mostly the women took care to note which of their lovers was likely to have fathered the child. It was a gift, from man to woman and from woman to man. And if he was of such a mind, the man might be rather a fool about it.

"As if," Rain said once, "he had devoted more than a few moments' effort to it." But she said it as gently as she said anything, with a shrug and a smile at Cloud. Cloud for once was taking notice of her rather than Keen, and he returned the smile, unabashed. He was quietly proud of the baby growing in her belly.

It was not his first, Sparrow discovered, though Rain had not had a child before. Half a dozen of the dark-eyed children running about the camp had his pleasant blunt features and his beautiful long-lashed eyes. Their mothers made no claim on him that Sparrow could see, nor thrust the children at him, but they appeared to know who was their father.

It was a strange, rather subtle way of doing things, but people seemed content with it. Since mother-clan was the only one that mattered, mothers' brothers helped raise the children, or if there were no brothers, elder sons or, rarely, fathers performed the duty. All of Cloud's children had uncles to teach them the ways of the tribe.

That maybe was why he was so intent on Rain's child. He was its father, but also its clan-uncle. He would raise it and seal it with its name, once its mother had told him what that was.

Sparrow, cherishing the secret within her, reflected that Kestrel was as close to a true heart's brother as she had ever had. Like Cloud, he could be both brother and lover. And he would help her raise this child. He was wonderful with children, patient and forbearing with the handful who followed him about; he was teaching them to hunt, and to make and fletch arrows, and to knap flint for arrowheads and spearheads and knifeblades. What joy he would take, she thought, in teaching his own child to do all of that; to make a hunter of it as his father had made of him.

+ +

Spring came all at once and almost unexpected. One day they were gripped in the icy heart of winter, suffering a blizzard so fierce that it plucked several tents from their moorings and froze one of the oxen where he stood among his fellows. The next morning rose clear and bright and unwontedly warm. The snow began to melt, the ice to slip from the branches of the trees. They were able to butcher the ox, and to share a feast, a rite of newborn spring.

That night Rain went into the birthing-house, which in this tribe was in the camp's center—not set apart and hidden from the eyes and ears of men, but full in their midst, so that everyone knew and shared in the birthing. By morning she had delivered a daughter, a fine strong creature who had, her mother swore, her father's eyes. Sparrow could not tell. Babies were babies, red squalling things of no beauty or charm. But its mother was vastly proud of it, and its father doted on it. It was, she conceded, a good omen, that winter's end should bring so strong a life into the world.

The child was named Spring, aptly enough. Her mother recovered quickly from the birth, suffered neither fever nor weakness, but was blessed of the gods and of Earth Mother. That too was an omen. It heartened the people, and brightened the rising spring.

⚬ ⚬

When the snows had melted and the snow-waters roared past, and the rivers quieted somewhat, Kestrel left the Grey Horse People. He rode out hunting, or so everyone thought. But he did not come back.

Sparrow had known. In her heart, she had felt it. His joy in her was as great as ever, his loving both passionate and tender. But after he had gone, she saw what she had been refusing to see.

He had agreed that he had no hope of taking the stallion back to the People. But he had never quite promised that he would stay. His duty bound him, and his given word. Once winter's long waiting was over, he had to go. He had no choice.

He said no farewells. He went hunting, that was all. But the trail he took led to the great river in the north, and over it, and on to the plains and the People.

Sparrow raged. She tried to raise magics, storms, floodwaters. But the gods were not listening. Earth Mother would not obey her. Whether this was ordained, or the gods simply did not care, Kestrel went unhindered; and she could not follow. The mare would not go. The stallion, who might have been willing, was in the mare's power. She kept him by her, nor suffered Sparrow to approach him.

Sparrow was bound to this camp and this tribe. Here Horse Goddess had sent her. Here she must stay.

No one could offer her comfort. None but Rain, who was neither

her friend nor her ally, but they were, in a fashion, sisters. "He'll come back," Rain said.

"Yes," said Sparrow bitterly. "At the head of an army. Or as a head on a spear."

"Then at least you'll see him again," Rain said: rough comfort indeed, but in its way it lessened her grief. Not her anger, never that, but it braced her spirit.

PART THREE

HORSE GODDESS' CHILDREN

.... ✦ ✦ ....

W HEN THE KING of the White Stone stallions was taken
away, the gathering of tribes rose up in revolt. A king
stripped of his stallion, cried his brother kings, was no
king at all. And if the White Stone People had lost their
king of stallions, they had lost their kingship. They were no longer
chief among the tribes.

Cliff Lion was swift to claim that eminence. Red Deer and Dun
Cow raised rival claims. Well before evening of the day after the stallion was stolen, the gathering had broken into a dozen squabbling
factions.

Linden had come back to the camp, riding behind Curlew on
that young man's sturdy bay, and halted in front of his tent, and shut
himself in it. His companions would not let even Walker pass. He
had to invoke the power of his office. Even then they made him
surrender such weapons as he allowed unsanctified eyes to see.

He took the insult to heart, and would remember it. But for now
he had greater matters to attend to.

Linden was deep inside the tent, pacing and snarling like a lion
in a cave. Every now and then he seized on something within reach,
tore it or kicked it or flung it.

Walker watched him with interest. For so equable a man, he had
a rather imposing temper. But there was a distinct air of petulance in
it. He did not have the gift of the grand passion, the towering wrath
that made a man terrible.

Walker, whose own anger was winter-cold, considered the uses
and misuses of this man whom he had made king. He had put aside
for the moment the other thing, the thing that ate at his spirit: the
discovery that his sister, the messenger of his visions, had taken his
wife and his king of stallions and ridden away. Curlew, who was far-

sighted, had seen who it was—impossible, preposterous, but there could be no denying it.

That would be dealt with in its due time. For the moment it mattered more that he rein in this pretty idiot of a king, and teach him to say the words that would quell the tribes.

"Lord king," Walker said in his sweetest voice.

Linden wheeled. "You! Get out."

"My lord," said Walker, "the tribes need their king."

"Pestilence take the tribes! Those—those *women* stole my horse!"

Walker suppressed a sigh. "My lord—"

Linden was not listening. "I've sent men after them. I'll send more. I'll raise an army. Any man who brings them back to me alive, and my stallion safe, I'll reward him—what shall I give him, shaman? Will women do? Cattle? Horses?"

"My lord," said Walker, raising his voice slightly in hope of catching the king's attention, "that is well thought of, and shall be done. But while your hunters pursue the thieves, you and only you must settle the tribes. I would suggest that—"

"You do that," Linden said. "Tell them the stallion will be back in a day or two. Then I'll show them how a king punishes such profanation."

"It's not that simple, my lord," Walker said. "The people—"

"Tell them," Linden said. "Leave me alone. Tell everyone to leave me alone. Except a woman. I will have a woman. Tell one of the servants. They'll fetch one for me."

Walker would dearly have loved to wring that pretty neck. But he needed this man still—not for terribly long, perhaps, but long enough. "I'll send you a woman, my lord," he said. "Be at ease. Rest as you can. And try to calm your spirit."

"Yes, yes," Linden said testily. "Go away. You're not bad to look at, mind, but I'd rather be looking at a woman."

+ +

Walker sent him a woman. He sent his father's wife White Bird, who was quite as pretty and fully as stupid as Linden. She did not care that another man than her husband had called her out of the tent and given her orders—for they were orders that she was glad to take. "The king!" she cried, clapping her hands. "Oh, yes. I'll go now. I'll make him forget all his grief. He'll love me, yes he will."

Walker was sure that he would. He stared down the crone who

had wandered in while he instructed White Bird. The crone met his stare brazenly, but she was only an old woman. He forgot her as soon as he had gone on the next of his errands.

The kings and shamans and some of the elders of the tribes had gathered in the sacred place round the stone of sacrifice. Their factions were obvious, small scowling knots of men, each separate from the other, with much shouting back and forth. Cliff Lion's king, who was called the Bull, had leaped up on the stone of sacrifice and begun to harangue the crowd.

He was, in his way, little more intelligent and hardly less foolish than Linden. Walker looked about for a man of greater sense. Red Deer and Dun Cow were ruled by warleaders, men for whom battle was meat and drink. Black Bull's king was old, with a pack of quarrelling sons. Tall Grass—Walker nodded to himself. Yes, there was an alliance he could use, and the king was comfortably in the shaman's power.

As he moved toward the western edge of the field, where Tall Grass stood with a gathering of lesser allies, a ripple ran through the crowd.

Someone new was coming. A man on a grey horse, one of the royal mares no less, and no shame that he, a man grown, an elder and a shaman, should stoop to ride so lowly a creature. He rode slowly down the track that priests took in procession. Silence followed in his wake.

Walker watched him in shock. Drinks-the-Wind should have been lying in the innermost space of his tent, lost to dreams and slow poison. He was pale, he was thin to emaciation, but his grey eyes burned in his white face. He was not only alive, he was stronger than he had any right to be.

The mare carried him to the stone of sacrifice. The Bull, whose speech had trailed off as the shaman drew closer, lowered his head and hunched his heavy shoulders and retreated from the stone.

The mare climbed up on it. She was a massive thing, and not young, with a heavy broodmare's belly, but she was agile and she was strong. The stone was just large enough to hold her and the man astride her back.

Drinks-the-Wind looked out over the gathered kings and elders and shamans. His eyes were full of light. Walker had not yet learned the trick of that. Maybe it needed the full pallor of white hair, white beard, and colorless skin, and the sun striking the eyes just so.

The shaman spoke. His voice was not particularly loud. It was clear, and carried well enough, if those on the edges moved in closer. Which they did, drawn as if by a spell, but it was only the power of curiosity. "My lords, my brothers, my kin. This is a terrible thing that has befallen us, and it dishonors us all. But if a spirit of ill-will wrought this thing, then it rejoices now to hear you. The breaking of the tribes would be its dearest hope, and war would give it great satisfaction."

"Surely!" shouted a man from among those of the Dun Cow. "It was *your* daughter who stole the kingship. What do you have to say to that, old man?"

Drinks-the-Wind did not seem dismayed. "I say, sir, that when she is found—and I pray that be quick—I will be foremost among those who call for her judgment. My fault that in naming her I gave her life. I will redeem that fault once she stands before us."

Men nodded at that, and muttered approval. But the man of the Dun Cow was not satisfied. "I hear tell she's a witch's child. What if she's in league with the dark gods? Can you protect us against them?"

"If that is so," said Drinks-the-Wind, "then all of us priests and shamans will protect you and your people. That I swear to you, as elder shaman of the White Stone People."

Maybe he had not won them all over, but he had won enough. When he dismissed them, and bade them wait, be patient, pray to their gods for guidance, they obeyed him. He had great presence, and great skill in wielding it: white man in white garment, mounted on white mare, standing on the stone of sacrifice.

Walker could admire the beauty of it, even as he brooded over the failure of his potions. He had had in mind to do something rather similar, but in the end it mattered little that his father had done it. It quieted the tribes, for a while; that was what mattered.

But he could see that he would have to dispose of the old man rather more directly, and rather soon. He could not have Drinks-the-Wind claiming back his old place beside the king. That belonged to Walker now, and Walker meant to keep it.

In the meantime Walker set about making use of the lull between the first shock of anger and the eruption that would follow. He sent word to the shaman of the Tall Grass that the wedding would proceed, and quickly. He sent word also to each of the kings, in his own king's name, proposing a great alliance, a royal wedding, with each king invited to send a daughter to the king of the White Stone People.

And while that was in train, he approached Linden again.

✦ ✦

Linden was lying in White Bird's arms. Her wonderful white breasts were bare, and he was suckling at them. Her face wore an expression of creamy pleasure, which altered not at all when she saw that Walker was watching. Indeed she smiled, heavy-lidded, and tilted her head just so: inviting him to partake, too, if he was so minded.

His lips twisted in disgust. He had perforce to wait until Linden, too, had noticed him—a time during which he was very well apprised of his king's tastes in womanflesh. Maybe, he thought, he should send new messages to the kings and bid them send daughters who had borne gods' children, rather than daughters who were at least publicly acknowledged to be maidens.

Linden emerged from his preoccupation at last, unperturbed to find that he had an audience. Like White Bird, he seemed minded to offer Walker a portion; but Walker forestalled him. "My lord," he said, "if you please, I've servants waiting to bathe and dress you."

"A bath would be pleasant," Linden said lazily. "But clothes? Why? I'm not leaving here."

"My lord, you are," said Walker. "Tonight you dance in front of the kings of the tribes. Tomorrow you take to wife a daughter of each. And tomorrow night," he said, smiling though his gorge rose, "you may rut like a bull in a herd of eager heifers."

Linden's eyes gleamed at that, but White Bird cried out in dismay—a sound far less like birdsong than like a hawk's scream. "You can't do that! He's mine!"

"Why, surely," said Linden. "And you are mine. But just think— all those pretty faces. All that soft skin. Won't you be glad to share it with me?"

"May I?" she asked, breathless.

He nodded.

She clapped her hands. "Oh! Yes, that would be so delightful. But," she said, sobering suddenly, "you must promise me. You are *mine*. The others can belong to you, but you cannot belong to them."

"You had me first," Linden said—which was by no means a promise, but she seemed content with it.

If he learned to seduce men as he seduced women, he would be a striking figure of a king. Walker pondered the advantages of that as he completed the last of his errands.

Drinks-the-Wind had left the stone of sacrifice and, it seemed, sent the mare back to her herd. He was not in his tent, nor in the shamans' tent. Walker had nearly lost patience with the hunt, when he found his father outside the camp, sitting by the old king's barrow. He looked like a ghost or wandering spirit, a white and motionless figure, with the wind plucking at his robe and running fingers through his beautiful long beard.

He was aware of Walker's coming, though he did not acknowledge it until Walker stood over him. Then he lifted those clear pale eyes and said, "If you're wise, you'll let me live a while."

Walker widened his own eyes, which he knew were neither as clear nor as pale as his father's; but his face, he thought, was more distinctly beautiful. "Let you live, Father? Surely it's the gods who do the letting."

"Don't play me for a fool," Drinks-the-Wind said. "Not that I haven't been one; I should have known long ago what was being slipped into my cup. The girl who did it is dead. Next time, if you must corrupt one of my daughters, find one with a little more courage. That one broke and wept before I laid a hand on her. It was a dreadful and noisy chore to force the whole of the vial down her throat. She took a long time to die, and not pleasantly, either."

Walker regarded his father in ungrudging admiration. "I see I underestimated you," he said.

"You do have that flaw in your character," said Drinks-the-Wind. "Now that that other of my daughters is gone, and your visions with her, what will you be doing about it?"

Walker had not been expecting that. It struck the wind from his breast, and left him gaping, bereft for a moment of words. When at last he could speak, his voice was thin and somewhat strangled. "The king's men will bring her back. How far can she go, after all?"

"That," said Drinks-the-Wind, "might be farther than you can imagine. You should consider it, youngling. If she is not brought back within a day, or two at the most, I won't be able to hold back the tribes."

"But I will," said Walker. "Tomorrow the king will take a tentful of wives. And I will take the daughter of the Tall Grass shaman. That will absorb the people for a while, even without a horse-thief to punish."

Drinks-the-Wind nodded. "Yes. Yes, that's not an ill thought. But after that, if there's no king stallion, and no thief—you had better find our king another horse."

"Surely the herds will do that," said Walker. "The royal mares will gain a stallion, even as our king gains wives."

"No," said Drinks-the-Wind. "The mares have driven off several already. Most strange, that is: who ever heard of mares refusing a stallion? But so they have."

"One will persist," Walker said. "One will win them."

"Maybe so," said Drinks-the-Wind, "and maybe not. These are not horses as we know horses. These are something else. Horse Goddess' children. Her spirit is in them."

"They are still horses," said Walker. "And mares need a stallion."

"O son of my loins," Drinks-the-Wind said, "believe me when I say this. If your sister goes where my heart tells me she will go, and does what my spirit fears she will do there, you will need me sorely— if for nothing else than that I am not blind to the gods' light."

"Nor am I blind," Walker began.

Drinks-the-Wind cut him off. "Without her eyes, you are. Do you think I don't know what she is and what you are? If she had been a man, you would be a hunter and warrior of no particular distinction, with no hope in the world of calling yourself a shaman. Because the gods chose to mock us all by giving their visions to a girlchild, you stole those visions, and I allowed it—because, as we agree, I am a fool."

"They are *my* visions," Walker said. "She is but the messenger. And she will be brought back."

Drinks-the-Wind regarded him in a kind of surprise. "Why," he said, "you believe that. Or you've convinced yourself that you do." He sighed heavily. "Ah gods. It would have been restful to drink your poison; I would have been glad to see my battle-brother again. But I am not to go yet. I will grant you your semblance of power, youngling, and feed it as I may, for the People's sake. But have a care. If you tire of me too soon, there will be no one to give you visions. She will not, never again."

"I will keep her alive," Walker said. "There will have to be the appearance of a sacrifice. We can't avoid that. But after she seems to die, I'll keep her hidden. I'll not blind my eyes that see the gods, however valueless the body in which they reside."

"I rather think," said Drinks-the-Wind as if to himself, "that you may be mad. Alas for my People! But you are what the gods have given them. Far be it from me to question the gods' purpose."

Walker was sore tempted to slit his throat as he sat babbling of follies. But he had spoken the truth, as unpleasant as it was to contemplate. Until Sparrow was brought back, Walker would have no visions. He would use Drinks-the-Wind as the old man bade him—warily always, alert for signs of a trap, but he would hardly waste the gift.

"Need commands," Walker said. "I accept your offer. Until my sister returns."

"If she returns," said Drinks-the-Wind; but Walker chose to take no notice.

· · · · · · · 42 · · · · · · ·

LINDEN THE KING took to wife a royal daughter from each of the greater tribes—and from Cliff Lion, which would not help but vaunt itself even in defeat, twin daughters. And while he enjoyed the nine days' riot of his wedding, Walker took the daughter of the Tall Grass shaman, spoke the words with her before her father and her tribe, and took her into his tent.

It was by no means the pleasantly austere place it had been while Keen was his only wife. Blossom had filled it with her belongings—enough to weigh down three oxen, and a flock of servants who would not go away even when Walker took his new wife to bed. Walker was coldly, grimly angry at Keen; she would die when he found her, at his own hand. But he could still remember what a quiet and undemanding presence she had been.

Blossom was neither. She proved, rather to his surprise, to be a maiden. She seemed also and by some miracle to have been prevented from discovering what every woman of the People learned as a child, how a man was made and what he did with a woman.

He wedded her in the daylight as was proper, led her into his tent and left her there in the care of her mother and her servants while he presided over the wedding feast. When, not overly long after sunset, he went in to her, he found the outer room full of giggling maidservants. She was in the inner room, watched over by her mother.

Walker knew a moment's horror. Was he to take this woman while her mother watched?

But it seemed that even that queen of meddlers would not go so far. She simpered—not an art in which she had any skill—and laid her daughter's hand in his, and said, "Be gentle to my flower, my lord. Love her. Cherish her as she deserves."

Walker inclined his head. The woman hung about for a moment that stretched interminably, but when he did not speak, at length she retreated.

Perhaps she reckoned to hover beyond the curtain, listening avidly to the proceedings. But Walker was in no mood for that. He left his bride where she sat, strode to the curtain and swept it aside. "Out," he said in the voice he had learned as a shaman. "Begone!"

The maids fled. The mother might have lingered, but his glare was too terrible even for her fortitude. She made herself scarce.

The tent was blessedly empty. Walker left the curtain as it was, and turned back toward his bride. She stared at him as if he had grown fangs.

He smiled at her, a smile as carefully cultivated as his voice. It soothed her somewhat.

She was beautiful. More beautiful than Keen, maybe. Certainly more vivid, with her fire-red hair and her green eyes. Keen was gold and blue, with skin like milk. Blossom's was cream. She was richer in the body, too, her breasts full and round, her hips wide, her thighs— visible through the thin robe that she wore—as ample as he had seen among their slender people. She would be a lusty armful, he had thought when he first was permitted to see her. It was for that that he had chosen her over several of her sisters.

His body was delighted at the prospect. He let fall his shaman's robe and approached her, still smiling. He was beautiful in his maleness, and substantial, too. *My bull,* Keen had been used to call him. *My stallion.*

Blossom shrieked. He recoiled, crouched, spun, searching shadows for the thing that had so horrified her.

There was nothing. Her shrieking stopped. Her finger stabbed at him. "That—*that*—"

His rod. She was pointing to his rod. Her screeching had shocked it into hiding. She was breathing hard, glaring at it. *"What is that?"*

"By the gods," Walker said, too startled to measure his words. "Haven't you ever seen a man before?"

"You are a man," she snapped. *"That* is an abomination. Is that your deformity? Is that why they made you a shaman?"

Walker rocked back on his heels. Gods. She meant what she said. She honestly did not know. "Tell me," he said to her. "Did anyone teach you what would be expected of you here?"

She drew herself up. "Of course they did! A man comes in to his wife. They kiss. He rubs her *here.*" She pointed to her lap. "He sets a baby in her. Then he goes away and lets her be."

"Did they tell you *how* he sets the baby in her?"

She shrugged. Her expression was sullen. "I suppose he keeps it in a bag. Or a box. You're a shaman—you do it by magic, don't you? I hope it won't hurt. I do so hate things that hurt."

Walker was truly, honestly amazed. This idiot's father had boasted to him that she was pristine, untouched, unsullied by any man—but he had never expected her to be utterly ignorant of the ways of men and women.

"My dear," he said, "this that horrified you—this is where the baby is. It's very, very small. It has to grow. Will you trust me? Will you try to be understanding when I do what I must do?"

She narrowed her eyes. She was not so beautiful now. In fact she looked distressingly like her mother. "Will it hurt?" she asked—that question again.

"At first," he admitted, "a little. But after that, not at all. And the gods give you a gift in return for your bravery."

Those narrowed eyes gleamed. "What kind of gift?"

"A wonderful gift. A glorious gift."

"Is it a necklace? I want a necklace. I liked the armlets you gave me for a bride-gift, but I do so love necklaces."

"I will give you a necklace," Walker said with careful patience. "The gods will give you something different. Wait, and you'll see."

"I hate to wait," she said. But then, magnanimously: "I suppose I shall have to. Get to it, then. And try not to hurt me!"

Walker had seldom been less inclined to get to it—and the more so when she realized that he was going to take off her tunic. She clutched it and beat off his hands. "No! No, you won't! Let me be!"

She was adamant. It was all he could do to lift the skirt enough for the purpose; then she did not see why she should open her thighs. "A maiden of breeding does not—"

"But you are not a maiden now," he said, struggling for calm. "You are a wife."

And not likely to be one in truth, if she did not stop getting in his way.

She screeched, of course, when he breached the gate. She clawed and fought, and kicked him quite painfully in the hip. He wrestled her down, took her hard and took her fast, and never mind the slow ascents of pleasure. Anything, he thought, to get it over.

His release when it came was quick, a handful of spasms and it was done. She had stilled, at least, lying limp beneath him. She could be taking no pleasure from it: she was dry, and she was clenched— he had to thrust hard to open her at all.

She did not move when he lifted his weight from her. Her face was set. There was blood on her thighs and on his manly parts. She had not seen that yet. Her eyes were small and hard. "Where is my gift from the gods?"

"That," he said, "you have to earn."

"I did earn it. It hurt."

He shook his head. "Pain is not the price. Pain is the test. When the pain goes away, you win the gift."

"That's not fair. I want it now!"

"You don't know how to win it," he said.

"So teach me."

"Not tonight," he said. He was tired of her—suddenly and profoundly.

"But I want my gift!"

He slapped her, to her lasting shock. In the silence that gained him, he took up his robe and left her.

He slept that night on the plain not far from the horses. First however he bathed in the river, wading out into the starlit water, scouring away the blood and the smell of her, and as much of the memory as he could. Then, clean and naked, he walked till he found a place that suited him, spread his robe for a blanket and lay in the sweet-scented grass.

He dreamed of Keen. In his dream she was her sweetest self, so modest and so seeming shy, but passionate in her loving. She had been a maiden, too, but she had known what a man was and what he did; and she took great joy in learning the ways of it.

+ +

Blossom did not know joy in anything a man did with a woman. In the morning he sent White Bird to her—for surely that of all women could teach her both the art and the pleasure. But when he came to her at night, she clung grimly to her garments, and she recoiled from his ardor. "It's disgusting," she said. "It hurts."

"Did my father's wife teach you nothing?" he demanded.

She shrugged. He had come to know and loathe that shrug. "She rubbed me *there*. That didn't hurt, and after a while it was rather nice, but I don't see how you can do it with *that*. It's ugly. I don't like it when it goes inside me. I don't like the way you kiss me, either. Your beard scratches. When *she* kissed me, her lips were soft, and her skin was lovely. Your skin isn't like that at all."

"That," he said low in his throat, "is because I am a man."

"I don't like it," she said. "She said I had to let you kiss me and do *that* with me, because that is what a wife does. But I don't want to."

"What you want matters very little," he said.

"I want the gods' gift."

"And that," he said with no little satisfaction, "is only given if you want a man, if you hunger for him, if you love the sight and smell and feel of his body. If when he comes to you, you open to him, and accept him, and give him of your heart. Then the gods give their gift. And only then."

"Then," said that astonishing creature, "I don't want it. I'll take a necklace instead."

"Not without the gods' gift," he said.

He had no desire for her after that. He slept again under the stars, and again dreamed of Keen; and when he woke, he had spent his seed in the earth. He hoped Mother Earth was glad of it; for indeed, that wife of his would never be.

A MAN LEARNED to endure what he must, if it gained him the ends he looked for. Blossom had brought with her the strength of the Tall Grass People. Between that and the alliances that Walker had forged for Linden, the tribes were mollified, for a while. Many of their young men went out hunting the thieves who had stolen the king of stallions, which quieted the gathering considerably, and let the older men set about making marriages and confirming alliances and making use of what remained of the gathering.

The king was still without a stallion. And, as Drinks-the-Wind had foretold, the royal herd refused all comers. Stallions who came with war in mind were given war indeed. The mares would have none of them. All were in foal and in no mood to suffer the rule of a stranger.

Walker pondered long and hard. Cliff Lion's example might be worth following: to declare that the gods had chosen another herd and another stallion to lead the herds of the People. But to succeed in that, he would have to remove the royal herd. All the mares looked to those, and where the grey mares went, the others followed.

He could arrange another theft. There were men who would do it, for the game or in the gods' name; and if any of them threatened betrayal, Walker would assure that he did not come back from a hunt, or that he died in his tent of something that he ate.

But in that, he reckoned without Drinks-the-Wind. The elder shaman made no effort to take Walker's place beside the king, or to reclaim the office of chief of shamans. Yet neither he nor Walker could prevent the king from seeking him out.

Linden emerged from his nine days' seclusion with his brides, by no means as lazy or as sated as Walker had meant for him to be. He was very well satisfied, but that satisfaction had only sharpened his anger at the women who had stolen his stallion. Especially since no one, not one of all the hunters who had gone out, had found any sign of the thieves. They spoke of sudden storms, unexpected floods, and attacks by wild beasts—"As if," they said in the gathering, "the gods were driving us back."

Linden sneered at that, without even Walker to prompt him. "Cowards," he said. "You gave up too soon."

But when he went in search of advice, he went to Drinks-the-Wind. It was happenstance, perhaps. Walker was laboring among the tribes, speaking softly to kings who again were losing patience, and expecting that Linden, like a good fool, would tup his wives or hunt with his companions or find himself a horse from among the unbroken stallions. All of which he would eventually do, but first he sought the elder shaman in his tent.

He stayed there, Walker was told, for most of a morning. When he came out, he went straight to the herds and inspected the young stallions, and chose one as pretty as one might expect: a lovely golden dun with glossy black mane and tail, and each leg perfectly black to knee or hock, and no white hair on him anywhere. Linden devoted the rest of the day to the horse, and the next day, too, taking his time about it, as if he had been advised to do just that.

While Linden was so occupied, Walker in his turn visited his father. Drinks-the-Wind received him politely, ordered his wives to wait on the guest, and in no way conducted himself as if he had anything to fear. But Walker took note that he was received not as a beloved son but as a guest of rank. Drinks-the-Wind was letting him know, subtly but clearly, that he had set aside the bond of blood kin.

It hurt. Walker was surprised at that. Drinks-the-Wind was an old fool and a weak one, but he was still Walker's father. That Walker had been undertaking to dispose of him, and would again when he no longer had need of such visions as the old man might have left in him, stood quite apart from the fact of their kinship.

But not, it seemed, to Drinks-the-Wind. He observed every courtesy with excruciating exactness, until Walker had had enough. "What did you say to the king?" he demanded abruptly.

Drinks-the-Wind raised his brows. "Why, did you think I would break my word?"

"The king went to you," Walker said. "Tell me why."

"Perhaps," said Drinks-the-Wind, "because he needed wisdom, and you were elsewhere."

"What did he say?"

"Nothing that you've not heard before, I'm sure. He's very troubled. He feels the loss of the stallion keenly. His spirit is bound to the stallion. But the stallion is bound to the mare, who is Horse Goddess."

Walker was not concerned with that. He focused on the heart of the matter, which was Linden's obsession and his folly. "And you told him to find another horse."

"I told him to distract himself as best he could. A new mount would be useful, I said. He agreed. I take it he's taken my advice?"

"You know he has." Walker fixed his eyes on his father. "Tell me what else you told him."

"Nothing," said Drinks-the-Wind. His gaze was unwavering.

"I don't believe you."

"Believe what you like."

Walker held tight to his temper. "I'll find it out. You may be sure of that."

"There's nothing to discover," Drinks-the-Wind said. And that was all he would say. Until, as Walker was leaving in disgust, he said, "You might consider that no one can find the thieves. And no one will—not before winter. The tribes should go when the time comes to go, and keep to their own runs. In the spring, the world will begin to change."

Walker stopped, turned on his heel. Drinks-the-Wind was not looking at him. The pale eyes were remote, lost in visions.

"Tell me how the world will change," Walker said.

"In the spring," Drinks-the-Wind said, "it will begin. Look for the one who left on four feet but comes back winged."

That was all Walker could get out of him. If he knew more, if he saw more, he would not speak of it.

It was maddening. It was the price the gods had laid on him for his power: that all his visions should come blurred and darkened through the eyes of another.

+ +

As vague as the vision had been, Walker made full use of it. He held the gathering together with his tireless passing from camp to camp and tribe to tribe, soothing kings, pacifying elders. That his efforts also kept him away from the tent that was nominally his, and gave him manifold excuse to sleep wherever he happened to be when exhaustion took him, he regarded as a blessing.

After the time of weddings and alliances and feasting was done, the tribes parted as they had since the dawn time, going each to its own fields and hunting runs. White Stone was first to go, roused by the peal of a horse's call. The old mare, the queen of the royal herd, had wearied of these grazed-out pastures. She called her kin and the lesser herds together and led them away northward.

They had always gone east before in summer. But north she went, and north they must go. That a mare led them was an omen Walker liked little and the priests liked less, but it was as the gods decreed.

Linden did not want to go. "My stallion went south!" he cried as his people broke camp around him. "I know he went south—I saw him. Why are we going north?"

"Because the gods will it," Walker said with studied patience.

Linden shook his yellow braids and stamped his foot like a child. "I will not go! Let the women go, and the old men. I'll take the warband. We'll go south. We'll find my stallion."

There was a certain strong logic in that. But it was not the first time Linden had proposed it, and the visions—as Drinks-the-Wind saw them—were clear. The People would go north.

"I am going south," Linden said. Nor would he be moved. When the People set off on the northward way, Linden and the warband galloped south.

Walker went with the People. He had debated it long, but without great doubt as to his course. Kings came and went. The People endured. And he was shaman of the People. While Linden pursued his revenge, Walker ruled in his place. He sat in the royal circle, though not on the royal horsehide. He wielded the royal justice. And he kept the People on their path, following the white mare to a new grazing-ground altogether, a rich and well-watered region which seemed empty of tribes. It was a gift of the gods, that place, and the hunting and the fishing were splendid. Even bereft of their kings, both man and stallion, they were manifestly content.

+ +

All that summer the People reveled in their new camp and their splendid good fortune. Come autumn the old mare led them to a more familiar camp, south and east toward the joining of two rivers. There Linden found them.

He had lost a dozen of his men and thrice that number of horses. The rest were gaunt and wild-eyed. They brought no booty, no fruits of their raiding. All the enemies they had fought were beasts of the earth and forces of the air: storm, flood, fire on the plain. They had never reached the great river of the south at all. "When we were closest," said one of the king's companions in dull wonder, "the earth opened up and swallowed five men."

"The gods were against us," another said. "At night when I tried to sleep, I could feel their eyes staring down."

"Nonsense!" Linden cried. He alone of all of them seemed almost his wonted self. He had gone straight to his tent when they first returned, and emerged much later, much cleaner, and much happier than he had been before. His wives, it was said, had mourned his absence and were delighted to have him back again. But the one he had taken to his bed was not his wife. It was the elder shaman's wayward wife, White Bird.

He was full of himself now by firelight, and full of *kumiss*, too. "The gods weren't against us," he said. "How could they be? Those thieves broke the gods' own law. It was a bad storm season, that's all. We'll go back in the spring. We'll find my stallion."

"Maybe lions got him," someone muttered. "Or a tribe in search of meat."

"He lives," Linden said. "He's in the south. I feel him. Come spring I'll go to him. And no god or storm will stop me."

People did not argue with that. Linden was a king robbed of his stallion. If he had been less than obsessed, they would have been less than pleased.

Walker would have been happier if Linden had stayed away through the winter. But while it was a nuisance to have the king back and getting in his way, it was useful, too. Decrees that had been difficult to uphold in the king's absence were now, with a compliant king, much simpler. Walker had only to see that Linden was well occupied with his women and his pleasures. The rest was Walker's to order as he pleased.

In the winter, he decided, Drinks-the-Wind would give way at last to the weakness of age. It would leave Walker without eyes to see visions, but surely the gods would provide. Or they would send Sparrow back, for him to use as he had before.

And in the spring, yes, the world would change. Walker would change it. Already he had chosen the means. One of the young men was even more biddable than Linden, but also slightly more intelligent. Walker was watching him, and occasionally offering him signs of favor: a lesson in herb-lore, the offer of a choice portion at the daymeal. Ash was of the royal clan, of course, Linden's brother of a wellborn mother. He would do well for the purpose Walker had in mind.

Walker was, all in all, content. Even when, at the gate of winter, he discovered that Drinks-the-Wind was gone. The elder shaman had vanished. His women did not mourn him, nor would any admit to knowing where he had gone. If the gods were kind, the old man had gone away to die. If not, then maybe his own age and frailty would settle it.

Walker decided to let it pass. Whatever the old man thought he was doing, he could not harm Walker or weaken his power over the People. He was more than king now. He ruled them in body and in spirit. And he would continue in that. That was his vision. He needed no more.

·········· **44** ··········

K ESTREL LEFT THE Grey Horse with a cold heart. His eyes were burning dry. His spirit wept.

But he had to go. He was bound. He could not bring back either Sparrow or the stallion, but he could bring back word of where they had gone.

It was betrayal. But it was also his duty. And maybe, he tried to tell himself, the People had recovered. There must be a new king of stallions, a new lord of horses to make Linden forget his silvermaned darling.

Kestrel went for a hunt of some days' length, mounted on his dark-maned grey and leading a second, likewise a grey, but still bearing the dapples of youth. It would have been a lovely ride if it had been the hunt it pretended to be: clear sky, warm sun, burgeoning spring. But there was deep winter in his heart.

He had thought—and indeed hoped rather than feared—that he might be prevented, either by men or by gods. But the ways were open. The floods of spring had passed. There were no storms. No wild beasts threatened him. Earth's blessing lay on him, when he would have given heart's blood to suffer her curse.

And no one pursued him. Sparrow did not come after him. He could not believe that she did not know. She must. But she let him go.

She must hate him. He hated himself—but his word was given.

The north was still somewhat in winter's grip, snow in the hollows, spats of cold rain over the steppe. He found that he missed the shadows of trees—strange, for he had thought little of them while he had them.

He passed by the Tall Grass camp and the Red Deer camp, but he did not stop in either. It was uncivil of him. He could not care. He was a solitary creature, a hawk in blue heaven. He had no desire to share travelers' tales, even with such friends as he had in those tribes.

Not far from the spring camp, Kestrel's solitude was broken. A rider met him on the plain, rising up out of a fold in the hillside and setting himself athwart Kestrel's path. He was a strange, wild figure, white hair and long beard streaming in the wind, clad in a long tunic of white doeskin, and mounted on an elderly white mare.

At first Kestrel did not know him. Apart from the tribe, without the flock of people about him, he seemed a stranger. But when he spoke, Kestrel knew his voice. "A fine morning to you, hunter," said Drinks-the-Wind.

Kestrel peered into the shaman's eyes, searching for a sign of recognition. He might almost have said that Drinks-the-Wind was blind, so pale were those eyes, and so full of light. But they met his stare keenly enough. "A fine morning to you, O speaker to gods," Kestrel said. "Are the People nearby, then? Will I find them soon?"

"Soon enough," Drinks-the-Wind said. "They've wandered somewhat astray this season. Everyone is off his reckoning, one way and another."

"Yes," said Kestrel. "Yes—I, too. The People are not in camp?"

"They wander," the shaman said, "where the horses lead them."

Kestrel paused. Something in the old man's manner was strange. "They—didn't—send you out, did they?"

Drinks-the-Wind laughed, sweet and empty of either bitterness or guile. "No, young hunter, I sent myself. It was time to go." He sighed a little. "Past time, maybe. This is a new world we've entered into, however little some may understand it."

"You've had visions," Kestrel said.

"I always have visions." Drinks-the-Wind reached down to the sere grass, last year's remnant, that brushed his knee. A few seeds clung to the head. He stripped them, scattered them to the wind. "You go," he said, "and wait for the People. They'll come to the spring camp late, but they will come. Then do what your heart bids you do."

"I am not fond of my heart now," Kestrel said.

The shaman patted him on the shoulder. "There, boy. Be brave. You're wiser than you know, and you have more power than you imagine. Trust to it."

Then Drinks-the-Wind turned, or his mare turned, and rode away across the plain. Kestrel's stallions would not follow. Like his late and lamented dun, they were bound by the will of a white mare, and by the gods' command.

So for that matter was Kestrel. He could exhaust himself in fighting it, or he could let it carry him where it would.

As the shaman had said, White Stone was not yet in spring camp when he came there. He made his own camp up the bend of the river. The hunting had been poor in much of this country, and was no better here. When the People came, it would be a lean season.

The grass at least was good, if less plentiful than it could be. The horses set about fattening their lean flanks, while Kestrel made shift with rabbits and a lone deer. He could hunt down the People, he supposed, against the shaman's advice, and come to them in another camp or on the march. But he elected to stay where he was. He was putting off the reckoning, to be sure.

When it was ready, it would come. He waited in a strange kind of contentment, with a hunter's studied patience. In that brief meeting, Drinks-the-Wind had soothed his spirit—not altogether, but enough to sustain him in his waiting. It was a gift, and he was grateful for it. Someday he hoped that he could tell the shaman so. Though he feared the old man had simply ridden away to die.

+ +

The People came to the spring camp on a day of mist and rain, nearly a moon's cycle later than they were wonted to. The lowing of cattle, the squeals of horses, drifted ahead of them. Kestrel watched from the hillside above the river, well hidden in the wet grass.

The horses led them as always. His eyes searched the royal herd that held the van, but found only mares, and an old white mare leading, who could have been sister to the mare who had carried Drinks-the-Wind into the south. They were all heavy with foal, some seeming close to their time.

They had no stallion. The lesser herds, trailing behind, were suitably graced with stallions, and the herd of the young stallions and the men's remounts jostled and squabbled in the rear. There was no lack of princes to be king, but none had claimed that eminence.

The People followed the horses as they had for time out of mind: women afoot, laden down or leading oxen; children perched atop packs or running alongside; men and boys mounted and ranging the edges. Linden the king led the warband, the gathering of young warriors in their fine tunics—wet and bedraggled now with rain—and their bristling array of spears.

Linden was mounted on a very pretty stallion indeed, but the horse was no king. Kestrel could see that clearly.

At first he thought Linden had not changed at all. But as the People passed by his hill and began to make camp where they had done so every spring since the dawn time, he saw that the fair and open face had grown a little hard, and the honest eyes were narrower than he remembered. When he had ridden to the center of the camping-ground and halted and sprung from his horse's back, he moved with a sharpness that had not been there before. Easygoing Linden had discovered a temper—though somehow Kestrel did not think that it had sharpened his wits as well as his gestures.

No king of stallions, and a king who had not grown well into his office. Kestrel lost somewhat of the calm that Drinks-the-Wind had laid on him. To gain it back if he could, he searched among the People for faces he knew. The king's companions were there, all but Spearhead who had died in front of Kestrel. His father's tent was going up, his father's women bustling about it—and he recognized his mother among them, ruling them as she always had. Of his father he saw nothing, but that was as it should be: Aurochs would be out hunting.

Walker was there, whom Kestrel least wished to see. His tent was larger now, nearly as large as the king's. A round dozen women raised it and prepared it, so that one who sat idle while they worked could be led in. That must be his new wife, the Tall Grass shaman's daughter. Kestrel glimpsed fire-red hair and white skin, but at this distance little else.

Walker did not go in once the tent and the wife were established. He was keeping company with the elders. When the camp was complete, the fires set to blazing, and women preparing the daymeal, Walker entered the king's tent, where Linden had gone some while since.

Kestrel retreated from his hill. He told himself that he should wait a day or two, or even three, for camp to be fully settled before he rode in. The truth, as he knew too well, was that he was a coward. He could not muster his courage to face what he knew he must face. It well might be his death.

He returned to his camp up the river, concealed as it was from casual eyes, and made a wan supper, and lay awake nightlong, except for brief dreams. Sparrow was in them, in his arms or being a shaman to the Grey Horse People.

Dawn brought him no greater courage, but his heart knew that he could not evade his fate. He prepared himself carefully. He washed in the river. He put on the clean tunic that he had carried from the south, and fine white leggings, and boots of good leather. He wore his boar's tusks and his lion's teeth, and the lionskin waited to be spread on the back of his dark-maned grey. He combed his hair, which was wet still from washing, and plaited it tidily.

He was as seemly then as he could ever be. He mounted his stallion, leaving the other loose; but that one elected to follow. He rode down the river into the camp of the People.

+ +

They did not know him. His garments were made in Grey Horse fashion, and his horses were strangers. And, it seemed, he had changed more than he knew.

Dogs barked. Children ran after him. Men called greetings in trader-tongue as they would to a stranger. Women watched him sidelong, heads bowed—and that startled him, not for what it was, but for what it did to him. He wanted to make them look up, to shout at them to stand tall, be proud, look him in the face.

Yes, he had changed. People were remarking on his looks, admiring them mostly, and reckoning his wealth and rank. The extreme plainness of his clothing might mark a man of low standing, but the fine stitching, the carving of his knife-hilt, the bow and bundled spears that he carried, and the lionskin on his horse's back, with the

tusks and the teeth that he wore as ornaments, led them to conclude
that he was a man of rank, perhaps even a prince traveling on some
errand of the gods. And his horses were very fine, royal horses—and
what was more, they were greys.

Some were even wondering if he was a shaman, or—and these
were the greatest fools of all—a god's messenger. Or a god himself.
At which he would have laughed, but his throat was too tight.

He rode straight through the camp to the king's tent. The king
had come out of it, drawn by the alteration in the camp's accustomed
rhythms. Linden had his full complement of royal women now, Kestrel had noted the day before, and he had been enjoying them as a
man should enjoy a woman. His hair was unbraided and tangled on
his shoulders, his face rumpled with sleep; he had pulled on a pair of
leggings, hastily, and was still fastening them as Kestrel halted and
slid from the stallion's back.

Linden, too, failed to recognize the man he had sent out hunting
for a thief. He managed something like royal courtesy, and a greeting
in trader-tongue: "Welcome, stranger, to the White Stone People.
Have you come searching for the king?"

"My lord," Kestrel said in the People's own language, "I have
come back to you."

Linden frowned, puzzled. It was Curlew, from among the companions, who cried out, "Wolfcub! By the gods, you came back."

"Wolfcub?" Linden peered. "Wolfcub! Gods, it is you!"

The others were all shouting at once, word running through the
camp, a quite astonishing tumult.

But for Kestrel, none of it mattered but the man in front of him.
The sound of his old name was like a voice heard from far away, a
drum beating across the hilltops: remote, familiar, but of little concern to the self that he was now.

Linden seized his arms in a bruising grip and shook him; then
embraced him so tight he could not breathe. "Wolfcub. Wolfcub! We
all thought you were dead."

He stood back, still gripping Kestrel's arms. His eyes flicked up
and down, taking in the fashion of his clothing; marking the horses
he had brought with him, and fixing with a kind of desperate hope
on the second, younger, and darker of the stallions. But although it
was a very handsome stallion, it was not the one whom he had lost.

Kestrel could have waited, and probably should have, until he was alone with the king, but he could see no profit in delaying the inevitable. "I found him," he said. "But I couldn't bring him back. I was forbidden."

"Forbidden!" Linden bridled. "Who in the gods' name would dare forbid you to bring back my king?"

"Horse Goddess," Kestrel said baldly.

That roused an even greater tumult than the fact of who he was. Linden gaped at him. "How could she do that? He is my king!"

"He is her consort," Kestrel said. "My lord, if I could have done it, I would."

"Would you?"

That was not Linden's, that smoothly beautiful voice. Walker had come—not from the tent near the king's, but from elsewhere in the camp. He was little changed if at all, with his ice-white beauty and his cold pale eyes. He looked remarkably like his father, and yet utterly unlike.

Drinks-the-Wind was a shaman. This was the shadow of one, an image painted on a tentwall. Kestrel had not known he could see so clearly, but it was as distinct as a track in snow.

Kestrel regarded him coolly, a stare that—to his surprise—made the shaman flinch and look away. But Walker's voice was strong enough, and his arrogance unshaken. "I find it difficult to believe," he said, "that you were unable to fulfill the king's command. Obviously you found help on the way, and horses of remarkable quality— royal horses, if my eye is not mistaken. I think that you come to mock us, and to betray us. Is there an army behind you? Or will it wait until you've lulled us with soft words, then fall on us in the night?"

"I am alone," Kestrel said. "These horses were given me, yes, by Horse Goddess' people. None of them followed me. They have no care for war, nor do they trouble themselves with the concerns of tribes so far away. I came because I owed it to my king, for honor and for nothing else."

"You're mad, then," Walker said, "because you came here only to die."

"Odd," said Kestrel. "She told me that, too."

He was not prepared for the violence of Walker's response. The shaman fell on him, all but striking aside the king. "*She? She is there? Why did you not bring her back?*"

Kestrel maintained his calm by sheer effort of will, in the face of that blazing anger. It was edged, he noticed, with desperation. And no wonder, if it was true what she had told him, that Walker had taken all his visions from her. "Horse Goddess forbade," he said, as he had said of the stallion.

Walker struck him. It was a weak blow, a woman's blow, not even worth evading. "You are lying," Walker spat at him.

"I don't lie," Kestrel said.

It was fortunate for Walker's reputation that he remembered where he was, and did not throttle Kestrel in front of the gathered People. Kestrel was oddly unafraid of him—and foolishly, too, for however negligible his powers as a shaman might be, he was a very dangerous man.

Kestrel had walked between the lion and the lightning, and had taken to his bed Horse Goddess' chosen servant. He had no fear to spare for a mere man, however venomous his hatred.

Maybe Walker saw it. Maybe he simply chose to bide his time. He drew back, leaving Kestrel to Linden. "You really are alone?" the king asked him.

Kestrel nodded.

"He's right," said Linden. "You're mad. You know I can't just let you back into the tribe. You found the king and left him there."

Kestrel bowed his head.

"But," said Linden with the air of one who has made a great discovery, "if he wouldn't come to us, we can go to him. You will lead us. He is in this world, yes? He's not somewhere in the gods' country?"

"He is in the world," Kestrel said through a closing throat.

"Thank the gods!" Linden had lit like a fire in the dark. He threw an arm about Kestrel's shoulders and pulled him in, holding him tight in an embrace of brothers. "We'll take the warband. We'll win him back again. But now," he said expansively, "we feast. Our boarslayer, our wolfling, our loved companion, has come home."

KESTREL WAS TRAPPED—and there was no one to blame for it but himself. If he had thought at all, he had thought that Linden would kill him with his own hand. Then of course the warband would go to take the stallion, but Kestrel would not be part of it. He would be safely and honorably dead.

Linden was not angry with him at all. "If Horse Goddess forbade," he said as the women hastened to prepare a feast, "of course you couldn't take him. But I'm the king, the one meant to ride him. She'll let me take him."

"And if she won't?" Kestrel asked.

Linden's clear brow darkened. For an instant he looked as he had the day before, harder and colder, with a faint, cruel edge. Then he was himself again, grinning and thumping Kestrel on the shoulder. "Of course she will! And if she resists, I'll woo her. She'll let me have my stallion."

Kestrel sighed and let be. Preparations went on while he sat by the king. No one had asked after Spearhead. At last he said it, because if this was to be a funeral feast or a day of mourning, the People would have to know. "The one who went with me," he said, "Spearhead. He—"

Brief sorrow crossed Linden's face. "He died. We know. Walker told us. We thought you'd died, too. He saw it in a vision: a terrible storm, and lightning. Then everything was dark, and you both had vanished."

"*Walker* told you?" Kestrel bit his tongue. "And Drinks-the-Wind? Did he say anything of it?"

"Drinks-the-Wind was old," Linden said, "and had grown feeble. He's gone now. We've mourned him as is proper. As we mourned Spearhead. And you." His eyes glinted. "We mourned you very splendidly. Some people are maybe disappointed that you came back—it was such a waste of grief."

Kestrel smiled thinly. "I may give you something to grieve for yet," he said.

It was not a jest, but Linden laughed at it, far more uproariously than it deserved. He was happy, Kestrel thought. He had a war ahead of him and his stallion to win back. A long grim winter had lifted from his spirit. He could let himself be a creature of the sunlight again.

Kestrel's winter of the heart had only begun. He feasted as joyously as he could. To be reunited with the People—that was not the pleasure it should have been. He kept remembering a different tribe, dark eyes and round faces, and strangers who had, in so short a time, become as dear as kin.

If his father had been there, he might have felt somewhat differently. But he had always been alone, walked alone, hunted alone. The place he had fallen into by slaying the boar had never been altogether his. Now, with what he had been and done, he felt no part of this tribe.

None of them understood. Of course Linden had to know of the lion's claws and the skin, and he had to see the scars and marvel over them. The rest of the companions professed gladness to have him back, and none too carefully concealed jealousy of all that he had done, or that they fancied he had done. Boarslayer and lionkiller: he was a great hero, and he had no desire to be any such thing. He wanted to be lying in his tent in the Grey Horse camp, with Sparrow in his arms and Rain singing one of her songs nearby.

Inevitably Linden offered him a woman. "I'm rich in them now," he said. "I've a dozen wives from all the greater tribes, and concubines innumerable. Choose yourself one. Or two or three, if you've a mind. I'm sure they'll be delighted."

But Kestrel was not the child he had been, to take what any man bade him take, even his king. He bowed and thanked Linden politely, but said, "Tonight I'm weary, and I've yet to visit my blood kin. Tomorrow, if you're still minded to give the gift . . ."

Linden waved his hand. "Oh, go, go! They'll still be there tomorrow, certainly. Go, do your duty—and beg your kinsmen's pardon for me, for keeping you away from them."

✢ ✢

Kestrel escaped while he could. He cared little for most of his kin, and most of those were at the feast, basking in the light of his glory.

But his mother, who as a woman could not join the revels, was waiting in his father's tent, and the rest of the wives seemed glad to see him.

Willow dismissed them after a blessedly short while, but stayed in the men's portion, regarding him with eyes that were too proud to weep, even for joy. "We did believe," she said, "that you had died."

"I think maybe I did," he said.

She waited in the way she had, that commanded him to speak again, and speak well.

He smiled at that, a broader smile than he had offered Linden. "I can't seem to find opportunity, and they keep calling me by the name I left behind, but it's not mine any longer. The goddess' people—they call me Kestrel."

Her brows rose. "Sparrowhawk? Because you hunted a Sparrow?"

"They didn't know that. I'm not sure they do even yet. But their shaman insisted that I'm no wolf, I'm a small swift falcon with a ruddy tail."

His mother tugged at one of his plaits. "Small you are not, but swift and ruddy? Yes, I see that. It was a good naming."

Kestrel sighed. He had been clenched tight for so long that it felt strange to unclench, to be at ease again. He lay propped on his elbow, banked in furs that he or his father had brought back from hunting.

"Is she well?" Willow asked.

"Sparrow?" He was flushing—and why he should do that, he could not imagine. "Yes, very well—very well indeed. The people there, they let women be shamans. She's a shaman. They say she's very powerful, the most powerful that they've known."

"Indeed," said Willow, without surprise. "So you were in her mother's country. That's where the stallion is."

"Yes," said Kestrel.

"You could have stayed there."

"I promised the king," he said with a resurgence of misery. "Damn that stubborn honor of mine! I couldn't stay where I was happy. I had to come back here."

He had not meant to strike her to the heart, nor had he thought he would: she was made of sterner stuff. But her face had gone stark. "You found kin there—kin of your spirit."

"I found Sparrow," he said. He took her hand and held it to his breast. "Mother, except for you I have no joy at all in this homecoming. But you, and Father when he comes back—you make it bearable. If I could take you—if there is a way—"

She shook her head slightly. "I belong here. So does he."

"No," he said. And more strongly: "No! There is a place worthy of you. Their king is a woman, Mother. Their shaman is a woman. The king's heir is a man—they walk side by side, women and men: rule alike, hunt alike, live alike. Nothing is forbidden to a woman that is permitted to a man."

"Then Sparrow must be profoundly happy," Willow said. "A woman who is a king. Imagine that. Is she beautiful?"

"In her way she is," said Kestrel. "She rides as well as a man."

"And does she fight?"

Kestrel's teeth clicked together.

"She is going to have to fight," Willow said, "when our men come raiding. When you lead them to her."

The knot was back in Kestrel's middle, tighter and harder and more painful than ever. "What am I supposed to do? Run away? I can do that. Maybe if they're busy chasing me, they'll forget about the stallion."

"You know that won't happen," Willow said.

"Then what do I do?"

"You should have stayed there," she said. "Since you wouldn't, then you pay whatever price your foolishness demands. Who knows? Maybe the warband will have no better luck than it did the first time it tried to find the stallion. The gods drove it back. Maybe they will again."

"Maybe they will," Kestrel said. It was a poor hope, but it was better than any he had had before.

············ 46 ············

EEN BORE A son in the midmost moon of spring, delivered him at moonrise after a long and exhausting labor; but when Cloud laid him in her arms, she forgot all her pain and exhaustion in the enchantment of that face. Even as small and red and wrinkled as it was, she saw the beauty it would have, the hair like sunlight in summer and the eyes as blue as flax-flowers. "Summer," she called him, defiant, in this place where the mother named the child and not the father.

He was year-brother and milk-kin to Rain's daughter Spring; for to Keen's grief, she had too little milk for a child so robust and so strong. But Rain had enough for three.

She cried over that, weak with the birth, and Cloud held her as he had held the baby, with gentle strength. She had been appalled to come to her time and find him acting as midwife, and no one found it strange or outrageous that a man should do such a thing. Storm was there, too, and Rain, and others of the women who had borne children, but it was Cloud who supported her through the long ordeal, and into whose hands, at last, the child seemed to leap, yelling lustily at the world.

Summer had taken all her strength. It was slow to come back, so slow that she wondered if it ever would. But Cloud would not let her despair. "You'll nurse your baby as you can," he said, "so that he knows who his mother is; and you'll eat what I tell you and when I tell you, and do as I bid you, and you'll be strong again."

"I'm weak," she said. "I could barely even do what—any woman—"

"Stop that," he said, so sharp that she stared. He who was always so gentle was not gentle now. "You did as well as any woman. Better than most—that's a big, strong, healthy little monster, and he'll run us ragged before he properly learns to walk."

"But I—" she began.

"He tore you when he came, because he was so big. You bled more than you should. But you haven't taken a fever and you're gaining strength. You're going to live and be strong, and bear other children, too."

She blushed at that, for no reason at all. Cloud took no notice. One of the children had brought a cup of something hot and savory. She was not hungry, but Cloud made her drink it, every drop. Then he brought her her baby, warm and replete with Rain's ample milk, and let her hold him till she fell asleep.

+ +

Keen regained strength as Cloud had promised. It seemed slow, but he said not; he was pleased. He fed her like a prized heifer, saw that she had her baby by her except when he had to eat, and often Spring was there, too, sleeping or babbling or being delightful. Summer, at so young an age, mostly slept; but when he was awake he was as lively as a newborn could be, and noisy, too.

"He'll be a warrior," Sparrow said. She had kept away from the birthing by custom of this tribe: they believed that a bearing woman should not see what was before her, lest it frighten her out of all due measure.

For she was bearing. It had become evident in the early spring, and was obvious now. No one asked who had fathered it. They all knew, as they knew that he had gone out hunting and had not come back.

Sparrow had not grieved where anyone could know of it, nor raged, either. "He did what his heart bade him do," she said when Keen ventured to ask.

She was much too calm. Keen watched her carefully, but she seemed as she always had, rather quiet, rather reserved, and inclined to wander off by herself. But unlike Kestrel, she always came back.

She was not a woman for children. Even with a child in her belly, she had little interest in babies. But she could hardly ignore Summer when she visited Keen; he was either asleep in her arms or yelling in his cradle. "This is a warrior king," Sparrow said.

Keen shivered. "Not—not a shaman?"

Sparrow frowned and looked closer. Keen held her breath. Sparrow straightened and shook her head. "That gift the gods have kept from him. It's as well. He'll be happier as he is."

Keen could not disagree. "His father really isn't a shaman, is he? He's all a lie."

"His father is a shaman's son of a line of shamans. It was his misfortune that when the magic passed, it passed elsewhere." Sparrow left the cradle to sit by Keen. Keen was stitching again, making a covering for the baby. "He's coming, you know."

Keen went still. "He—"

"Walker. He's coming. They're coming, Linden and the warband, to take back the stallion."

"And you'll give the stallion to them," Keen said, "and let them go away."

"No," said Sparrow.

"But—"

"Horse Goddess has purposes of her own. And she has little love for the men of our people. They try her patience."

"But if they come with war, the people here will die. They're not warriors. There's not even a warband."

"I know that," Sparrow said. "I have to trust the goddess. And so should you."

Keen bit her lip. That was true. She should try harder to trust in Horse Goddess' will. But she could only think of Walker, how relentless he was in pursuit of a goal. What he wanted, he had. No matter what it was.

Would he want her?

Her eyes fell on the cradle, and on the child in it. That, he would want. A son of his body, a strong and kingly child. Maybe, for Summer's sake, he would want Keen again.

And did she want him?

That was a question she would never have thought to ask before she crossed the river into the south. She should not be thinking it now. And yet there it was.

She had loved Walker so much, and been so eager for his touch, his loving, his regard. All of that was gone. When she remembered him, she remembered how he had abandoned her in the spring camp, and forgotten her thereafter, pursuing his advantage through a loftier marriage. If he would take her back—which she rather doubted—it would be as a lesser wife, subject to the Tall Grass woman.

Keen had not known she could be so bitter, or could cherish her anger so long. What she wanted . . .

While she was maundering, Sparrow had risen quietly and gone away. Someone else was sitting in the place that she had left, waiting patiently for her to notice him.

Her heart leaped at the sight of him. Her smile was sudden and heartfelt. He returned it without an instant's hesitation.

She wanted Cloud.

It was a terrible thought. She had to put it aside while he was there, as difficult as that was. She wanted to touch him, run fingers through his curly beard, feel the surprising softness of his skin. She wanted to know with her hands the width of his shoulders, the muscled strength of his arms. She wanted to feel his arms about her, and hers about him. She wanted—

She wanted to taste the salt of his skin. She wanted to kiss him till she was like to drown. She wanted to feel him inside her, hot and strong, filling her, making another child.

She was Walker's wife. She belonged to him. But people here grew angry when she said such things, and insisted that she belonged to no one except herself. Cloud lay with Rain, she knew that. Rain lay with other men—had lain with Kestrel, people said, before Sparrow came. Then, they said, Rain no longer lay with him. He was a single-hearted man as they put it; he was a man for one woman, a rarity and much admired, though most of them did not understand it.

They were so free here—so wanton. Women walked about with their breasts bare, flaunting themselves, and no one disapproved. The queen herself did it, proud of her big round breasts with their dark nipples, and the king-marks and shaman-marks swirling on them. She took men to her bed nearly every night, and seldom the same man twice running. It was a kingly thing to do, if she had been a man— to take many lovers and never devote herself to one. It proved her strength before the people.

Keen could not do such a thing. It was not in her. But one man of all the dark lovely men in this tribe, him she could dream of, and did.

Not long after she understood that she wanted him, he came to her as she sat in the sun, rocking the cradle with her foot, and Spring was in one end and Summer in the other, both blessedly asleep. Rain was gone somewhere, not too far or for too long, but it was something to do with being a shaman. It was very warm that day, the new moon before the moon of midsummer when the tribes of the north would gather for the great sacrifice.

Tribes here did not gather so. Two or three or four would meet sometimes on common ground, dance together and sing together and share their young men and women. They would linger for a day or three, then part, returning to their own lands. Only a month before, a tribe called Laurel had met the Grey Horse on its journey from camp to camp, and they had danced and sung together for a hand of days. Keen, still weak from the baby, had stayed apart from most of it, but she remembered the singing; it had been wonderful.

Cloud as always was patient with her, and let her remember him in her own time. The sight of him in the flesh, after the dreams she had had, was almost too much to bear. Dreams could make a man more than he was, more beautiful, more gentle, and far stronger. But Cloud was just as he had been in the dreams. Completely without willing it, she leaned toward him and stroked fingers down his cheek. His beard was crisp and yet soft, as she had dreamed it would be.

She snatched her hand back with a gasp, stammering an apology. "I'm sorry. I didn't—I don't know—what I—"

"I do," he said, warm and rich with—laughter? No, nothing as slighting as that. It was joy. "I did come to tell you that you're well, as if you couldn't tell. And that, if you're minded—"

He did not finish. He did not need to. Keen knotted her fingers together in her lap. Her traitor fingers, that would have loved to finish what they had done, run down his cheek to his breast, down and down, until—

She hammered the thought down and sat on it. "My husband is far away," she said.

"One who would be your lover is here."

She caught her breath at such boldness. As wanton as these people could be, she had never expected him to be so direct. Rain, yes. But Cloud was a man of exquisite discretion.

Not, it seemed, in such a state as he was in now. He was not at all embarrassed by it. He carried himself, in fact, as if it were something she should be pleased to see: as if it were his gift to her. A tribute. A homage to her beauty.

Part of her reveled in it. But the part of her that was a properly brought up wife was appalled. She should not even look at a man not her husband, let alone lust after him.

He reached across the slight space between them and took her hands in his. It was a simple gesture. Anyone could do it, friend or kin. But it made her heart shudder and threaten to leap out of her breast. He leaned the last of the distance, and lightly, oh so lightly, touched his lips to hers.

She should recoil. She should escape. She should not open her own lips to meet his kiss, nor observe with dizzy delight that he tasted of sweet grass and herbs.

He drew back. She followed by no will of her own. Her hands freed themselves from his, to clasp behind his neck. He was only a little less tall than she: a tall man among these southern people. He was much broader, much stronger.

And yet he was so gentle. He was rampant between them, but he made no move to seize her and fling her down. He kept his wits about him.

That, as small as it was, was her downfall. If he had moved, if he had forced himself on her at all, she would have torn herself away and fled. But he left it entirely to her. It was her choice, to go or to stay.

She had never been given a choice. When her husband wanted her, she was expected to oblige him. She had never approached him. She had learned to want him, and to want him sorely, but always it was he who had come to her. It would have been unthinkable of her to go to him.

Here, a woman could ask. Or if a man asked, she could refuse. It made her head swim to have so much power. She could send him away, and he would go.

Or she could say, "Show me how a man loves a woman, here in the southlands."

He was quiet in his joy, but his eyes were almost too bright to meet. He kissed her softly but thoroughly, taking his time about it, letting her understand how many ways there were to take pleasure in a kiss. And when she understood that, he drew back. He said, "That is the lesson. Tonight I'll come to you. You may refuse me. Remember."

Her shock was so great that he had gone before she found words to speak. Summer woke then and began to bellow, and Spring, thus roused, shrieked with him. In settling them, and with Rain's coming to distract her, she almost forgot what Cloud had said and done to her.

······· **47** ·······

CLOUD CAME AS he had promised, slipping into the tent that Keen shared with Sparrow. Sparrow was not there: she was gone from the camp again. Summer was asleep in the queen's tent, close by Spring and her mother. Keen was alone.

She had decided that she would not do it. She would sleep in the queen's tent, or go away somewhere as Sparrow had. But when night came, she went to bed as always. As always, she plaited her hair neatly and folded her tunic as a pillow, and lay down in the darkened tent.

He brought light with him. He had one of his people's clay lamps that burned rendered fat from the cattle, its flame so dim and so flickering that it did little to banish the dark. But that little was enough. He set it atop a lidded basket and knelt beside her.

She rolled onto her face to cover her nakedness, blushing furiously. But she kept an eye on him—for wariness, she told herself. He had, somehow, shed his tunic.

She had not seen him all naked before. He was much the same below as above: not so broad in the hips as in the shoulders, by far, but well-muscled, with strong black-furred thighs. His manly parts were as substantial as the rest of him. He was beautiful as a bull is, or a stallion.

More than ever she felt like a peeled wand, thin and pale, with no strength in her. But he regarded her in open admiration. "So beautiful," he said. "Like a white lily. Do you not show yourself to a man? Is it something your people forbid?"

She hid her burning face; but inside her something cracked. Something tight and hard.

She thrust herself up. She let him see what there was to see: narrow hips, narrow shoulders, breasts not small as the People reckoned it but little enough here. They were empty now, their little milk dried; they were not quite as firm as they had been, and her belly was a little slack still, scarred from carrying the baby.

His expression was so fierce and yet so tender that her heart nearly stopped. He reached to run a finger down her cheek, down the slender length of her neck to her shoulders, pausing just where her breast began its soft swell. "Beautiful and beloved," he said in his voice that was full of slow music. "Will you let me love you?"

She could not speak. Her throat was shut.

"Well then," he said as if that had been an answer. "I will let you love me. Here, see. Touch me."

She could not.

He took her hand in his and raised it to his cheek; then drew it down as he had done to her, to his breast over the heart. "That is a beginning," he said. "Have you never loved a man of your own will?"

She shook her head.

"Then you must learn."

She wanted to learn. She was afraid to learn. It was too bold. It expected too much.

He would not stop until she had done it. He coaxed her till she kissed him, herself, leaning toward him, touching her lips shyly to his. Something in the touch made her bolder. She ventured to lay her hands on his breast, to run fingers through the curly hair. She had never touched a man so before.

And he was letting her—he was glad of it. He knelt quietly while she explored him, doing what she had dreamed of: spanning the width of his shoulders, testing the strength of his arms, and shyly, shakily, freeing his hair from its plaits. Once freed, it sprang into a mass of curls, thick and wonderfully soft.

He shivered at that, with a murmur of pleasure. It seemed he liked her hands in his hair, combing fingers through it, trying to make order but only making it more riotously unkempt. The slide of it against his shoulders roused a gasp from him. She followed it down his back, finding the places that made him gasp anew, stroking slow circles along his spine and across his shoulders, then down into the hollow of his back. She should have flinched from that; from taut buttocks and firm thighs, and the discovery that, rather to her startlement, his ribs were wickedly tender. Fingers brushed across them made him flinch and shiver. Persistence made him collapse in helpless laughter.

Laughter—in this. And he took revenge, too. He snaked out a sly hand and found her own vulnerable portions, till they rolled together like puppies, he laughing, she giggling with no control over it at all.

They came to a halt against a heap of bundled hides, he on his back, she half-sprawled across him. One small shift, one turn of the hips, and the hard hot thing between them would be inside her.

She could not move. His laughter had died somewhat after hers had. He lay quietly. All but his rod, which knew well what it wanted.

She rose over him. She shifted, she turned. She did—herself, with no aid from him—what no proper wife should ever do. She danced the rest of the ancient dance with a man not her husband.

The gods did not strike her down. Her flesh did not wither from her bones. Nor did her womanly parts shrivel and grow cold. Not at all.

This man was large, and filled her almost too full; but as he matched her slow and rather tentative rhythm, it seemed she had never been filled, or satisfied, before. He took heed of her. He noticed what made her flinch, and what made her quiver, however slightly, with pleasure. She had not known how lovely it would feel to be stroked along the back and flanks while he was inside her, or how exquisitely sensitive her breasts would be, sparking with delight at the quick dart and flick of his tongue. He loved her everywhere, not only in her secret place. And she, belatedly, tried to do the same. She was awkward; she lacked the sense of what to do. But she did try.

The summit when she reached it was sudden; it caught her by surprise. She had been so intent on him that she had hardly taken notice of her own body.

But he was intent on it. He raised her slowly, step by step, higher than she had ever known it was possible to go. And when she was near to crying aloud with the intensity of it, he held her there. And met her, in a hot swift rush that sent them both swooping down into breathless stillness.

She lay for a long while, all her body thrumming. Little by little she remembered how to breathe again.

He was holding her in his arms. Her head lay on his shoulder. It fit perfectly there. His warmth, the scent of him, the strength that he never flaunted, were all perfectly as they should be.

Guilt was there, no doubt of it, but faint and far away. Her hand found his. She wound her long fingers in his shorter, broader ones. Her spirit felt as if it had done the same. Woven with his. Become a part of it.

⁕ ⁕

Keen was a terrible creature, a monster, a woman who had betrayed her husband. And she was as happy as she had ever been. It burst out of her in song, in a voice she had barely known she had: clear, pure, and surprisingly strong. She sang as she tended the children. She sang as she plied her needle, fetched wood or dung for the fire, gutted fish or plucked fowl or skinned rabbits for the pot.

"We should call you Linnet," Sparrow said with every evidence of amusement, as she came on Keen rocking the cradle with her foot, sewing a tunic, and singing a song that had come to her out of the sunlight and the birdsong and Cloud's presence in her arms the night before.

Keen blushed. He always came well after dark, and never when there was anybody about. And Sparrow had not been in her own tent in days.

Still, Sparrow was a shaman. She must know. And though she hated her brother, surely what her brother's wife did to dishonor him—

She did not seem angry or outraged. She was smiling, not as brightly as she would have before Kestrel went away, but warmly enough for any purpose. "It's good to see you happy," she said.

Keen could not look at her till her hand tipped Keen's chin up, making her meet Sparrow's eyes.

"I know," Sparrow said. "Everybody does. It's a wonderful thing; a great joy, too. Do you know what the Grey Horse People say? Men and women are made for one another, and often in great numbers. But when a man is made for one woman, and a woman for one man, the gods have given their greatest gift."

"I haven't—" Keen said.

"I forgot—you can't see it, can you? Wherever you go, his shadow goes with you. Where he walks, your shadow walks beside him."

Keen shook her head. All the brightness had vanished from her heart. "It can't be so. I belong to someone else."

"Not any longer," Sparrow said, "if in fact you ever did. Are you tormenting yourself over my brother? Silly fool. He never thought twice before he supplanted you with a richer wife. Would you like to wager that's he's taken another already? Or that if he hasn't, come the gathering he'll find himself an even more advantageous match?"

"I'm sure he will," Keen murmured. "But I still belong to him."

Sparrow shook her head. "You always were a stubborn thing—even when you seemed most pliant. Promise me something, Keen. Promise that whatever you do, you won't harm Cloud."

"What, do you love him, too?"

Sparrow bared teeth at her. "Not as you do—but he's a good man and will be a very good king. Promise."

"I'll try," said Keen. It was as much as she could do.

And if she did harm him, if anything she had done caused him any suffering, she would die. She contemplated it with perfect calm. If it must be, then so it would be. The gods would do as the gods chose to do.

THE GODS WERE against Linden's riding into the south. Walker swore that it was not so, but Kestrel knew what Walker was, and that was not a shaman. The waves of storms that swept spring into summer, the flooded rivers, the unwonted cold and the delay of summer's warmth, kept the king in camp long after he would have been gone. And the hunting was as bad as Kestrel had known it would be—worse, once the storms began.

The People would not have suffered terribly for that, for they had their herds, which were numerous. But the storms brought a plague in among them. Calves and kids, such as were born alive, died of sickness. So too the foals, which were the People's greatest treasure.

Only the royal herd seemed to escape the curse that was on the rest. The white mares foaled in proper time and brought forth strong young—and every one a filly. No colt was born to them, no stallion who would be. And when each came to the foal-heat, her sisters drove off the stallions who came courting, savaging any who persisted.

"This is a curse indeed," Walker said. "And we know who laid it on us. We must go. We must destroy the thief who stole our king of stallions, the witch who has afflicted us with this plague of ill fortune."

Linden heard him avidly. So, by then, did the elders. The young men of course were all afire to be gone. No one pressed him to stay, to wait until the gathering, when he could muster the warbands of the lesser tribes and ride southward with an army. "That's too late," he said, and Walker abetted him. "We'll go now—as soon as there's a break in the rain."

That break came, by chance, within a day of Linden's saying so. The clouds lifted in the night. The sun rose over a sodden earth, rivers swollen beyond their banks, and drowned things floating in them. But Linden did not care. The light was brilliant, and warmer than it had been in all that bleak season. "An omen!" he cried. "The gods are with us after all."

His men cheered. The elders and those who would stay behind echoed them. The women in their tents were silent. Only when the warband had gathered and mounted and ridden out did they lift up the song that every man heard as he rode to war: the shrill and piercing keen that was half dirge, half war-cry.

Kestrel's mother had told him that morning as she plaited his hair in the war-braids that she would not sing for him, or for his father either—for Aurochs was riding with the warband as guide and guard. "If we could bring you with us—" Kestrel began.

"A woman in a war-party?" Willow shook her head sharply. "Not unless she's a captive—and I refuse to be that. Stay alive, child. You and your father both."

The memory of her face followed him as he rode away from the camp. She was refusing to weep. Tears were a weakness. She sent him out firmly, and his father after him, the two of them so alike, she declared, that if they lingered she would be calling each by the other's name.

Kestrel eyed his father sidelong. It did not seem likely that he was as handsome as that. He was certainly not as calm or as beautifully composed. Aurochs had greeted his return with an entirely uncharacteristic display of emotion: brimming eyes and a long, breathlessly tight embrace. Since then he had been much his usual self, except that he kept to the camp much more than Kestrel might have expected. But with the hunting so bad, there was little enough profit in going out.

Kestrel had not looked for him to come on this riding. Most of the older men stayed with the tribe, to rule and guard it, and to escort it safely to the gathering. But Aurochs prepared for war with the younger men, chose his remounts, mounted and rode with the warband. Kestrel wondered briefly and unbecomingly if he did it to keep watch over his son. But that was hardly likely. He wanted to go to war, that was all. Men did, even men of substance, husbands and fathers. He was welcomed gladly. Before he was a hunter he had been a famous warrior. His skill with weapons was if anything greater than it had been then, and he was still a young man after all, still in his prime.

Strange to ride with Aurochs as an equal, not as father and son but as warrior and warrior. Other people than his mother remarked that they looked alike; that Kestrel seemed older and his father younger than he was. Aurochs said nothing to that. Kestrel had nothing to say.

The weather held as they rode south. They had somewhat to do to ford the one or two greater rivers, which should have been sinking to their summer levels but were flood-high. That delayed them, but not by as much as Kestrel would have liked.

The time for gathering was coming, but they had passed the great camping-place already. They paused there to pay respect to the sacred places. Linden offered a young stallion on the stone—the beast had gone lame beyond repair, but he was fine enough to please the gods, once his blood had been let and his bones laid on the fire. They ate his consecrated flesh and raised the hide above the altar-stone for the People to find when they came, such of it as the beasts and birds might have left. Its stripped skull they raised on a spear and left on guard, the king's promise and his boast, that he would come back riding his own royal stallion.

Linden was sure of it. He rode as one possessed by the gods, in a white fire of certainty.

Walker abetted him. Kestrel wondered when people would begin to notice that the shaman had no visions to give them. Those that he spoke of were old, from before Drinks-the-Wind left the tribe. The vision that led the warband was Linden's.

Kestrel was not asked to guide them. Not yet. South of the river was all Linden needed to know until he came there. Kestrel rode as a warrior. Most days he even managed to pretend that that was all he was. Then memory would strike, or some glint of the sun or ripple of the wind through grass would remind him of what he was, and of what he went to.

Sparrow was there. When he let himself, he could feel her, a warmth of presence, cooling if he turned east or west, going cold if he turned north; but while his face looked southward, it was as if he stood in front of a fire. He dreamed of her as he always had, and that was strange, because she never upbraided him for what he had done. She came into his arms with a sigh of homecoming, loved him with as much passion as ever, and never, not once, called him what he was, which was betrayer of his faith to her.

+ +

The weather grew gentler and the hunting better as they made their way south. They met the Red Deer on their way to the gathering,

paused in their camp for a night, and in the morning took with them
a good portion of the tribe's warband. Its king did not come, which
was as well. Two kings were too many on such a raid as this. But the
young men were delighted with the adventure. They brightened the
air immensely with their laughter and singing, their fresh horses and
their lively spirits. They had not had such a spring as the People had.
All the storms had kept to the north.

Tall Grass must have passed them by. Kestrel could not tell if
Walker was glad or sorry for that. Glad, maybe, that he did not have
to pretend to his wife's father that she was a frequent occupant of
his bed. He had not gone to her, people said, since soon after he
married her. She was known not to be with child, nor was she likely
to be. "Some women have no use for men," Willow had said when
Kestrel happened to ask.

"Maybe she has no use for *that* man," Kestrel had said.

"That's possible, too," said his mother.

Whatever the truth of that, they passed the place of the Tall Grass
spring camp, but the tribe was gone. They camped southward of it,
near the river. In the morning they would cross.

Some of the men went down to the ford to see how deep the
water was. It ran high, but not, Kestrel reckoned, high enough to be
impassable.

His father agreed with his reckoning. "We'll manage," he said,
"though we might lose a horse or two. It's treacherous toward the
middle, if you don't know the way of it."

"You know this river?" Kestrel asked.

"I've crossed it," said Aurochs. "There's good hunting in the
woods beyond."

Kestrel nodded. His breath was coming short. It had struck him
rather too suddenly, if far from the first time, that past this crossing
there was no turning back. Linden would not stop until he had his
stallion.

But there was nothing at all Kestrel could think of, that would
turn Linden from his course. The gods' own storms had only been
able to delay him. They had given up—or were biding their time.
That could well be so. Had they not waited till he crossed before, to
smite his companion with lightning and to sweep his horses away?

"There's death in your eyes," his father said.

Kestrel closed them. "I am thinking," he said in the blood-tinged
dark, "of the gods and their playthings."

"Yes," said Aurochs.

Kestrel opened his eyes again and turned them on his father. "Would you have done it? Or would you have stayed?"

"I would have done it," Aurochs said.

It did not comfort Kestrel as much as he had hoped, but it soothed him a little. There was another man in the world at least, who was as stiff-necked as he was.

⁕ ⁕

That night in camp, Walker approached Kestrel as he sat apart. Others had tried to persuade him to join in the dancing and singing about the fire, but he had ignored them.

Walker he could not ignore. The shaman sat beside Kestrel, took the skin of *kumiss* that he had been trying to drink himself senseless with, and drank deep. "You'll be our guide once we cross the river," he said. "Is it far, where we'll be going?"

"Far enough," said Kestrel. *Kumiss* had lost its allure even before Walker drank a good portion of it. His head ached, but was damnably clear nevertheless.

"Will we come there before midsummer?"

Kestrel slanted a glance at him. He was too casual. This question mattered. "Why?" he asked. "Are you hoping we'll have gone there and back again in time for the gathering? That's not likely."

"I didn't think it was." Walker drank again from the skin. He had been drinking before that: he was steady and his voice was un-blurred, but his eyes were a little too bright. "We'll have our sacrifice in the warband. The gathering has been seen to."

Kestrel raised a brow. "Yes, I thought it would have been. The elders, who speak for the king—"

"The elders will speak," said Walker, "and the shamans will pro-claim their visions. *My* visions, O hawk of the gods. But that matters little. What matters is here. After gathering, the tribes will gather again here, in this place, to wait for us."

Both of Kestrel's brows went up. For some reason he was calm, though this was a thing he had not known. "Do the others know of this? Does Linden?"

"Oh, no," said Walker. "The word has gone through the sha-mans, from the Red Deer onward. Their gathering is for the gods, and for the making of marriages among the tribes. The other, the new gathering . . . that is for something else."

He put Kestrel rather vividly in mind of a dog who has stolen a bone and carries it off to bury. Whatever he plotted, it pleased him very much indeed.

"I don't suppose," said Kestrel, "that you're mounting a war against the southern tribes."

"Oh, no," said Walker. "Not at all. We don't need the southlands yet. This is for the north."

Kestrel's breath left him slowly. He had not even known he was holding it. "That . . . may be wise," he said.

"It's very wise," said Walker. "It's my plan. Mine. You'll see. You might even marvel with the rest of them. Though you're not the sort to marvel at much, are you? You have a cold heart."

Not where he loved. But Kestrel did not say that. He sat in silence, watching the dancers about the fire. They were dancing the wardance, leaping high, whooping and chanting their vaunts. As he watched, Linden sprang up in their midst, naked, gleaming with oil, hair loose and streaming bright sun-gold. Whatever he lacked in wit, he lacked nothing in beauty, or in virility either. And he was incontestably fierce in battle.

"Pretty, isn't he?" said Walker beside him. "We should put him to stud like a fine stallion, and breed lovely fools for the warbands."

"He is the king," Kestrel said. "You raised him up. Are you regretting it now?"

"Not at all," Walker said. "Maybe we'll have our stud-service, at that. He's got all his wives with child, and most of his women, too."

"Even the old shaman's wife?"

"No," Walker said. "Not White Bird. Pity, too. She's the most like him of any."

Since Kestrel had often thought the same, he held his peace.

There was a pause. He dared to hope that Walker would grow weary of silence and wander off, but Walker seemed determined to torment him to the utmost. "Tell me, hunter. Tell me the truth. Is my wife—out there? With the others?"

Kestrel could not see the use in denying it. "Yes. She is."

"She was stolen, too," Walker said. "Taken from me, to mock me as the stallion was a mockery of the king. She's mad, you know—my sister. She hates us."

"I wouldn't call it hatred," Kestrel said.

"What would you call it, then? Malice? Contempt?"

Kestrel did not answer.

Walker grinned mirthlessly at him. "You did find her, didn't you? Did you ever lie with her? Southern women are wanton, it's said. Her mother would have lain with half the men of the People if my father hadn't keep her muzzled and bound."

Kestrel set his teeth.

"You did, didn't you? Was she worth it? Because of course, you know, I should geld you, since you dishonored my sister."

That was a jest, or Kestrel was meant to take it so. But he had little enough humor when all was considered. His smile was completely without mirth: a baring of teeth, no more. "You'd do better to kill me. Because if you did less, I would hunt you down and kill *you*."

"And you are a great hunter, of men as of beasts." Walker's glance took in the boar's tusks and the lion's claws. "Will you add a shaman's skull to your ornaments?"

Kestrel had a moment's flash of Sparrow standing by the fire in the Grey Horse camp, holding up a skull-cup set with blue stones and carved with swirling signs. Those signs he knew very well. They were limned in her flesh, sealing her power. Out of that vision he said, "Never fear that, shaman's son. If I should take a skull, it would be to drink true power."

With that he rose and walked away, it little mattered where. Nor did he look back, to see what Walker made of his words.

············· **49** ·············

SPARROW STOOD BY the fire on the eve of midsummer. The Grey Horse People were camped at the northernmost edge of their lands, by a grove that was sacred to Earth Mother.

In the daylight, Cloud had sacrificed to the great goddess: slitting the throat of a snow-white bull and letting the blood pour out on the ground. Time was, they had said, when it was not a bull who died but a youth of the people; but that custom was forsaken. Just so in the north, each year a young king had gone to the altar-stone and given his life for the people; and the one who took his life took with it his kingship.

The world had grown soft in its age. And yet Sparrow felt no softness in it tonight. The stars were fierce in their multitudes. The fire leaped high. The scent of roasting bull was strong.

She lifted the cup of Old Woman's skull, offering it to the ravenous stars. It was full of berry wine, leavened with a sprinkling of blood. The people watched in silence. Even the horses were watching: the mare, the silvermaned stallion. The mare was vastly in foal, and uncomfortable with it, but she had come in from the herds to see this offering to her goddess mother.

The stars found the offering good. Sparrow poured out a little on the ground for Earth Mother to drink. Then she sipped the sweet strong wine and passed it to Storm who stood nearest. Storm bowed low over the cup, sipped, passed it to Cloud, and he to Rain; and so on through the circle of the people. It came back not quite empty. One drop lingered. Sparrow offered it to the fire, which hissed in response.

So was the feast blessed and consecrated. Sparrow laid the cup away in its wrappings and gave it to one of the children to take back to her tent. At that signal, the silence burst in a torrent of sound: singing, skirling of pipes and beating of drums, and the pounding of feet on earth as the people began to dance.

Sparrow was not too heavy with child yet to dance, but her mood was strange. When she held the cup to the stars, in the fire's flare she had seen for a moment Kestrel's face. It was stern and might have seemed cold, but he always looked so when he was heart-sore. She wanted to reach out to him, to touch him, to assure him that all was well; but he was gone.

She retreated from the firelight and revelry toward the white gleam of the mare. The mare had no greeting for her. She was intent on something altogether more important than her servant. Her tail lashed; she stamped, snapping at her sides.

Sparrow might have withdrawn, but the mare made it clear: she was to stay. So too the stallion, though not too close—she lunged at him when he ventured nearer.

She foaled there on the outskirts of the firelight, while the people danced and sang in Earth Mother's honor. From the glimmering caul emerged a dark nose and dark feet, elegant curling ears and shoulders broad enough to give her pause. Sparrow eased the foal from its mother's womb till it lay on the grass, glimmering wet, struggling already to stand.

It was a colt. He was all dark but for a star on his brow; he would be grey, she knew, though in youth he would be black. He was the very image of his sire, who stood well apart, neck arched, nostrils flared, alert in every muscle. As his son drew breath in the world of the living, he loosed a peal, a trumpet of greeting and of triumph.

The dancing paused. The music faltered. The fire flared, catching the small dark thing and the recumbent mare. The stallion stamped and tossed his head.

Somewhere among the people, a young man whooped. A woman answered him. They whirled into a wilder dance than before, a dance of greeting and of gladness, welcoming this new prince, this omen, this promise of glory, Horse Goddess' firstborn.

+ +

On the day of midsummer, as Sparrow lingered with the mare and the new colt, teaching the colt to trust and never to fear a human touch, one of the children came running, shrilling her name. "Sparrow! Sparrow! Sparrow!"

"Yes," said Sparrow when the child was close enough to speak to without shouting. "That is my name. What is it? Does someone need me?"

It took the child a moment to recover her breath, and with it such dignity as she had. "Storm needs you," she said. "There's a messenger. He comes from Greenwood clan. He says—"

Greenwood was north of Grey Horse, not far from the river. Sparrow remembered to thank the child, even as she sprang into a run.

The man was sitting with Storm, drinking herb-tea and eating berry cakes. He did not look as if war or terror had overcome him; he was a stolid person, unassuming, but something about him said that he could speak and be obeyed.

Storm greeted Sparrow politely, but she did not wander off in indirection as elders could in council. "This is Bracken, king's heir of Greenwood. He brings word that you should hear."

Bracken inclined his head to Sparrow with the respect that everyone showed her here; they all knew who she was. "Horsemen," he said, as direct as Storm had been. "They've crossed the river west of us. We counted a hundred, riding as in a warband. Their king has yellow hair."

Sparrow nodded. She had been expecting it. Hearing it, knowing that it had come, gave her a feeling almost of peace. "I thank you," she said. "If I may ask . . . were there others riding near the king?"

"Kings are always well accompanied," Bracken said solemnly. She could not tell if his eyes glinted. He did not seem the sort of man to jest on such an errand, but one never knew. "This one rode in a band within the band. All men, no women. I noticed one close by who was paler than I've seen before, like a bleached bone; and two together like twin falcons, keen-faced, with ruddy hair."

"Two?" Sparrow blinked. Two of Kestrel?

No; of course not. Everyone knew how much he looked like his father. Aurochs had come, then. And that was interesting in ways she would examine later, after she had spoken to this messenger.

Aurochs and Kestrel. And Walker. Of course he had come. He must need her visions sorely, as sorely as Linden needed his stallion.

Storm and the stranger were silent while Sparrow pondered. They were waiting for her to tell them what to do. It was not a weak thing, indeed it was a kind of strength. She bowed her head to it. "If you will," she said to Bracken, "or can, tell the tribes between here and the river to withdraw. Let them leave the way open, and clear the path for the warband."

"I can see to that," Bracken said.

"Good," said Sparrow. And to Storm she said, "I'm not commanding you. I'm asking. Are you willing to stay, to wait for them? You need not. You can go, and protect your people."

Storm nodded slowly. "Yes, I can. Perhaps I should. But this is our place. We belong in it. We've camped here every summer for time out of mind."

"These are men who live to fight," Sparrow said.

"Such men as your Kestrel?"

"No," said Sparrow. "Kestrel is reckoned odd and rather soft."

Storm laughed, incredulous. "Soft? Your Sparrowhawk? He's as hard as a flint blade. Although," she conceded, "he has a gentle heart."

"These men have hearts of flint," Sparrow said. "They kill for joy."

"And you will face them." Storm sighed, and shrugged a little.

"We fight better than maybe you think. And maybe there will be no need to fight. We'll stay."

She was not to be moved. She saw Bracken tended, fed, and given a fresh horse. She would have been glad to offer him a bed for the night, but he would not stay. "I've messages to run," he said, "and tribes to visit. Best I begin now."

There were preparations to make. The people had to be told, and offered the choice: to retreat to a more distant camp, or to stay. Nearly all of them elected to stay. The ill, the old, those who feared for their children, took horses and oxen and a strong store of provisions and rode away south and eastward. The rest, men and women both, brought out weapons Sparrow had not known they had: short bows but strong, for shooting from horseback; spears of fire-hardened wood, sharpened or else tipped with flint; quivers full of arrows. They had knives and clubs and darts. They were well equipped to face a war.

"Raiders come," Storm said, "and not all them on two feet. Wolves in winter, too, and lions, and once a herd of aurochs. Their bull had a taste for manflesh."

Sparrow was rather properly humbled. She had been thinking of these people as strangers to war. But peace was a choice they made. They would fight if so compelled.

⚜ ⚜

Keen had not gone away to the safer camp. Sparrow tried to persuade her, but she refused to go. "Rain is staying," she said. "She's Summer's milk-mother. Summer is much too young yet to wean."

And no matter that one of the other women would have been pleased to take Summer to her breast. Keen was adamant. "When Walker sees Summer," Sparrow warned her, "he'll want him. And if he sees what is between you and Cloud—"

Keen paled, but she would not give in. "You'll look after them," she said, "whatever happens to me."

"I'd rather look after you," Sparrow said, but the battle was over. Keen stayed.

And they waited. Bracken's people sent word of the horsemen's passage. It was not as swift as Sparrow might have expected. They were advancing warily. Sparrow wondered if that was Kestrel's doing, or Walker's. Linden must be fretting endlessly at the delay. But someone among his advisors was counseling caution—as if this were war indeed, and they could expect an army to fall upon them.

She hoped that they were growing more unhappy rather than less, the farther they rode, and the emptier the land was. Complacency might serve her purpose, but mounting fear of the unseen would serve it best.

·········· 50 ··········

W ALKER COUNSELED CAUTION in the warband's passage through the southlands. Linden would have ridden straight on, but when scouts brought word of camps discovered but empty of people, Walker insisted that they stop at each one. Some had been abandoned as recently as a day or two before, but they never found the inhabitants, even when they sent bands of riders to track the tribes. Half a day or a day away from the camp, the trail invariably vanished, or proved to be false.

"They know we're coming," Walker said by the king's fire at night. He could not sit still; he paced and fretted, as restless as everyone would have expected Linden to be. But Linden, apart from an expressed and rather obvious desire for a woman, was at ease.

"What makes you think they're expecting us?" he asked.

Walker looked as if he would burst out in words of unfortunate consequence, but he had a little self-control left. He answered with tight-drawn patience, "People don't just walk away from camps in summer, not without cause. And we are that cause. They've seen us. They're running away from us."

"Pity," drawled Curlew from the depths of a skin of *kumiss*. "The king's not the only one who'd be glad of a woman. Or a nice side of beef, either. I'd be glad to raid some southlander's cattle. Take his daughter, take a fat heifer, have myself a feast."

The king's companions sighed at that. "Kestrel," said the king, "do you think they'll run, too—the ones we're hunting?"

Kestrel began to regret that he had taken a place at the king's fire. He should have spread his lionskin on the camp's edge and gone undisturbed to sleep. But he had had a desire for *kumiss* and a hunger for the gazelle that roasted over the fire.

Linden wanted an answer to his question. Kestrel gave it unwillingly but honestly enough. "I can't tell you. They're not warriors, I know that. They see no dishonor in flight, if it keeps the children safe."

"Weaklings," Linden said. "If they run, you'll track them. You found them before. You can do it again."

"They found me," Kestrel said. "I was half-dead on a riverbank."

"You'll find them," Linden said.

It was lightly spoken, but Kestrel heard the growl beneath. The king had laid a command on him—the same as before, but stronger now, because Linden would ride wherever he rode. This time he could not escape his duty.

Kestrel escaped soon after that. Walker was still pacing and snarling. For all that it was his caution that had slowed their advance, he was aquiver with impatience. He was in rather a terrible state, Kestrel thought. Was it just that he was blind to visions, and must have his sister's eyes to see them? Or was there something else that drove him to distraction?

Kestrel was not particularly inclined, tonight, to concern himself with Walker's anxieties. He had enough of his own.

Aurochs was asleep near where Kestrel had in mind to spread his own bed. Kestrel unrolled the lionskin at arm's length from his father and smoothed it on the flattened grass. He lay on it, yawning hugely, stretching till he felt the pull in his scarred ribs.

Sleep eluded him. People had begun to sing by the fire. After a while he saw Linden leave it and walk not far from him, pausing just within sight. A second figure crept from the camp to join him: from voice and movement, one of the younger men of the Red Deer, so young his beard was barely sprouted. He had a face as pretty as a girl's, and a girl's giggle, too. The two of them went down in the grass, taking such comfort as warriors would take on the march when women were far away.

Kestrel sighed inaudibly and rolled onto his belly, head on folded arms. He did not need a girlish boy to ease his discomfort. What he needed was close now, so close that when he closed his eyes he could see her. But whether she would want to see him ever again—that, he did not know. He could only pray. And hope that, somehow, she would forgive him.

The two in the grass were noisy enough to wake the dead. It amazed him that his father slept through it. When at last they were done, Linden left the boy panting and still giggling, and walked quickly back toward the camp.

He paused by Kestrel. Kestrel considered feigning sleep, but Linden seemed determined to wait him out. He opened his eyes. There was just enough firelight, at this distance, to see the king's face. It was a little slack with satisfaction, its smile lazy. "He'll go another round if you've a mind. My taste is for finer meat, or I'd have stayed."

"I have no taste for such meat at all," said Kestrel.

Linden dropped down beside him. "Truly? I've heard some say you must prefer men, since you're so seldom seen with women. Though from what Fawn was saying after you had her that night . . ." His voice trailed off. Fawn, as he must have remembered, was dead, buried with his father. He shrugged, sighed. "Is it true, what Walker said? Did you lie with his sister?"

Kestrel would not lie to this man, whom in his fashion he trusted. "Yes," he said.

"Did you lie with her in the south? Was that why you took so long to come back?"

Far too often, Kestrel thought, one did underestimate this man. Quick he was not. Stupid? Not in certain ways. When it came to the ways of men with women, Linden was not stupid at all. "Yes," he said again.

"I thought so," Linden said without anger. "You know, I never noticed her, except that she was different—little and dark. And people said her mother was a witch. Did she turn out beautiful?"

"Not particularly," Kestrel said. "Not to most eyes."

"But you think she is."

"Her spirit is a white fire," Kestrel said. "She really is a shaman. Far more of one than her brother ever was or could hope to be."

"A woman can't be a shaman," Linden said.

"In the south she can be."

"That's hard to believe," said Linden.

"Believe it," Kestrel said.

He thought Linden might leave then, but the king stayed. "Walker says that I should kill you once we find the stallion. You betrayed us, he says. You're leading us into a trap."

"Do you think that?" asked Kestrel.

Linden lifted a shoulder. "I think it's strange that this country is empty. We could be going to an ambush. But we're strong. We'll fight our way out if we have to."

"And will you kill me if it is an ambush?"

"Yes," Linden said. "I'll hate to do it. I like you, Sparrowhawk. You always tell me the truth. And you never treat me like a fool."

"I don't think you are a fool," said Kestrel. "You could be a better king, but I've heard of worse. You've the wits to let others rule where it's sensible, and you keep the women happy; and the young warriors love you. Nobody loved the old king. Only you and Drinks-the-Wind mourned him when he died."

"My father was a good king," Linden said. "Tell me. Did Walker kill him?"

Kestrel's eyes widened. "How did you know that?"

"I told him," Aurochs said.

Kestrel started half out of his skin. His father was awake, had perhaps been awake from the beginning. He lay on his side, eyes open and clear of sleep.

"*Did* Walker kill him?" Linden pressed.

"Yes," Kestrel said. "He did. Sparrow saw it—she was watching. And Spearhead who is dead. He used a dart to sting the horse."

"Do you think he'll do something to me?"

Linden did not sound afraid. Kestrel, who had been thinking such thoughts for a long while, was taken off his guard, so that he could not for a while think of anything sensible to say.

It was Aurochs who said, "I am thinking that it is near midsummer, and in the old time they sacrificed the king on the Stallion's day—the third day, the day of the greatest sacrifice. I am also thinking that Walker bade the shamans bring all the tribes to the river after the gathering. He'll be making a new king there, if I'm not mistaken."

Kestrel shook his head to clear it of fogs that had been filling it since he came back to the People. "Of course. That's what he's up to. But he can't kill Linden out here. He'll want to do it where the tribes can see."

"The warband would do," Aurochs said.

"But first he has to have the stallion." Kestrel frowned, pondering that. "It's too close to midsummer. We won't find the Grey Horse before then, not if they're camped where I think they are—

and supposing they stay there and don't vanish into the hills and woodlands."

"Midsummer this year is mid-moon," Aurochs said. "It's not the time of power that the new moon would be—and Walker is a new-moon shaman. Would you like to wager that he'll push to find the stallion before the new moon, and ordain that the sacrifice be then and not on the day of midsummer?"

Kestrel's belly tightened. "Yes. Yes, that's when he'll do it, if he does it. Then take the king's head and the stallion's head back to the river, and raise up a new king there. But how is he going to make the royal mares accept a stallion for his new king to ride?"

"Simple enough," said Aurochs. "He'll name a new royal herd, and have the old one sacrificed. A great sacrifice, a mighty holocaust before the gods."

"The People would never allow that," Kestrel said, appalled.

"They would if he declared that the royal herd was a deception, a plot on the part of the southern witches, and cited as proof that these witches are Grey Horse People. If their women took the shape of mares and came to deceive us, and in the fullness of time stole away our kingship through our stallion—who'd not believe that?"

"I would not," Kestrel said. "No Grey Horse woman would do such a thing, even if she could. What would she know of the People, or care?"

"My son," said Aurochs dryly, "the People are the world's heart and center, its divine rulers. How could anyone, even a southern tribe, fail to acknowledge their power?"

"That's ridiculous," said Kestrel.

"To you it is."

And Linden said, "That's not true, is it? About the witches? Because if it is—"

"Believe me," Kestrel said, "the Grey Horse had never heard of White Stone until I came there, and it has no care at all for our kings or our troubles, except when we force them upon it. Anything the royal herd is or does is Horse Goddess' doing. No mortal man or woman has a part in it except by her will."

"But those are Horse Goddess' children," Linden said. "You've told us so."

Aurochs spoke before Kestrel could, in his quiet voice. "Believe this, my lord. Walker lies as he breathes, for his very life. And he'll destroy yours to feed his power."

"Then what do we do?" Linden asked. He was afraid, maybe. Maybe he was only confused. But he believed—and that was what mattered.

"I think," said Kestrel, since Aurochs' glance passed the question to him, "that we need to watch and wait. And decide whom we can trust. Keep the companions by you always, my lord."

"We should tell them," said Linden.

Kestrel nodded. "I think so. They're to be trusted. Some of the warband, too. Not the men of the Red Deer. I think they're his. I think Tall Grass is serving him in the gathering while Red Deer serves him here. And . . ." He hesitated. "I think . . . my lord, would you be willing to make alliance with the Grey Horse?"

"But we're going to raid them," Linden said in surprise, "and steal back my stallion."

"We may not need to raid," said Kestrel. "If they're ready for us, and I think they are, they won't attack us before we attack them. We can ride in as guests."

"I don't know," Linden said. "The men are expecting a fight. They won't like this."

"Tell them," said Kestrel, "that Grey Horse women are as free as men, and that if a man asks, and asks politely, a woman will happily lie with him. But he must ask—he can't take."

Linden's eyes gleamed even in the near-dark. "Really? They really will?"

"Truly," said Kestrel. "Their younger shaman, who is a woman, came to me and lay with me, bold as a man, and skilled—my lord, you never knew such skill."

"Gods," breathed Linden. "Do you think—would she—?"

"She would like you very much," said Kestrel. "And she would find you quite amazingly beautiful."

"Is she beautiful?"

"Like a fine bay mare," Kestrel said.

"Ah," said Linden. He rose as if in a dream and wandered back to his fire and his companions.

There was a pause. Kestrel could feel his father's amusement.

"That," said Aurochs at length, "was divinely inspired. Did you just think of it?"

"Didn't you?"

Aurochs laughed softly. "I confess I didn't. I was hoping we'd be able to sweep in, raid, and get out; then pray we could gather enough of the warband to fight off Walker's faction. I'm thinking that what the people have done in this country, he's done north of the river—it's most suspicious that we met only the Red Deer and never passed by any other camps at all, except Tall Grass; and that was empty."

"You think he's got another warband following us?"

"It's possible," Aurochs said. "I've scouted as I can, but if they're following, they're farther back than I like to go."

"Then even if the Grey Horse unites with us against Walker's men, we'll be faced with a war when we try to go back home."

"Not if Walker is dead."

Kestrel stared at his father. "You'd do that?"

"I'm not sure I dare," said Aurochs. "But if his sister is as you say, she well may be willing. And able. How strong is she? Truly?"

"Stronger than any shaman I've known," Kestrel said.

"Stronger than her father?"

"Much stronger."

"And she hates her brother."

Kestrel found that his fists were clenched. "I don't know if I can do that—or if I'll let anyone else do it, either. What would it do to her spirit to kill her own kin?"

"Her brother was doing his best to kill their father."

"Walker's spirit is a dark and twisted thing," Kestrel said. "Hers is beautiful, and bright as the sun at noon. Brighter."

"You do love her," Aurochs said musingly. "I think we should find her. Then we'll see what we can see."

"Maybe I should do the killing," Kestrel said. "Or arrange an accident."

"That one is too canny for accidents," said Aurochs. "And if it's known that you killed him, you'll die for it. It's a terrible crime to kill a shaman."

"Worse than killing a king?" Kestrel lay on his back, hands laced beneath his head, filling his eyes with stars. "I've killed a boar by accident and a lion by necessity. Why not a shaman by both? I'll have his skull for a drinking cup."

"I think," said Aurochs, "that you should wait until we've found his sister."

"She won't let me do it."

"Yes," Aurochs said.

Kestrel drew a deep breath, held it, let it go all at once. "Do you know what I'm thinking? Beyond all the rest? That she'll help us not for me but for Linden. She's always been besotted with that pretty face."

"Has she?" said Aurochs.

"Yes. Ever since we were children. He never looked at her—why should he? He could have any woman he wanted. But now she's what she is. He likes a prettier face than she has, but he loves power. And I'm thinking . . . here in the south, a woman may have as many men as she pleases."

"You think she'll bed him."

Kestrel nodded. "I'm a fool, aren't I? Jealous of a king. I don't want to be one, not ever in the world. But if I could have Linden's face—"

"You wouldn't want it," Aurochs said. "He'll be losing his hair in a few years, and his sort runs to fat. You'll only get better as you age."

Kestrel laughed, catching painfully in his ribs. "Oh, yes! They all say I look like you. But that's years away, and he's beautiful now, with that yellow hair. She's a shaman, she's a woman of great power and wisdom, and I love her beyond endurance—and she is still infatuated with him."

"Youth," said Aurochs, "is a dire thing. Go to sleep, boy, and stop your fretting. I'll lay you a wager. If she lies with him, she'll do it once, just to have done it. Then she'll come back to you—and she'll never look away from you again."

"You think I should let it happen."

"I doubt you can stop it, if she's set on it."

"There is that," Kestrel sighed. "Do you think I—"

"I think you should sleep. We'll be tracking a tribe tomorrow, and beginning a game that could end in death for us all. Best we be rested before we begin."

That was wise. Of course it was. Aurochs was the wisest man Kestrel knew; wiser than any shaman.

But Kestrel was still inclined to fret over Sparrow and Linden. It was better than some of the other things, and Walker most of all. Walker could not be allowed to live. Not after all this was done. It was a cold truth, and a hard one. But in the end there was no escaping it.

THREE DAYS BEFORE the new moon, they found the camp of the Grey Horse People. It was nearer than Kestrel had expected; indeed they had camped very far north. They were waiting, he knew. Facing what they were destined to face.

Linden had done his best, and that, among the warriors, was very good indeed. Most of the warband were eager to approach as guests and to share the vaunted generosity of these southern women.

Walker offered no objection. Kestrel had not expected that he would. For what Aurochs thought he had in mind, it only mattered that both Linden and the stallion be in his power on the night of the new moon.

Kestrel noticed that one of the Red Deer men—the girlish boy, in fact, who had pleasured the king—was missing. He must have gone, then, to bear a message. Which meant that there was indeed a second warband behind them.

There was a kind of calm in it. This long hunt was nearing its end. Kestrel was ready for whatever might come.

They camped for the night not far from the Grey Horse camp. Some of the greater fools wanted to press on, to reach the dark-eyed wanton women sooner. But Linden for once was determined to be patient. "We'll come to them in the morning," he said, "with our best faces on, and no threat of war. And remember—don't take any of these women. *Ask*. We want allies, not enemies."

They all agreed to that, some less willingly than others. Linden appeared to be satisfied. Kestrel determined to be.

Tomorrow he would see Sparrow. However great her anger, however bitter her condemnation of what he had done, even if she turned from him to Linden, still he would see her. The thought made him dizzy with a mingling of joy and fear.

✦ ✦

They were up at dawn and riding by full light. All of them were arrayed as if for a festival, or as much as they could be after so long a riding. Such ornaments as they had, they wore. Their hair was plaited, their coats cleaned as much as could be. Their horses' manes were braided with feathers and bright stones and even flowers. All their weapons were put away, bows unstrung and riding in their cases, only their knives close to hand for a fight.

They were a handsome company, and their king was glorious to see. He had managed to bring with him a kingly coat and clean white leggings, and a great collar of shells and bone and beads, and other, lesser ornaments that were still impressively rich. He looked as a king should look, tall and golden and proud, mounted on his lovely dun stallion.

He insisted that Kestrel ride at his right hand. People murmured only lightly at that, and some was for the fact that Aurochs rode close behind: the two so alike, father and son, and Aurochs mounted on the younger of Kestrel's greys besides, to heighten the resemblance. They made a brave show, everyone agreed.

Walker was part of it. He rode on Linden's left in his long white tunic, with his hair blowing free, looking the very image of a shaman. But to Kestrel's eyes he was a shadow, a glimmer without substance.

The Grey Horse People were waiting for them. Their camp was ordered as Kestrel remembered, no defenses, nothing changed or darkened in preparation for attack. But he noticed that the back of it lay under the eaves of a wood. The people could retreat within if there was need.

It seemed a full camp, with children and dogs running out to greet the strangers, and their elders following, many afoot, but some mounted on fine grey horses. Those came together, Storm on her heavy-boned mare, Cloud and Rain on smaller, lighter horses, and a few others behind.

Sparrow was not there. Kestrel could not see or feel her. She might have been gone from the world; except that if she had died, he would know it. She had simply vanished.

Storm rode from among her people with her air of royal ease that was so disconcerting at first to a man from the north. The way she approached, the ornaments she wore, the leggings of doeskin tanned as soft as butter, made it clear who she was. There was also no question that she was a woman; she was bare-breasted as always in warm weather. So too was Rain in the shaman's place at her left hand.

Linden's eyes were like to fall from his head; Kestrel could well imagine what the men were doing behind. Some of them he could hear: they were panting like dogs.

Storm appeared to take no notice. But Rain knew well what she was doing to these outland warriors. She rode straighter than she was wont to do, and kept her shoulders well back. Her eyes had a gleam in them that Kestrel knew well. She would make mischief as she could. He only hoped that she did not provoke one of the warband into something everyone would regret.

"Welcome," said Storm in trader-tongue, "king of the White Stone People. You've been long awaited."

Linden looked ready to swallow his tongue. But he managed to stammer, "You—you were waiting for us?"

Storm inclined her head. "Will you be our guests? We've prepared a feast for you, and a place for your men to camp, and for your horses. Though if you will, I would be pleased to welcome you into my tent as my honored guest and my brother king."

"I—would be pleased to—" Linden shook himself. "Yes. Yes, you're very generous."

Storm smiled. "Come then," she said.

She led them somewhat away from the camp to a broad field. There a fire was built, and an ox roasting whole, and wild game, and a boar turning slowly on a spit. Kestrel glanced at Cloud when he saw that. Cloud was dressed as the women were; he bore no new scars, nor wore the boar's tusks. But Kestrel did not doubt that the boar was his kill.

There in the field they set up camp, centering it on the fire and the feast. The Grey Horse People streamed after them and past them, to help with the tents and the lesser fires and to tantalize the warriors with the sight of bold-eyed bare-breasted girls and women. But the warband remembered the command Linden had laid on it. No one offered impertinence, or tried to seize a woman. Kestrel was rather proud of them.

The king and the shaman and the king's companions had no need to raise a tent; Storm insisted that they must be guests in hers. For them there was a canopy near the great fire, rolls of furs to recline on, and boys and young girls to serve them baskets of fruit, cups of *kumiss* and berry wine, and bits of cheese and sweet cake while they waited for the feast to be prepared.

The child who waited on Kestrel and his father had a familiar face, though she was trying to be dignified. When she knelt to offer them her basket of berries, Kestrel scooped up a handful and said as casually as he could, "So tell me where the shaman is."

"Why," said the child, whose name, he recalled, was Squirrel, "she's yonder." She tipped her chin toward Rain, who sat beside the king. There was a child in her arms, suckling at the breast: a dark-eyed, dark-curled infant who reminded Kestrel, somehow, of Cloud.

But he would think of that later, and admire Rain's firstborn, too. His mind now was on another thing. "Not that one," he said to Squirrel. "The other one. The foreign one."

Squirrel's round eyes were guileless. "I'm sure I don't know, lord hunter," she said.

Kestrel bit his tongue and kept silent. She went on to serve Cloud, who must have overheard; but like everyone else, he was pretending to be oblivious. When he spoke, it was of trivial things, as if Kestrel had been a stranger.

That, Kestrel could not bear. "Stop it," he said. He kept his voice down, but it was sharp nonetheless. "I'll let her reveal herself when she deigns to do it, but I won't be treated as if you never saw me before. I don't care if you hate me—at least be honest about it."

"I don't hate you," Cloud said. He sounded surprised and a little dismayed. "Is that what you've been thinking? I'd be a hard man indeed if I hated you for this."

"For leading a warband against you?"

"There's no war yet," said Cloud. "You're guests. We're honored to serve you."

"Once," said Kestrel, "I was somewhat more than a guest."

"Once," Cloud said, "you were."

Kestrel flinched beneath the mask he had made of his face. So few words, to smite so deep. They were not spoken in anger or with intent to be cruel. In Cloud's eyes, they were the simple truth. They pierced Kestrel to the heart.

Cloud did not know, and Kestrel would not tell him. The prince had turned to Aurochs with an air of evident pleasure. "And you are the great hunter, yes? The Lord Sparrowhawk's father?"

Aurochs bowed assent.

Cloud smiled at him. "You are welcome here, my lord. Very welcome indeed."

"And why is that?" asked Aurochs.

Cloud's smile widened. "For your son's sake," he said, "and for the sake of another who has been a guest and more. But come, eat; be merry. There's ample time later for higher things."

Kestrel determined to be patient. Linden was more than pleased to do it: he sat between Storm and Rain, and his servant was an older girl than the others, lissome still but with her breasts sweetly budding. She was not shy, either, as maidens of the People were taught to be. When she had served him, she sat in his lap and played with his yellow braids, clearly fascinated.

Linden was a happy man. So were the rest of the companions whom Kestrel could see. But Walker, despite the offices of a lovely young thing and the attentions of several more, all captivated by his ice-pale beauty, wore the expression of a man on the raw edge of endurance. When his servant took her lead from Linden's and twined herself about him, he rose abruptly, spilling her to the ground, and stalked away.

Kestrel half-rose to follow, but Cloud's hand stopped him. Cloud's eye slid. Kestrel saw what he indicated: a nearly imperceptible drift of certain people in the shaman's wake. Walker was being watched. Kestrel should stay where he could be seen, and betray none of his suspicions.

Kestrel sank down reluctantly, but he could not deny the prince's wisdom.

The girl who had so discomfited Walker came to join those about Linden, with no sign of offense to have been cast off so rudely. "Such an odd man," she said to Linden. "Do you have many like him?"

"I think he's the only one," Linden said.

"Good," she said.

Kestrel began to see a great many things. Fortunately no one saw him fall back, laughing soundlessly; or if anyone did, he did not speak of it.

T REACHERY."

The hiss brought Kestrel starting awake. For a moment he lay in confusion. Then he remembered: he lay in the outer room of the queen's tent in the Grey Horse camp, with his father beside him and the king's companions beyond. Linden was in the inner room with Storm, who had claimed him from among the rest and taken him to a fate most of them could well imagine. They had heard it clearly enough from beyond the curtain.

Morning light slanted now through the open tentflap. Kestrel heard voices without, the soft clamor of a camp rising, dressing, breaking its fast. One of the voices was Storm's, warm, deep for a woman's, and rich with contentment.

But Linden was still in the inner room. Walker was with him— and none of the companions had roused.

None but Aurochs. The space beside Kestrel was empty. Kestrel's father knelt close by the curtain, listening as unashamedly as Kestrel went to do.

"Treachery," Walker said again, barely above a whisper. "They've trapped you here, separated you from your warband, and lulled you with strong drink and willing women. Where do you think my sister is? Wouldn't you wager that she's leading an army against you?"

Linden yawned audibly, and must have stretched: Kestrel heard a soft and distinct cracking of waking bones. "Walker," he said with a slight edge of petulance, "you woke me up to tell me that? You worry too much. Storm told me, your sister is a shaman now—can you believe that? A woman, a shaman. She's gone to a holy place to do whatever shamans do. When she comes back, she'll bring my stallion. Storm promised. I made her promise that he'll be alive and fit for me to ride. That was clever, don't you think?"

"Very clever," Walker said without conviction. "My lord, you believe what the she-king of an enemy people tells you? Of course she'll say what you want to hear. That's part of the plot."

"There's no plot," said Linden. "Guests are sacred here. We've eaten their bread, drunk their wine. They can't kill us. It's against their religion."

"So they told you," Walker said.

"Lord Sparrowhawk told me, too. He knows these people. And he's loyal."

"Is he?"

"I trust him," Linden said. "Now go away, please. I want to sleep a little longer."

"You'll sleep long in your death," Walker said tightly. "My lord—"

"Go away," said Linden.

Kestrel and Aurochs were well away from the curtain and feigning sleep when Walker burst through it. He was beyond knowing or caring who listened, Kestrel suspected.

When he was gone, sweeping through like a wind across the plain, Linden emerged from the inner room. He was naked, and his hair was a sun-colored tangle. He did not look near as sleepy as he had sounded. "Sparrowhawk," he said.

Kestrel sat up. Linden frowned at him. "Come in here. Help me."

He meant more than that Kestrel should help him dress and make some order of his hair. Between them, Aurochs and Kestrel made short enough work of that. Linden frowned through it, as troubled as Kestrel had ever seen him.

At last, as Kestrel finished plaiting his hair, he said, "Walker's going to crack."

"That's the intention," Kestrel said.

Linden shook his head. "I don't like the way he feels. He should be happier. His other army is coming. He has me safe, until he needs to take me away. I think he knows about the rest of it."

"It is possible," Aurochs said.

"Then you can do something about it?"

"We'll think of something," said Aurochs.

Linden's frown relaxed at last. He sighed heavily. "I'm not good at this game. I think I'd rather have come in and raided, and never mind all this."

"If you had come in so," said Kestrel, "you wouldn't have found the stallion. They've hidden him away. And Walker would still be plotting to give you to the gods at the new moon."

Linden shivered. But he said, "He can't do that without the stallion."

"Which means he'll set himself to find the horse." Kestrel sighed himself, almost as heavily as Linden had. "Storm's people are watching him. Our part is to pretend to be joyful guests—and to watch our backs. Do I have your leave to send scouts? Walker's army will be near, if it's coming. I'd like to know how near."

"Yes," Linden said. "Yes, do whatever you need to do. Am I safe with Storm?"

"As safe as you'll be anywhere," said Kestrel.

Linden smiled. "Oh, that's good. That's very good." He paused. Then: "She's old, and I don't know that she's beautiful, but . . . aaahhh!" It was a sigh of rapture.

That startled laughter out of Kestrel. "Was I right, then?"

"You were very right," said Linden.

+ +

Sparrow rode into the camp at midmorning. She came without fanfare. She was riding a dark grey stallion with a silver mane, with a small dark colt gamboling after. She had no escort but a single rider, a woman mounted on the moon-grey mare who had come with her from the north.

Linden was learning to shoot the shorter, stronger bow of these people, afoot for now; later, Cloud had promised him, he would try it from horseback. They had set up targets on the open field, and had mounted a contest, men and women of the Grey Horse against the men of Linden's warband.

Sparrow rode straight across the field, taking no notice of arrows that flew about her. They all flew wide. And yet some, it seemed to Kestrel, came very close; one should have struck, but a trick of the wind sent it veering aside.

He shivered lightly. The sight of her was like rain on dry land. She was as she had always been, small, dark, unprepossessing until one met her eyes.

She rode up to the king, with the other following. Linden's eyes were fixed on the stallion, ignoring for the moment the woman who rode him as easily as any man. The stallion did not notice. He was nibbling the neck of the colt who could not but be his son: the foal was his image in miniature, with already a glint of silver about the eyes and in the tail.

Linden approached him blindly. No one else moved. They were

all watching him, except Kestrel, who was watching Sparrow. She was almost smiling, doting as always on that handsome face.

Linden laid his hand on the stallion's bridle. The stallion noticed him then, and snorted at him, warning him away from the colt. The colt nosed inquisitively at the end of one of his braids. "You are riding my horse," Linden said to Sparrow. His voice was light and calm, but it made Kestrel's shoulders tighten.

"This is the goddess' horse," Sparrow said with equal calm.

"He belongs to me."

"Are you greater than a goddess?"

Linden blinked. "I am a king."

"You should be careful," said Sparrow, "that you don't anger her."

"This is my horse," Linden said again.

Sparrow shrugged, swung her leg over the stallion's neck, slid lightly to the ground. "He doesn't belong to any man," she said.

"You'll have to die," he said, "because you rode the king of stallions. You, a woman."

"I, Horse Goddess' child." Sparrow smiled at him, completely without fear. "I'll lay you a wager, king of men. We'll turn him loose and let him wander. You finish your archery. Then when the field is clear, call him. If he comes, he has chosen you. If not, you forsake your claim to him. Will you wager so? Are you as bold as that?"

"He is *mine*," Linden said.

"Then prove it," said Sparrow.

She had him. Kestrel could see how it rankled at him to be casting the bones with a woman, but her boldness, it seemed, intrigued him. And it was an easy wager, if his claim was true.

"I'll do it," he said. He slipped the bridle from the stallion's head and let him go. The stallion snorted, tossed his mane, lifted his tail and pranced down the field, reveling in men's admiration. His son loosed a high whinny and sprang after him. They danced together, the stallion gentle in his strength, the colt springing into the air and making a great show of ferocity.

No one could shoot while they were there, nor was anyone minded to venture it. They put away their arrows, unstrung their bows. Those who had wine or *kumiss* passed it round.

But Linden had eyes and mind for only one thing. "Now?" he asked Sparrow.

She spread her hands. "When you will."

Linden shouldered the bridle and walked out across the field. The stallion was grazing, the mare nearby, nursing the colt. Linden approached as a horseman should, easily, expecting no trouble.

The stallion grazed unperturbed. The mare had not seemed to move, but somehow, where Linden wished to go, she was there, with her colt at her side.

Across the field, somewhat apart from the rest of those who watched, Sparrow was smiling.

It was not a chase. None of the horses ran from the man. But he could not come near the stallion. Either the mare impeded him, or the colt. Or the stallion moved away just as he came close.

Linden persisted. He was not a man to surrender without a fight—even if that fight was as subtle as shifting mist.

At last Sparrow walked calmly over the trampled grass, straight up to the stallion; stroked his neck and his inquiring nose; and swung easily onto his back. She rode him up in front of Linden. Linden's face was slack with shock. "My lord king," she said, "what belongs to Horse Goddess can never belong to a man. And yet . . ." She held out her hand. "Come up," she said.

He hesitated so long that Kestrel thought he would refuse, but in the end he took the proffered hand. He swung up behind her. He sat on his own stallion—but only by her leave.

She laughed. The stallion wheeled, flagged his tail, and sprang into a gallop.

Not everyone was frozen in astonishment. A few cried out, even ran after them. But no one had a bow strung, even if he would have dared to shoot the woman without fear of striking the king.

"Gods," said Curlew of the companions. "Gods, she's stolen the king, too."

"She has not."

That clear voice startled them all. No one had noticed the mare's rider: she had slipped down before the game began, and effaced herself near Storm and her heir. But when she spoke, she drew every eye; and the sight of her was dazzling.

By the gods, she was beautiful. More beautiful than the king, and in the same mode: sunlight and summer sky. Kestrel had not known Keen could stand so tall or speak so distinctly, as if she had been a queen of this country. "She has not stolen your king," she said.

"She'll bring him back before too long. I give you my word on it—
and myself as hostage, if you have need of such."

Men looked down abashed—those who were not gaping at her
as if they had never seen a woman before. Maybe they had not: not
a woman of their own kind, standing with head up, eyes level, bold
as a man.

"You!"

Walker had retreated to his tent after he left Linden that morning,
there, no doubt, to brew up poisons and to ponder his myriad plots.
But something had brought him out. Maybe he was enough of a
shaman after all to know when his sister had come.

But his eyes were on Keen now. "You," he said, his voice as harsh
as anyone had ever heard it. "Wife. Come here."

Keen went white. She did not move. Cloud was standing close,
not touching her, but the bond that had been between them from
the beginning was as strong and nigh as solid as a rope of braided
hide.

That bond was her strength. Even with it, she looked near to
fainting.

"Come here," Walker repeated. "Now."

Still she did not.

He strode toward her. And as the mare had done for the stallion,
Cloud arranged to be between. If Walker would touch her, he must
do it through that much shorter but much broader and no doubt
stronger man.

Walker glared down his long white nose at what, his expression
declared, was a creature beneath contempt. "Out of my way," he said.

Cloud smiled his sweet and guileless smile. "Sir," he said, "far be
it from me to be rude to a guest; but this too is our guest. She is
under our protection."

"She is my wife," Walker gritted. "Stand aside."

Cloud shrugged slightly, spread his hands, and stood immovable.
He was still smiling.

Walker raised a fist.

"I would not do that," Aurochs said mildly, "all things considered. Since this is, after all, the prince of the tribe."

Walker wheeled. Aurochs stood at ease, offering no threat, ven-
turing no command. But there was no evading the truth he had spoken. Walker, who lived for power as Linden lived for women, stood

stiff. It must be a terrible dilemma, Kestrel thought: torn between his wife's defection and his passion for princes.

Kestrel watched him measure where he was, count the numbers who stood at Cloud's back, and recall what he had plotted—with, no doubt, the lovely memory of the army that was coming. It must have torn at him to retreat, but retreat he did, though not without casting a final, poisoned dart. "The woman is mine," he said to Cloud. "If I find that any man has touched her, that man's privates shall shrivel, and he shall enjoy no other woman."

Cloud seemed unperturbed. "You should have a care," he said. "Curses have a way of rebounding on those who cast them."

"Are you threatening me?" Walker asked, as if he honestly wished to know.

"I only warn," Cloud said, "as I would any guest whose safety was my concern."

Walker's lip curled. He turned on his heel and left the field.

Keen's knees gave way. Cloud wheeled to catch her. They touched only for a moment, she leaning, he supporting. Then they drew apart. But Kestrel had seen enough.

For Cloud's sake, he hoped that Walker's curse had no power to harm.

················· 53 ·················

SPARROW DID NOT ask the stallion to carry his doubled burden far: only as far as the wood, and somewhat within, away from eyes that could pry or ears that could hear.

Then she let him halt in a clearing with grass for him to graze on and a stream from which to drink. She knelt by that herself, slaked her thirst, laved her face.

Linden had dismounted when she did, and stood as if dazed, looking about. He was fully as lovely as she remembered, indeed perhaps more so. He was taller and his shoulders were broader. His beard had come in thicker, almost thick enough to braid as the great warriors did.

He was still as much boy as man, and no great marvel of intellect, either. "Is this where your magic is?" he asked.

Sparrow raised her brows. "My magic is wherever I am. Why? Did you think I'd sweep you off to my lair?"

He nodded. "And do unspeakable things to me. Kill me, even. Isn't king's blood the strongest of magical potions?"

"Who told you that? Walker?" She sat on her heels, looking up at him. He was very pleasant to look at. "I don't need your blood. I do need your alliance."

"My—" He seemed astonished. "But that's what I came here for! Or," he said with the hint of a frown, "that's what Aurochs and Kestrel said I should come for. Walker wants to kill me, you know. At the new moon. So he can make a new year-king. We're not sure who it will be. Maybe someone from the Red Deer, since they came with us."

Sparrow nodded. Cold walked down her spine, but her heart was steady. "Or a man of the Tall Grass. That's who's following you. Tall Grass, Cliff Lion, Dun Cow. But Cliff Lion won't be allowed to take the kingship—it's too arrogant. And Dun Cow isn't bound by marriage to Walker."

"But it is to me," said Linden.

"So it is," Sparrow said. Amid all the crowding visions and the intoxication of his presence, it was hard to think, let alone speak.

"You really are a shaman, aren't you?" Linden seemed to have recovered command of his body: he went down on one knee in front of her, peering into her face. His fear had retreated in favor of curiosity. "Kestrel said. But a woman—who'd have thought it? And you. He's right. You're not beautiful. But you shine."

"You can see, too?"

She had puzzled him. "I'm not blind. You're like Storm. Your beauty is inside. It's strange, but rather wonderful. Different."

"You don't talk to your wives, do you?"

That baffled him, too. "Why would I want to do that?"

Sparrow shook her head. "I suppose you wouldn't," she said.

"This really is your country," said Linden. "You must have been wretched among the People."

That took her aback. "I wasn't—" She had to start again. "I wasn't unhappy. I wasn't happy, either; but I didn't wallow in misery."

"You needed to be here." He touched her hair, which was rioting out of its braid as usual, and brushed her cheek: light, daring much, but as if unable to help himself. "You're not my enemy. Are you?"

"Never," she said.

"And Walker is." His fair brows drew together. "It's all very difficult to keep track of. Kestrel and Aurochs, they can do it; it's easy for them. Kestrel said you wouldn't hurt me. But you stole my stallion. You're keeping him away from me still. How can I be king before the People if I let you live?"

"That," said Sparrow, "I can show you how to do. Will you trust me?"

"Kestrel said I could."

"You trust him."

Linden nodded. "With my life."

"Why?"

"Because," said Linden, "he never lies to me. He never flatters me. And he came back, even knowing I could kill him."

"But you didn't."

"How could I? I needed him for a guide. And," Linden said, "he turned out to be so much more than that."

"Yes," said Sparrow, "there is a great deal to him." It hurt, almost, to sit here with this man whom she had yearned after all her life, and to speak Kestrel's praises. Kestrel, whom she loved to the heart's core. But she loved Linden, too.

The child stirred in her, restless, stretching beneath her ribs. Kestrel's child. She still wanted Linden; and rather strongly as she sat there, close enough to feel the heat of his body, and to catch his scent of musk and sweat and horses. Kestrel's was different, less strong, and somewhat cleaner. Kestrel was a fastidious man.

It did not matter. Nor did it matter to know that if she lay with this man once, then once would be enough. She wanted that once.

He was looking at her as she had dreamed he would, in something like wonder and something that most definitely was desire. He touched her hair again.

She moved into his arms. He was broader than she was used to, and taller; much larger than she was. He surprised her with gentleness, with forbearing to fall on her like a bull in rut. He had some skill, and some regard for her pleasure. He did not adore every inch of her as Kestrel did, but he admired her full round breasts and her ample hips, and he kissed her thighs.

She took him inside her. His broad breast above her, almost as thick with tawny hair as a southerner's, struck her rather piercingly with memory of one narrower, smoother, and dearly beloved. She buried her face in the hollow of his shoulder and let their bodies finish it.

He dropped away without lingering—and without, at least, falling asleep at once. His hand stroked the domed curve of her belly. "Kestrel's?"

She nodded.

"He's lucky," Linden said. "Though he doesn't know it. He thinks you must hate him."

"I love him," she said.

"I can tell."

"Why?" she asked in dismay. "Was I—"

"No, no," he said, patting her as if she had been a hound. "You pleased me very much. But when you talk about him, your eyes go all soft."

She began to laugh. Once she had started, she could not stop, even when he dashed water in her face. She was alarming him. She had to stop.

It took a long while and another cold drenching from the stream. Linden was eyeing her wildly, as if she had gone mad.

"No," she said. "No. It's only—I've wanted you so long. And when I have you . . . we talk about someone else."

"That's because you're his," he said. "I suppose I should arrange it that you two can marry, once this is over."

"I don't want to marry," she said.

"But—"

"This is the south," Sparrow said. "Things are different here."

"But how will your children know their father?"

"They'll know," she said.

He shook his head. He did not believe her.

With Kestrel she could have said what she was thinking, which was that if a man had to keep his wives imprisoned in order to be certain his children were his own, then the man was hardly the lord and master that he fancied himself. But Linden would not understand.

Beautiful Linden, who had given her pleasure, but not as Kestrel could. "Let's go back," she said.

He frowned. "No. Not yet. Tell me why you brought me here. It wasn't just to lie with me. Was it?"

"Actually," she said, "it was." And as he stared at her: "Also, to talk to you. To see what you knew. To know if you were honest—if you really meant to turn against the shaman who made you king."

"The stallion made me king," Linden said. "He was mine before Walker touched him."

"He was never yours," said Sparrow. "But your spirit calls to him. You know what he is. You really are a king."

"But I need him to—"

"Not to be king," Sparrow said. "That is in you, and always was. But to be king in front of the tribes: yes, you need something obvious. A horsehide to sit on. A stallion to ride."

"Then you'll let me have him?"

"I do no letting," Sparrow said. "That's for Horse Goddess to decide."

"Make her give him to me."

"I can't do that," Sparrow said.

His face darkened. "You won't."

"Can't." She laid her hands on his shoulders, stroking along them, soothing him as if he had been a large and restless hound. "You have to ask her yourself."

"Yes? Then I'm asking. I want my stallion back."

"One asks the gods in proper wise," she said. "At the new moon—"

"Are you going to sacrifice me?"

"Not likely," she said in the face of his fierce wariness. "You should have your full span as king, and be given opportunity to become wise. Earth Mother loves the blood of her children, but kings' blood is no sweeter to her than any other. She'll be as glad of a fine young bull or a stallion."

"She doesn't care if it's a king?"

Sparrow shook her head. "Men's laws mean nothing to her. When she asks for a human life in sacrifice, she wants it wholly willing. It must go to her gladly, in its full time."

"What if I did that?"

"Someday you will," Sparrow said. "But not now. You're young. Your blood is hot. You have great handfuls of life still to eat."

His gratitude was as simple as the rest of him. "I don't want to die," he said. "But Walker—"

"Walker will be dealt with. And you will help to deal with him.

Can you play the game a while longer? Can you pretend that I laid a spell on you, and bent you to my will?"

"Didn't you?"

She laughed—startled again by his flash of perception. About most things, she was coming to understand, he was rather slow-witted. But people he understood. And women best of all.

She reached suddenly and pulled him toward her, and kissed him until he gasped. Then she rose and held out her hand. He took it, drawing himself up. He was smiling, rather to her surprise. "I'm sorry I never noticed you," he said.

"I'm not," she said. "I could watch you, you see, and you couldn't stop me."

"Not any more."

"No," she said a little sadly. "Not any more."

················ 54 ················

L INDEN CAME BACK as he had left, riding behind Sparrow on the back of the silvermaned stallion. Sparrow dismounted on the camp's edge and walked calmly to her tent. Linden rode on as if in a dream, till he came to the warband's camp and the herd of stallions beyond. There he left the stallion.

No one could mistake the meaning of that. Linden, in what way no one knew—but there was ample speculation—had won back his silvermaned king.

But he insisted that he had not. "He's not mine," he said. "I was allowed to borrow him, that was all. I have to earn him back."

"And how will you do that?" Walker demanded. He had come out at Linden's return, composed as if he had never lost his temper so strikingly in front of the warband.

Linden shrugged at the question. "Horse Goddess will tell me," he said.

"Through whom will she tell you?"

"She'll tell me," said Linden. "Here, I'm thirsty. Who's got a skin of *kumiss*?"

Kestrel did not have one, but he was the first to find one. Linden smiled as he brought it. "You," he said, "should go to her."

Kestrel flushed. "Go? To her?"

"Yes, go," said Linden.

"But I can't—"

"Go," said his king.

Kestrel went, and with a fair portion of sullenness, too. What those two had been doing alone in the wood, he could well imagine. She had been dreaming of it all her life. And Linden had a look—he would not fail to notice Sparrow again. Oh, no.

The Grey Horse camp welcomed him with every evidence of gladness, and none of the cool distance that Kestrel had met earlier. But of course: he came alone. None of the People came with him. He was dressed in their fashion, too, and walking as they would remember, striding long-legged among these shorter, quicker people.

This was his homecoming. They did not make a show of it. There was no dancing, no feasting. But people greeted him, smiled at him. His escort of children appeared as it always had, running on as if he had never been gone: "We went hunting. We shot a squirrel. Would you like to see?"

"In a while," Kestrel said.

He saw how they glanced at one another and winked broadly. His teeth set. It would be a sore disappointment to them if Sparrow cast him out before he could speak a word, or refused to let him enter her tent at all.

She did not drive him away from the tent. The flap was not fastened; he lifted it and slipped within, pausing in the sudden dark after the bright daylight. As his eyes found their balance, he saw her sitting against the far wall, lit by a lamp, doing nothing. Waiting for him.

His temper had cooled remarkably in his passage through the camp. All that was left of it was the tightening of his brows in a frown. And the words he spoke, which he knew were not wise at all. "You must be happy. He finally noticed you. Was he as good as in your dreams?"

"No," she said.

Kestrel stopped short. "Then you did—then he—but—"

She rose. Before he knew what she was doing, she was in front of him. She pulled his head down. She kissed him till he reeled. And while he was reeling, she sat him down next to her accustomed place, and stood over him, dark steady eyes and expressionless face, and said, "It's your fault. If it weren't for you, I would have been satisfied."

"What?" He glared at her. "What in the gods' name does that mean?"

"It means," she said, "that after you, no man will ever truly please me."

The heat rushed to his face. "You're poking fun at me."

"No," she said.

"But you hate me. I abandoned you. I—" At last his mind comprehended what his eyes had been seeing since he came back. "You're bearing!"

"You noticed." Her voice was dry. "Of course it's yours. You were the first man I ever lay with, and the only one, until today. If there is a third, I doubt it will be soon. All he did was make me want you the more."

"You can't want me. You hate me."

"Why, because you would hate me if I left as you did?"

His mind was in a roil. His heart was beating wildly. He could not seem to breathe properly. So much to understand. So much to see differently. No hate. Linden. A child.

A child.

Her cool hands soothed his cheeks. Her lips brushed his forehead. "There," she said. "There."

His head rested against the curve of her middle. Inside it, something stirred. He recoiled.

She stood still. He came back slowly, trembling, laying his head where it had been before. The small presence stirred again, tapping against his cheek.

He burst into tears.

Sparrow was patient—which was the most remarkable of all the things she had done. She held him and stroked him and let him find his own way back to calm. He lost it for a while in remembering who had just this morning been lying in those arms, but her words had sunk in deep.

"I thought," he said when he could speak, "that because I betrayed you—"

"You would have betrayed your honor if you had stayed. No," she said, "you did as you had to do. I tried to keep you here, but the goddess wanted you to go. She was rather angry with me for using her name against you. Your leaving was her will. What you did, what you do now, you do by her leave."

"She was angry?" Kestrel's heart constricted. "Did she hurt you?"

"Of course not," Sparrow said. "I was rebuked. I had to endure your absence—and she let me know what you were thinking of me. *That* hurt."

"I'd rather you hated me than hurt for me."

"I deserved it. I lied in the goddess' name." Sparrow shrugged it away. She sank to her knees, face to face with him. She had laid aside her priestess-mask. The light in her eyes came near to felling him. "Oh, my beloved. It's been so long, and my arms so empty."

"And when you filled them first, it was with another man."

That was petty, and cruel. Kestrel bit his wayward tongue until it bled.

"I deserved that, too," she said steadily. "I'm not sorry I did it. Don't try to make me say I am. But he did prove what I should have known. I'm not as Storm is, or Rain. I'm not a woman for many men. One is all I need."

"Does it matter which one?"

She slapped him lightly, but hard enough to sting. "You know it does."

"Will you promise not to lie with another man?"

"No," she said.

Kestrel cursed his tongue. It kept saying the worst possible thing, the thing he knew better than to say. "And if—I promised not to lie with another woman?"

Her eyes went wide. "You would do that?"

He nodded—not too reluctantly, either.

"Don't," she said. "What we have, what we know of one another—it's enough. Leave it at that."

Her tone was clear. She was not to be moved. He traced her cheek with his finger. Her eyes closed. He kissed her softly—barely reflecting on who else had touched those lips since the day began. "Now," he said, "I am home."

Y THE EVE of the new moon, the scouts had brought word: there was an army riding toward the Grey Horse lands. But something else was riding ahead of it.

It came in between noon and sundown: a pair of white mares, and a pair of riders on their backs.

Kestrel could not say he was astonished to see Drinks-the-Wind, though he had thought the old shaman long dead. But the other—

"White Bird!" Linden spoke for all who knew her, with lasting astonishment.

She smiled at him. "Linden," she said. "You look well. Are the women keeping you happy?"

He flushed crimson. Even if he could have answered, he would have been forestalled: Walker was standing in front of his father, quivering with what could only be fury. "What, by the gods," he asked in a voice so soft it was nearly a hiss, "are you doing here?"

Drinks-the-Wind smiled down at his son from the white mare's back. "Well met again, my child. Are you prospering? Is all going as you would will it?"

"It will be," Walker said grimly.

"Then you must be very pleased with yourself," said Drinks-the-Wind. He left Walker to white-faced silence, turning to bow low to Storm, and lower to Sparrow.

Sparrow seemed as startled as Walker, but considerably less furious. "Father," she said. "I did not expect—"

"It seems no one did," Drinks-the-Wind said. "Come, shall we settle the horses? Then I think my wife would be glad to bathe and eat and rest. We've ridden far. Farther I think than she bargained on when she asked to come with me."

Sparrow's brows rose, but she held back her questions as they all did, until everything was done as he had asked—as indeed was only proper in welcoming guests from far away.

This they had not been prepared for. Even Sparrow. Kestrel asked her when there was a moment, when Drinks-the-Wind had been taken away, and White Bird, too, and food and drink were being prepared for them. "No," she said. "I had no foreseeing of it at all. It . . . changes things."

"How?"

"I don't know," she said. She sounded uneasy. "I only know that it does. I've got to think. Will you do something for me?"

"Anything," he said.

"Warn everyone you trust, beginning with the king. In the morning we'll go to a sacred place for the new-moon sacrifice—a place that happens to be north of here, and on the path of Walker's second army. Let our people go armed. And watch Walker! If he grows suspicious, he may turn on us too soon. I want us to reach the place of sacrifice before sunset tomorrow. And be ready. There will be no fighting if I can avoid it—but there well may be bloodshed."

Kestrel nodded. "May I ask . . . ?"

"Tomorrow we face one another, he and I. Today I'll see he's distracted."

"Be careful," he said.

She smiled and took his hand, and set a kiss in the palm. She folded his fingers over it. "Beloved," she said.

+ +

Walker's tent had been a frequent refuge since he came to this impossible country. Something in the air here threw him endlessly off his balance. Women's magic, he thought. Dark, secret, odorous magic like a woman's private parts, overwhelming men's strength by subtle degrees, till they sank down gibbering in corners.

He was still strong, though his temper was far less certain than he would wish it to be. His men here were ready for what was to come. His army was riding southward. Tomorrow it would halt at a useful distance, and there wait until he sent a man with the signal. His chosen one, his young king, rode at their head—not entirely to the liking of Cliff Lion or Red Deer, but they had been appeased with promises of greatness once the new year-king was raised up.

He should be well content. But that Drinks-the-Wind had come back, as it were from the dead, disconcerted him sorely. And his sister . . .

She was not a shaman. And yet she rode about as if she had been a king of men, a great lord of shamans. Everyone, even his own people, bowed to her. The visions she gave them were his visions. His. She had stolen them as she had stolen the king of stallions.

And now Linden was seduced by her spells. Walker knew the look: the vague, dreaming eyes; the sudden lapses in speech or movement. He knew what she must have done when she took him away. Women's magic again: magic of her body, trapping a man in coils of flesh.

That, Walker thought, might serve him better than she dreamed. Linden weakened and corrupted by magic would be all the easier to lead to the slaughter. But Walker was not entirely easy in his mind. It was this country, these people. Their magic was not stronger than his, it could not be, but it cast spells of confusion. And he had to be perfectly clear in mind and power, come the new moon.

What he needed, he knew in a flare of sudden light, a vision surely, such as were given to him most often through others' eyes. He went seeking it, passing quietly, keeping to less traveled ways.

She was not in the tent which he had been told she shared with Sparrow. He tracked her through the children, who would tell him what their elders would not, though they stared round-eyed at his pale beauty. He must seem to them like a god or a spirit.

They led him past the camp's edge to the eaves of the wood. Women gathered berries there—men, too, doing women's work as if it could not sully them. He could see that some of them were using it as an excuse: baskets abandoned, rustles and giggles coming from the undergrowth.

She had gone farther in than any, to a clearing edged with brambles and difficult of access, but she had found a way in. Her basket was full; she had sat down in the grass to rest. Another had come with her, was still gathering berries, eating as many as he let fall into his basket.

As Walker paused, watching, he bent over Keen and dropped a ripe red berry in her opened mouth. She swallowed it. He sweetened it with a kiss. Her laughter rippled. She lay back still laughing, arms stretched above her head, wanton and merry.

The man, who was no less than the prince-heir—difficult as it was to tell one black-bearded savage from another, this one Walker remembered, because he was a man of rank—lay down with her and lifted her tunic. She wriggled till she was rid of it. He cast off his own leggings and mounted her, and rode her as a man rides a woman, but long and slow. She did not giggle as her sister harlots did. She smiled, sweet and rapturous, and covered that blunt bearded face with kisses.

Walker watched it to its end, which was an unconscionable time in coming. Then he watched as they lay together, murmuring inaudibly, the prince's broad brown hand caressing her white breast. This was not the first time, he could well see, that they had lain together. They had an air of ease that came only from long familiarity.

They were still lying so, shamelessly naked, when a newcomer slipped through the brambles. It was a woman, carrying a black-eyed baby on her back and another swaddled in her arms. Keen flushed very faintly and half-moved to cover herself with her arms, but her lover laughed and kissed her until she remembered again to be wanton. The newcomer was no less so herself, half-clad as women went in this place, in leggings but no tunic. She sat near the lovers and began calmly to nurse the child in her arms.

The prince lifted the other from its cradleboard on her back, set it in his naked lap and dandled it till it crowed with laughter. Keen leaned against him, smiling down at the baby, which grinned back up at her.

Walker was so intent on them, so appalled and yet so fiercely aroused, that it was some few moments before he truly saw the infant whom the second woman was nursing. It was a perfectly ordinary child, fair-skinned, fair-haired.

Ordinary for one of the People. Not for these dark southerners.

The child finished its dinner. Keen reached for it, drawing it to her, slipping it free of its swaddlings. It was a fair child indeed, as fair as she was herself, golden-haired, longer and more slender than the other, darker infant. If it was not her own, then there must be another woman of the People among these tribesmen.

And if it was hers, then . . .

Only the thickness of brambles kept Walker from bursting in upon them. With that to stop him, he had time to think, to grow calmer, to understand a number of things.

It was an infant, but not a newborn. As it lay in its mother's lap, he saw that it was a manchild. A son. Beautiful and perfect, and clearly robust: when the dark girlchild cooed and crowed, he roared his strength to the world.

The second woman took the girlchild from the man's lap and set to nursing her as she had the other. She did it without fuss, smiling and chattering with the man while Keen rocked the golden manchild to sleep.

Walker slipped away then, but not to his own tent. He was waiting in Keen's tent when she came back, decorously clad, hair in a tidy plait, arms empty of the child. Nor was her lover with her. She was alone.

She did not see him at first. It was dim in the tent, and she was not expecting to find anyone there. She slipped off her tunic and searched in a basket for another, drawing out one fit for a festival, or for welcoming strangers to the camp.

She saw him then as she stood naked with the tunic in her hands. She lifted it quickly to cover her breasts.

Walker looked her up and down. "What, are you so modest then? And you my wife, whom the gods know I've seen the whole of, and more than once."

Her face was stark white. "What are you doing here? What do you want?"

"Why," he said, "to visit my wife. And, I rather hoped, my son. It is true, yes? I have a son?"

She gasped. "How did you—"

"I know these things," he said. "Were you going to present him to me? It must be a difficulty for him, to have lived so long without a name."

"He has a name," she said, low and tight. "Mothers name their children here."

"Do they? And do they give their children to others to nurse, as well?"

"I had no milk," she said. "A—dear friend offered to be his milk-mother."

"No milk? You? And why is that? Did the gods curse you? Or did you see to it that your lovely breasts would not be ruined?"

"Get out," she said.

"But I am your husband," Walker said.

"I said get out."

"No," said Walker. "I need the power you can give. Even as stained as you are, you are a woman of the People, and my wife. No one else will do as well."

Beneath the new boldness that she must have learned from southern women, she was stiff with terror. It was delicious, that mingling of bravery and fear. It aroused him even more strongly than the vision among the brambles. He surged up. She whirled to run, but she was too slow. He caught her. She twisted, kicking, clawing at his face. He laughed. "O beautiful! What a lioness you've become."

"Let her go."

Walker looked from her to a dark figure standing in the shaft of light from the opened tentflap. In his moment of inattention, Keen tore free and flung herself into her lover's arms.

He put her gently but firmly behind him. "Go," he said.

She obeyed him—a marvel, and maddening.

The prince braced his legs well apart and folded his arms. He was a fine figure of a man. Walker could admit that, even in his anger. And he had seen all of this man that there was to see; even the size of him when he rose in tribute to a woman.

"It seems," the prince said, "that you failed to understand my warning. This woman is a guest here. She is not yours to take."

"That woman is my wife," said Walker levelly. "Among my people, that bears with it certain rights and privileges."

"But you are among my people now," the prince said. His voice was soft, his expression amiable.

"Indeed," said Walker. "And in this country, does the king claim any woman who comes to him without a man?"

"Not at all," the prince said.

"In my country," Walker said, "a man who lies with another man's wife can be gelded or killed. Or both."

"Truly?" said the prince with no sign of fear. "Yes, you did speak of that. You'll pardon me for thinking it rather barbarous. And rather insulting, too, to the wife—as if she were incapable of deciding for herself whether a man was worthy to lie with her."

"A wife lies only with her husband."

"And a husband only with his wife?"

"Of course not."

"How unfair," said the prince. "Tell me. If your king claimed her, would you have to give her to him?"

Walker's mouth opened. He shut it with a snap. "No king would dare touch my wife."

"But if he did. Would you geld and kill him?"

"A king may claim another man's wife. Even a shaman's—if he has no fear of the shaman's curse." Walker spoke the words sharply, biting off each one.

The prince smiled with all the sweetness in the world. "I am not afraid of your curse," he said.

He stepped aside. Men stood behind him, two tall ruddy-haired men with long stern faces.

"Come, my lord," the elder of them said. "The king is asking for you."

Walker gritted his teeth. "Is he really?"

"Really," said the younger. "He wants you to help him give your father a proper welcome."

"Tell him—" Walker broke off. His temper was slipping free again. He brought it back to hand.

One more day. Only one. He put on as calm a face as he could, smoothed his tunic and straightened his shoulders. "Take me to him," he said.

56

AUROCHS SERVED AS Walker's escort to the king's circle where Drinks-the-Wind was receiving his welcome. Kestrel lingered for a moment with Cloud. He had not seen that face so dark before, or so grim. Cloud was a formidable man when he chose to be.

"How bad was it?" Kestrel asked him.

"Not as bad as it might be," said Cloud. "He hadn't raped her yet."

"Gods," said Kestrel. "I suppose you have a fittingly severe punishment for rape."

"We do," Cloud said. "We feed the rapist to the vultures." He drew a deep breath and flexed his shoulders. "By the gods, my lord falcon, if there were not so many plots riding on that man's head, I would have ripped it from his neck."

He said it calmly. It was the exact truth. Kestrel regarded him in respect. "I salute your restraint," he said.

"Salute your beloved. She'd turn me into a toad if I took her prey away from her."

"She can't do that," Kestrel said.

"Would you care to wager on it?"

"No," Kestrel said after a moment. "After all, no."

Cloud grinned with almost his old insouciance, and clapped him on the shoulder. "See? You're a wise man after all. Shall we go and be princes? It should be amusing, if it's true as I'm told, that the old man ought to be dead and the young one has been doing his best to make sure of it."

I am not a prince. Kestrel shaped the words in his mind, but did not say them. Here, he supposed he was. After a fashion. Arm in arm with Cloud, who truly was a prince, he went to be courteous to these latest and strangest guests in the Grey Horse camp.

Cloud did not stay long: only long enough to greet Drinks-the-Wind and his strange, half-mad wife. He would go, Kestrel knew, to comfort Keen. Kestrel would have liked to do the same, but he had duties here. Walker had escaped his watchfulness once. Not again.

Aurochs had him in hand, not openly holding him prisoner, but seeing to it that he stayed in the circle, near the king but not near enough to do harm. Linden was ignoring him, fixed on Sparrow, who sat beside the Grey Horse king.

So too was Drinks-the-Wind. As Kestrel settled beside Aurochs, the old shaman said in slow wonder, "The more fool I, child, for not seeing what you were."

Sparrow looked him in the face. She betrayed no awe of him, and little enough respect, either. "Men are blind," she said.

"It would seem so," he said. "And I was looking elsewhere to find the blaze of light among my children."

"Do you regret that?"

She did not seem to care that Walker could hear. Nor did Drinks-the-Wind. "It was the gods' will," he said. "Even if I had seen, there was little I could have done. No one would accept a woman as a shaman."

"You could have sent me to my own people," she said.

"But I never knew," he said. He sighed. "Too late. Too late to undo it. The path I marked for myself, I follow to its end. So, too, shall you."

Something in her changed. Her expression was the same, her body still, but her eyes were burning. "Are you—"

"Yes," he said.

"Tomorrow?"

He nodded.

Her shoulders drooped a fraction. She looked suddenly weary. "I don't know if—"

"You will," he said. "You can."

"She said that to me, too," Sparrow said. "Nor was she any more merciful."

"That is the way of us elder shamans," said Drinks-the-Wind. "When your time comes, you will do the same."

"Yes," she said.

✤ ✤

It was some while before Kestrel could speak to Sparrow alone. Drinks-the-Wind was with the Grey Horse king still, conversing of a myriad things. Walker by then was shut in his tent—and how safe that was, with all the poisons he could be brewing, Kestrel was less than certain. Aurochs, wise man, had set the king's companions on both sides of the tent, to forestall an escape from behind.

Kestrel went from there to find Keen, but met Rain on the way. She said, "Cloud is looking after her."

"Is she—"

"She's angry," Rain said. "Anger makes the spirit stronger. Don't fret, my falcon. She only looks fragile—and too often fancies that she is. My cousin has disabused her of that notion."

Kestrel had to be satisfied with that. With a clearer conscience, he went looking for Sparrow.

She was in her tent for once, preparing for the morning. He lent a hand with her packing, raising his brows at some of the things she was taking, but asking no questions. She was deeply preoccupied; she barely glanced at him.

When the bundle was made and bound and ready to carry, Kestrel laid it aside and set about preparing one of his own. He did not expect Sparrow to help, nor did she. She sat on her heels, hands on her thighs, staring straight ahead. When he passed in front of her, her eyelids did not flicker.

He wrapped and bundled what he expected to need on a riding of indeterminate length. When he was done, he sat facing her, cross-legged, elbows on knees, chin propped on fists, waiting for her to come back from wherever she had been.

She took her time about it. He was nearly asleep, but with a flicker of hunter's alertness, when she said, "Promise me something."

"Yes."

"No," she said. "Think first. Promise that, whatever I do tomorrow, you will still love me."

"Always."

She glowered. "You didn't think."

"I don't need to."

"You should."

"Some people think too much," he said.

"Most don't think enough." She straightened, stretched a little, lay with her head in his lap. As he stroked her soft curling hair she said, "I'm not afraid of what will happen. Not for me. But some of it will not be easy, and some will be terrible. I can't alter that. I can only do what's required of me."

"Yes," he said.

"You don't understand. You can't."

"Maybe not," he said. "But I can love you."

"Oh, gods." She buried her face in his lap. He could not tell if she wept. Maybe she only needed to shut out the light, and such visions as she could.

Whatever comfort he had, he gave to her. He hoped that it was of use.

+ +

The morning dawned bright and clear. It was a fine morning of midsummer, cool before sunrise but promising to be hot when the sun had risen to its zenith. Word had gone out as Sparrow commanded. Those whom she trusted knew that they rode to meet the army. The rest were given to believe that she intended a great sacrifice in the moon's dark, in a sacred place northward of the Grey Horse camp.

Drinks-the-Wind rode with them on his white mare, and White Bird followed. She had spent the night with Linden, everybody knew but no one chose to remark on, least of all her husband. Drinks-the-Wind himself had kept to the inner room of the king's tent. As to what he did there, some of the warband laid wagers.

"Talked all night," Curlew said.

"Lay with her," countered Bullcalf.

"Both!" Brighteyes cried. He had been into the *kumiss* already and was waxing silly with it.

Linden, who on most occasions would have been joining in the banter, was unwontedly silent. When he looked at anything at all apart from the plain or the sky, he looked at Sparrow. His eyes did not turn toward Walker at all, though the shaman rode nearby.

Linden was not riding the king of stallions. Sparrow rode him— and it was a wonder to many that the king said nothing. He sat astride his pretty dun like a man under a spell. Kestrel hoped that Sparrow knew what she was doing, because the glances darted at her were not friendly.

Keen rode beyond her on the mare, close by the prince and the king and the shaman of the Grey Horse People, protected among them, with her son strapped to a cradleboard on her back. She never glanced at Walker or acknowledged his presence, though his eyes rested often on her and on the child she carried.

It was a strange and complicated riding in the bright sunlight. Kestrel's belly was in knots. He untangled it carefully, breathed deep and slow, and willed himself to be calm as before a battle. Everything was ordered as Sparrow would have it. She had not tried to prevent the Red Deer men from mingling with the White Stone men and the men and women of the Grey Horse, nor seemed to notice that they kept their weapons close to hand. The taste of treachery was bitter in Kestrel's mouth; but Sparrow's command had been clear. "Let his plan unfold. Move only when I bid you."

Kestrel would do that. But when young warriors of the Red Deer insinuated themselves among Linden's companions, they found that web of casual banter and easy revelry to be impenetrable. One fine tall fellow on a spotted horse tried to force his way past Aurochs toward the king. His horse tripped on a stone, perhaps, and went down, sending the rider sprawling. Even his fellows laughed at that, till it dawned on them that he had not moved. His neck was broken.

Aurochs was profuse in his apologies, promising great reparations, even shedding a tear for the fallen man—and that, in Kestrel's mind, was perhaps a trifle excessive. But it staved off bloodshed, and sent knives back into sheaths. The Red Deer warriors remained behind to tend their fallen kinsman, while the rest ordered themselves once more and rode on.

"The gods are hungry for blood and souls today," Drinks-the-Wind said. He had ridden up beside Kestrel, as light on his white mare's back as a young man. He turned his face to the sun and smiled. "Are you not, my lords of light and darkness?"

Beyond him Kestrel saw some of the companions make swift signs against ill fortune. But he did not think the shaman was cursing them, nor was he mad, either. Drinks-the-Wind seemed as much in the world as he ever was, and in great good humor, too. "We've paid our day's passage," he said. "As for the night . . ."

Kestrel shivered in spite of himself.

Drinks-the-Wind's smile warmed and broadened. "There, lad. You've little to fear. Death is a simple thing. The gate opens. You pass through. Then you journey—far, sometimes, but that should never dismay you, great wanderer and hunter that you are. The game in that country, they say, is better than any in this one: swifter, stronger, and far sweeter to the taste."

"You've hunted there," Kestrel said.

Drinks-the-Wind shrugged. "A little. In dreams. Enough to lose my fear of the life beyond life."

"I think I'm too young for that," said Kestrel.

The shaman laughed. He looked and sounded uncannily like his son Walker, but Walker made Kestrel's hackles rise. Drinks-the-Wind made him uneasy, but not as an enemy would. He was a strange creature, powerful, and perhaps beyond Kestrel's comprehension. But he meant Kestrel no harm. "Child," he said, "do you think I am old? To the gods I am a child, an infant, a creature of a mere day's span. I feel it in my spirit. I'm as young as the morning."

"And I," said Kestrel, "was born a heartbeat ago."

Drinks-the-Wind applauded him. "Always remember that," he said. "It may not help you to understand the gods, but it will help you to survive their notice."

"Does any man survive that?"

"In the end," said Drinks-the-Wind, "sooner or later, we all die."

He left Kestrel to ponder that, riding off to regale Walker with his uncomfortable wisdom. Walker seemed rather less appreciative of it than Kestrel was.

Kestrel, watching, caught himself wondering again what the night would bring. Sparrow would not tell him. No one else seemed to know. But that it was a matter of shamans, and a great matter, too, he had no doubt. He could only pray that the rest of them would come out of it alive and sane.

THEY STOPPED IN the heat of the day and made a few hours' camp by a little river. Trees overhung the bank, offering a green shade. It was a cool and sweet-scented place, and there was a thicket of brambles somewhat up the river. While the horses grazed and drank, they ate a midday feast of berries and journeycake, and rested for a while.

Not all of them were sleeping. Walker, looking for a place to relieve himself in peace, passed by no few Grey Horse women sharing their favors with men of their tribe and any other who happened by. He turned his face away from them.

He was aware that he had an escort. Aurochs the hunter seemed to have appointed himself Walker's guardian hound—or perhaps Keen's protector. Walker was keeping a careful distance from his wife. She, he noticed, was clinging to her black-bearded lover, and hiding as best she could among the Grey Horse People—like a tall young mare in a flock of goats, foolish and cowardly and altogether like a woman.

He could be patient, now that it was too late to feed his power in coupling with her. By the next day's dawning, everything would be his. All the power, all the gods' favor. Then she would come to him, and remember at last that she belonged to him. And if the Grey Horse prince tried to stop her then, he would die.

Walker paused on the riverbank and made water into the stream. Aurochs' eyes were on him, tireless in their fixity. He smiled sweetly at the hunter and wandered along the bank, with no intention of escaping, but not minded to stay put, either.

Aurochs simply followed like the two-legged hound he was. Walker toyed with the thought of disposing of him. But that would cause a great deal of fuss. Time enough later, when all was won.

Some distance upstream, under a tree with fronds that trailed in the water, Sparrow sat with her own guardian hound—waiting for him. Walker regarded her in something close to contentment. "So," he said. "You have visions for me."

"Crowds and hordes of them," she said.

He smiled. She was almost good to look on, sitting there in her mockery of a shaman's robe, with her hair escaping as always from its plait. He had noticed before this that she was either growing plump or growing a child; from the way her hound hovered, and the way she carried herself, it was rather clear which it was. He would enjoy exacting the punishment for that, come the time. But for now he chose not to speak of it.

It was a pity, too, that they were both so well guarded. Two of them, brother and sister, a shaman's children, on the day of the new moon, could have raised great power in their coupling—power that Walker could well use.

But he would have to settle for mere words. He sat a little distance from her on a bank of grass and flowers, and let his smile widen. "You've been making good use of my visions," he said.

"They were never yours," she said: so tiresome, and so untrue.

"You play shaman very well," he said.

"Because I am one."

"There is more to a shaman than visions," he said.

"Yes."

Truly, he thought, she had grown insolent among these southern women. "My visions," he said. "Give them to me."

She smiled, the first time that he could recall that she had ever smiled at him. It made the small hairs rise on the back of his neck. From a bag that had lain half-hidden in the grass, she took a cup. It was a skull-cup, somewhat small but very rich, beautifully and magically ornamented. His fingers twitched toward it. This, they knew, was a thing of great power.

She filled it with water from the stream, holding it without awe, as if it had been a plain cup of wood or clay. She brought it back to him, still smiling, and set it in his waiting hands.

He bowed under the weight of it. The pain—the crushing burden—

Her hand passed before his face. He could see again. The cup was a cup, cool and round in his hands, brimming with water. Some of it had spilled. It was cold.

"Look into the cup," she said.

"What, scrying like a crone by a campfire?"

"Look," she said, unruffled by his contempt. "See."

He looked, not to obey her but to prove that it was folly.

The cup was full of fire.

It was water—water, cold within the white bone.

Cold fire. And in it, such things—such visions—

They were too many. They were too fast. They were too terrible. And he could not look away from them. They seared through his eyes into his spirit. Blood and fire, fire and water, stone and blood. A black knife raised against a starlit sky. Blood springing, glistening black in firelight. Kings and princes, warriors, armies riding. And horses. White horses. A white mare in the heart of the moon.

"Enough."

Her voice, as cold as the moon. His eyes lifted of themselves. He gasped.

She was full of light. It filled her to brimming and overflowed. The touch of it was pain so terrible he could not even cry out.

"Now you have visions," she said in that cold, still voice. She took the cup from his slack fingers, bowed over it, poured the water out upon the grass. Then she put the cup away, rose and left him to his shock and waxing terror.

He mastered himself. He was a shaman of a line of shamans that went back to the dawn time. His power was great and would be greater still. And now he had visions.

Visions . . .

He staggered to his feet. Aurochs made no move to help him. The hunter's arms were folded, his eyes flat. If Walker had ever doubted that this was his enemy, he would have known it now.

Tonight, Walker thought. He had power such as he had not known a man could have. And all his enemies would know the force of it.

✦ ✦

"Do you think that was wise?"

Sparrow stumbled. Kestrel caught her, pulling her into his arms. She let him hold her. She had been strong enough when she faced her brother, but now that she had left him, she could feel the weakness in her knees. "Horse Goddess wanted it," she said.

"Horse Goddess is going to get you killed."

"Hush." She could feel the anger in him, but greater than that was fear. Fear for her; fear of her brother. She tried to reassure him.

"He still is no shaman, no matter what he thinks. These visions will confuse him."

"And they don't confuse you?"

"They're mine," she said. "They're part of me."

He lifted her suddenly, carrying her in his arms. She folded her own arms about his neck and let her head rest on his shoulder. Pride did not matter here; and if people thought her weak, that was not an ill thing. Particularly if Walker thought it. "I'm afraid for you," he said.

"I suppose you should be. It's not going to be an easy night."

"If you will let me—"

"No," she said. "I've told you what to do."

"But to stand by—to—"

"You will do it," she said, putting the force of command in it; but then and perhaps not so wisely she softened. "My love, my beautiful one, this is the gods' will. Be as strong as you know how to be, and help me. Do what I ask."

"Do I have a choice?"

"Yes," she said.

He did not believe her. But he set his lips and left off arguing.

She kissed his shoulder and sighed. "Oh gods," she said. "I love you."

✤ ✤

It was summer in the world, but Keen's heart was cold and bitter winter. When she looked at her son whom she—she, not his father—had named Summer, and at her lover, with whom she had broken the laws of the People so often and in such gladness, she warmed a very little. But Walker had taken away her joy. His hands on her, his eyes that had no love in them, only the certainty that he owned her—she had washed and washed, scrubbed herself till she was raw, but she could not scour away the memory.

Cloud tried to comfort her. His touch was balm for her wounds, but it could not take the pain away. She had tried to lie with him; but when he took her in his arms, she gasped as if she were drowning, and struggled frantically to escape. He, blessed man, had let her go. And such pain in his face, such love and such deep anger against the one who had done this to her: oh, by the gods, she did not deserve him.

She wanted Walker dead. It was a terrible thing, an unholy thing, but it was the truth. If he died, she would be happy. Even if she died for it—it would free the world of him.

Tonight, she thought, it would be settled. Sparrow had said so. And Sparrow saw what no one else could see.

· · · · · · · · 58 · · · · · · · ·

THERE WAS INDEED a sacred place, as Sparrow had known from Old Woman's teaching. It was a hill crowned with a thin ring of trees, and a great thing of power within: a black stone sunk deep in the hilltop, heavy and cold and throbbing with potency. The black stone in Old Woman's belongings, Sparrow had come to understand, was such a stone. It had fallen from the sky, it was said; it was the burnt cinder of a star.

Sparrow wore Old Woman's piece of it in a bag about her neck. It hung between her breasts, heavier than anything so small should be. The mother stone called to it, drawing Sparrow with it.

They came to the hill somewhat before sundown. Sparrow bade them make camp at the hill's foot, where a spring bubbled from beneath a rock and poured into a broad shallow pool. From there it ran in a stream down to a greater stream. There was water in plenty for the horses, and grazing, and space to pitch tents.

The scouts found them there as the campfires flared in the sun's sinking. They had the word that Sparrow had been waiting for: Walker's allies were camped down the stream and over a low ridge. A Red Deer warrior had crept out of the camp as it was being made, and been seen entering the outland camp.

Sparrow nodded, satisfied. "Good. It's ready, then. Come full dark, we'll ascend the hill."

"All of us?" Rain asked. "No guards? No one to look after the horses?"

"Every one of us," Sparrow said. "It's not horse-stealing these raiders have in mind tonight."

Rain bowed to that. She was headstrong and inclined to argue, but only in lesser matters. In greater ones, she knew when to keep still. She was a good shaman, Sparrow thought, and would be better as she grew past her youthful impatience.

Everything was as ready as it could be. Those with the stomach for it, and those innocent of what Sparrow expected to pass come nightfall, ate a quick daymeal while the sunset poured blood across the horizon. Drinks-the-Wind ate well and drank an imposing quantity of *kumiss*. He was the lightest of heart of any of them. He told tales and even sang, and kept the warband and the Red Deer riders rather well entertained.

But in the twilight he managed to leave them for a while on pretext of a full bladder. After he had relieved himself he came upon Sparrow sitting a little apart. She had just sent Kestrel to keep watch on Linden. Drinks-the-Wind watched him go with an appreciative eye. "That's a handsome young stallion," he said.

"I do think so," said Sparrow.

"But you won't marry him."

"No."

"Would he like you to?"

She shrugged. "I don't know. He seems content."

"You're fortunate." The old man laid his hand on her head, briefly: a father's blessing. "I regret now that I took so little notice of you. There are things I could have taught you. Paths I could have smoothed under your feet."

"I needed the roughness," she said, "and the lack of regard. If you had singled me out, I would have been too much preoccupied in dealing with envy. And people would have noticed if I was missing—and I often was, out among the horses."

"That is so," he conceded. "I still wish. . . ."

"Don't," she said. "The gods chose me for what I was. I bear you no ill-will."

He raised his brows. "What, none?"

"None at all." And that was the truth. "The Grandmother did everything that you should have done, and in comfortable obscurity. Old Woman did the rest. In between, the horses raised me."

"You had no need of me at all."

She could hardly deny it.

He sighed. "But I matter to you now. Don't I?"

"You always did."

His glance was dubious.

She laid a hand briefly atop his where it rested on his knee: a daughter's blessing. "If you need forgiveness, you have it. If not . . . it's yours regardless."

He looked long at her, and steadily, as if he would remember every line of her face. Then he nodded as if one of them had spoken, rose and went away.

She sighed and rose herself. It was time. The mare was waiting for her—the mare tonight, not the stallion, who stood aside in proper deference. Sparrow mounted her.

That was the signal for the rest. She heard but paid no heed to the muted tumult of people gathering to follow. They were not to ride up the hill—there was no room for so many horses. She was the only one mounted, apart from Drinks-the-Wind on the old white mare who was, as it happened, the young mare's grandmother.

Walker was not allowed to approach the horses. He objected, but not for long: he saw soon enough that if he tarried he would be left behind. He strode angrily afoot, shouldering his way through the gathering, till they grew wise and left his path open. Sparrow could feel his temper behind her, like a spearpoint aimed at her shoulderblades.

She rode up the hill. The black stone was calling, heavy with the moon's dark, dragging at the daughter-stone between her breasts. The stars were brilliant. Her eyes were a shaman's eyes; they saw as clearly as in daylight, though their sight was different, greyer, no color in them; everything was tinged with shadow.

Drinks-the-Wind had drawn ahead of her. She was aware of that; of Walker drawing closer behind, though his breath came short on the slope; of the people trailing in back of him, and below, in the dark, Walker's allies approaching the camp. They would discover soon enough that it was empty, and ride up the hill.

It was all as inevitable as the wheeling of stars overhead. She breathed deep and held it for a few heartbeats, then let it go. All her worries, her weariness, the concerns of the world, poured out with it. She was empty as Old Woman had taught her to be, open to any wind of power that blew.

Drinks-the-Wind was even emptier than she. He was a shell, a shadow. All that was in him was joy.

They ascended the last steep slope and came out on the broad round level. The stone was set in it like an eye in a vast face, a black orb staring up to heaven. Sparrow slid from the mare's back, staggering as her feet struck earth. It was humming underfoot, singing upward through her bones.

The mare took no notice of it. Once Drinks-the-Wind had dismounted from his own mare's back, the two white mares wandered together toward the stone. They grazed as they went, concerned as horses always were with true matters of consequence: grass, the herd, contentment. But the goddess in the younger mare was awake, focused on the stone with a deep calm, a white stillness.

That focus held Sparrow in place. People were ascending as she had done, clambering up, panting, straggling in a circle. Walker was not the first among them. When he did come, he had a look of serious discontent. He had fallen; his hands and knees were bruised. The gods were not choosing to be kind.

He was the more dangerous for it. His people were closing in behind. For what she must do, she must be focused; she could not let her spirit wander or fret or be distracted. Her own people knew what they were to do. She had to trust them—and pray that nothing went amiss.

She turned her eyes and her mind on the circle's center. Drinks-the-Wind had gone to it as if drawn by a hand, and knelt by the black stone. His eyes were wide, his face empty of expression. The stone had him. If his spirit was not to be taken into it, she must move, and quickly.

It was as it had been with Old Woman—as it would be in her turn, when her time had come. The great sacrifice, the willing surrender of life in the gods' name. What Old Woman had done at midwinter, now in the new moon of midsummer the elder shaman of the northern tribes offered to do.

Two such sacrifices within one turning of the year was a great thing, a thing of power, a thing that could shift the world. Sparrow did not know what its long outcome would be. That was for the gods. She only knew that if she did it now, and Walker did not prevent her, the world would change. Horse Goddess would not only walk in it. She would rule.

And if Sparrow failed, these people of the Grey Horse would die. And so would she. Walker's people would overrun them all. True power would dwindle, fade. The gods would become but masks for petty men, shadows through whom such men played out their games of earthly glory.

It was a sad grey world she saw on that path, and Walker a great lord in it. She drew the black blade against it, the knife that had been tempered in Old Woman's blood. Drinks-the-Wind, kneeling at her feet, looked up at her and smiled.

A weight struck her from behind. It had a voice, crying out: "Stop! By the gods, stop! That's your own father!"

Walker's voice. Walker's body hurled against hers, grappling for the knife.

Sparrow had been too slow, too little watchful. She fell hard beneath him, gasping and twisting, desperate to protect the baby in her belly.

He flew free of her. She lay for a moment in shock, till she saw the two shapes tangled, pale hair and dark, but who the dark one was, she could not tell.

Nor should she tarry for it. She groped in the trampled grass. The knife—goddess, where was the knife?

There. She gripped its blade first, gasped at the sudden sting of pain, found hilt and gripped it as she stumbled to her feet. Her whole body hurt.

She must not feel pain. She must be empty, open, for the power to come in. Drinks-the-Wind had not moved. He waited on fate and time and the gods. His spirit was slipping free, powerless to resist the call of the stone.

She had no grace, no dignity, but the knife was sharp and her hand, after all, was steady. It struck straight and true, full to the heart. The last sound he made, his last utterance in the world, was a sudden, sweet ripple of laughter.

It was a sound of pure joy. It poured strength into her. It held her up as she freed his blood to flow over the stone, and took his head to raise in tribute to the gods.

All about her, the world burst into a torrent of sound: the roar of battle, sudden and deafening. Men grappled with men, and men with women. She saw Kestrel locked in combat with a tall fair boy, and Aurochs set upon by two men dressed in the fashion of the Cliff Lion warriors. Walker's army had come, swarming up the hill, overwhelming the people on the summit. Their mingled war-cries shook the sky.

A new sound pierced it, high enough and strong enough to split a man's skull: a scream of rage.

The mare stood on the black stone, balanced on the smooth

rounded surface as no hooved creature should have been able to do. She loosed another peal, loud enough to shatter the sky. And again, a third, terrible in its strength.

Then she smote the stone. The sound it made had never been heard in the world before: a clear, ringing clang. It echoed impossibly. It shook men from their feet. It cast down the men of Cliff Lion and Dun Cow who had come to see a king-killing and been moved by a shaman-killing to attack the people who were there before them.

But Walker kept his feet. Whoever had freed Sparrow from him was gone. He had a second figure by the throat: Linden, white-faced and helpless, frozen in fear of the black blade that rested, oh so lightly, on the great vein of his neck. Sparrow, with shaman's eyes, could see the life pulsing in it, rapid as a bird's.

"Brother," Sparrow said, clear and cold—words that did not belong to her at all, but were spoken through her—"if it's kingmaking you would be doing, your hand cannot be the one that takes his life. Where is your new king, then? What's become of him?"

"Here." Kestrel said it in something like sorrow, standing over a crumpled shape. As people stared at the black blood on the pale hair, he sighed. "He came at me while I was driving your brother away from you. I struck before I thought. I only meant to stun."

"Pity he wasn't king already," said Rain behind him. "His kingship would have been the briefest in the world—and you would have won it."

Kestrel shuddered. "Gods forbid," he said.

"No matter." Walker snapped the words, drawing their eyes back to him. "In this country, a shaman can be a king. Why not in the north as well?"

"In this country also," said Sparrow, "a woman can be a shaman. And your power is a lie."

"All the power I need," he said, "is in my hands."

"If you kill him, the gods will curse you."

"Empty threats," he said.

And all the while she held him with words, shadows stalked him, softer than wind in the grass.

One leaped. He whipped about. His knife bit deep. The figure fell.

Linden was free. Another of the shadows thrust him aside and sprang on Walker.

Linden reeled toward Sparrow. His weight drove her backward, spinning out of the battle, till they stumbled and fell beside the black stone. He was alive and unhurt, breathing in gasps.

The stone's power was so strong that Sparrow could barely see. She crawled toward it, pulling herself up onto it. Her bones felt as heavy as the world. But the stone, for all its cold darkness, had fire in its heart. She called it up into her bones and drew it into the stone about her neck. And when both stone and bones were burning, burning with a terrible beauty, she set it free.

······· **59** ·······

KESTREL WAS ONE of those who stalked Walker, but it was another who sprang first—and suffered for it. As small as it was, and quick, he thought it might be Rain; Cloud he saw circling, and Aurochs crouched low and closing in when Rain fell. He grappled with Walker. The knife dropped. Kestrel swept it up before Walker could win it back.

Then the fire came down. The stars descended in tongues of flame. Walker's allies had come armed with spears, that now blazed up like torches.

The spears' bearers recoiled. The spears stood erect with no hand holding them, a ring of fire. It blazed as bright almost as daylight, but redder, as if tinged with blood.

Rain was down, Cloud crouched over her. Walker twisted free of Aurochs' grip, wheeled and bolted straight through the ring of spears. Fire licked at him, but he darted away from it. It caught the end of his long white-gold plait. He ran on, trailing fire and smoke and a pungent stench.

Kestrel sprang in pursuit. But his way was blocked, and not only by Walker's allies. His own people were standing stunned, staring at the fire from heaven and at the figure who stood on the black stone. Sparrow was a flame herself, fire licking from her fingertips, from her lips, from the crown of her head. It streamed down her body like water. It poured back into the stone.

Kestrel too was caught by the sight of her—briefly, but long enough. When he looked again, Walker was gone. He had vanished into the night.

+ +

In that rain of fire, the battle ended. There were wounded: tribe had fought with tribe before the fire came down. And there were dead, two figures lying crumpled near the stone. One was a man whom Kestrel vaguely recalled, a man of the White Stone People—not of Red Deer or Cliff Lion—whose name had been Ash. He was prettier than Linden, and if possible less quick of wit. Kestrel had been astonished when he learned what life he had taken, not even meaning it, thinking only to defend himself. *That* was Walker's year-king?

And the other who had died was Rain. Cloud tried still, as if possessed, to bring her back to life, but her throat was cut across.

She had died as Ash had, in a backwards stroke without particular intent. Drinks-the-Wind, as great a shaman as he was, had not been enough to sate the gods. They had been terribly hungry, and thirsty for blood.

Now surely they were sated. They had had a great sacrifice, the greatest since the dawn time: two shamans and a man who was to have been king, felled beside the black stone that fell out of the sky.

+ +

Walker's allies, deserted by their shaman and bereft of their would-be king, with their spears burning down now and crumbling to ash, were easy enough to subdue and take captive. Kestrel saw to it, and Linden recovering from his confusion. Fear and the imminence of death had affected him strangely: he was, if not swifter of wit, then certainly clearer of mind. He called his men together with such an air of command that Red Deer came, too, and even some of the Cliff Lion and Dun Cow warriors. Those would not lay hands on their own tribesmen, but they stood back and did not interfere while the rest were taken and bound and led down off the hilltop. Grey Horse followed, bearing the dead; all but the old shaman. Sparrow stayed behind to see to him, a duty that only she could perform, as both daughter and priestess.

+ +

Walker's allies were secured under guard for what remained of the night. Walker was nowhere to be found. A few of the warband searched for him, but most were preoccupied with the captives and with mourning for the dead. No one had much to say of it, but most were weary of him, and inclined to let him go. The few who reckoned that unwise were not heeded. There was too much else to think of. Too much grief. Too much anger. Time enough, they told one another, to hunt the traitor down and kill him.

Those who could sleep slept—more than Keen might have expected, in the peculiar horror of that night and its ending. She had her own horror piled on grief: both Summer and Spring were reft of their milk-mother. One of the Grey Horse women, whose name Keen did not even know, came to help as she could; she had weaned her own daughter but yesterday and was glad, she said, to relieve the ache in her breasts.

The children were looked after. But Keen, whose breasts had never been enough to keep a child alive, and whose friend was dead, could only sit in the small traveling-tent, staring into the dark. Cloud never came, nor did she expect him. He had the offices of the dead to perform, he and his mother. He had no time or strength to spare for a lover.

She did not begrudge him the need to consider his own kin and people. But it was cold, sitting here without him, and bleak. The children slept fitfully. Spring made her uneasy: staring dark-eyed and silent, as if her mother's death had struck her mute.

Keen rocked them and sang, and waited for the night to end. There was no sleep in her.

Late in the night, a step brought her alert from a half-doze. She turned expecting Cloud, or maybe even Kestrel, who looked out for her in quiet ways. It was a tall man, one of the People, but it was not Kestrel.

He did not even look at her. His eyes were on the cradle, and on the bright-haired child sleeping in it. Keen saw what he was doing in the instant before he did it. She flung herself at him. But it was too late. He had Summer in his arms. He bowled her over, running past her, trampling her underfoot. She snatched wildly at him, raked flesh—heard his gasp and curse. He did not even pause.

He was gone. She lay bruised and sore, and in her heart a great and swelling cry. It rose up and up. When it reached the brim of her heart, it poured out.

It seemed a very long time before anyone came. She knew that she should go out and find someone—Kestrel, maybe, to hunt down the thief and bring him back—but she dared not leave Spring alone. Rain's daughter—and Cloud's, too—had made no sound, nor moved, when her milk-brother was taken away.

Cloud came at last, and Sparrow behind him, and Kestrel loping long-legged in the rear. None of them needed her to explain. They saw the dark-eyed child alone in the cradle, and Keen's bruises, and knew.

Kestrel smote his thigh with his fist and cursed. "Gods and goddesses and black spirits below! I *knew* he wouldn't just go away. But I didn't—"

"We all knew. But we thought him cowed—we reckoned that we could hunt him at our leisure. We should have known that Walker of all people would strike like a snake the moment our backs were turned." Sparrow spoke calmly, but her eyes were fierce. "We'll get Summer back. Kestrel—"

"I'll go," he said. "When I find him I'll kill him—once the baby is safe."

"Not alone," she said. "Take the fastest riders in the warband. The rest will follow in the morning as we had intended. We'll all go north, all of us who can, or who can be trusted. This will be settled at the river."

"Not if I find that baby-thief sooner," Kestrel gritted.

"At the river," she said. "Now go, ask Linden to give you the riders. And tell him what I told you."

"Linden is asleep," Kestrel said.

"Happy man," said Sparrow, hard-hearted. "Wake him."

Kestrel snorted, not quite laughter, and went to do as she bade.

While they settled that, Keen crouched where Walker had left her. Cloud came, knelt, gathered her into his arms. She laid her head on his breast and wept, not loudly, not particularly long, but deep. It did little to comfort her.

He was weeping, too, quietly, as he held her. He had lost his clan-sister this night, the mother of his child, the shaman who had been meant to stand beside him when at last he was king. And now the son of his heart was gone.

She wept for Rain then, as she had not been able to before; and that did ease the terrible aching in her heart. But the place in it where Summer had been was an open wound, too deep and terrible to heal with tears.

When after a long while she could speak, she said, "I have to go, even if I go with the slower riders. I can't stay here."

He nodded. "We'll both go."

"But the burying—Rain—"

"Rain is—was—a shaman. Their burials are shamans' rites. Such farewells as I can say, I have said. In the morning I'll be ready to ride, I and others of the Grey Horse."

He met Sparrow's eyes as he said that, as if he defied her to stop him. But she said, "Tell them to bring their bows. We may need them."

He inclined his head. If he was grateful not to be laughed at, he did not show it. But then, thought Keen, Sparrow would never mock a Grey Horse man or woman for lack of prowess in war. She knew how well they hunted, and how skilled they were with weapons.

So it was settled. Cloud stayed with Keen after all, though she urged him to go back to his kin. "They know where I am," he said. "They'll know why soon enough. Let be. Rest. It's a hard ride we'll have ahead of us."

Hard not because it was long or the journey arduous; it was short enough by ways his people knew. But to hunt Keen's child, in such fear as was in her of the child's father, was bitter indeed.

Not even a memory of love remained, or a flicker of desire. Not even for duty would Keen take Walker back as a husband.

✦ ✦

Two dozen of Linden's warriors mounted the swiftest horses, took what was needful and readied to ride. Sparrow would have taken the silvermaned stallion, leaving the mare to her colt, but the mare would not hear of it. She did a thing that no mortal mare would willingly do: she passed her son to one of the Grey Horse mares who had lost a foal not long ago, left him and bade Sparrow mount her and ride.

While the mare proved herself other than simple earthly creature, Linden approached the stallion whom the mare had forced Sparrow to abandon, and mounted him. The stallion offered no objection. Linden met Sparrow's glance, once she herself was mounted, with a flat and defiant stare. This time, his expression said, nothing in heaven or earth would keep him from the back of his beloved king.

She astonished him with laughter. Still laughing, she swept them all together, gathered them and loosed them into the north.

✦ ✦

It was strange to be riding those ways again, that only a year before she had taken going southward. In that little time, the world had died and been born again. She had become a shaman, and was to be a mother. And here she was, riding with the king's warband of the White Stone, and the Grey Horse to follow come morning—armies that rode where she bade them, and kings and kings' heirs who looked to her for guidance.

The riders' laughter as they went was bright and rather mad, laughter masking a sacred anger. Their quarry was in front of them: he had stolen a swift horse, and it seemed he had no care to keep it alive.

In the dawn Kestrel found a sign that Walker had met a company of horsemen and set off again at a killing pace. "Cliff Lion," he said, pointing to a fallen bit of rein. It was braided in the colors and fashion of the tribe.

Some distance past this, they found the first horse. Vultures' circling led them to it. It was still alive, its foreleg shattered. It called to their horses as they came near.

Aurochs put it out of its misery. They could not stay to bury or to butcher it; they had perforce to leave it to the vultures.

Sparrow would not let them ride as fast as Walker was riding. "We'll need mounts that can still stand, when we come to the river," she said.

"Two dozen riders against the full gathering of tribes," Linden said. He shook his head, but he was smiling. "We're mad."

"Two dozen riders, a shaman, and," said Sparrow, "a king mounted on a king. Remember what you are, my lord."

"What I should be is dead," Linden said.

"Only in the world as Walker would have it."

"Then we must make a new world," said Linden.

F OR ALL HER air of headlong confidence, Sparrow was caught out of her reckoning. What Drinks-the-Wind had done, what had followed upon it, had shaken her visions, blurring and scattering them like images in water. Walker's allies were subdued, his kingmaking ruined, but he was alive, like a snake that, crushed and stabbed almost to death, still revives and strikes at its enemies.

And he should not have lived. In every vision that showed the kingmaking failed, it had failed because both Walker and Ash were killed. In none of them had Walker lived, nor had he lived to seize Keen's child and carry him away into the north. When Sparrow sought foreseeing, or even guidance, in that act, she saw things that appalled her. Great wars, armies, conquests sweeping across the world—and a monster at the head of them, a golden creature with a face of light and a heart that was black darkness. This was the thing that Walker would make of his son, this king of blood and slaughter.

In only one respect did the confusion of her visions serve her. Walker, blind and deaf to things of the spirit, could not know that it was all changed; that the foreseeings she had given him of both his defeat and his victory were no longer certain.

Drinks-the-Wind's spirit stood athwart them. In her arrogance and her softness of heart, she had trusted him. She had reckoned him an ally. But he had, after all, been the great shaman of the People. He would serve the People first and himself after, and the rest as it pleased him. In his eyes, a king of battles would not be an ill thing, even a king as blackly cruel as Sparrow foresaw.

She fought to remember the vision that had guided her before Drinks-the-Wind rode into the Grey Horse camp. Walker defeated, the northern tribes overcome, Horse Goddess worshipped from the south to the farthest north. And Sparrow as shaman and priestess of the goddess, serene among the people whom above all she had made her own: the Grey Horse People, the white mare's following, Horse Goddess' children.

She could still make that come to pass. She must. And the golden king, Keen's son, raised by his mother and accepted by Cloud as his heir, would rule according to her teaching, both wise and just.

It must be so. No other way was possible. So she told herself as she rode north on her tireless mare, with her companions trailing exhausted behind.

⁕ ⁕

They did not catch Walker before he crossed the river. It was close—they were almost near enough to see him; his track in the tall grass was fresh. But he was gone and the river still some distance away, and the light was fading.

The others would have pressed on. Sparrow would have flown if she could. But she caught Aurochs' eye, and something in it focused her spirit. "We'll stop till morning," she said. "We know where he's going."

"But if we catch him before he comes to the gathering," Linden said, "won't it be better? We won't have to fight all the tribes to get our hands on him."

"I think," said Sparrow slowly, "that it would be worse if we did kill him on the plain. He has committed great crimes against you and the People. Let the People know that, and share in his judgment."

"He'll seduce them," Linden said. "He always has."

"Not if I can help it," said Sparrow.

She hoped she sounded stronger than she felt. She was worn down. The power that had burned in her on the hilltop was sunk to an ember. She still wore the bit of black stone, but it was only an oddly heavy, rather clumsy amulet about her neck.

They all needed sleep, and badly. As she considered that, she decided something else. "Tomorrow we'll stay here. We'll hunt, and eat well. The morning after, we'll ride."

"But—" said Linden for them all.

"We have to be strong," she said. "We can't stumble in as we are now. They'll cut us down and reckon it good riddance. We should ride among the tribes as people of consequence, rested and fed and as clean as we may be. As a king and his escort, not as a band of wild raiders."

Linden acceded to that, after a while: perhaps because he was as tired as she, as much as that he was allured by the vision of himself as king. When he went at last to sleep, Sparrow sought her own rough bed, with Kestrel in it.

But she did not slip at once into a dream. Kestrel was awake, with such a look about him that she wanted to hit him. "What?" she demanded crossly. "What are you thinking?"

"Nothing," he said.

"Don't lie to me."

"I'm not."

"Then why are you staring?"

"Because I love to look at your face," he said.

She fixed him with her fiercest glare. "You're thinking I'll leave you all here, creep out, and get myself killed. Aren't you?"

"I . . . had thought of it," he admitted.

"Don't."

"I thought that, too." He brushed his finger across her set lips, and followed it with a kiss. "I think I'll trust you."

"Good," she said, biting off the word.

He grinned, which truly made her want to hit him; then he took her in his arms. Her body, the fool, did not struggle at all. It melted against him and sighed.

"Sometimes I hate you," she said.

"No matter," he said, "if most times you love me."

† †

They rested, then, and gathered strength. And as they did that, a rider came in on a hard-ridden horse, one of the king's warband who had stayed to ride in the morning after the new moon. Grey Horse was indeed riding with them, with Cloud at their head, and Storm remaining behind to look after her people. This day's pause would bring the slower riders close, though not quite together.

Sparrow nodded at that, and sent another of the king's men back with messages which she made him repeat over and over till he had them perfect. Then she was a little more at ease, and a little less confused in her mind.

That night they ate the flesh of two fat stags that Aurochs had brought down, and drank the last of the *kumiss*. The next fresh meat or strong drink they would have would be in the camp of the gathering—or among the warrior dead.

Then they slept as the just sleep, deep and dreamless—even Spar-

row for once freed of the burden of visions. Dawn woke them with
dark and starlight and a keen wind blowing, as if it would carry them
across the river. Sparrow heard voices in it, faint cries, the murmur-
ings of spirits. They were close then, all of them, to the land of the
dead. When another morning came, some of them, and maybe all,
would walk or ride there.

Sparrow, too. Sparrow perhaps most of all. She was to have lived
long and died old, with her successor ready to take her life and carve
a cup out of her skull. But in the world that Drinks-the-Wind's sacrifice and Walker's escape had made, it was rather more likely that
she would fall before evening with her brother's knife in her heart.

Even the gods were divided, tumbling in confusion. She shut her
mind to them all and fixed herself on the world of the living: dawn
wind, scent and sound of horses, men rising and groaning and read-
ying to ride. They remembered what they had sworn when they
paused to rest, that they would approach the gathering with pride.
They had all cleaned and mended their garments yesterday, brushed
their horses, plaited one another's hair.

Now they dressed and made themselves seemly, undid the dam-
age the night's sleep had done to the hide or hair of man and horse,
and made certain that their weapons were ready and close to hand.
Some of them sang softly as they did it, war-songs, and here and
there a death-song. Someone had a drum, someone else a bone flute.
To that skirling and drumming, they mounted and rode. Their hearts
were strangely light.

Linden rode beside Sparrow on the king of stallions. They were
both as beautiful as Sparrow had ever seen them. Linden smiled at
her, the warm smile he kept for women he fancied. "It's a fair morning," he said.

"And a fair day coming," she agreed. "We'll find the gathering
somewhat after noon, if we ride neither too fast nor too slow."

"Is *he* already in it?" asked Linden, with a flicker of shadow across
his bright face.

Sparrow nodded. "He'll have come there a day or two ago."

"Then," Linden said, "anything we could say or do, now he's
had time to brew his poison—"

"You are the king," she said firmly. "Remember that."

She watched him remember it: sitting taller, smoothing the frown
from his brow. If fear still troubled him, he had buried it deep. He

would be as strong as she needed him to be, if Horse Goddess was kind.

A new messenger came as they rode on in the rising morning. The others were not far behind now; they had ridden for part of the night, were resting, would ride on at full morning. That was later than Sparrow would have liked, but they would reach the gathering soon enough after she would—well before sunset, certainly.

Which left nothing but the riding, and a scout or two sent ahead to watch for spies and ambushes; but there was none. If Walker knew that they followed, he was waiting in camp for them, secure among all his allies.

+ +

They came to the river somewhat after noon on a fine hot day of summer. The river was still a little swollen from the spring rains, even so late in the year, but the ford looked passable.

The gathering camped beyond, spreading up and down the bank and straggling away onto the plain. A pall of smoke hung over it, a reek of cooking fires, dust from the hooves of horses and cattle, and massed humanity.

They had been seen: movement stirred in the camp, surging of figures afoot and figures on horseback toward the riverbank and the ford. Kestrel eyed the way they must take, and shivered. They would be open targets for arrows and thrown spears, trapped like a herd of antelope in a ravine.

But there was no other way. Bravely then, heads high, they rode as Sparrow had bidden them ride: king's companions foremost in an arc like a bow, warriors behind, king between them like the arrow set to the string. Sparrow rode beside the king, white mare beside grey stallion. She was not armed. The king had not strung his bow or taken spear in hand. The others rode with bows strung but arrows in quivers, shoulders stiff, eyes alert.

They went down the bank into the water. It was knee-deep on the horses, swift but not so much that it would carry them off if they went slowly. And slowly they had to go, while the tribes waited on the far bank, a long line now of men and horses. Kestrel marked the sigils of the tribes: Cliff Lion, Tall Grass, Dun Cow, Red Deer, White Stone, and other, lesser people among them. They, like Linden's warriors, carried strung bows, but none nocked arrow to string.

The king's companions reached the middle of the river. It was deeper here, the current stronger, waves lapping the riders' knees. Their horses braced, slipping a little but holding. The riders kept their eyes on the men who waited.

They passed midstream. Still no arrow flew. The foremost man reached shallow water, started up the bank.

The men atop the bank seemed disinclined to let him by, but at the last instant they drew back, horses jostling, leaving a space wide enough for one rider to pass.

Linden set heels to the grey stallion's sides, so suddenly that he took Sparrow by surprise. The stallion leaped forward, spraying water, surging up the bank behind that first bold man. Linden was shouting with laughter, whooping like a mad thing, whirling a spear about his head.

Men scattered. The silvermaned stallion danced, curvetting, tossing his head.

Linden's warriors rode up through the space he had opened, into the midst of a wary army. They spread behind him as they could.

The stallion stood still, motionless, neck arched, snorting softly. Linden smoothed his water-dampened mane and smiled sunnily at the gathered tribesmen. "Well met, my people," he said. "And such a welcome! Are you glad, then, to see your king again?"

They seemed notably more amazed than glad. Linden rode forward. Men gave way before him.

And, Kestrel noticed, closed in behind. There was no escape now. They could only go on toward the camp's center, where the king's tent of the White Stone stood tall among the rest.

✢ ✢

Walker was waiting for them there, with the kings of Cliff Lion and Dun Cow and Red Deer, and the Tall Grass king standing at his right hand. He was dressed as a shaman, but he stood on the royal horsehide. If any memory remained of his defeat on the gods' hill, he had buried it deep.

"Take them," he said to the men behind Linden's warriors.

They closed in. The king's men nocked arrows at last, bending the shorter, stronger bows of the Grey Horse People, which could shoot far and shoot hard.

"Now then," Linden said easily, addressing the kings as brother to brothers, "isn't this a bit ridiculous? Brothers, brothers, if it's my kingship you're wanting, there's a way to get it, and with little enough bloodshed, too."

Cliff Lion's king rumbled laughter. "What, you'd fight us all?"

Linden spread his hands in deprecation. "Oh, I'm not that great a hero. One at a time—or two if you like. Whoever's still standing at the end, he takes this beauty of mine, and the kingship, too. Not," he said with his sweet, maddening smile, "that I expect anyone else to take him, but you can dream."

"We can *take*," said Cliff Lion's king.

"You can try," said Linden. "Here, I've been riding a while and I'm thirsty. Shall we share a skin of *kumiss* before we fight, and a bite or two with it?"

"Hungry for a last meal, boy?" sneered the Red Deer king.

"Starved," Linden said brightly.

He had them, whether they knew it or no. They all dismounted, but each man kept his horse near to hand, and his weapons, as women brought food and drink. It was a strange feast for a battlefield, there in the middle of the great camp.

Linden ate with relish, nor would he go when Sparrow tried to draw him aside. Kestrel would have liked to do it himself. Linden had been advised to offer combat with a single champion—not with every one of the kings, still less one after the other. One man he could defeat; he was a great fighter. But a dozen, or more if the lesser kings took it into their heads to try for the prize—that was wholly unreasonable.

Kestrel managed to say so under cover of offering Linden a cut of roast ox. Linden grinned at him, altogether unrepentant. "I know, I know. But I couldn't fight just one—it wouldn't be enough. It's got to be all of them."

"To the death?"

Linden shrugged. "I'm married to a sister or daughter of each. My wives are all with child. I'll name the offspring heirs and myself regent for them—and appoint good men to play king while the babies grow up."

That was breathtakingly ambitious and rather brilliant. But it had a signal flaw. "All or most of those children could be daughters," Kestrel said.

"Then I'll find husbands for them, yes?" Linden patted his arm. "There, there. Would you like to be king in all but name of, say, Cliff Lion? Or Tall Grass—I know you have friends there."

"I don't want to be king of anything," Kestrel said. "I want you to be alive and king of the People."

"The gods will make sure of it," said that gleeful madman, biting into the haunch of antelope, and grinning as the red juices ran down his beard.

Kestrel sighed deeply and withdrew.

+ +

Just before Linden could be accused of avoiding the inevitable by prolonging the feast, he rose and drained the last of a skin of *kumiss*. He belched enormously, laughed, and stretched. "Well now. Who'll begin?"

Men moved hastily to mark out a circle before the king's tent, where the people could see the battle clearly, and the combatants could see what prize they stood first to win: the king's wealth and all his women, bright eyes and shy faces peering out from the tent's flap.

Linden stepped into the circle even as it was complete, stripped and tossed his garments wherever they happened to fall, wound his yellow plaits about his head and bound them, and stood waiting, smiling, gleaming in the sun. He could not but know how splendid he looked, with his broad muscled shoulders and his strong rider's thighs, and his rod, even at rest, as long and nigh as thick as many a man's at full stretch.

He rolled those shoulders, flexed his muscled arms. He smiled his infuriating smile. "What, no one wants to fight me after all? Am I so terrifying? Is it so obvious that I can't but win?"

Cliff Lion's king snarled and sprang into the circle. He was a bull to Linden's young lion, taller, broader, and notably heavier. His strength was famous, likewise his ruthlessness. He loved to seize his enemies in such a circle as this, and break them over his knee.

Linden beside him seemed a stripling, a golden child with too little sense to know when he was overmatched. But Kestrel, studying the larger man, noted that he was no longer young, and that for all his massive strength, he had grown soft about the middle. If Linden could withstand the first mighty charges, he could wear that bull of a man down.

But there were other, younger, fitter men waiting, and Linden had agreed, in his folly, to fight them all. He could not play out the game too long. He had to fell each opponent quickly, and hope to keep his strength for the next.

He eluded the Bull's charges, light on his feet, laughing, which enraged the Bull. Then his foot slipped, and his rival caught him, grappled him and flung them both bruisingly to the ground.

Linden twisted, so that the Cliff Lion king was beneath him when they struck. While the Bull lay winded, he paused as if hesitating— with his own men screaming at him to make the kill now, do it *now*, and get it over. When he did strike, it was too late; a heavy arm swung up to turn the blow aside, and a massive hand reached for his throat.

He flung himself backward, staggering, rolling, scrambling to his feet. The Bull charged again. He might have had long curving horns and great hooves, he was so like the beast of his name.

Linden let him thunder past, but caught him just before he passed out of reach, whirling with the force of his speed, letting it carry him down again. He was already turning in midair. Linden struck rather wildly. The Bull ran full into that flailing fist, and dropped without a sound.

He was not dead. His breast heaved, though he was unconscious. All about the circle, men roared, bellowing for his blood.

Kestrel bit the insides of his cheeks. The pain helped him to focus, to keep his distance from that surge of sound. Linden could not let the Cliff Lion king live—not that one of them all.

Whether he understood it or simply did as he was told, Linden sank to one knee and took that massive head in his arms. His jaw set. The muscles rippled across his back. He broke the man's neck.

.... **61** ....

LINDEN WAS GIVEN no time to recover from the battle or from the killing. Red Deer's king leaped into the circle.

This was a much younger man than the Bull, hot-tempered, lean and quick. He had a flint knife in his hand.

Linden was unarmed. Kestrel caught his eye and tossed his own knife into the waiting hand. Linden grinned at its balance. It was a fine knife—Aurochs had made it.

The Red Deer king circled, stepping as light as a stag. Linden was heavier, slower, and still breathing hard from the earlier fight. But this circling let him get his breath back. When his rival darted in for a stab, he was ready, beating the blow aside, thrusting underhand. The Red Deer king twisted out of reach.

Linden pressed after him. Wise, Kestrel thought. The smaller man was much faster, but if Linden could catch him, he would fall to greater weight and strength.

But he was so very fast. The second dart of the knife found flesh, slashed Linden's shoulder. The third caught his arm. The fourth he eluded, but barely: it was aimed at his throat. He was like a lion beset by a small and determined hound, too slow to turn, to run, to leap. The Red Deer king was everywhere at once.

Linden stopped in the circle's center, not far from the fallen Bull. He was breathing hard, bleeding from numerous small cuts and slashes. He had never even touched his enemy. He crouched down as he could, and set himself to parry each thrust as it came. He did not try to strike, simply to defend.

The Red Deer king laughed in scorn. He made a dance of it, leaping, whirling, stamping, striking. Linden for his part stood as heavy as a stone, moving only to protect himself.

Kestrel nodded slowly. A truly wise man would have lured Linden back around the circle, harrying him until he fell. But the Red Deer king exerted himself mightily while Linden, for all purposes, rested. And waited. And watched.

Kestrel's eye was quick. He saw it as soon as Linden did: a slight hesitation, the hint of a stumble. The Red Deer king was tiring. Linden smiled faintly. He did not look a pretty fool then, but a man in his element: a warrior fighting for his life.

A blow, slipping slightly wild, bounced off his blade and raked down his arm, aimed for the heart.

He caught the knife-hand in his free hand. At the last possible instant, he leaned away from the blade that almost—but only almost—had pierced his breast.

The Red Deer king struggled. But he was tired, and Linden was strong. Linden pulled him in, clasping him in a bear's embrace, turning the knife inexorably, inescapably, toward his rival's own heart.

The Red Deer king was, after all, a king. He did not beg for mercy. He met Linden's eyes as he died, met them without flinching.

Linden lowered him to the ground beside Cliff Lion's king. He closed the wide eyes, arranged the slackened limbs. He straightened slowly.

Dun Cow's king entered the circle without haste. He had two spears in his hands. He tossed one. Linden caught it.

This was a great warrior, one of the great ones of the plains. His name was Spear; and that was his weapon. He balanced it in his hand as if it had been as light as a stem of grass. Then he began to work his magic with it: whirling it, spinning it on his palm, letting it dance humming up his arm and over his shoulders and down to his free hand.

Linden leaned on the spear he had been given, and watched. When Spear balanced the whole length of the weapon on his finger, Linden straightened. When it came spinning down into Spear's free hand, Linden was ready. Shaft smote shaft with a clatter audible even above the watchers' tumult.

Spear was not to be deceived into flailing at Linden while Linden rested. He forced the White Stone king to follow him, to dance with him, to defend his head and neck and shoulders from the haft and his vitals from the sharp flint head. Linden was flagging. He had lost blood; he had taken blows from the Bull's fists. Now the spear battered him, blow on blow. There was no opening, no path to Spear's body.

As Spear swept his weapon high, Linden swept low. Spear, braced for a stab to the heart, fell astonished. His spear dropped and spun away. Linden set spearhead to his throat, and smiled.

Spear smiled in return. "The gods favor you," he said.

"Yes," said Linden. He drove the spearpoint home.

✛ ✛

Three kings down. Three tribes taken. But there were so many more. Kestrel regarded them in despair. Linden was no longer the glorious young warrior he had been so little a while before. He was covered in bruises, stained with blood both fresh and dried. One eye was swollen shut. His lip was split.

But he grinned nonetheless, and beckoned with hand and spear. "Come. Come here. I'll fight the lot of you—I swore it, I'll do it. Come and take me!"

Eyes slid. Some of the kings who had pressed so boldly to the front were nowhere to be seen. Some of the others graciously gave

way to their fellows. Tall Grass, who might have been expected to
defend the honor of the greater tribes, was an old man. He should
have given himself to the knife at the midsummer sacrifice; that he
had not, spoke ill of his courage.

There were younger kings in plenty, and some cocky enough to
reckon Linden an easy target now that he had exhausted himself in
defeating the greatest warriors of them all. As they jostled among one
another, squabbling over precedence, a new sound brought the rest
about.

Kestrel's knees nearly gave way. At last, but somewhat sooner
than he had dared to hope, the rest of Linden's warband had come.
Men of Red Deer and Cliff Lion rode with it. The Grey Horse led
it, men and bold bare-breasted women on fine grey horses, armed
with their strong bows, driving back the people who crowded near
the circle. No one at all had thought to post guards at the river.
Everyone was here, watching the battle for the kingship.

The shock held them rooted. No one was mounted, no one
armed except the kings. And here was an army in their midst, with
strangers at the head of it, and two foremost who made a striking
pair: a black-bearded man and a golden-braided woman. Sparrow was
riding beside them on her moon-white mare—and when had she
slipped away from the crowd about the circle?

Kestrel wondered too how many people would recognize Keen.
She was not at all the same woman who had run away from her
husband. She rode as no woman of the People was allowed to do,
and she rode armed with a bow, arrow nocked to string, aimed at
the heart of the shaman who stood beside the Tall Grass king.

Walker, Kestrel would wager, had been advising his ally to wait
Linden out, to let the younger kings destroy him, then claim the
kingship for himself. How he would do it without winning it by
combat, Kestrel did not know, nor much care. Walker would have
conceived a way.

Walker seemed not at all dismayed to face a bow in the hands of
his erstwhile wife. He murmured in the old king's ear. The old king
frowned and seemed to protest, but Walker persisted.

The Tall Grass king spoke then in a voice that wavered before it
steadied. "My people! Seize them."

No one moved. Linden in the circle, leaning on the spear with
an air of insouciant ease, laughed lightly and said, "You're forgetting
something, my lord. Until someone proves otherwise, I am the king

of kings here. And these are my allies—my kindred and my friends."
He turned his eyes to them. "You are very welcome, but you have
interrupted our game. Will you dismount and watch?"

"Not," said Keen, "while that one lives to poison your hope."

There could be no doubt as to whom she meant. Her arrow did
not waver, even when her eyes rested briefly on Linden.

"You had better not kill him," Linden said reasonably. "He's a
shaman."

"He is a liar and a stealer of children. He is no more a true
shaman than I am."

"There now," said Linden. "That's not—"

"It is true," Keen said. "You may go on with your kingmaking,
if that is what it is. But first I will take his life."

Kestrel believed that she would. But Walker laughed, rich with
scorn. "Fool of a woman! Get off that horse and put down the bow
and have some sense. If you kill me, no one will save you. All the
shamans will sing you to your death."

"It will be worth it," she said, clear and cold.

It was Sparrow who said, "Not to us who love you. And what of
your son? Who will raise him?"

That stopped Keen. Her arm wavered. Her face went white.

Kestrel saw Walker tense, saw the hand creep under the shaman's
robe.

The width of the circle was between them. It was forbidden any
man to enter it unless he would contest for the kingship. But Walker
reached for a weapon—to kill Keen, to kill Sparrow, to kill both, it
did not matter.

Before Kestrel set foot in the circle and doomed himself, someone
else moved, too swift almost to see. Walker gasped. His arm dropped
limp. His shoulder had grown a length of carved bone: the haft of a
knife. Cloud smiled at him, sweet and terrible, and balanced a second
knife in his hand, twin to the first. That one, his smile said, would
be delighted to pierce Walker's heart.

Cloud was a king's heir. He could take a shaman's life and be
suffered to live.

"Take them!" Walker cried in a voice gone thin with pain. "Take
them as you took the others. You outnumber them, curse you! Swarm
over them and bring them down!"

Some few men moved then, perhaps in fear of a shaman's curse.
Kestrel saw how one was given pause. He found himself breast to

point with a flint arrowhead. The archer was a slip of a girl, a curly-headed beauty whose breasts were just budded. Her smile was as sweetly deadly as Cloud's.

Others were not so easily halted. They surged toward the horses.

A piercing cry stopped them short. It was a woman's keen, shrill enough to split a man's skull.

All the kings, the warriors, the strong men of the tribe, were engulfed in women. Wives and concubines, sisters, daughters, even captives, surrounded them, impeded them, bound them in slender arms and long braided hair. The kings were overwhelmed.

Not one of them could move. Kestrel, whom none had touched, realized with a faint and penetrating shock that his mother stood in front of him, and that his father was beside him. "Don't tell me you did this," Kestrel said.

Willow tilted her head toward Sparrow. "No, not I. She found her way to us while the kings were strutting and flaunting their manly parts."

"But," said Kestrel, "in that little time, she could not possibly have—"

"She is a shaman," Willow said. She turned away from him, such a thing as a woman did not do to a man among the People, but Kestrel had to stop to remember it.

Sparrow was speaking, not loudly but her voice was clear. It carried remarkably far. "It's over now. If any king still believes that he can claim the title from the king of the White Stone People, let him remember that after he takes the king's life, he must ride the king's stallion. And that, I promise you, none but Linden may do. Even he does it only on Horse Goddess' sufferance."

"Pay no heed to her!" Walker cried out over the excessive noise that the woman nearest him was making. Her fiery hair and strident voice left Kestrel in no doubt as to who she was. Blossom of the Tall Grass had come to claim her husband.

Her husband struck her aside with his unwounded arm, ignored her shrieks—which were more of rage than of pain—and lifted his voice in the full force of which a shaman was capable. "This is a liar, an outcast, a stealer of kings. Look at her! She profanes the very earth she walks on. She slew our father, O my people. She cut his throat with her own hand, and took his head. She destroyed the great shaman, the wisest of us all, Drinks-the-Wind whom we loved."

"So she did."

Kestrel had not seen White Bird come, but she was unmistakably there, sitting astride the old white mare who must have carried her across the river. Her hair was loose, streaming down her back. Her garment was a shaman's robe, one of her dead husband's, most likely. In her arms like a terrible child she carried his head, its long white hair and its white beard streaming. From either side of the mare's shoulders hung the others: Ash who would have been king, and—great shock and no little horror to Kestrel who had, after all, loved her—Rain the young shaman of the Grey Horse.

They were mighty in death, white and terrible, nor had the passage of days disfigured them. It was clear to see who they had been, and how they had died: the shamans fearless, in exaltation; the warrior in enormous surprise.

White Bird rocked her husband's head and crooned to it under all their stares. "She did kill you," she said, "oh yes, my lord, she took your life. You offered it—you gave it into her hands. You commanded her to take it. Because, my lord, my husband, great shaman of the People, she and only she could take the power that was in you. No one else had the strength. No one else was brave enough."

"The woman is mad," Walker said. "Remove her."

She laughed, sweet and high. "Oh, I am mad. Divine madness. The gods whirl in me, sing to me, promise me . . . oh, wonders! But no son." Great grief crossed her face. "No son." She rocked her husband's head even more tenderly than before.

Walker stirred. Perhaps he thought to remove her himself, cast her from the mare's back and hand her over to someone suitably strong and suitably inured to such sights as she was. But he had forgotten, perhaps, the knife in his shoulder. The movement set him reeling.

"You are no shaman," White Bird said as in a dream. "You never were. Look, sister of the Tall Grass, what you married. Is he not beautiful, for a lie? Is he not wonderful? Is he not a great bull of the inner room?"

"Bull?" Blossom had picked herself up, nursing a bruised cheek. Her glare was baleful. "No bull, that. That is an ox, and in shaman's clothing, yet. He is no shaman. He has no magic. He has no visions. He has nothing but a web of lies."

"Indeed," said Keen in her new, cold voice. "He raped you, too, did he? And left you forgotten?"

"He lies," Blossom said, "and lies, and lies." Her lips drew back from her teeth. "We know. Women know. Men—men are fools."

Walker struck at her again, to batter her down. She shrieked and sprang. She found the knife in his shoulder; pulled it free in a bright rush of blood; and stabbed, stabbed and stabbed, shrieking in pure mindless fury.

People shrank away. No one moved to stop her. Not the kings, not the shamans. Not the Tall Grass king or his shaman, though he had been ally and kin to both. They watched in horror, with their hands at their sides.

Even if they had ventured to move, their women would have prevented them. They stood in a wall about Walker as he died. Every one had turned her back, rejecting him and all that he had been.

·········· 62 ··········

A T LAST BLOSSOM stopped shrieking. She stood over the bloodied body. Her face was a perfect blank, like the mask of a priest.

The silence was enormous. In it, Willow made her way across the circle—breaking the ban of kings without a thought or a flicker of fear—and with great gentleness laid her arm about Blossom's shoulders and led her away. A path was cleared for her, women pressing back the men, watching without sound.

It was Sparrow who spoke, softly, but every one of them heard her. "Thus falls a world," she said. "I am my father's heir. If any shaman fails to see it, then I reckon him blind, as blind as my late brother. There will be no more lies, people of the plain. No more falsehoods. No more thieves of visions."

Woman she might be, but they were greatly cowed, all those strong warriors. They had seen the Walker Between the Worlds fall, struck down by a woman. And there was White Bird with her terrible burden, smiling, singing softly to herself.

Her eye fell on the Tall Grass shaman. Her smile sharpened. She rode toward him. He shrank back, but his wives and daughters impeded him. White Bird halted the mare in front of him and held out her husband's head. "Take it," she said. "Drink from its cup. There's a little power left, that he kept for you. He said—he says to me, you are not wise, not yet, but you may be. And you are all these people have."

The Tall Grass shaman had little choice but to take the grisly gift. It had dawned on him, perhaps, what he was being given. His eyes flicked toward Sparrow.

"Take it," Sparrow said. "All that he had to give, he has given me."

The shaman bowed—not willingly, but he was not one of those who were blind. His eyes on her were briefly dazzled as he undertook to see what power she had from her father.

She turned from him, leaving him to his new eminence, and faced Linden in the circle. He was standing quietly, leaning on the spear, patient as she had seldom seen him. He was not terribly wounded, though there was a great deal of blood about him.

He smiled at her, as honest as a child, but she had learned how strong he could be in that simplicity. The mare shifted beneath her. She nodded, though there were no words between them.

She called the silvermaned stallion. He came obediently, snorting at the stench of blood and death, but his heart was strong and his courage high. "This," she said, "is a king, and a maker of kings. Only one man of the plains is granted leave to be his rider—both his master and his servant. So Horse Goddess has decreed."

She nodded to Linden. He barely needed encouragement. Naked and wounded as he was, he swung onto the broad dappled back. The stallion arched his neck and pawed. Linden slapped his shoulder in pure love.

Someone—it might have been one of the companions, or one of Linden's warband—raised a whoop, the war-cry of the royal following. Others took it up, in pairs and handfuls and dozens, till the earth rocked with it, and the sky rang.

The People had their king again. All of him.

✢ ✢

There were kings to bury, and a shaman, however false, to send to Earth Mother's breast. Linden, with the elders of Cliff Lion and Red Deer and Dun Cow, saw to the burial of the three kings. The tribes he disposed of as he had promised: naming each wife of that tribe regent for the heir unborn, and giving her a warrior to rule where men must rule. Cliff Lion and Dun Cow had had prince-heirs already, one a brother and one the father of the royal wife. The brother Linden put to death, for he was intransigent. The father was offered a place of great honor as grandfather to the heir. He, who was not an unwise man, chose to accept it.

While that was settled, the shamans saw to their own. Sparrow sought no part of it. She had retreated among the Grey Horse People where they had camped on the southern side of the river. Kestrel followed her there silently, and stayed with her, offering nothing she did not ask for, except his return to the People. "You are my People," he said, "and all the tribe I'll ever need."

She looked him in the face. "Truly?" she asked him.

His eyes were steady. "By my heart," he said.

More might have come of that, but one of the wild children who had ridden with the Grey Horse came calling at the tentflap. "Sparrow! Someone's come for you."

Sparrow did not want to listen. But Kestrel was a man of excessively dutiful temper. "Go on," he said. "I'll be behind you."

Daylight still lingered in the sky, though the sun had set. Fires were lit, oxen roasting—the Grey Horse had been given great gifts of Linden's generosity, and the first of them was a herd of fine white cattle.

The messenger stood by the king-fire, eyes fixed rigidly on his feet, while a circle of bold young women remarked on his looks. He was quite the pretty thing, paler even than Walker had been, and all but beardless. He wore the tunic and leggings of an apprentice shaman, with the necklace of bones that proclaimed him within a season of his trial and ascent to full power.

He did not like at all to be forced to pay reverence to a woman, but like the Tall Grass shaman, he had eyes that could see. He glared at her, outraged, and said with stiff politeness, "Lady, the shamans of the peoples bid me ask you, if you will—they would speak with you."

"They could not come to me?" Sparrow asked. "It's late; I've traveled far. I'm going nowhere tonight. Tell them, come morning, I will receive them here. They have safe passage. In the goddess' name I promise it."

The apprentice flushed. "Lady! You cannot—"

"I can do," said Sparrow gently, "whatever the gods permit me to do. If the shamans would speak with me, they may come to me here."

The apprentice left at that, all politeness forgotten. Sparrow found that she was shaking—with weariness, she was sure. She slid her arm about Kestrel's middle and leaned on him. "Gods," she said. "I could sleep till the dark of the year."

Kestrel might have ventured commentary on her treatment of the shamans, but wisely elected to keep silent. She kissed his shoulder to thank him; decided that that was barely sufficient; pulled his head down and kissed him on the lips.

✦ ✦

Keen watched them from inside Cloud's tent, torn between joy for them and a deep sense of her heart being torn in two. When the Grey Horse rode away from the gathering, she had seen no reasonable way to separate herself, though her spirit cried out toward her son. Wherever he was, whatever Walker had done with him—oh, gods, what if he had been killed? What if, even as Walker died, his son lay dead in some forgotten place?

No. He was alive. He must be. Someone kept him, someone in the vast camp that spread across the river. Its fires were myriad, its pall of smoke and dust thick even in the dusk. Cloud had not wanted to stay there. She reckoned him wise. Best he keep to this side of the river, with free escape southward if somehow the gathering should turn against him.

Tonight it was preoccupied with all that had happened: kings fallen, shamans dead, lies uncovered and power laid bare. The sounds that carried over the water were muted, the singing faint. Not many were celebrating tonight, even round the king's fire. Linden was in his own tent at last, ministered to by his many wives, all of whom seemed besotted with him.

Somewhere in that camp was Keen's son, the light of her heart, for whose sake alone she had come so far. Her other dearly beloved was outside by the fire, being prince to his people. He would not come to bed till late, if he came at all.

She slipped out the back, taking with her a thing or two that she might need. No one was on guard, though she had heard Cloud post sentries. Those could not watch every fingerbreadth of the river; and clouds had gathered to veil the stars and the waxing moon.

She forded the river in the dark, entering the cold swift water carefully, placing each foot solidly before she essayed another step. The river tugged at her, wrapping chill soft hands about her breasts and belly; for she crossed naked, with her clothes and the rest of her belongings on her head, to keep them dry.

At midstream the river nearly had her. Its softness turned to terrible strength. She braced, dug toes into the river-mud, and pressed on as fast as she could before the current plucked her loose and flung her downstream.

She staggered the last few steps, dragged herself up the bank and lay for a long count of breaths, emptied of strength. Slowly she came back to herself. The night wind dried her. She shivered, remembering the cold clutch of water, and sat up, fumbling into her tunic and leggings. Their warmth was greatly welcome.

She went on as a hunter might, making herself small, stepping soft, fitting into the sough of wind in the grass, the lap of water in the river, the night-sounds of the great camp. There were guards, but those had not been watching the river. They were intent on matters closer to hand, on watching the camp's edges. She slipped through them like a shadow, unseen and unheard.

The camp dogs had troubled her mind; they were better guards by far than human men. But any that might have been roving by the river were gathered tonight near the fires, alert for such scraps as might come their way. She kept her distance from the fires and did her best not to seem furtive in ways that would rouse a dog's suspicion. Men, too; once she was inside the camp, she was better advised to walk tall and seem unconcerned than to slink and creep and look as if she had something to hide.

She did not know precisely where to go. But one place would make a beginning. It was a larger tent than she remembered, by a considerable degree, and it was pitched not far from the king's. Walker, as king's shaman, had preferred not to keep to the edges. He wanted a clear view of the power that he had claimed, and the tent that maybe, in the end, he would have taken for himself.

Now he would take nothing but the road into the gods' country; and if the gods were just, that would be a long and bitter journey, beset with torments. But there was a fire burning in front of his tent, and signs about it that someone still lived within.

Keen stood straight in deep shadow, breathed deep, smoothed her tunic and leggings. After a moment's thought she loosed the bone pins that had held her plait wound about her head, and let it slither down her back to brush her thighs behind. She must look as much at ease as she could, and as empty of either anger or hate, though both were roiling deep within her.

Calmly then, as if she had every right in the world, she entered Walker's tent.

It was brightly lit, prodigal with lamps—proof in itself of his new wife's wealth. The reek of burning fat, scented with some sickeningly sweet herb, made her gorge rise. But she kept it down.

There was no one here in the outer room. No one on guard, no one watching for just such an invasion as this. Blossom's belongings were everywhere in towering heaps. Only one corner was cleanly bare, with a bed spread there, and a single basket near it. Of Walker's possessions there was nothing else.

Keen's lips thinned. So. He had not lived here. But his wife had— and she would know what Keen needed to know.

She was rather obviously within. Her shrieking had stopped, but her voice rang out at intervals, snapping orders, reprimanding someone for clumsiness, lamenting her grievous fate. Her father, it seemed, had not sent anyone to fetch her back to him, nor had her mother come to comfort her in her widowhood.

Another voice spoke briskly and with an air of one who had said such things many times since Blossom was led away from the king's circle. "My dear," said Willow, "you can hardly expect your family to come for you, in the circumstances. The king and the shamans will have to judge you first, and decide what is to become of you."

"*Judge* me?" Blossom's voice rose sharply. "What is there to judge? The man was a liar. He deceived us all. His death was just."

"Women do not have that power of life or death," Willow said. "We bring forth life, yes, raise it and nurture it, and when it ends, we lay it in the earth. But we are not permitted to take it with our own hands."

"Men kill men," Blossom said, "and boast of it at tedious length. Should I be out by the fire, then? Should I be boasting? I have blood on my hands, just like a man. Just—like—a man!"

She shrieked the last of it, quickly muffled, but not before she had roused someone else.

That voice of all in the world, Keen knew as she knew her own. Summer's glorious bellow quelled even Blossom's carrying on.

Keen was moving before she even thought, bursting into the inner room. She took no notice at all of the women who filled it, the eyes staring, faces white, astonished. She saw only one thing: her son in a stranger's arms, roaring his rage.

She swept him into her embrace, clasped him tight, covered him with kisses. His tears were salt, his hair sweet, its scent so blessedly familiar that she wept.

His outcry had stopped. Summer always had been less inclined to cry if she was there. He knew his mother, Rain had liked to say, even as she gave him the breast that he was clamoring for.

Keen sank down where she was, not caring if women had to scramble out of the way, and cradled him in her lap. He was staring at her, wide blue eyes beneath a crown of yellow curls. She found a smile for him. He smiled back, a broad reckless grin. There was none of Walker's close-mouthed caution in this child. He was as brilliantly easy a creature as Linden. That grin was strikingly like Linden's, sun-bright and utterly free of care or fear.

"Thank the gods you came!"

Keen looked up startled. Blossom had pulled away from Willow's embrace, and found her wits again, too.

"I was beside myself," she said. "In he came, no warning, no greeting, just dropped this *thing* in my lap and ordered me to look after it. And no reason why, either. What did he do, steal it from you? Is it his?"

"Yes," said Keen. It seemed answer enough. Whatever she had expected, it was not this perfect self-righteousness—though it made her want to laugh till her sides ached. Oh, what a match for Walker this woman had been!

And she had killed him. She was clean now, the blood washed away. She had no more remorse than a warrior after a battle, and no more concern for the rights or wrongs of it, either.

Blossom's eyes rested on the child in Keen's arms. He was fed: he had the look. The woman from whom Keen had taken him was one of those who seemed to be always bearing or nursing, and often both at once. Her belly was swollen, her breasts full even after Summer had drunk his fill.

Blossom made a sound, drawing Keen's attention back to her. "You will take it away, won't you? It bellows like a bull. I can't sleep for the racket it makes."

"I will take him," Keen said. "You need have no fear as to that."

"Good, then go," said Blossom. "I want to sleep. I need to sleep. My head aches. Oh, it aches so terribly!"

Keen had not thought much past finding Summer. If she had, she would have supposed that it would take her hours, perhaps into daylight, to find him. Then she would go back to Cloud in the southern camp, and whatever followed would be no affair of hers.

He had been in the first place she came to, cast there with so little regard for his life or comfort that if Walker had been alive, Keen would have happily gutted him all over again. She wanted desperately to take her child away from it. But it was night still, and Summer would not take kindly to the river crossing.

Willow seemed to see her trouble. "Come," she said, "I'll take you to my husband's tent. Aurochs is there. He'll look after you."

"You can't leave me!" Blossom shrilled. "You have to stay here!"

"I do not," said Willow. "Come, child."

But Keen paused. "This is a dead man's son. A dead shaman—however discredited he may be. What if—"

Willow would not let her finish. "Aurochs can protect him. Come."

Keen went, because she could think of nothing better to do. Blossom tried to follow, but Willow restrained her firmly, handed her to the burliest of the women, and bade them guard her till morning. Only one came with them: the silent and sleepy-eyed nurse, whom Summer would need again before long.

※ ※

Aurochs was asleep, but he woke quickly enough at his wife's touch. Nor did he need overmuch explanation. "I'll send a man to watch her," he said of Blossom—"and the more fool I for not doing it sooner."

"Yes, you are a fool," Willow said without sympathy. "I've had my fill of her, myself. If you don't terribly mind, I'm going to sleep—and, child, so should you. We'll keep the baby between us. No one will touch him or take him away."

Keen sighed. The fist that had been clenched inside her was opening slowly. She was suddenly, profoundly exhausted. She barely noticed where she was taken, except that it was deep within Aurochs' tent, surrounded by his women, and Aurochs himself stood watch without.

Then, with Summer in her arms, she could rest. It mattered little what came after, if only he was safe, and she could be sure of it.

THE SHAMANS OF the plains came late in the morning, but come they did, crossing the river in a sour-faced company and entering the Grey Horse camp with the air of men who stooped far below their proper station. That a woman forced it upon them, none of them was likely to forget.

But Sparrow was her father's heir, and her station therefore was far above theirs. It must gripe them sorely to look at her among these outlandish people, and to know that she was stronger than any of them.

After she sent the shamans' messenger away, she had tormented herself with doubts and fears. If she had judged wrongly, not only she would suffer for it. And shamans' curses were never to be taken lightly.

Yet as she watched that small company of men on horses ride up out of the river, her spirit eased a little. Most of them were old. All had some deformity or some strangeness of face or form. Many carried in them the light of the spirit that she had always been able to see, and that Walker had never had. None could match her strength. What she did as she breathed, simply by emptying herself of thought, they had to win by great workings of magic, invocations of gods and spirits, raisings of sacred smoke, even sacrifices of blood.

Her spirit was washed in the blood of two great shamans. The life of a third had been given in her name. She needed no sacrifice. She needed simply to be.

She received them in simple state, dressed in the fashion of the Grey Horse. Kestrel's brows had climbed when she came out of the tent, but he had mercifully kept silent. No one else remarked on it. All the women here were in leggings and nothing else, this time of year.

Sparrow had never flaunted herself so. She had to fight the urge to cover her breasts, even as fine as Kestrel averred they were. She wanted—needed—the shamans to see all that she was: woman, and bearing, and marked richly with the signs of a shaman. Where the other women wore necklaces or collars of bone or beads or stone, she wore only Old Woman's stone in a cage of woven thongs, white deerhide clasping the black starstone.

It was easier if she thought of herself as clothed in power. That, after all, was what she wanted the shamans to see. She lifted her chin and squared her shoulders. The child shifted inside her as if in sympathy.

Cloud welcomed the shamans as they entered the camp, saw that they dismounted and their horses were tended, and offered them a greeting-cup full of the berry wine of his people. They were not displeased to be so greeted: he was a man, and it was known that he was a prince.

When they had drunk from the cup, though warily and only after he had drunk himself, he led them into the circle of tents. Sparrow waited there under a canopy, seated on a white horsehide as if she had been a king.

She was not going to be gentle with them. She could not afford to be. She let them stand in front of her, with the sun beating down on bald or greying heads. When after a stretching while she spoke, it was not to invite them to sit in the shade. She said, "You summoned me in the night. Why?"

"Surely you know why," said a tall man with a face marred by a wide blood-red stain—Red Deer shaman, as she recalled. His lip curled slightly, though his tone was polite enough.

She tilted her head. "I prefer that you tell me," she said.

"Such were the sleights your brother made use of," said Red Deer shaman, "and so deceived us all."

Sparrow's brows rose. "Even you, sir? You have eyes; you could see. And yet he deceived you."

Red Deer shaman lowered those eyes she spoke of, but not in submission. There was anger beneath the smoothness as he said, "Some of us are so powerful that we can conceal it utterly, and seem as nothing in the spirit. So we reckoned him. And his visions were true."

"Indeed they were," she said. "They were mine."

He might have thought to sneer at that, but when he looked up to speak, she let him see all of what she was. He flung up his hand with a cry.

She smiled, a stretching of lips over teeth. "Did you think," she asked him, "that what you saw before was the whole of it? I, too, can hide. I, too, can pretend, if there is need. For years I hid and pretended and let my brother steal my visions. What could I do, after all? I was only a woman. I could never be a shaman."

"Nor can you be one now," said Red Deer shaman. "Not among us."

"No?" Sparrow shrugged slightly. "Maybe not. Maybe I'm meant to be more. Priestess, servant of the gods. Horse Goddess' chosen."

"A woman cannot be—" one of the lesser shamans began.

It was not Red Deer shaman who silenced him. Tall Grass shaman had let the other speak for them all. He looked terribly weary, worn down with the duties that she had laid on him, and with grief, too: for it was his daughter who had killed the false shaman, and his ally and son-in-law whom she had killed.

Now he spoke, slowly but clearly, and more strongly as he went on. "Woman rode the mare long before man rode the stallion." Some of his fellows gasped: shock or surprise, or outrage at his speaking so publicly of a mystery? Sparrow thought perhaps the last. "Horse is a goddess, and not a god. So it has been known to us from the dawn time. But to speak of it before all the people, to confess it to those who knew nothing of the mystery, and nothing of the truth—"

"—must be done," Sparrow said. "The lies have gone on long enough. A man took the horse away from a woman, and earned Horse Goddess' wrath, though that was terribly slow to rise. Then a man took the visions from a woman, stole the power that was hers, that the goddess had given her; and that roused her ire far more swiftly. Horse Goddess is not pleased with the people of the plains. That they worship her children, she reckons right and proper. But how they choose to do it, and what they have done to her chosen— that, she likes not at all."

"Are you demanding," said Red Deer shaman, "that we lift the ban on the women? What will follow? Women riding to war? Women claiming to be kings?"

"Why not?" said Sparrow, though it was hardly wise.

"Surely," Tall Grass shaman said, "all that will not be necessary. No warriors; no kings. But if women could ride the mares, or mount children on them, think, brother, how much swifter the marches would be, and how much easier to defend against raiders."

"Women *riding?*" Red Deer shaman looked as if he had swallowed a live coal.

"You will settle that," Sparrow said levelly, "in as little time and with as much plain sense as possible. So the goddess bids you. You will begin today. You will do it now."

But they were not so easily dismissed. "There is still another matter," Tall Grass shaman said. "Your brother—"

"He lies still above ground?" Sparrow could not call herself surprised. Angry, yes. "You did not entrust him to Earth Mother as soon as the sun fell? And did his spirit walk? Whom did he beset, then? Whom did he drive mad?"

"No—no one." That was a young shaman, strikingly young for that company, and pleasant to look at, too, but for a twisted arm. He seemed startled that he had spoken, but once he began, he gathered courage to go on. "Lady, my brothers and I, we watched over him all night long. His spirit hid inside his body and pretended that it was alive. That was why—that's what—we couldn't bury him. Because, you see. He wouldn't leave."

Sparrow believed him. She had not foreseen it, but much of what Walker did had skirted the edges of visions.

She glanced at Tall Grass shaman. He nodded, though she had not needed him to assure her that the boy spoke truth. "We performed the rite of opening and the rite of freeing. He only held the tighter to the bars of his body. We called on the dark gods to fetch their own. They bade us do it ourselves. If the dead will not go, the gods have no concern with them."

"And that," said Sparrow, "was why you sent to me in the night. To do what you could not."

"He was your brother," said Red Deer shaman. "He stole your visions. We thought that that might be holding him."

"That, or fear of the punishments waiting for him." Sparrow sighed. "Very well. I'll do what I can. But first, tell me. What have you done with his wife?"

They glanced at one another. "Done?" said Tall Grass shaman. "We hardly had time to—"

"You are in great disarray," Sparrow said almost gently. She rose. The mare had come and was waiting, none too patient to be kept standing about in the sun. Sparrow smiled at that, stroked her lovely head and smoothed her mane and mounted her. The others had to scramble to find their horses and follow.

✦ ✦

Walker lay where Blossom had felled him. There was a bull's hide over him now, and the roof of a tent, and a circle of shamans to keep away the curious. Those were many as Sparrow rode into the broken circle; she felt their eyes on her like a myriad small groping hands.

She put aside the thought, slid from the mare's back beside the still shape under the spotted hide. She stood for a moment, steadying herself on the earth. The sun clamored at her, all bright male strength.

She had to put that aside, too; to go quiet inside.

Then she could see. He was there, yes. He coiled inside the broken body like a worm in a shell, dreaming that he dreamed; that he had entered the mystical dark of the shaman, and awaited the visions that would lead him anew to the light. The strength of will that held him there, the sheer selfishness of his spirit, roused her almost to awe. Nothing in his world existed but through him. Even death could not conquer him. The body would crumble about him, but he would endure, certain to the end of time that he would wake and be alive again.

It was a perfect fate for the Walker Between the Worlds. Even in death he would live a lie, and persist in self-deception.

"Will you free him?"

Sparrow started slightly, staring for a while without recognition at the Tall Grass shaman. The old man could see as clearly as she.

"He seems perfectly content," she said.

"Yes," said the Tall Grass shaman.

He let the moment stretch, and the meaning of the word with it. Contentment for such a creature as Walker had been. And if she freed him, she sent him to long torment.

Justice would dictate that she free him. Mercy . . . the gods were not merciful. Nor had Sparrow thought she could be. And yet as she knelt on one knee, staring at what was left of her brother whom she had hated so long and so fiercely, she could only think of the sun beating on her shoulders, the breeze playing about her, the living world that she had and he would never have again. Darkness and silence, crumbling slowly into Earth Mother's arms. No name, no memory; no hope of cleansing, or of rare rebirth.

She straightened. "Bury him," she said. "Heap the earth high over his bones. Make it a warning and a reminder to all who would claim the name of shaman. Unless they claim true, this, too, will they become. To this will they go."

T HE SHAMANS TOOK the bull's hide and what it had concealed, and carried it away to be laid in a secret place.
Sparrow stayed where she was. She was still rather disconcerted when people did as she bade them, even in Horse
Goddess' name. And whether the goddess had spoken through her
just now, or whether it had been her own troubled spirit, she did
not know.

She looked up into Linden's face. She had not heard him come.
He held out his hand. She took it and let him draw her up. His eyes
on her were openly appreciative. "It's very immodest," he said, "but
I think I like it."

She caught herself blushing.

He smiled. "Come," he said. "The priests will close the circle and
end it. You come and let me play the king for you. There are so many
things I've thought of, so many things I want to do. And with you—"

"I'm not staying," she said.

He stared.

"I'm going," she said. "When the Grey Horse goes, I go. They're
my people now."

"But you're of *our* People!" Linden protested. "And what will
we do for a shaman?"

"Tall Grass shaman belongs to you," she said. "Did you forget?
Command him to find one for you. A true one, an honest man and
a loyal child of the gods. There is one whom he might consider: a
tall boy of the Dun Cow, with a withered arm. You'd like that one,
I think. He's young but he's strong, and he has the courage to speak
when no one else will."

She hoped that Linden was listening. If not, she would send the
message to Tall Grass shaman herself.

Linden shook his head, not at what she had said, but that she
had said it at all. "You have to stay. You're strong. We need you."

"Grey Horse has lost a shaman, too," Sparrow said. "It needs me—and it won't mind that I'm not a man. That will matter, my lord. Not to you, maybe; but to everyone else."

"Then it will change," Linden said firmly.

She shook her head. "Not in this age of the world. What I can do, I have done. The ban on women with the horses—that is ended. You can see to it. But a woman who is a shaman? No. That's too much. They'll accept me as Horse Goddess' priestess, and as Drinks-the-Wind's daughter. While I'm out of their reckoning, and out of their tribe, and come only at intervals—for great rites or great visions, for gatherings or festivals—I'm bearable. But as a shaman, living among them, working magic for them, they need someone whose manhood they can be sure of."

Linden was beginning to see, though he did not want to. He scowled formidably. "You just don't want to stay."

"If I only had to think of you," she said, "I would stay."

He shook his head, obstinate. She tugged lightly at one of his plaits, which in truth was a great insolence, and coaxed him with a smile.

He was not to be cajoled. "Who will advise me, then? Who will help me to be wise? Because you know Kestrel will go wherever you go."

"But his father won't," Sparrow said. "He belongs to the People, he and his senior wife. They can help you as we children never could."

Linden gave way slowly, with great reluctance. But she had an answer for his every argument, and he was not a man for wars of words. He flung up his hands. "Very well. Very well! You'll never do what I tell you, I know that. But if I ask—will you stay a little while? Will you at least help me make sense of this gathering, and send the tribes to their lands?"

"That," she said, "I can do."

"Then come and begin," he said.

+ +

Linden's first beginning was the judgment of Walker's slayer. It should have been a matter for shamans, but the shamans had surrendered the task to the king. "I cannot judge," Tall Grass shaman said as chief of them. "This is my daughter. I cannot condemn her."

Linden was not visibly delighted at the prospect, either. But he had the woman brought to him as he sat on his royal horsehide with his companions about him and the elders of all the tribes gathered in a great circle. And the women were there, too, standing back, making no spectacle of themselves, but unquestionably present. He made no move to dismiss them, though he was clearly aware of them: his eyes kept wandering toward them.

Blossom had taken time to make herself presentable as befit a woman of wealth and standing, even a widow without kin to acknowledge her. The light of day well suited her bold beauty. She moderated her voice as much as she could, bowing before the king and murmuring politeness.

Kestrel wondered uncharitably if she had had instruction. He had heard a great deal of Walker's second wife, and heard no little from her, either, while he was with the People. Her voice carried far, particularly when she was hectoring her husband.

She conducted herself in no respect as a woman who repents the murder of her husband. She faced the king squarely, without the wanton edge that another woman might have offered; if she was affected at all by his fine male beauty, she concealed it well.

"Woman of the Tall Grass," Linden said, "bound in marriage to the White Stone People, by your own hand your husband fell. Will you defend that action?"

"It needs no defense," she said. "You were there. You saw what he was. How could I have done other than I did?"

People murmured at that. Linden frowned. "A woman cannot kill her husband. It's against the gods' law."

"But I did," she said. "He needed killing, for the things he had done. No one else would do it. Therefore I did."

"A woman cannot—" Linden began.

"My lord," said someone from the circle's edge. "May I speak?"

Keen was standing there with Summer in her arms. Kestrel had not even known she was on this side of the river—had thought her in the Grey Horse camp, left behind and grieving for her child and, maybe, her fallen husband.

And yet she was here, head high, speaking out before the king as the Keen of a year past would never have dreamed of doing. She was magnificent in her golden beauty, cradling her golden child.

Linden seemed as dazzled as the rest. "You may speak," he said somewhat belatedly. "Certainly you may."

Keen inclined her head to him. "My lord, may I enter the circle, then?"

Linden beckoned. She entered slowly, stepping with care as if the earth might buckle underfoot. She stopped at a little distance from Linden, not far from Blossom.

Blossom looked her up and down. "So. Are you here to make these men see reason? Did our husband not deserve killing?"

"He deserved it richly," Keen said. "But men keep the killing for themselves. They need trials and defenses, or battles in proper order. They are not happy that you, a woman and his wife, performed the execution."

"Indeed we are not," Linden said. "For if every woman could put her husband to death so readily, there would be few men left."

"That is true," Blossom said. "But now it's done, you should thank me. It's spared you the trouble of doing it yourself."

Linden shook his head at that. Keen spoke before he could muddle matters further. "You have to be judged. There isn't any choice—not in the world as it is. They're going to want to put you to death. As a lesson, you see. So that other wives know better than to kill their husbands. Even husbands who deserve it."

Blossom's head came up. Her nostrils flared. "Death? Put me to death? But why?"

"Justice," said Keen.

"Justice," said Blossom, "was that man dead at my feet. You knew what he was. Do you know what he did to me? Do you?"

"I know," said Keen.

This, Kestrel noticed, was doing odd things to those who listened. Their anger was changing. They were beginning to whisper among themselves. *Mad*, they said. *The woman is mad.*

"I am not!" said Blossom, whose ears were too keen for her own good. "The rest of you are lacking in sense and reason. Does any one of you truly believe that that man should have been permitted to live?"

"Only a king or a shaman," said Linden, "or the elders in council, should have determined that." He spoke sorrowfully, but he did not waver. "We can't have wives passing judgment on their husbands. No matter how just that judgment may be. You are condemned to death, woman of the Tall Grass People. It will be gentle. That I swear to you. You will know no pain."

"You can't do that," said Blossom.

"I am the king," said Linden. "I can do whatever is best for the People."

"But this is not—"

Linden beckoned. Two of his companions came forward, took her gently but firmly by the arms, and began to lead her from the circle.

She twisted. They held on tighter. She began to shriek.

It sounded stark mad. But Kestrel, watching her, was put most in mind of a small and deeply spoiled child. She did not believe that she could die, or indeed that she could suffer any harm. She had always won her way before by the perfection of her intransigence.

Now she had no escape, but she did not know it. Curlew, who was one of those who held her captive, clapped a hand over her mouth. Bullcalf, the other, followed it swiftly with his belt, gagging her with it. That silenced her as much with shock as with the stopping of her mouth. They began again to carry her away.

This time it was Sparrow who stopped them. She spoke to Linden, not pleading, simply speaking calmly. "Is there no other way?"

"None that I can see," he answered.

"Not even exile?"

"No," he said. "If she lives, then other women will imagine that they can escape, too."

"Exile is not an easy sentence," Sparrow said.

"No, it is not. Separated from the tribe, from all that she ever knew—how would she live? What would she do? No, lady. Death is kinder. She'll be taken to a quiet place and given a potion to drink—one of her husband's, I suppose. He always did brew the best poisons. Then she'll sleep, and never wake."

Sparrow looked as if she might have resisted further, but Linden's eyes were unyielding. She bowed her head and was silent. This after all was the same mercy she had given Walker. It was fair, in its fashion: that he should be trapped forever in his body, and Blossom should be set free.

※ ※

No one else spoke as Blossom was carried off to her sentence. The silence persisted after she had gone. Its breaking came from outside: a murmur that resolved into the sound of hooves on earth, and took shape as a company of riders making its way through the camp toward the king's circle.

Linden rose. His face forgot to be somber. He opened his arms wide in welcome.

Cloud opened his own arms from the back of his grey stallion, riding to the circle's edge and springing down. Linden was there, pulling him into a glad embrace, drawing him inward, setting him down on the royal horsehide.

It was done altogether without thought, and it shocked the elders and the lesser kings. Cloud was not even yet a king, still less a king of the plains; yet he was set as an equal beside the king of kings.

Nor did he refuse that equality. Cloud had no arrogance, but he knew what he was, and what he was worth. He inclined his head to the lords of the plains. He smiled at the king's companions. His smile warmed on Kestrel. And when it fell on Keen, who was still in the circle, rocking Summer who had begun to fuss, it went wonderfully soft.

Summer stretched arms toward him, straining, proclaiming at the top of his ample lungs where he wished to go. Keen had little choice but to set him in Cloud's lap. There he subsided to a contented gurgle.

When she would have withdrawn, Cloud caught her hand. "Stay," he said.

She blushed and shook her head. "I can't—"

He would not let her go. "My lord," he said to Linden, "it's not our custom, but since we are here, and since she is of your people, I'm minded to ask . . . would you give me leave to court this woman?"

"Court?" Linden asked.

"Approach her," Cloud said, "and persuade her to make a marriage with me."

Linden's eyes were wide. "You want to marry her?"

"Shouldn't I?"

"But I didn't think you—"

"Sometimes we do," Cloud said. "She has to agree. But if I have your leave—her king can do that, yes? Or should I ask her father?"

"The king can do that," Linden said. "But—"

"Then will you?"

"Why are you asking me? You took her long ago. Why does it matter now?"

"It matters to her," Cloud said.

Linden turned his baffled blue gaze on Keen. "Has he spoken to you of this?"

Keen shook her head. She seemed stunned.

"Do you want it?"

"Yes," she said, "but—"

"He wants to marry you," Linden said. "That would make you a prince's wife. It would also make a great alliance between our people and his—between the plains and the south, and between Sky-father's children and Horse Goddess' children."

"Did you think of that?" Keen demanded of Cloud.

"No," he said. "Not . . . at first."

She slipped her hand out of his. He sat with her son falling asleep in his lap, such a sight as the People had never seen in the king's circle before, and such a look on his face that if Kestrel had been a woman he would have melted.

But Keen was proof against it. "Is that why you want me? For the alliance?"

"No!" he said.

"Then why?"

"Because," he said, "I know you would want this."

"I never said—"

"You never needed to."

She sank down, forgetting that it was the royal horsehide she sank to. Linden made no move to stop her. She knelt in front of Cloud. "I will marry you," she said. "But if you ever doubted it—"

"Never," he said.

"Good," said Keen.

"And if I won't give my leave?" said Linden.

They both turned to stare. They had forgotten him, maybe. He laughed at their expressions. "Do you care if I give it or deny it?" he asked Keen.

She frowned. "You are my king."

"Not if you've given yourself to this one," Linden said.

"I am still of the People," she said. "Until—"

"Yes," said Linden. "Until marriage makes you one of his people."

"Will you allow that?"

"I think," said Linden, "that it would be a very good thing."

"You won't raid the Grey Horse if they're your allies," Keen said.

"Yes," said Linden.

"And it would make you free of the south, which is rich country, with fine grazing."

Linden nodded. "And Horse Goddess rules us all, and Horse Goddess' priestess is mighty and holy and will keep us as honest as we can be, but if we have a marriage to make us happy, it makes everything better, somehow. Don't you agree?"

Keen nodded gravely. "I'll take him," she said, "if I have your leave."

"You have it," said Linden.

"Now? Will you do it now? Say the words. Do what's needed."

"But that needs nine days. And—"

"We can take nine days," Cloud said. "We can hold a festival. A great marriage, and an alliance. The end of a world—the world that Walker would have made."

"And what is this world we make?" Keen asked.

"Anything we choose," Cloud answered over the head of her son that Walker had made—but Cloud had been more truly a father to the child than Walker could ever be. "Anything at all."

················ **65** ················

THEY WENT ABOUT it properly after all, because the women, led by Willow, raised a great objection to preparing a wedding feast on a moment's notice. The morrow would be soon enough, Willow declared as she swept Keen away into the seclusion proper to a bride.

Cloud was greatly amused—and Keen's father undertook to be, once he was found and informed of what his king had done with his daughter. He was aging sadly; he had grown deaf. But he had still had a wonderful roar of a laugh. "Widowed a day and she's found herself a prince? There's my girl!" Cloud he seemed to like rather well, for a foreigner. No one quite ventured to remind him of what it meant that Keen was binding herself to a foreign king's heir. The woman went with her husband, wherever he happened to be.

Tonight the bride was hidden among the women. The bridegroom found himself celebrated among the men, a nightlong carouse that struck him as strange. "There are no women," he said to Kestrel. "It's only men."

Kestrel was corrupted. He was missing lighter voices, too, and beardless faces, and sweet rounded bodies caressed by the firelight. One body in particular . . .

"Do you think," Cloud asked him, "that your people would object terribly if I disappeared before middle night and found my way to my lady? She's put on a brave face, but what that man did to her—it left scars."

"You'll not be let near her till tomorrow," Kestrel said.

Cloud's face darkened. "That's cruel."

"It's custom." Kestrel spoke again quickly, because Cloud looked ready to leap up and charge like a bull through the crowd of revelers. "My mother is with her. Whatever comfort she needs, whatever healing she will accept, Willow will give her. Sometimes," Kestrel said carefully, "it's not a man a woman needs to talk to. Even the man who holds her heart."

"Because it was a man who wounded her?"

Kestrel nodded.

Cloud's brows drew together. "Is she kept away from *all* men? Or only from me?"

"Well," Kestrel said, "men who are her kin can—"

"You are her kin," Cloud said. "She's in your mother's tent. Will you go? Will you speak to her for me?"

"I shouldn't—"

"Speak to your mother, then. Let her carry the message."

Kestrel sighed. Cloud was clearly determined, and Kestrel, if he was honest with himself, was in no mood to linger over *kumiss* and bawdy songs. Time was when he would have gone hunting to get away from it, but he was a king's companion and a shaman's lover. He had to stay in the camp at least until Keen was well and truly married.

✦ ✦

The world was a quiet place away from the king's circle, a vault of stars over the camp, a whisper of wind. Willow's tent—there; Kestrel was corrupted again, calling it his mother's rather than his father's—showed a gleam of light within.

He had heard that the women could carouse as long and hard as the men. But this was a quiet gathering, and small: Willow, Sparrow, one or two of his father's lesser wives, and, most oddly, White Bird.

She had put aside her mad wild look and returned to the seeming of a proper wife. But the eyes she turned on Kestrel were as strange as ever. Not quite shaman's eyes, but not simple mortal woman's either.

Keen sat in the middle of them with Summer asleep beside her. Her face was unexpectedly serene. It brightened at Kestrel's coming; her smile had no shadow in it.

"Are you well?" he asked her.

She nodded. "It's over, you see," she said. "He can't touch me ever again."

Kestrel glanced at his mother. She shrugged slightly. It would be as the gods willed, her expression said.

But Keen seemed much calmer than Kestrel could remember— gods, since she was a child. "Cloud sent me," he said. "He'd come himself, if he could."

"He would," Keen said. Her smile deepened and warmed. "Is he terribly worried?"

"He won't be, once I take word back to him," Kestrel said.

"My poor love." Keen shook her head. "I scared him, I know. I was so cold inside. But now that one is dead and I have Summer back, all the cold is gone. When we join hands tomorrow, I'll have to take care, or the sun will have a rival."

"You're happy," Kestrel said.

It blazed in her. It made her laugh. "Oh! Is that what it is? I keep wanting to sing."

"Happiness," said Kestrel. He stooped and kissed her forehead. "For Cloud," he said, "who will give you more and better tomorrow. And for me—" He took her hands in his and kissed them, and held them briefly to his heart. "I'm glad to see you glad."

⚜ ⚜

Sparrow went with him back to the king's circle, and waited in the shadows while he delivered Keen's message. Cloud's joy was as great as Keen's. It made him all the more eager for the morrow; but he was a strong man. He could wait.

Kestrel did not need to be strong, nor did he need to wait, either. He walked with Sparrow toward the river, close enough to feel her warmth, but not touching. Not yet. When they had come to the bank, in the rustle of reeds and the lapping of water he said, "I don't suppose you want to make it proper, too."

"No," said Sparrow. She stooped and dipped a handful of water and drank.

"Why?" he asked. "Because a wife stays with her husband?"

"Because I can't stay, and if you want to—"

"I told you," he said. "Wherever you go, I go."

"You'd leave the People for me?"

"I already did."

"Do you really want a wife?"

"I want you," he said. "Whatever you call yourself, whatever you are to the world. If you won't be a wife, then I'll have you as a lover, or mistress, or priestess and queen. It doesn't matter. Nothing matters but you."

She turned suddenly and wrapped her arms about him, pressing close. He could feel the shape of the child in her, protesting mildly at the sudden narrowing of its world. "I could live without you," she said, muffled against his chest, "but I would much rather not."

"And I," he said, "have forgotten how to live apart from you."

She raised her head. "That's not sensible."

"No," he said.

"You're a hunter. You can't be living constantly in my shadow. You certainly can't—"

He silenced her with a finger on her lips. "I'm not *that* besotted. I'll run off often enough, no fear of that. But I'll always come back."

"Promise."

"By my heart. By this child between us."

"Your daughter," she said.

His heart leaped like a stag. "It is? Truly? You see it?"

"I see her," Sparrow said. "She looks like you."

"Ah, poor child."

"She'll be beautiful when she's grown."

"Maybe. But the getting there . . ."

"Oh, hush," said Sparrow, half in exasperation, half in unwilling amusement.

"Well then; and what shall I name her? It should be something lovely, but not too soft. Maybe—"

"*I* shall name her," Sparrow said. "You may name the sons."

"Sons? There will be—"

"If you're willing to help me make them."

"Sons?" Kestrel could not stop repeating it. "And—daughters?"

He had not known there was tension in her until he felt it ease. She sighed against him. "You don't mind," she said. "That the first-born is—"

"You expected me to mind?"

"Men are strange," she said. "Even you. And when it comes to sons, you can be impossible."

"A man shouldn't want sons?"

"A man should want daughters, too. Except he seldom does."

"Your father wanted you."

"He did, didn't he?" She let him go, turning slowly, face to the stars. "This one is a shaman, too, or more than a shaman. Priestess; Horse Goddess' servant. And the next one a hunter. And the one after that—"

Kestrel stopped her with a kiss. "I shall be delighted to help you make any and all of them. But tonight, if you please, we'll keep for ourselves. And tomorrow . . ."

"Tomorrow Grey Horse and White Stone unite in marriage." Sparrow smiled. "They don't know yet what that will do. Women riding horses—that's only the beginning."

"A good beginning."

"Very good indeed." Her smile widened. "Oh, the things I see!"

"Will you be letting Linden keep the stallion?"

"The stallion chose him," Sparrow said. "But the royal herd—that, we take back with us, as Keen's marriage-gift."

Kestrel's breath hissed between his teeth. "You'll ask for that? But that's almost worse than taking the kingship from the People!"

"Almost," she said. "We won't take them all. We'll leave a mare or two. And the stallion. Linden will be content with that. The rest will learn to be. It's only mares, after all, and an excess of fillies."

"*Only* mares." Kestrel shook his head. "Someday, my love, the men of the People will wake and see what you've done to them."

"I'll wait eagerly for that," she said. With a sudden movement she stripped off her shaman's tunic, standing naked in starlight. The shaman-marks on her breasts and belly seemed to stir like living things. She stretched, whirled about, danced along the riverbank.

Kestrel caught her sudden wild mood, the joy that was in her, the dizzy gladness. He shed his own garments and laughed for the pleasure of the night wind on his bare skin. When she leaped into the water and struck off swimming, he was hard on her heels.

They played like otters, tumbling, laughing, till Kestrel swallowed a gulletful of water and came up gasping. He scrambled toward the shore, found purchase for his feet, and paused to breathe.

She floated into his arms. She had always swum more easily than he, as if water were her element. Truly, she did look like an otter, with her wide dark eyes and her round mischievous face. And he, he supposed, looked like a bedraggled falcon, all wet feathers and dampened dignity, and water dripping from his long arched nose.

She did not seem to find him unpleasant to look at, though her eyes danced upon him. "Beloved," she said, "it's a long life we'll have together, and laughter enough to brighten a world."

"That is true seeing?"

She kissed him so long and so very well that he almost forgot what he had asked. But in the end she answered him. "Pure truth," she said, "in the goddess' name."